TERRA

a standalone novel in the Tales of Tempus series

E. Solofoni

ISBN 978-0-6458541-0-7

Cover art – Paul Davies
https://www.instagram.com/pmdavies_artist/

For Poppy.

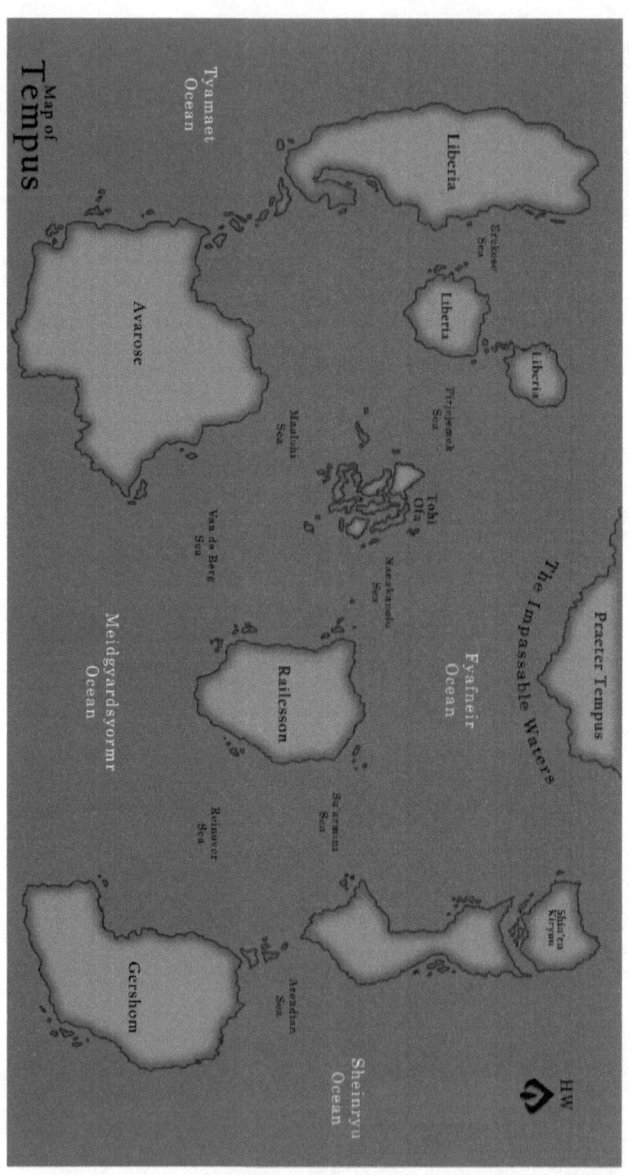

Fig 1. Map of our world. Printed outline of initial cartography work by
Eulyus Van de Berg in the final spell of Draco Aetate, 1253.

Fig 2. Rough sketch of Railesson post-sun's death. Outline based on cartography work by Eulyus Van de Berg in 1253DA. As there is scholarly dispute on the use of established Pateran compass directions, I've listed both Old and New World directions. Heavenward North, Ezerforth East, Heavensent South, Spiritrest West.

In the beginning was the One with Many Names.

One was filled with boundless love. This love he wished to share. Thus, he created. Into these creations he poured his fathomless love.

For a time, theirs was a perfect relationship. But it was not long before the created spurned its Creator.

- *A Collective History I: Railesson, The People of Old and Scriptura* by E. Yelnorin.

PROLOGUE
8 BSD (*Spells* Before Sun's Death)
Or 203 EB (*Spells After the* Empty Ben'min Throne)

In the hot afternoon sun, a silver-haired lady lingered on the bank of The Mare, attempting a conversation with Joseph's young son.

Joseph disembarked from the opposing dock, grinding his teeth and straining against the boat oars. It was in moments such as these where he longed to have the blood of Vei. Merely being a descendant of Veirya's was not enough to be blessed with her gift. But even as he thought this, the presence of the silver-haired lady was enough to dissuade him—the once honourable title was almost entirely synonymous with a curse nowadays.

When Joseph finally reached the bank, his white-haired son scampered to his side, face noticeably flushed. Then, with trembling fingers, the young boy helped secure the boat to the dock with a rope. He fumbled with the new knot Joseph had taught him just yesterday and Joseph felt a surge of joy watching him.

"Thank you, Adam." Joseph patted his son's head but his eyes were fixed on the silver-haired woman.

The sound of heavy heels stretched along the wooden dock between them, hidden beneath an indigo dress. If not for the clunk of her shoes, Joseph would be forgiven for believing the lady glided towards him above the susurration of satin, carrying an air of gentle serenity.

Joseph's mouth twisted into a grimace. He would not play any of her games.

Maremortums were all the same.

He cleared his throat. "Are you looking to depart to the heavenward bank?"

The Maremortum attempted a smile but Joseph tensed, knowing better than to trust appearances. "I was hoping you would appeal to Pater." She pursed her lips, unable to meet Joseph's gaze. "On my behalf."

Folding his arms across his chest, Joseph crinkled his nose and pressed his lips firmly together. "You're overexposed."

The Maremortum fiddled with the white ribbon that secured her wide brim hat under her chin. "I know," she whispered, eyes lowered. She laid a hand across her stomach. "But I still want to try."

Joseph allowed several beats of silence to pass before he spoke again: "I've heard that the last heirs with the blood of Vei now share a marriage bed." He spat to the side, his lip curling in disgust. "And yet, you still dare to ask me to intercede on your behalf."

The calm mask fell from the Maremortum's face, and her expression darkened as she stepped toward him.

"Two seeds shall be planted in a barren land and from it two plants shall take root."

The Maremortum halted, her grey eyes wide.

Faint blue runes emanated from Joseph's body and he sighed, closing his eyes, body tingling with energy and words that were not his own. "And from one, a sword shall be used to bring judgement upon you and all in Tempus. From the other, division and death." Joseph opened his eyes. The runes continued to circle him and filled him with a power that hardened him against the tears that sprang up in the Maremortum's eyes.

"No," she whispered, falling to her knees. "I don't want them to suffer."

"Throughout Tempus their names will be known and they will be resilient even in their desire to uproot themselves." The runes dissipated and Joseph took a deep breath, eyes narrowed. "So says One."

"I will raise a sword among my people. A perfect sword to cast out all evil."

- Lines from the *Seers of Paegaelai, Scriptura*. Translated by C. Yelnorin

1
0 ASD (*Spells* After Sun's Death)

The hazy glowing sun of Tempus rested for the last time on the horizon, casting lengthy shadows across the grassy fields of Attero.

It sank in a fizzling display of colour; dazzling yolk seeping from a broken shell before it burst in a flash of blinding light, sparking an horrific chain of events. The night sky blazed like fire. Stars erupted. Meteors hurtled towards the land at a frightening speed, destroying the homes and lives of humans and beasts alike.

The rich farmlands of Attero were eradicated.

That day marked the end of the sun and the beginning of The Stillness.

Darkness had engulfed all the world of Tempus.

On the third day of The Stillness, an old ox in a rundown café contemplated closing early. The inky quiet that had swallowed the world was unsettling and the town of Lacuna was in disarray. Word on the wind was the rest of the country of Railesson was in the same state.

Still, the old ox peered out at the dark, lamp-lit street, running a cleaning rag over the same spot on the counter. He heaved a long sigh and turned back to the cabinet of valuables, idly rearranging the contents in the drawers.

He would have to find something suitable to charm Rebekah with—he would convince her he was content with not buying a child slave from the beastmasters.

Running his humanoid fingers over a silk cloth, the old ox jumped with the jingling of the door's bell. A grin broke out on his face when he looked up to see a relatively tall, lantern-bearing man amble in. "Agnus—"

The welcome died on the ox's lips when his gleaming eyes fell on the young girl's sleeping face resting over the man's shoulder. Her arms were slung around his neck and her legs wrapped around his waist, bare feet dangling at his sides.

"Lamina, my friend," greeted Agnus, adjusting his top hat with the back of the hand holding the lantern. "Can you book a room at the inn for this child?"

Lamina held his tongue while Agnus offered a silk cravat to the innkeeper. There were too many questions, but he didn't want to add any more rumours to the fiery whirlwind that dogged Agnus wherever he travelled.

The innkeeper had other ideas. He flicked off the golden switch on the small radio perched on the counter and rested an elbow on top of it.

"Back so soon from Attero, Mr Dayton?" the innkeeper asked, voice seemingly nonchalant. His charcoal eyes blazed in the light of the counter's lamp and they flitted to the young girl Lamina begrudgingly offered to hold. "With a child in tow. I hope she isn't masterless."

The pointed remark was not lost on Lamina, who hoped his face gave nothing away.

But Agnus smiled quietly, holding the innkeeper's gaze.

The latter looked away first, scanning the cravat with a danyekza. The exposed gears within the hand-held machine whirred, glowing a soft green from somewhere within, and the innkeeper focused intently on the circular face of the meter, its thin black needle settling on a white circle.

Nodding approvingly, the innkeeper slotted the cravat on a glass shelf within his cabinet of valuables. "Don't misunderstand me, Mr Dayton. Lacuna will always support your strange antics—no matter what the rest of Tempus says about you. But I'm not the only one who thinks you should be more careful. Especially with the death of the sun. The world leaders are bound to clash in a bid to save Tempus and your wander to Attero better have been worth sticking your neck out."

Agnus' smile remained. "I had my armour."

"And Spiritus, I hope!" Dangling a room key in one hand and a lantern in another, the innkeeper waved for the pair to follow him to the allocated room, apologising for the darkness of the halls. "The lights need repairing. There's been a lot of strain on the town generators the past two days."

Agnus stopped beside Lamina, gesturing for the girl. "I will take her from here. Wait for me at your café."

Lamina inhaled sharply, nostrils flaring and eyes hard as he regarded Agnus. After a moment, he shook his head with a grunt. "Fine."

It was later that day—the café clock read 3.38 sun down—when the dark-haired Agnus Dayton stumbled through the doors again, dressed in his grey double-breasted coat. Dusting his top hat off, he seated himself at a table far from the door, the café's only customer for the day.

"It would have been better if you had left her where you had found her," grunted Lamina, pouring a cup of hot tea.

Agnus languidly stretched his legs out and laid his top hat on the faded wooden tabletop.

"Did you hear me, Agnus?" Lamina growled when he approached with the teacup in hand. "You should have left her in the hands of Death."

Hanging light bulbs, like little jewels, adorned the leaky ceiling and tinkled quietly above their heads, keeping the muggy café well-lit despite the blanket of darkness that currently engulfed Tempus.

The amount of lighting could not, however, brighten the stiff smile that crossed Agnus' lips at Lamina's words. "Mors Mortis does not guarantee a painless death, Lamina."

Dumping the teacup on the table, the old ox shook his large horned head, his shaggy mane of hair whipping about him with his grunts of disapproval. "Only you can get away with mentioning that name in my café, Agnus. If anyone else said it—I'd send them flying out!"

Chuckling lightly, Agnus drew the cup of tea towards him and blew gently on the dark liquid. "Shall I pay with something personal?" he seemingly asked the cup, sipping the contents.

"I would not accept! I will only take other items of value from you!" Lamina clicked his tongue, mouth tugging down into a frown. "And even with Attero gone, if The Conqueror orders Lacuna to accept blood, I will refuse that too!"

Agnus shook his head, placing his cup down. "Even in these circumstances, it is unlikely that he will drastically change Currency Law."

"Doesn't seem beneath him to do that. The blasted sun has died, and the world will never know peace with that usurper on the throne! Like Marius said, the world leaders are going to fight it out—Tempus will devolve into unbridled chaos! If you ask me, this world isn't worth the effort of breathing."

"You know better than others that life is always worth living. If you accept the reasons for it." Pausing, Agnus frowned at his reflection in his cup and shifted in his seat. He sighed. "The girl cannot stay with me, Lamina."

Lamina shook his head knowingly. "I told you Agnus, it's too much of a burden for you!" He bustled to the sink to douse his dishrag in soap and water. "Everyone knows the fate of a child without a registered master."

Agnus said nothing.

"Is she awake yet?" Lamina returned to the table where Agnus sat and wiped it down.

"I have not woken her yet."

"Well, if she hasn't woken up on her own in two days then I say get her off your hands quickly, Agnus!"

Grabbing his top hat from where it rested on the table, the dark-haired man rose from his seat. He spun the hat slowly in his hands. "I'm going to place her in the care of Van de Berg."

The dishrag fell from the ox's hairy human-like hand. "Van de Berg?" he repeated, his voice rising in alarm. "Gustav Van de Berg? You're really tossing the child directly to those Magian wolves? It would've been more merciful for Death to claim her!"

Agnus said nothing, choosing instead to rummage through his coat pockets. The old ox hovered anxiously around him.

"Why not throw her to the beastmasters? At least guarantee Libertas for her. No, forget the girl! What about you, Agnus? You do know that they require blood in Magia, don't you? Surely you don't intend to go through with that payment!"

Agnus gave a small, bemused smile, his eyes twinkling as he pulled out a neat lock of wavy brown hair from his pocket. "I have plenty of blood to give away, my dear friend." He held the hair out to Lamina. "Here. For the tea."

Lamina squinted at the lock of hair. "Whose is that?"

"The girl's."

Brow furrowing, Lamina waved Agnus' hand away. "I can't accept that!"

"I insist," said Agnus, taking Lamina's hand and dropping the lock of hair into it.

"You know how this works, Agnus! You can only surrender things of value to you! Therefore, this doesn't pay for anything."

Agnus gently closed Lamina's fingers over the lock of hair and steadily returned the ox's gaze. "She *is* of value to me."

Surprised, Lamina averted his eyes, uncomfortable under Agnus' earnest stare. Sighing heavily, he turned away, payment in hand. "I don't understand you, Agnus." He shuffled across the worn and aged wooden floorboards towards the sleek, mahogany cabinet of valuables.

Agnus merely smiled, watching Lamina run a danyekza over the girl's lock of hair. He donned his top hat and exited the café.

On the fourth day of The Stillness, Agnus carried the young girl through the streets of Lacuna.

Humans and beasts alike made a wide berth around them, with the cleared path lit by electric street-lamps. Some of the crowd whispered as he passed, wondering if he had found her in the ruins of Attero or if she were masterless. Many stared openly.

None of this concerned Agnus, his steps never faltering as he passed through the wrought-iron gates of Lacuna. He left the safety of the Old World town and strove on into the depths of the inky black that haunted the rest of Railesson and the world beyond.

Darkness swallowed the area outside of the light of the lantern held high in Agnus' right hand, his left supporting the young girl he carried on his back. The small electrical buzz of the lantern light seemed insignificant in the darkness that threatened to strangle it, yet Agnus strode on confidently.

The hot air thickened the further he travelled along the deserted dirt road, riddled with overgrown weeds crawling across it. Agnus' once crisp white shirt stuck unpleasantly to his skin and his limbs had grown weary from carrying the girl. However, he faithfully plodded along, his gaze fixed ahead of him while beads of sweat trickled down his brow.

As the terrain slowly morphed around Agnus, the air grew heavier and pressed upon his chest. Breathing was increasingly difficult, breaks more frequent and the need for water more desperate. Yet, he strove on, cheerful as he relayed the history of Tempus to his unconscious companion. The earth below his feet responded to his chatter and sprang to life, glowing grass illuminating wherever he trod. It allowed him to easily point out sections of the landscape and share the stories behind them.

The light-hearted chatter went on until they reached The Mare, the sole body of water flowing over the surface of Railesson. Agnus solemnly explained its significance when they crossed in an old rickety boat manned by a dirty-faced beggar. After giving his grey vest as payment, Agnus added, with a smile, "Your son is well" and the beggar thanked him profusely.

On the river's bank, Agnus sat the girl against a tree, and in the yellow light of the lantern, he told her of The Mare's role in ancient times. The land's resting place for the dead. The respected tradition of only disturbing the water with the boat that had borne them across. The long line of seers who upheld these customs.

For a moment, he fell silent, staring into the darkness of The Stillness and listening intently to the soothing sounds of the river's flowing water. Quietly, he turned to the girl and kissed her softly on the forehead before gathering both her and the lantern up, continuing his journey to the mountainous area of Magia.

In the distance, the dark silhouette of an imposing tower came into view, barely noticeable in The Stillness, wedged between two dark, jagged mountains.

"The Lost Languages," Agnus murmured. "It was once part of the Old World. But now, it's part of Magia." A hint of sadness tinged his voice.

The journey towards the ominous silhouette continued in silence, the tower looming threateningly above the pair's heads. At the very foot of it, faint hues of lights dotted the gate rising from the depths. Immediately before the gate, an outpost station sat, lit by the blaze of torches sagging in old wall brackets, revealing peeling white paint on the chipped rock slab walls. The small orbs that flickered along the gate that edged into view. Squinting into the darkness, he saw the orbs were in fact more lit torches, the style of the New World.

Before the outpost station sat a small, worn obsidian desk with a hand mould formed by crystal at its centre. Behind the desk, a man dressed in a navy-blue uniform sat quietly, his cold gaze fixed on Agnus' approach.

"Halt."

Agnus slowed to a stop and the guard rose from the seat behind his desk with an air of self-assurance. Though Agnus studied the guard carefully, he ensured his expression gave nothing away.

The guard was tall in stature with smooth and neatly combed ebony hair, a stark contrast to Agnus' unkempt and unruly style. His eyes, which sternly regarded Agnus, were a cruel icy-blue set into a finely chiselled face and accentuated by long dark lashes.

"State your name and your business here," the guard demanded, his pointed nose crinkling as he gazed at the child on Agnus' back.

"I have come to see General Gustav Van de Berg," Agnus answered, ignoring the frown that furrowed the guard's brow. "Tell him that Mr Dayton has arrived as forewarned."

The guard shot him a look of distrust and instructed Agnus to remain where he was before sidling off to the small spherical scarlet crystal sitting on a metal cabinet which, Agnus noted, was fashioned from the same material as the hand mould on the guard's desk.

There were a few grumbled exchanges between the guard and the crystal sphere which had assumed a deep purple colour. The colour faded suddenly when the young man turned away, annoyed.

Upon returning to the desk, the guard slapped his hand into the crystal mould. The crystal began to emit an eerie green glow in response to the guard's touch and Agnus pressed his lips firmly together. Glancing up at Agnus, the guard nodded in the direction of the station's door that was now slowly sliding open, the sound of grinding stone filling the still night air.

"General Van de Berg is waiting inside."

Agnus swept silently into the dim candle-lit room beyond the stone door where the Magian General waited, poised by a bookcase.

At the sight of the girl Agnus carried, the General flinched and ushered him to the leather lounge in the far corner.

Agnus gingerly laid the unconscious girl down and removed his coat, dusting it off before folding it over his arm. Stooping to the level of the sofa, he yanked out a handkerchief from beneath his shirt's wrist cuff and dabbed lightly at the sweat gleaming on the girl's forehead.

"We're here, my child," he whispered.

He straightened, glancing over his shoulder. The Magian General hovered uncertainly near a chair at the shiny mahogany table in the adjoining kitchen.

Gustav was small, with an undeniable air of indecisiveness. Age, and perhaps, something else, seemed to have slowly gnawed away at the remaining logic the balding, grey-haired man was graced with. His back was slightly hunched and he kept his pale hands clasped together.

The General cleared his throat awkwardly and gestured to the chair opposite his. Agnus obediently approached it, seating himself calmly.

Gustav extended his trembling hand. "Allow me to take your coat, Mr Dayton."

Agnus shook his head, voice steady and even when he spoke, "I have come to ask a favour of you, General Van de Berg."

The general involuntarily shifted back in his seat, the corners of his lips tightening into a frown. "Would... would you like some tea, Mr Dayton?" His watery eyes darted about, unable to meet Agnus'. "It's an honour to have you here." His hands shook violently, spilling tea onto the desk as he poured out two cups.

"General Van de Berg," called Agnus, his tone firm yet gentle. "I have come, as promised, to place a certain child into your care."

Gustav froze, looking anywhere but Agnus. "T-tea, Mr Dayton?"

Without waiting for a response, Gustav slid the filled cup and a chipped wooden coaster to Agnus. Taking up his own cup and sipping from it, Gustav seemed to regain a degree of composure. He placed his cup calmly down on a wooden coaster and slicked back the few strands of grizzly grey hair on his head with his free hand.

"Mr Dayton," he began, the corners of his mouth pulled to form a tight smile. He leaned forward in his seat, lacing his pudgy fingers together and rested his elbows on the table, watery eyes still slightly hesitant to meet Agnus'. "I will accept your burden. It is law that Magia must open its arms to any masterless child and blemished that stray onto its path. If you leave the blemished here, she will be raised to happily work to help Magia eradicate The Stillness."

Agnus lifted his hand in a silencing gesture. "General Van de Berg, I understand the laws instituted in Tempus. Specifically, the ones that govern Magia and prevent you from using this particular child for labour."

The amount of composure Gustav had regained appeared to slip, a deep frown embedding itself on his worn and weathered face. "What do you mean by that?"

Gesturing to Gustav with upturned hands, Agnus held his gaze, smiling. "She is without blemish."

The General recoiled, his eyes flickering to his tea and then to his tightly clasped hands. Sweat collected on his forehead.

After a few breaths, he cleared his throat, his gaze rising to meet Agnus' briefly. "W-well…what is the point of bringing her here? She is of no use to Magia in that state." There was a beat and then he leaned across the table, this time unflinchingly locking eyes with Agnus. "You could make it easier for us, Mr Dayton," he breathed, an unnerving look passing over his face.

Agnus was silent as the older man reached into his breast pocket and withdrew a handkerchief to dab his drenched forehead—as if maintaining eye contact with Agnus was a test of endurance. The General mumbled incoherently to himself, his eyes wide and wild as his head bobbed.

"General," said Agnus, his voice quiet. "You will not spill a single drop of this child's blood. If harm comes to this child, I *will* hold you responsible."

The hairs on the back of Gustav's neck stood on end and he shrunk back into his seat. His body trembled and sweat again poured down his stricken face.

"Do not spill a single drop of this child's blood. The girl will return to me," said Agnus, enunciating each word carefully and steadily holding Gustav's petrified gaze. "She does not belong to Magia. She will not work for

Magia. She belongs to only one person and will only work for that person."

Agnus rose from his seat and reached into his vest pocket, pulling out a sealed vial containing a thick, dark red liquid. He held it out to the quivering General who eyed it with a mixture of horror and, to Agnus' disgust, greed.

"The payment?" Gustav asked, unable to wrench his eyes away from the vial. He licked his lips and slowly reached out. "Your blood. For the child's?"

Gustav grabbed the sealed vial but when Agnus did not let go, the General's eyes wandered up to meet his which studied him critically.

"Do not spill a single drop of her blood, General."

Gustav swallowed nervously. "The bl-blood of Agnus Dayton! Wh-what a tale to tell! Of course, I won't! O-of course!"

Agnus scrutinised Gustav for a moment longer. He slowly released the vial of blood which the General clung to with trembling hands, eyes glinting with undisguised greed. Turning away from the wretched sight, Agnus paced over to the sofa where the girl continued to sleep.

"This child will wake soon." Agnus rested his hand on the youth's wavy chestnut hair. He was still for a moment, observing the unconscious child quietly. He turned back to Gustav who was busily examining the blood in the firelight. "Remember what I have told you, General Van de Berg."

Nodding insistently and expressing his earnest gratitude, Gustav saw Agnus out of the station, watching as the younger man slung his coat back on and strode out into the dark of The Stillness, his humming lantern held up high before him.

Standing by the station doorway, Gustav watched until the light of Agnus' lantern became a small speck in the distance and then slipped back inside.

Absentmindedly stroking the vial of blood, he walked slowly to the armchair adjacent to the sofa where the unconscious child lay. Pausing, he reached into his coat pocket, drawing out a small jagged scarlet crystal. A replica of the ones used by the guard.

Marvelling at the precious stone, he sat in the armchair, balancing the scarlet stone carefully on his lap. His breathing quickened and his eyes grew wide with anticipation. His hands, slick with sweat, shook violently as he grasped the stopper of the vial and rotated it slowly. It easily came undone and a sense of trepidation mingled with excitement pulsed through him. His eyes widened further and his lips moved rapidly and anxiously as if in fervent prayer.

Without another thought, he grabbed the shard of crystal and tipped the vial over it, its thick, red contents spilling over the jagged stone.

Immediately, the crystal shard oscillated vigorously in Gustav's grip.

He yelped when it suddenly shattered, the pieces embedding themselves hungrily into the palm of his hand.

Gustav's shriek was followed by a crash, the alarmed guard charging into the outpost station.

"General!" he cried, hurrying to Gustav's side.

Gustav shook uncontrollably, unable to wrench his eyes away from the horrifying sight of the scarlet pieces of crystal slithering under the skin of his hand. The veins beneath his skin throbbed angrily as the lumps of crystal crawled up his arm.

A petrified scream tore from his throat.

The young girl stirred on the sofa and Gustav's tear-filled eyes shifted to her.

"It was her!" he howled, scratching at the wriggling lumps in his arm. "Agnus has cursed Magia again!"

"Cursed?" repeated the guard, the little colour left in his face draining away. "Mr Dayton. That was Agnus Dayton?"

"Who else you fool? And he brought that cursed child with him!" bellowed Gustav, his voice rising ridiculously in octaves as the lumps slithered up to his neck.

There was a terrifying pause where Gustav froze, his eyes bulging and mouth gaping. A terrible gurgling noise filled the air and for a second, Gustav appeared to reach for his throat before there was a sickening sound of flesh ripping and the crystal pieces burst out of his neck.

The guard flinched, reflexively closing his eyes as blood splattered his face and the front of his uniform. He turned away from the grotesque sight of the dead General, bile rising into the back of his throat, causing his eyes to sting. Trembling from head to toe, he glanced back at the General before quickly looking away again, a wave of nausea washing over him.

His eyes fell on the crystal pieces that had torn through the General's throat. He watched in fascination as the pieces melted, losing their scarlet appearance and assuming an obsidian hue. The black puddle hissed and faded to a pure white. A lump stuck in the guard's throat.

A loud humming filled the air and the guard, still visibly shaken, approached the now purple spherical crystal on the cabinet behind his desk, the object from which the sound came.

"Major General Tres," answered the guard, his throat dry.

"Officer Cadet Simeon Van de Berg, The Oracle claims that General Gustav Van de Berg has died. Please confirm the claim."

Simeon swallowed hard and, with a shaky hand, brushed back a strand of hair that had fallen out of place. "Claim confirmed. I witnessed a horrid curse take the General's life."

"A curse?"

"Placed on the child that Agnus Dayton had left in Gustav's care. I'm certain she caused the E132 to attack the General. He stated that she was cursed before his death."

"A-Agnus Dayton?" spluttered the Major-General. "What was *he* doing *here*?"

"I believe it was to dump his cursed burden on Magia. And it appears that this curse made the E132 change, too."

"Change?"

"Into a strange white substance."

"Gather it up for review."

"And the girl?"

"What state is she in?"

"I can confirm that she is unblemished. The child is currently unconscious. What are your orders, sir?"

There was a lengthy pause before the Major spoke, his voice crisp and unsympathetic: "Make her work."

Simeon nodded gravely, turning away and re-entering the station, his eyes darting towards the sofa where the young child continued to lay. He approached her, his hand sliding into his coat pocket and eyes steely as he gazed upon the sleeping youth. From his pocket, he drew out a scarlet stone—carved of the same crystal the communication sphere and the now pearly liquid had been.

Breathing deeply, he closed his eyes, his hand closing over the crystal piece he had drawn out.

From between his fingers, a strong scarlet light ballooned out, vibrant and ominous. Slowly, he slid his fingers across the crystal and a long, jagged blade formed, glowing maliciously in the firelight.

From the sofa, the youth stirred, her eyelids fluttering.

Simeon grabbed her wrist, waking the girl as he drew her arm out towards him and swiftly brought the scarlet blade down.

A scream pierced the night air and blood soaked the floor of the station.

The youth's first memory was of pain.

In that time, the thralls of the Other thrived and their gruesome deeds cursed the land.

- Lines from *The Wisdom of Aurelius, Scriptura*. Translated by T. Lowenthal

2

2 ASD

The unhurried shuffling of countless leaves of paper occupied a very insignificant portion of Lieutenant Simeon's day.

Occasionally he stood from his work desk and, with a chipped mug of hot coffee in hand, paced to the recently polished front window. He would peer out at the pathway through the loosely tied curtains, barely able to see through the ink black darkness that still enveloped the entire world of Tempus.

It had been two long spells since The Stillness had begun, and from his position at the window, Simeon glimpsed the silhouette of The Lost Languages. A tower of the Old World, erected in Magia when the Lieutenant had been a child himself. He quietly surveyed the scarlet crystal that sat at the peak of the tower.

He wondered whether Magia would successfully restore the sunless black sky of Tempus to a replica of its original state, solidifying their country's place of power against the likes of Liberia and Avarose. Where they had failed, Railesson could not. Here was the ruling kingdom of Tempus. They did not have the luxury of failure.

During his musings, a flicker of a small, distant flame caught his icy-blue eyes.

He sipped his coffee, eyes fixated on the firelight that steadily grew as it danced up the pathway. Passing by the window, its light illuminated the face of an older, uniformed man, escorting a thin young girl. Trailing slightly behind the officer, her gaze was focused on the ground and her left arm, which stopped just above the elbow, hung uselessly at her side.

There was a succession of four rapid knocks on the door and, taking a generous swig of his coffee, Simeon walked leisurely to it. Upon opening the door, he was met with the sight of the man and child he had seen from the window and he murmured a cold greeting.

"Special delivery for Lieutenant-Colonel Simeon," greeted the man at the door, a mocking smile lighting his face.

Simeon did not return any pleasantries. His eyes flickered to the man's arm, which wound around the girl's back, hand resting on her shoulder.

"0792 was well behaved today," remarked the man, noticing the Lieutenant's stare and releasing the girl before nudging her forward. "Despite her being the oldest of the children mining out the E132. We'll soon have enough to complete the crystal on top of the tower and bring an end to The Stillness," rambled the man, seemingly amused and satisfied with the sound of his voice.

Nodding mutely, Simeon gestured for the girl to enter, his eyes still trained on the man before him.

After a beat, the girl stepped hesitatingly over the threshold and Simeon reflexively stroked her brunette head as she passed by him. She wordlessly headed to the sofa.

"Thank you for taking care of her, Colonel," said Simeon, stepping aside to allow room for the man to enter. "Please, come in. I promised you a coffee last time we spoke."

"I really shouldn't—"

"But I insist," pressed Simeon, motioning for the Colonel to enter.

The Colonel smiled politely and thanked Simeon before stepping inside.

"We'll have coffee in the back room so that the girl may rest."

The Colonel thanked him again and ambled through to the next room.

As Simeon closed the front door, he turned to find the girl quietly watching him from beside the sofa.

"Is it a good day today, Lieutenant?" asked the girl tentatively, taking a step back.

"Why do you ask, 0792?"

"You're humming." The girl positioned herself behind the coffee table.

"My dear girl," breathed the Lieutenant, smiling in a manner that caused the girl to shudder. "Do you know that I will be promoted, today?"

For a moment, the girl fell silent. She returned Simeon's gaze evenly and he felt his breath hitch momentarily in his throat. "I'm sorry, I thought you were promoted five months ago…" she began uncertainly. Her eyes lowered briefly before glancing back up at him. "…congratulations."

Simeon crossed the room and pressed her hand with his, his icy blue eyes holding her grey ones. "Thank you."

Turning away, he clasped his hands behind his back and steered himself into the back room. At the sight of the Colonel standing awkwardly there, Simeon invited him to the dining table where a steaming pot of coffee sat.

The Colonel slipped into one of the chairs, idly glancing about the small room as Simeon took the opposing chair. Filling a cup, Simeon handed it to the Colonel with a smile.

"I hear the Sominiums may be in favour of extending the olive branch to Shin'en Kiryuu." Simeon refilled his mug stealing a glance at the Colonel, who took that moment to sip his coffee. After a beat he continued, "I assume that this bodes well for the General's plans, Johansson?"

Simeon suppressed a smirk when Johansson finally met his gaze, whose lips were pressed firmly together. Johansson set his cup down and leaned back in his chair, arms folded over his chest.

Giving a dismissive shake of his head, Johansson sighed, "So, this is the benefit of having family in higher positions of authority?"

Grimacing, Simeon's mouth puckered, the Colonel's words sour. "One of the very few benefits."

Johansson studied him wordlessly and Simeon returned his gaze unflinchingly.

"Well." Johansson sat forward again, arms spread as he shrugged. "There's no benefit in you questioning me." He leaned over his teacup, a glint of mirth in his eyes. "Unlike some, I respect ranks."

His words hanging in the air, Johansson leaned back and picked up his cup. He sipped the coffee leisurely, ignoring Simeon's long stare from across the table.

There was a shine of scarlet as Simeon unsheathed his blade from the scabbard at his side and Johansson jumped to his feet at the sight of it.

"Lieutenant-Colonel, what are you—"

Johansson froze his mouth agape and eyes bulging out of their sockets. A small choking gasp issued from his mouth.

"Hush now, Colonel," urged Simeon, pushing his blade into the older man's ribcage. Blood spurted out, scattering small liquid jewels on the waxed wooden floorboards.

Johansson gasped again, his hands weakly pressing against Simeon's shoulders, chest and face in a futile struggle.

"Hush Colonel. I told someone special that I was going to be promoted today." Simeon's lips curled up into a cruel smile.

He expertly twisted the blade inside Johansson and withdrew it with ease, pushing his superior away and watching his body slump lifelessly to the floor, eyes still and wide in death.

"And now," said Simeon calmly. "I can be."

He reached into his pocket and drew out a handkerchief to clean his bloodied blade. Wiped clean of blood the vibrant scarlet colour remained. It was a blade formed from the same type of crystal that was perched on top of the Old World's tower.

From the front room, the young girl turned her eyes away from the back-room door, blocking out any unwanted sound. She listened intently to the sound of her own breathing—it comforted her.

Gathering herself, she tiptoed across to the window and pushed the curtains carefully to the side, her eyes focused on the large scarlet crystal sitting at the pinnacle of the tower of Lost Languages.

She contemplated pushing the window open and bounding out in a second of fleeting madness. Instead, she stood motionless by the window, staring listlessly at the tower, her right hand massaging the stump end of her left arm.

Her mind drifted to the area beyond the tower and her grip on her arm tightened as fear awakened within her. North of the Old World's tower stood the outpost station where the entries and exits to and from Magia were monitored.

Thinking back to the outpost station itself, the building was a symbol of terror for the girl. It had been within its walls that she had met Lieutenant Simeon. Since then, she had been entrusted to his guardianship and had quickly learnt to be wary of his fluctuating moods.

The abrupt screeching, like an otherworldly alarm, shook the girl out of her thoughts and her eyes darted to the pitch black beyond the tower. She desperately squinted, unable to see a thing.

Movement behind her caught her attention and she glanced over her shoulder to see the Lieutenant tossing a bloodied handkerchief into a bin as he re-entered the room.

"Seems like there is a misbehaving child," he muttered more to himself than to the girl. "They know that we will detect any attempts at escape and yet they still try." He smiled wryly, approaching the front door. Opening it, he paused and shot a meaningful look at the girl. "Don't even let the thought enter your head. I'll be right back after I see this child's blood on the mine's walls with my own eyes."

The door snapped shut, leaving the girl to stare silently after the Lieutenant from her place near the window. She watched his silhouette cut through the pathless ground to the current mines and decided to turn away, trying to ignore the inhuman shrieks in the distance.

Heading over to the sofa, she laid down and closed her eyes, willing sleep to take her where the serenity of a desolated barren desert and the kind smile of a familiar stranger would greet her.

"Prayer?"

08387, a young boy with one odd milky eye, nodded, ignoring the disdainful look of the blonde girl, 08385, mining the wall beside him. "I overheard Mr Ridley saying he does it to try and revive some old tradition his great grandmother used to do," 08387 whispered excitedly, his nose not as physically big as his busy body nature demanded.

The brunette girl, 0792, who was missing part of her left arm, screwed up her face in confusion. "What's prayer?"

The boy clapped his hands together and stifled giggles at the stern look the blonde girl shot him. Then, with his eyes closed, he began to mumble incoherently.

"What on Tempus are you doing?" scorned the blonde, and what remained of her mangled nose crinkled in disgust.

"Prayer!" insisted the boy with a boyish grin. "Mr Wayman said, 'Why do you sit there with your hands together, muttering nonsense?'"

The blonde rolled her eyes. "He probably didn't mean it literally."

Suppressing a laugh, the brunette urgently gestured for them to continue working as a Magian officer peered around the corner.

She never knew how the boy could maintain such high spirits. It kept her heart light despite how long she had been working in the mines.

Glancing over, the brunette noticed her blonde-haired friend looking about surreptitiously. When the officer's back was far enough away, the blonde leaned forward, whispering, "When I was younger and before this—," she pointed at her nose, "—my Gershomite master prayed every day to Ezer. He said his great, great grandparents were Paterans." She paused, her eyes growing distant. "He was a lovely man."

The brunette girl and the boy exchanged worried looks over their blonde friend's downcast face and all three said nothing as they returned to their work, another officer patrolling past them.

Biting her lip, the girl found herself wondering what kind of life her friend could've led without her blemish.

It was a panicked Lieutenant Wayman who informed Simeon of the sudden arrival of The Oracle and her husband in Magia. He squashed his hat anxiously in his hands and Simeon looked away, rolling his eyes.

As Simeon made to dismiss the gaping man from his office—"I have five new groups of blemished to process"—, the door to his office flew open and a silver-haired woman in a burgundy petticoat stormed in, her feather plumed hat waving wildly like an antenna. She was followed by a silver-haired man who cautiously slid the end of a cane around the floor before him, his cloudy eyes fixed on the ground.

At the sight of the silver-haired woman, Simeon jumped up from his seat, meeting her cold stare. "The Oracle," he spat. "To what do I owe the displeasure?"

Lieutenant Wayman excused himself and awkwardly scuttled out of the room.

Adjusting the shawl draped across her arms, The Oracle stuck her chin out, her nose crinkled in the air. "Fool. You know exactly why we're here," she sniffed. She begrudgingly took a seat when the man beside her nudged her with the end of his cane as he sat down.

Simeon held the woman's gaze, his eyes thin. "It seems that the seat of Colonel is now empty."

"How convenient! The Lieutenant-Colonel seat was empty five months ago too!"

"Yes, and similarly, I would be more than happy to fill said seat."

Folding her arms over her chest, The Oracle scrunched her nose, repulsed, her grey eyes scathing. "I will not excuse you for free."

"When have you ever given me anything freely?"

The silver-haired man beside The Oracle quickly raised his hand to stop her as she made to inch forward. She shot him a look, but he did not turn to her, eyes fixed on the tabletop.

"Simeon, please," was all the man said.

"Fine. I apologise." Simeon dropped back down into his chair, his brow knotted. "But I would be indebted to you if you allow me to fill Johansson's seat." Straightening, Simeon raised his eyes and held The Oracle's icy gaze, fingers itching to quiet the humming of his sheathed blade.

"Get on you two," the silver-haired man growled when the silence carried on, slamming the bottom of his cane against the wooden floor. "We are at a pivotal moment of The Stillness and we need to remain a united front in the eyes of Tempus."

At those words, Simeon leaned forward, a real smile playing on his lips. "So, The Conqueror *has* reached an agreement with Shin'en Kiryuu's Sora." His smile widened at the sour look The Oracle gave him. "Who would've thought that our countries would ally with each other in the darkness."

The Oracle chewed her bottom lip and huffed when the silver-haired man placed a hand on her knee. "Yes, I will try to get on with this fool." Her foot jittered impatiently as she continued, glaring at Simeon as she spoke. "The seat is yours. Tomorrow, you can overlook temperature control with the Avarosan techies—they will be arriving in the afternoon." The Oracle's scowl deepened. "And then, you can help with forming the Council of Magia."

"The Council of Magia?"

"Well, we will need a steady supply of blood for the E132 on top of the tower."

"I see."

The Oracle sneered, uncrossing and recrossing her legs. "Do you really?" The silver-haired man squeezed her knee.

Inhaling deeply through her flared nostrils, The Oracle continued through clenched teeth. "We'll go through all the details for your role tomorrow... together."

"Thank you."

"Don't thank me yet," snapped The Oracle, jumping to her feet and almost knocking the chair over as she moved around it. She turned on her heel, calling over her shoulder, "A meeting will be organised to smooth this nonsense over. I expect you to attend when you are called upon."

Simeon inclined his head to the silver-haired beauty in a mock bow as she strode to the door. "I will make it up to you." His lip curled as he watched The Oracle leave.

Turning to the silver-haired man, he walked over to him and clasped his shoulder wordlessly. They exchanged a brief and wordless hug before the silver-haired man took his cane and sought his way out.

The months following Simeon's promotion as Colonel left his office emptier than usual and his absence was enjoyed by the girl. Whenever he happened to be in the office, the now Colonel would snap at her more often than previously, so she was relieved to have the small building to herself most nights, especially after gruelling days in the mines.

On one of those hot sticky nights, the girl stretched out on the office sofa, trying to ignore the dull throbbing of her head. She idly wondered if the

Colonel would allow her access to a washing facility—the heat made it harder to avoid smelling herself.

Her thoughts wandered from the lively boy, 08387, impersonating the officer named Ridley on their walk back from the mines, earning him a solid whack from said officer, and the blonde-haired 08385 and her quiet agreement to call 08387, "Ridley", when it was just the three of them.

Thoughts blending into one, the girl's eyes slowly closed and she drifted off, dreaming of a man in a top hat and a large barren plain.

It was the odd notion that light was hitting her face that caused the young girl to stir. As her eyes fluttered open and grew accustomed to the light, it dawned on her that it was not from any source within the room. Bolting upright on the sofa, her eyes widened at the sight of light streaming in through the window of Simeon's office.

Leaping up, she scurried to the window, blanket strewn across the wooden floorboards. Eyes wide, she stared at the large azure orb hanging high up in the blackened sky above, lighting the land as far as she could see.

Touching the glass before her, she marvelled at the miracle of the light in the sky and reasoned that this was a sign of hope.

That there was something worth believing in, in all the insanity of Tempus.

She clenched her fist and rested her forehead against the glass of the window, the azure sun beginning to warm it.

Perhaps, even for a blemished, life was worth living.

To what are we beholden? The world and all within it passes away and yet we strain against the constraints of the flesh. For what purpose?

- Lines from the *Laments of Lerielle, Scriptura*. Translated by J. Talis

3

3 ASD

In the filthy mines of Magia, the brunette girl bent over the whimpering form of her friend. The thin boy was laid out along the rough, rocky floor of the mine, his body caked with dirt and his eyes—one dark and the other milky in colour—glistened with tears. His bony arms wrapped securely around his stomach as if to protect it.

A single torch, abandoned on the floor behind the pair, lit the small area of the mine. The boy's agonised moaning bounced off the mine walls.

"Hush, hush, Ridley," whispered the girl, the stump of her left arm, gently patting Ridley's shoulder. "Hush or they will find us."

Ridley bit his lip and squeezed his eyes shut, attempting to contain the small sobs that shook his worn body.

The girl glanced nervously over her shoulder and then back to the boy. "Let me see your stomach."

A small whimper escaped Ridley's lips. "I'm sorry, 0792. It was my mistake—I shouldn't have been so reckless with the mining tools—"

"Let me see."

Obediently, Ridley slowly slid his arms off his stomach, enough for the girl to glimpse the bloody gash and his shirt, soaked crimson. The boy sobbed at her worried expression. "It's terrible, isn't it? They're going to leave me here to die like all the others. They'll paint the walls of this mine with my blood, won't they?"

The girl swallowed thickly. Summoning the courage to look the boy in the eyes, a smile forced its way onto her face. "It's okay. You're okay, Ridley," she lied, gently stroking Ridley's head. "The wound's not too bad. You'll be better in no time."

Tears streamed down Ridley's face. "Really?"

The girl gave the brightest smile she could muster, yet it did not reach her grey eyes. "Really," she whispered, continuing to stroke the boy's head, and sweeping the long dark strands of hair out of his eyes.

Returning her smile, Ridley cried earnestly, his arms wrapping around his stomach as he rolled onto his side and hunched over. "Th-thanks 0792," he stammered gratefully, yet the girl could hear his disbelief. "Thanks."

Gulping nervously, she glanced over her shoulder again, her body shivering at a sudden idea.

Bending over, she slipped her right arm under her friend and hoisted him up with all the strength her thin arm would lend. "Come on then," she breathed heavily, supporting his weight and standing them both up, her wobbly knees threatening to cave in under her. "We'll get you some help—some medical attention. You won't die here."

Ridley leaned heavily on her shoulder before howling as he grasped his stomach. "It's too late!" he sobbed, his gaze on the rocky floor below them.

Droplets of his blood adorned the mine floor, glittering darkly in the lone flickering light of the torch. Gradually, it was absorbed into the rock, and in the distance a terrifying round of screeches filled the air, striking fear into both children's hearts.

"Quickly!" yelled the girl, heart pounding as she struggled across the mine floor, her arms already weary from supporting the wounded boy. "Quickly before they find us!" The idea of the Colonel appearing turned her blood cold.

"Don't! Just leave me behind 0792! We'll never be able to get away from the Colonel!" Ridley's body quivered, sweat mingling with the tears that poured down his face. "They'll paint these mines with your blood too!"

Ignoring his pleas, the girl continued to drag him along down the dimly torch-lit corridors, her eyes darting fearfully about her, imaginary shadows chasing them.

The ear-splitting screeches continued to cut through the air, reverberating throughout the mine and causing the girl's teeth to anxiously click together.

Maintaining her balance and keeping a firm grip on her friend was difficult as she staggered across the mine. After the meagre meal they had that night, the gurgling of the girl's stomach was hard to ignore. She shook her head, squinting into the dark to focus.

Having spent most of her life in the mines, the girl was well-acquainted with the darkness of it, knowing her way through it like the back of her hand. Silently, she hoped that this knowledge would be to their advantage. That, somehow, they could escape without encountering any officers. Especially not the Colonel.

Sweat trickled down the girl's brow as she trudged along, shifting her weight painfully from one foot to the other, her limbs aching and her lungs burning for air.

As if motivated by the girl's determination, Ridley began to limp forward along with her, clasping a hand tightly over his stomach. "Where—will we—go?" he gasped, wincing with each step.

"To a place where people can help you."

"Away from—Magia?"

There was a pause where the girl pursed her lips together, sweat dripping into her eyes. "Somewhere safe for the blemished."

The distant crunching of boots on rocks was like a stab of terror through the girl's system.

Driven by their fear, the two children picked up speed, stumbling around the corner to the next section of the long winding mine.

As they raced across the corridor, the girl's head spun from fatigue and hunger and she reeled back momentarily, arms flying out to catch herself.

Ridley seized her hand, squeezing it gently. "There is a person we can run to that all of Magia fears. I've heard officers like Mr Ridley speak about this person and whenever they did, they sounded afraid. Imagine that." His eyes gleamed, a weak smile lighting his worn face.

The story made the girl uneasy. "Run to who?"

The smile on Ridley's face widened. "Agnus," he answered brightly, eyes lit with delight as he pulled her along behind him.

The girl frowned. "But he isn't real, is he? Most of the officers say he's a myth—they say he doesn't even exist!"

"How little the children of Magia know."

The children skidded to a stop and the girl felt the vice grip of fear on her heart, her stomach plummeting.

A man of tall stature stepped out from the shadows, his hands clasped calmly behind his back and his icy-blue eyes trained on the two trembling children who were rooted to the spot. Behind him, two officers followed, each bearing a torch, casting dark shadows across the walls. "Are you on a night stroll?"

"C-Colonel," stuttered Ridley, eyes wide with dread as the man paced slowly towards them.

"Were you thinking of running away with my girl, 08387?" the Colonel asked coldly, raising his hand and signalling to the two officers who drew from their coat pockets small scarlet crystal shards.

Their shadows along the walls seemed to morph, mutating into a form unrecognisable, the crystals luminescent as they were reshaped.

The girl shrunk back into herself, wanting to make herself smaller. She was sure that the hammering sound of her heart was loud enough to be like deafening music in the Colonel's ears. Her body broke out in a sweat. Unconsciously, she grabbed the stump of her left arm. Feeling the Colonel's eyes following her movements, she quickly let go.

"You remember that moment in the station, don't you, 0792?" the Colonel asked, his eyes boring into her soul. "You remember it clearly now, don't you?"

The girl took a shaky step back, unable to wrench her wide terrified eyes from the Colonel's wild ones.

The Colonel took another step towards the two children, but his attention was focused solely on the girl. "I found you myself and brought you to Magia. I removed your withered hand with the E132. You remember all of that, don't you, 0792?" His voice was dangerously soft and low as he approached. "Aren't you indebted to me?"

Without warning, he grabbed Ridley by the hair and flung him backwards onto the floor behind him, kicking him roughly in the stomach. Ridley howled but fell silent when one of the officers pointed their scarlet sword at him.

The girl instinctively charged towards Ridley's fallen body, but the two officers shot forward, torches clattering on the ground as they caught both her arms.

"Colonel Simeon, please!" She thrashed against the arms that withheld her. "Please! He needs help—"

Her words died on her lips when Simeon turned his stony face to her.

"Help?" He stepped forward and seized the girl's chin. "Tell me 0792, why does the world continue to turn?" he asked, looking scornfully down at her.

"Wh-why does the world turn?" she repeated, her lips trembling.

"Yes." Simeon stepped back and spread his arms out wide. "There is no sun. Yet we continue to turn. Why is that?"

The girl lowered her gaze fearfully, unable to return the Colonel's piercing one. "B-because the Council of Magia constructed an artificial sun?" she murmured, staring at her dirty bare feet.

Simeon forced her chin up, her eyes returning to his. "Are you mocking me, girl? That isn't why."

Gulping, the girl racked her brain. "Then the scarlet element. Element

132."

"Incorrect."

"Then I don't know, sir," she whispered, her heart threatening to leap out of her chest. "I don't know why the world still turns."

"Well, 0792," began the Colonel, his grip loosening on her chin and his hand sliding down to her neck. "It certainly doesn't turn for *you*." His hand closed tightly around her throat.

Coughing and spluttering, the girl fought frantically against the arms that held her tight. But the hand on her throat tightened and the girl's eyes began to burn.

"Did you know, 0792, that the world will continue turning even after someone dies? Life for others doesn't end just because another person dies. So why should we care?" asked the Colonel calmly, maintaining his hold on the girl's neck despite her face changing colour as she gasped hopelessly for air. "What value is there in any life if the world can continue turning without it, hm?"

The girl's eyes slowly rolled up into her head.

The Colonel's grip on the girl's neck slackened. He let go and the girl felt her restraints slip away. She fell heavily to the floor, utterly still. Colourful spots floated in the back of her eyelids.

A foot slid under her limp body, rolling her over.

She could not move.

A voice that had to belong to one of the officers nervously asked, "Colonel, is that alright? If she's really his curse—" A sound like the shifting of feet and the officer fell silent.

There was shuffling and the girl felt light breaths near her ear. She was too weak to budge.

"My dear little girl," he murmured, cold fingers caressing her cheek. "How long have you lived since *he* was here? Far longer than any child has ever lived while working in the mines of Magia. What does it matter if you see another of your friends die here? Haven't you grown used to the pain yet?" he asked quietly, fingers now searching her throat for a pulse.

The girl internally screamed for strength to bat his hand away, but her body did not respond. She heard the Colonel rise and panic flared within her at the unmistakable shine of scarlet against her eyelids. Gravel crackled underfoot and her heart pounded in her chest, realisation dawning on her. Grinding her teeth, she cracked open an eye.

"What does another life mean to you, *Agnus' Curse*? The world will continue to turn regardless of whether this boy lives or dies. The only thing that matters is if we dance to Tempus' tune," said the Colonel, emotionless as he strode towards Ridley's unconscious form.

Heaving herself back onto her belly, the girl scrabbled for anything within reach, teeth clenched as she hurled a small rock. It landed harmlessly a couple of inches away from the Colonel's boot.

He glanced over his shoulder, apathetic as the girl struggled to hold herself up on her elbows.

The urge to be sick surged into the back of her throat, pulsing through her head. "Colonel Simeon," she wheezed, tears forming in the corners of her eyes from exertion. Her tearful gaze met the Colonel's. "He needs help. Please."

As if mesmerised, the Colonel stood motionless, his eyes fixed on the girl's.

It took her a moment to register the squelching of the Colonel's blade as he plunged it through the boy's heart.

The girl screamed, flinging herself across the floor towards her friend, tears spilling from her eyes.

The Colonel quickly sheathed his bloody blade and stepped in front of the despairing girl, barring her path. She furiously clawed at his legs, no longer aware of what she was doing anymore. She only knew the white-hot anger that boiled within her and the cold hopelessness of reality.

She was wrong. There was no hope in all of the insanity of Tempus.

The Colonel kicked her scratching hand away with a savagery that sent the girl spiralling to the floor, shrieking as she cradled her throbbing fingers. She wasn't sure if they were broken but it didn't matter. She still wanted to wrap them, broken or not, around his throat—the world would turn without him.

"Paint the walls with his blood," barked the Colonel over the howls of the girl. He nodded to the two officers. "We'll have a new team of children mine the E132 that will form on the walls afterwards. Meanwhile, I'll take care of this one."

Someone, the girl pleaded as the Colonel approached her, stooping to pick her up. *Someone, help. Please…*

She balled her hand into a fist, rising to strike the Colonel. But he caught her wrist effortlessly and his eyes flashed warningly, reminding her of her powerlessness, sapping any resistance that remained in her. When she slumped in resignation, he grabbed her, tossing her over his shoulder. She raised her head weakly, numbly watching the officers carry her friend's body in the other direction.

The thoughts of killing the Colonel rounded on her, melting into an oppressive wave of shame and self-hate. To want something like that made her like him. No, life was not worth living if she became like Colonel Simeon.

Is it even worth living at all?

Her ears rung with her own despairing cries and a sinking feeling of emptiness and loneliness pervaded her being.

The long walk from the mines to the Colonel's office was tormentingly silent except for the soft cries of the girl and the hurried salutes of officers at their posts as they passed.

In the Colonel's office, an officer was stationed by a door close to a large mahogany bookshelf. At a look from the Colonel, the officer opened the door, allowing him to enter the filthy tiled room beyond.

The cracked tiles on the floor and the stony walls were streaked with blood and other unpleasant substances but the sight of these did not prepare the girl for the odour that assaulted her nose. She gagged mid sob, but the Colonel strode undeterred across the tiled floor towards the lone metallic operation table in the centre of the room. There, he gently laid the girl down.

Pulling away, he paused for a moment, studying the girl's face as she continued to silently mourn, her eyes staring bleakly at the ceiling. She did not move when his hand touched the side of her face. Nor did she move when he drew himself closer, his cool breath fanning her cheek.

"My dear girl," he began softly, his voice seemingly distant to the despairing girl. "Your attempt to escape cannot go unpunished." He paused, as if expecting a response but did not receive any. "Have you given up then?"

A silent tear slid down the girl's face.

After a moment, the Colonel lowered his head, his lips close to the girl's ear. "How disappointing Agnus has proven to be."

Straightening, he unsheathed his blade.

The temple we still have. All of history had begun in this place. But One no longer walks its halls. One's voice we can no longer hear.

- Lines from *The Wisdom of Aurelius, Scriptura*. Translated by T. Lowenthal

4

She stood alone.

The endless expanse of the sky was dark and sunless. The devastated terrain below it was pockmarked with craters.

Her eye flitted across the horizon. No other soul remained.

No one except a lone figure that strode through the dusty plains towards her.

The longing twinge in her heart told her she knew him.

The top hat upon his head cast a shadow over his face and the long, grey double-breasted coat he wore flapped about his ankles as he slowly approached her.

The dust below his feet changed briefly into lush, green grass as he passed over it. His voice resonated in her mind, searing through her scattered thoughts.

"You, my child, are to be the Third."

The young girl awoke in the cold and dimly lit tiled room, the fine hairs on her arm at attention. As a shiver rippled through her and the metallic operation table rattled beneath her slender frame.

A four-armed chandelier—the only source of light in the room—sagged from the high ceiling, filled with candles, its flames prancing, almost wickedly gleeful.

The girl scanned the room with one eye, the events of the night before returning in vivid detail. A storm of emotions lapped at the edges of her mind when she dwelt on the empty socket beneath her left eyelid. She took several breaths, nails biting into the palm of her hand, and switched off the storm. Surviving meant suppression.

This permanent reminder was surely her penance. Her friends had pestered her to keep her head down. It kept her alive. Even when her blonde-haired friend, 08385, succumbed to illness and the girl had to mine the resulting E132. She had retched until nothing would come up. But she had never tried to attack Colonel Simeon.

Sitting up slowly, a thin sheet that had been lazily draped over her collected in a bundle on her lap. Swinging her legs over the side of the table, she slid off it. Her pale feet tingled when it met the cold tiled floor, the white sheet flecked with crimson spots coiling in a delicate heap nearby. The specks were also on her filthy, tattered dress.

The chill in the air prompted her to reach down and gather the sheet up, wrapping it securely around herself. It covered her from her bony shoulders down, with the remainder of the thin material trailing along the floor behind her.

Pattering to the door, she lamented waking from her recurring dream— the only place she felt safe during her time in Magia.

No matter how she mulled over it, she could not decipher the dream's meaning, nor could she make sense of its relation to an insignificant girl like her.

A blemished that had lived for far too long. That's all that she was.

Agnus' Curse.

The Colonel's words reverberated through her mind and she scowled, shaking her head to clear it as she grasped the door handle. His words were decidedly poisonous. If she allowed them to burrow any deeper into her being, there would be no point in her existence.

Even if she questioned this 'existence' herself.

It was strange though, she thought, her focus shifting back to the dream. The top-hat man had never spoken before.

Shaking her head again, she turned the door handle and wrenched it open. Beyond was the Colonel's office and the young girl entered, stopping dead in her tracks.

Colonel Simeon was seated at his desk, busily shuffling through leaves of paper.

The silence was suffocating and the girl trembled from head to toe, scarcely daring to breathe.

"Come here, dear girl," drawled Simeon without looking up.

The girl jumped. She bit her lip, clenching a fistful of sheet to steady herself and, with her knees knocking loudly together, she shuffled towards the Colonel's desk. As she came nearer, she spotted a new item upon the shiny mahogany desk. Displayed as if it were some grotesque trophy, the girl's left eye stared back at her from within a light-blue fluid-filled jar.

Bile rose into the back of the girl's throat and she tore her remaining eye away from the sight.

Stopping a foot away from his desk, the girl hesitated before nervously clearing her throat. "Colonel Simeon."

The sound of shuffling papers continued to highlight the silence within the room. The girl squirmed under the stare of her own eye from its place on the Colonel's desk.

The Colonel paused briefly, glancing over his papers at the girl. "Come to my side," he said loudly.

Gulping, the girl made her way around the Colonel's desk and obediently stopped at his side, feeling self-conscious as he watched her.

Abandoning his papers, Colonel Simeon rose from his seat and an unpleasant smile crept onto his face as he towered over the girl. Reaching into his long coat pocket, he drew out a piece of material and held it out to the girl. It was shaped as a semi-circle with a string of cloth attached on either side.

Her look turned from one of apprehension to confusion and she made no move to take the item.

"It's an eye-patch," explained the Colonel, stooping down to sweep the girl's shoulder-length hair back. Ignoring her flinching, he looped the strings of the eye-patch around her head and tied it neatly in place.

Stepping back to admire his work, the Colonel nodded in satisfaction and returned to his seat, missing the disconcerted look the girl shot him. "A new team of children have been assigned to the mines—Lieutenant Wayman went out late last night to purchase them from beastmasters. You are to be part of this new team." He resumed his perusal of papers and the girl noted that they had profile sketches of the new children. "You've been cycled through five teams already. You know the mines better than any child."

The girl gave a stiff nod, still adjusting to having only one eye and concerned with the Colonel's uncharacteristic display of kindness. She resisted touching the eye-patch. It felt out of place. She wondered why he would give her such a thing. And why would he specifically remove her eye. Perhaps there were no limits to cruelty in Magia.

As if reading her mind, Colonel Simeon stood from his seat and lightly touched her shoulder, making the girl's skin crawl—it was difficult to disguise her displeasure. Again, the Colonel overlooked her reaction and proceeded to gently touch the eye-patch.

"It's a lucky charm," he said with another unsettling smile. "I won't let *anyone* reach you."

The girl was far from believing that the eye-patch was anything close to a lucky charm.

She tried to inch back but a wave of nausea drained her. "Am I going to work now?" she asked, putting on a front.

The Colonel eyed her carefully. Touching her gleaming forehead with the back of his hand, he mopped up some sweat. "You must be hungry, 0792," he said, disinterested. "Well, there's no time to waste. It's already evening. Let's meet the new team then."

As the Colonel strode to the door, the girl was acutely aware of her stomach cramping. She could not recall when she had last eaten a filling meal.

Letting the stained sheet fall from her shoulders, the girl took a deep breath and stumbled to the door which Simeon held open.

Stepping out into the light of the artificial sun, she squinted against the brightness. The miraculous orb was perched high in its midnight canvas, denying the stories of an once azure sky. Instead, it was as if the azure had been peeled away completely, leaving behind a blank slate of inky darkness. Then was absorbed into the ball of E132 that had taken on its hue—an unheard of colour interaction for the scarlet stone.

Beside the artificial sun she could make out the moon behind her raised hand, a sinister blood-red since the sun's death.

Tearing her eye away, the girl followed the Colonel along the path leading away from his office. The thick and humid air of Magia was causing the eye-patch to stick to her skin and she absentmindedly scuffed a pebble past a scuttling skink.

Further they travelled, finally reaching the current mines and they began to weave through its numerous corridors; spells of picking into the earth to retrieve the brown stone that formed the basis for the scarlet Element 132.

The events of last night plagued the girl's mind and with her heart throbbing painfully fast, she scanned all the walls they passed for a glimmer of the scarlet element—a sign that they had saturated them with Ridley's blood.

However, it was not until they reached the deepest part of the mine that the girl saw the walls bleeding scarlet, gluggy chunks hanging in masses from the rocky faces.

The little colour in her face drained away.

The officers had been thorough.

This was how life ended for all blemished—a mineral resource for the rest of Tempus. Another wave of nausea struck her square in the chest.

Simeon cleared his throat. "You will be the leader of this group of children."

The girl lowered her dazed gaze, glancing about herself. Twelve dirty-faced children—younger than her—worked, drenched in sweat as they chiselled away at the rocky walls with their pickaxes, aided by the light of a few torches laying astray on the mine floor. Crammed into each corner of the mining area was an officer wielding a scarlet weapon, surveying the children's work.

Walking around the blemished children, the girl felt her heart ache as nostalgia dogged her steps. The faces of her friends, whom she met in a similar manner, swam to the front of her mind.

The blemishes ranged from small to great: a missing finger, a significantly curved spine, a half-burnt face exposing a jawbone where flesh hung like melted wax.

"That is 08396, the oldest of the team," remarked Simeon, following the girl's gaze. "He's around your assumed age—perhaps in his 10th spell. Major General Tres is hoping he'll survive to enter the Council."

"The Council? The Council of Magia?"

"Yes. Only the lucky ones are moved into the Council. They then live in The Lost Languages, finally becoming invaluable despite their blemishes," explained the Colonel, pacing slowly around the mining area, scrutinising the children. A look of concern passed so quickly over his face that the girl thought she had imagined it. "Make sure that the children mine all the E132 from the walls. Once that's complete, report back to me. The children may then be rewarded with food. The amount depends on the speed which they extract all the E132."

If possible, the girl turned paler. "Colonel Simeon, how long have they been working for?" she asked, returning the Colonel's gaze evenly.

Digging into his pocket as if he hadn't heard her, the Colonel pulled out an oval item securely wrapped in paper and held it out to the girl. "Do not remove your eye-patch," he said in a low voice as the girl accepted the item. "And make sure the work is done."

"Colonel—"

Before she could get another word out, Simeon seized her chin, his eyes boring madly into hers. "If *they* don't make you work, *I'll* do it myself," he hissed angrily. "Do *not* take the eye-patch off."

He released her, turning on his heel and marching away.

The girl stared after him for a while before looking down at the wrapped item in her hand. She balanced the item against her stump arm and side, slowly peeling back the paper wrapping until it fell gracefully to the floor and she stared at the small loaf of bread in her hand.

She clenched the bread tightly, gritting her teeth. A rebellious idea possessed her.

After a moment's hesitation, she cleared her throat and began to tear the bread as carefully and as evenly as she could with one hand while pinning it to her side. "Excuse me!" she declared boldly, her voice bounding back at her in the small area.

The children stopped, turning to look at the girl in surprise.

With all eyes on her, uncertainty plagued the girl and she swallowed the stuck words in her throat, her heart beating erratically. "There is some bread here to share. If you'd like some," she announced, legs wobbling as the children stared blankly at her.

One of the officers closest to the girl stepped forward, clutching the hilt of his sword tightly. "We are under the order of Lieutenant Wayman to ensure that these children work ceaselessly. Do not interfere," he warned, drawing the scarlet sabre.

An unusual calm fell over the girl as a thought struck her. She turned to face the officer coolly, noticing the other officers had followed suit, drawing their weapons formed from Element 132. She stared the officer with the sabre square in the eye. "I am sure you've heard of me then," replied the girl, standing tall. "Colonel Simeon says that I am 'Agnus' Curse'. I'm sure you've all heard of Agnus."

The officers halted and the girl could see fear in their eyes. There was something beyond what the girl knew about this 'Agnus' that frightened people.

Enthralled, the girl hurriedly continued, "It's only a small piece of bread to share with the children. It'll only take a minute."

She felt sure that the officers would deny her, yet they said nothing, returning to their posts, weapons stowed away. Pushing questions to the back of her mind, she scurried over to the children to share the broken bread, her heart hammering and soaring higher than it ever had before.

As day bled into late sun up and all the E132 had been extracted, the girl raced the sinking artificial sun to the Colonel's office. Throwing open the door, her voice died mid-sentence when her eye fell on an unfamiliar mousy brown-haired woman glaring over her shoulder from in front of the Colonel's desk.

Simeon grimaced, shifting in his seat. He cleared his throat. "Perhaps we should have this conversation at another time, Brigadier."

The girl decided the Brigadier's glare was the natural set of her face when she turned to fix her piercing stare on the Colonel.

"I don't think so. As I was saying, Major Casdaine expressed concern. He mentioned you passed him last night with the child, 0792."

The girl pursed her lips and furrowed her brow—was she invisible?

The Brigadier continued, her tone cutting. "Why did you spare her?"

She thinks he spared me? The girl shook her head. That was far too generous a word. Her hand curled into a fist and she bit her chapped lip, body trembling as she recalled the pain of losing her eye.

"She was sufficiently punished, Brigadier."

The Brigadier slapped her hand against the tabletop. "I mentioned this girl to The Oracle and she claims that she has never seen her." She sat back in her chair, tone cool. Her nail-bitten fingers beat rhythmically against the desk. "Why would that be?"

Simeon attempted a light shrug, the corners of his lips tightening.

"We can't play favourites here, Colonel Simeon. A blemished is a blemished and the law is the law. Her blood should have been on those walls today."

Simeon lowered his gaze and muttered under his breath.

"Yes, we wouldn't want you to be late to your dinner," quipped the Brigadier, sliding out of her seat and squaring her slim shoulders. She was far shorter than her presence suggested.

The girl stiffened when the Brigadier turned around, her angry brown eyes settling on her. Lip curling, the Brigadier's eyes, if possible, narrowed further. She glanced back over her shoulder. "Have you touched—"

Leaping to his feet, Simeon sent his chair clattering to the floor, his teeth bared as he growled. "I have not and will not break any clause from the Charter of Protection."

"So says many an adult, but there's reason certain clauses exist."

Simeon turned his face away, red with fury and jaw clenched.

"I advise you to stop hiding her from The Oracle." The Brigadier marched towards the door, not sparing the girl another look. "Don't be late to your dinner now."

The door slammed shut behind her and Simeon slumped back into his seat, massaging his forehead, his face drawn.

The girl fiddled with the strap of her eye-patch. She felt conflicted, wanting to laugh at the Colonel's apparent discomfort but aware that if the Brigadier had her way, she would be dead along with Ridley.

Perhaps that would've been better.

Sighing, she strode forward. "Colonel Simeon, we finished mining all of the E132."

"Yes, I know. I've already ordered the officers to prepare their dinner." Colonel Simeon rose from his desk where a bomb of parchments and books had gone off. The girl cast a curious glance over the mess of book spines. The Colonel yanked her arm and the girl inhaled sharply at the clicking of her shoulder. "Nosy girls may be punished," he growled, his eyes flashing warningly.

"I'm sorry!" spluttered the girl reflexively. She bit her lip, holding back her indignation. He knew she couldn't read! Forcing down a retort, she opted to placate the Colonel, trying to change the subject. "How did you know we were already finished?"

The girl let out a sudden yelp when Colonel Simeon twisted her arm, his teeth bared in a furious snarl.

"Am I a clown to you? Some harlequin in a play?" he snapped, shaking the girl.

"I'm not sure what a harlequin is, Colonel," answered the girl, cringing at her honest reply. She wanted to snap at him.

But her response seemed to calm the Colonel and his face emptied of emotion again before he let her go. "A harlequin is like a clown." He turned away, grabbing his coat from its place on his chair. "A person who does silly things."

"Silly things?" The girl's mind shifted to the Colonel's reactions to whenever she did something he deemed 'silly'. "Why would people want to do that?"

Colonel Simeon slipped on his coat and smoothed out his hair, shrugging with disinterest. "*Libertas.* The Freedom law established when the kingdom's throne was taken over. Adults are free to pursue whatever career and home they want. And a job like a harlequin is to 'entertain' people. Although, I don't find anything amusing about them." Heading to the office door, he gestured for the girl to follow. "Come 0792, the Major General has requested that I dine with him tonight at The Lost Languages. And he specifically asked to meet you."

The girl quirked an eyebrow but hurried out the door after the Colonel, her tongue rolling over the word Libertas and relishing it. She quickly fell in step with the taciturn Colonel, brimming with questions. She wondered how long she could take advantage of this tolerant mood. "What do they look like?"

"Who?"

"The harlequins."

The Colonel glanced at her as if to check if the question was a serious one. Deciding that it was, he continued to give her short answers. "They wear masks and colourful clothing."

"Have you ever seen one?"

"In the other cities of Railesson."

"Why don't they amuse you?"

Stopping abruptly, Colonel Simeon slammed his hand against the girl's throat, choking her momentarily before releasing her. "Am I a child? Only children are amused by such nonsense."

He turned away, tramping along the path that led to The Lost Languages.

The girl followed, anger simmering as she rubbed her sore neck. Staring up at the E132 that sat perched at the very top of the looming tower, she felt her anger dissolve into a wave of pity for the Colonel. Perhaps, he had forgotten what it was like to be joyful over anything. The understanding that she had nearly forgotten that too made her unbearably sad. She wondered if she would become like this man.

She didn't realise she was crying until the Colonel had stopped outside of the door leading into The Lost Languages, his outstretched hand touching the side of her face.

"Is it him?" he asked, voice barely above a whisper. He scrunched her hair in his shaking hand. "Is he finally reaching you? Because I won't let him."

The girl swiped at the tears that fell from her eye. "I don't understand." She took a breath, her stomach twisting into knots as her mind wanted to fold in on itself. "Why do I bother...why do I hope?"

Maybe it would've been better to join Ridley.

Colonel Simeon's grip on the girl's hair loosened.

The officer beside the tower door cleared his throat loudly and Colonel Simeon visibly relaxed, stepping away from the girl and regaining his composure.

"Colonel Van de Berg, here to see Major General Tres," he stated calmly. "This is 0792. She is to accompany me."

The officer nodded the pair in and Simeon led the way into the tower, ignoring all of the different lavish rooms that the flight of stairs connected to and marched briskly up.

The young girl occasionally stopped at doors that were ajar to catch a glimpse of the elaborate rooms—from a busy kitchen to an intricate magitech laboratory—and trailed behind, eye wide with wonder. However, at Colonel Simeon's snappish voice, she clambered to keep up, sneaking peeks as she raced after the Colonel's flapping coat.

The staircase seemed never-ending and ran from the bottom of the tower to the very top. Just when the girl felt her jelly-like legs would rupture in a gelatinous puddle of fatigue, the Colonel stopped outside of a room where an officer saluted them.

"Colonel Van de Berg, the Major General is ready to see you." The officer stepped aside, allowing the pair entrance.

Turning to the girl and grasping her arm, the Colonel tugged her close enough to whisper in her ear. "From here on, do not go anywhere alone. Stay close to me at all times."

And with that, he pulled away, entering the dining area that awaited.

Confused and suppressing her irritation, the girl entered in after him, finding a large, neat room, glowing with the light from a fireplace. At the centre of the room sat a round table, covered with a white satin sheet where food—more than the young girl could ever hope to see in a month—sat untouched and ready.

At the opposite end of the table sat a portly man with greasy grey hair, his hands clasped together in what the girl decided was undisguised greed. She found herself distracted from ogling the selection of food and instead staring at the golden rings wedged onto Major General Tres' thick fingers and the terribly distracting wobbling of his second chin as he greeted Colonel Simeon with open arms.

"Ahh, Simeon—forgive me—Colonel Van de Berg! You have come— and with this lovely delight too!" he exclaimed salivating as his eyes roamed over the girl who instinctively edged towards Colonel Simeon. "Why, you should have brought her last time with you! Had I known she looked so much like Arche, I wouldn't have let you—well, you know—three spells ago—"

"Major General," Simeon said dryly. "You said you wished to dine together? I'm sure we're not here to idly chat. You know I despise that."

"Yes, of course. Sit, sit," said the Major General rapidly, waving them over to the table. "The more I can learn about his curse, the better!"

Taking a seat beside Colonel Simeon, the girl felt uneasy. She found herself more fearful of this man than the Colonel and grasped some understanding of why he had ordered her to remain close to him. In his own twisted way, he cared. The very idea made her palms slick with sweat. She silently hoped that the dinner would end quickly.

"Tea, Colonel Van de Berg?" asked Tres cursorily, teapot and cups at the ready. "The finest from Shin'en Kiryuu."

"Yes. No tea for the girl." Simeon glanced at the nervous girl. "Get some food for yourself."

As the Major General poured out the tea, the girl leaned forward to resume gaping at the endless dishes laid out for them. Though her senses were delighted by the plethora of food, she felt a sting of embarrassment that there was so much for just three people. The thought of the children in the mine supping on hunks of dry bread and chalky cheese, that she could still taste, made her throat close up. She sank back in her chair, appetite lost.

"Such a lavish meal for three." Simeon pursed his lips and proceeded to take a swig of his tea. "I wonder how our currency can compete against the rest of the lands' when we are eager to waste fine imported food."

Tres chortled. "I never waste any of the food." He eased back and patted his robust belly.

Simeon fixed Tres with a sharp stare. "With Attero eradicated, the demand for imported food is higher than ever."

"Yes, it's such a shame that Railesson's farmlands and livestock were wiped out with the Sun's death," Tres lamented, his bottom lip pushed out in an exaggerated manner.

"You would mock our failing currency? So many places in Tempus are now declining blood and that's what you have to say?"

"Oh Simeon, you were always so serious." Tres waved the matter away.

"How can I not be? Especially when you ordered *this* much food—you're willing to drain our resources over frivolity!"

"Come now, Simeon. There are still many in Tempus who are willing to do business with us—take Avarose for example, they still pay in blood. Granted, they don't provide the majority of imported food to our country, but their technological contributions to Tempus as a whole are invaluable. And, with magitech still on the rise, the rocks from our mines are widely coveted—we will not struggle to find buyers in this world!" Tres turned his gaze to the girl. "Besides, I was simply ensuring the best for this flower."

"0792," called Simeon, and the girl glanced at him, anticipating his next words. "*Eat.*"

Mechanically, the girl took her empty plate and heaped food onto it until the Colonel fixed his attention elsewhere.

The Major General, sipped quietly from his teacup. "She looks to be the oldest of the blemished." He balanced his bloated rump precariously on the edge of his seat, eyes trained on the girl in the way a predator watches its prey. "Surely she's of age now?" he asked, keeping his voice light.

"There are no physical changes," Simeon said curtly, his voice spiky.

"No changes? Are you certain?"

"I'm certain."

At this, Tres sat up straighter, eyes sparkling. "Colonel Van de Berg, I wasn't aware that you were so—," there was a pause where he gave a leering grin, "—attached."

"I was simply stating facts, Major General."

Tres nodded, grin still plastered to his face. "Do you plan to keep this child as your own then? Since you have come to know her *so* well."

The girl looked from the Major General to the Colonel. The direction of the conversation was confusing, yet she suspected it was an unpleasant one. At a glance from Simeon however, she dug back into her sausages.

"I do believe that that is none of your concern." Simeon drank deeply from his cup as if to signal that was the end of that particular discussion.

Tres chuckled. Picking up a carving set, he began to undress a slab of meat. Nursing a chunk of meat, he nestled it in the folds of lettuce on his plate. "And you've responded quite quickly to the rumours."

"Not in front of the girl, please." Simeon reached forward and took a slice of cheesecake.

With a smirk, Tres sneaked a look at the young girl who, though curious of the rumours he spoke of, was unable to meet his gaze. "But everyone in Magia is saying that his death-defying reappearance in Tempus is because of this girl. Nearly every officer is trembling at the very thought. Why I wonder if she already knew he would return in the flesh—"

"Major General," Simeon cut in, jaw clenched. "Please do not speak about that rumour in front of the girl. It's a rumour and that's all." He stabbed the cheesecake slice viciously with his fork and shoved a piece of it into his mouth.

Tres smiled smugly to himself before turning to the girl who continued to avoid his gaze. "You do know what I mean by you being of age, don't you?" he asked and for a moment the girl wasn't sure whether she was meant to engage him or not.

Glancing sideways at Simeon, who stoically began to pile his plate with food, the young girl struggled to swallow down a piece of potato, nerves getting the better of her. "I'm not sure what you mean by that, sir," she mumbled, lowering her eye to the table. She fidgeted under the older man's stare, feeling as if he were devouring her every movement.

"Here in Magia, the blemished have the unique opportunity to prove themselves worthy by surviving their team cycle despite their imperfect bodies. Once proven, we allow them to contribute to sustaining the hope of Magia—the Council of Magia is a gathering of all the worthy survivors! It is here, in the tower of the great city Babylonia, that the children make efficient use of their blood by feeding it to the E132 attached to the top of The Lost Languages." The Major General poured himself another cup as if to slake sudden thirst.

The young girl was silent as Tres drained his cup, her mind reeling from the information. The question of why she had worked through five team cycles rose to her lips, yet she found she couldn't speak and that a terrible ache in her stomach had begun.

"As a girl, you would continue to work in the Council until you are in your 13th spell—when you are of age. Ahh, 0792, it is simply a privilege to be an unblemished adult," the Major General cackled, wagging his pudgy finger at the girl. "Tempus is not a place for the pitiful likes of blemished children. They're only here for the continual creation, extraction and empowering of the E132. That man—resurrected or not—was a fool to think of using you as his 'curse'! Blemished children have no power here!" He leaned forward and patted the girl's cheek mockingly.

The pained girl looked from the laughing Major General to the quiet Colonel and a strange emptiness seeped into her. She found herself gazing pleadingly at Simeon.

"Colonel Simeon," she moaned. "My stomach. It hurts."

The Major General leapt to his feet and made to bound to the girl's aid when Simeon wound an arm around her, glaring murderously at the older man.

"I didn't make her sick," said Tres defensively, throwing his hands up innocently.

Simeon shook his head, jaw clenched as he turned back to the girl. "Her stomach isn't accustomed to eating so much, that's all."

"Why did you force her to eat then?"

"Does it matter?" snapped Simeon, pulling the girl up with him as he stood.

"I say you should leave her here with me," suggested the Major General. "It would be a great pleasure to take good care of her until she recovers."

The Colonel snorted, turning gingerly and allowing the girl to lean heavily against him. She clutched her aching stomach, resisting the need to curl up on the spot.

"Dear Colonel, you do realise that I can easily pluck her from your care if I wish to," muttered Tres sinisterly, his hand dropping to the sword loosely strapped to his hip. "We could make real use of her as his curse. And we can learn how and why she looks the way she does."

Simeon halted in his tracks, looking back over his shoulder. Anger seemed to radiate from every cell in his body and through her pain, the girl could see the Colonel's blade glow brightly in its scabbard. "You do remember how I became Colonel, don't you, Major General? They say that there's no other person in Magia with such a natural gift for manipulating E132."

Beads of sweat trickled down the Major General's face as Simeon stared coldly at him, his eyes briefly flashing red.

Without another word, Simeon strode out of the room, supporting the girl.

Ω

After the girl had purged the food from her stomach, Simeon urged her to lie down and rest on the sofa at the back of his office—though she was sure that it was not purely out of concern.

He settled on the edge of the sofa and handed her a flask filled with water which she was careful to only take sips from, uncertain of what would set off the Colonel. Even his kindness was unnerving.

Instead of snapping at her, the Colonel touched her eye-patch, his brow furrowed as he studied it. "Is it bothering you?" he asked in a quiet voice, surprising the girl.

She shook her head. Staring at the Colonel, she tried to understand where this abrupt gentleness came from, unable to suppress her suspicions. Her mind drifted back to the conversation between Tres and Simeon and she found the words leaving her lips before she could stop them, "The rumoured man you were talking about—were you talking about Agnus?"

Before she knew what was happening, the girl found herself staring at the ceiling and struggling to regain the breath that had been knocked out of her, her head and back throbbing from having been viciously thrown to the floor.

Simeon's furious face appeared inches away from hers as he kneeled over her, straddling her thin body, his hands gripping her shoulders painfully tight as he shook her violently, slamming the back of her head against the wooden floor. "HAS HE REACHED YOU ALREADY?" he yelled, spit flying from his mouth and the girl could see the vibrant scarlet of his sheathed sword. "IS HE HERE ALREADY? I WON'T—I'LL KILL HIM—"

"C-Colonel S-Simeon!" cried the girl, tears streaming from her eye, her head threatening to split open from the pain. "Pl-please st-stop! I don't know where he is! Please!"

Releasing her suddenly, Simeon grabbed his head, his eyes squeezed shut as a deep and agonised groan escaped his mouth. He remained this way for a while and the girl hastily wiped away her tears, relieved that his sword had stopped glowing.

"Colonel Simeon?"

Running his hands slowly down his face, Simeon opened his eyes, a weary expression on his handsome face. "We'll be returning to work in the mines tomorrow. I'll wake you up early," he muttered, rising to his feet and stripping off his coat which he tossed over the girl. "It's cold," he explained at her dazed stare.

There was a moment of silence where the girl fought off the spots in her vision and Simeon cleared his throat as if to speak. Seemingly deciding against it, Simeon paced to the office door, snapping it shut behind him.

Finally alone, the girl sat up, her head ready to roll off from the excruciating pain. Despite it, the girl crawled to the sofa, determined to haul herself up onto it with a lot of grunting and gritting of teeth. Once on the sofa, she pulled up the still warm coat and sank back into the cushions, bleary eyed.

In the stillness of the night, thoughts tormented the girl. She wondered, in the quiet torch-lit office whether this was to be her lot in life—if all that she would ever amount to would be the girl of the unstable Colonel Simeon. She wondered, if this Agnus was truly a great man that everyone in Magia feared, why had he not freed her or any other child. Was his 'death-defying reappearance' real or was it all just a rumour like Simeon insisted?

And even if he were real, why would he care about a blemished? the girl thought, the harsh words of the Major General returning to her.

Sadness swept over her and she lay down on the sofa, curling up as tears welled in her eye.

Loneliness smothered her, its icy fingers firm around her throat and the girl pressed her hand over her aching heart, as if willing it to stop. Willing herself to stop existing if this was all that she was meant to be.

A reminder of Libertas and harlequins pierced through the gloomy soil of her mind, striking and wonderful, a tiny flower of hope blooming above her despairing heart.

But why?

Grinding her teeth, the girl's hand curled into a fist and she beat the cushion beneath her. Crushing that image. Begging the flower to die.

Why do I still have hope? What is there to believe in?

She tossed and turned, crying herself to sleep.

To murder a man in one's heart is no different from committing the deed itself.

- Lines from *The Wisdom of Aurelius, Scriptura.* Translated by T. Lowenthal

5
4 ASD

Another spell passed in Magia.

The harsh conditions were the norm—any goodness posed as a threat—and the girl's anger was tempered with a repentant certainty that she was doomed to a fate inextricably tied to Magia.

Sometimes she entertained herself with thoughts of a harlequin—the only piece of knowledge she had gathered of the outside world, shaping her view of it.

She dreamt of impossible wonders that demanded exploration in Tempus and could not conclude what lay in wait in Shin'en Kiryuu, Gershom, Avarose—let alone the country she had never left, Railesson. She could only picture what she knew from spells of eavesdropping.

Despite her constant grappling with elusive hope and grisly reality, she continued to dream of the mysterious top-hat man and still wondered if it had any meaning at all.

Whenever the girl became consumed with any of these thoughts, she found the Colonel watching her, his expression and attitude igniting a flaming pillar of revulsion in her. He insisted that a change was gradually occurring in her and the girl squashed every incensed argument she wanted to start, knowing how badly they would end for her.

At times she'd try to catch a glimpse of her reflection on the polished surface of the Element 132 she dug out of mine walls. The Colonel was right—she felt the change approaching herself. But she couldn't understand why this intrigued him.

The days and nights blurred together and one day at the top of the path that wound down towards the old dark mine shafts, the girl gazed up at the expansive starless sky and wondered about the meaning of existence and the frailty of life.

What was life that a blemished could be easily crushed by the whim of an adult?

The girl raised her hand up to the sky, stretching her fingers out as wide as she could, trying to grasp the blood-red moon in her hand and leave an imprint on a world that refused to hear the cries of a lonely blemished.

Maybe this time, she thought morosely, *someone will hear.*

In the dead of the night, during the seventh sun down hour, there were several resounding knocks on the office door and at the Colonel's direction the girl bustled over to answer it.

Framed in the doorway was the most beautiful woman the girl had ever seen. She was dressed finely in a fitted long-sleeved blue flared dress under a matching buttoned bolero jacket. Balanced on her head was a large straw hat, with an upturned brim trimmed with delicate white feathers.

Behind the lady stood a tall shaggy-maned ox, who the girl noticed stood on hooves yet had human-like hands. He seemed to stare at the girl but she was too distracted to think more of it. She was transfixed, unable to tear her eye away from the lady's grey eyes.

"Oh!" the lady said, mouth agape at the girl's identically coloured eye. "Oh!" Her mouth flapped repeatedly in stunned silence.

"Hello, ma'am," greeted the girl politely. "If you're here to see the Colonel, he's just inside."

"Oh—ah yes, I'm here to see the Colonel," the lady trailed off, head tilted to the side while searching the girl's face.

The girl mustered a smile and stepped back to provide the lady and her guard, the silent ox, room to enter.

Passing over the threshold, the lady glanced back at the girl before turning to the Colonel who wordlessly rose from his desk. As the lady slowly approached him, the girl crept towards the side of the room to get a better view of the visitor. Briefly, she caught Simeon's glare and bit her tongue, patiently reminding herself that he would not scold her in front of such company.

From the side of the room, the girl studied the woman's obviously forced smile and how her eyes were suddenly drawn to the jar on the Colonel's desk.

The lady paused. "I see. We're finally even."

Simeon nodded, rounding the desk to stand beside her, his eyes scrutinising. "I'm thankful that you overlooked the minor issue with Johansson, Oracle," he said smoothly, ignoring the ox who stationed himself at the door. He licked his lips and spoke slowly, feigning care, "and I assume that the recent sightings of the man once dead would have caused some distress."

"Obviously!" grumbled The Oracle as Simeon took a spare seat from the side of the room and dumped it in front of his desk. She gave a stiff thank you before sitting and racing to speak again, "Lachesis can't sleep much. That awful man is plaguing her dreams, saying terrible things to her! Claims he knows more about the future than she does. It's him, I tell you! He plans to harm the girls, I know it!"

Simeon had returned to his seat, fingers laced together under his chin. "Hm. I'll need Lachesis to provide a description of him."

The Oracle's eyes narrowed. "Are you calling my daughter a liar?"

"Well, who knows if he has changed since I last saw him."

The girl was sure Colonel Simeon was resisting the urge to roll his eyes.

The Oracle fell into an unhappy silence, arms folded and sullenly staring at the jar containing the girl's eye.

Following her gaze, Simeon cleared his throat, mirroring her as he folded his arms casually across his chest. "So, what is The Oracle doing here at this time of night?"

A muscle in The Oracle's cheek twitched. Reaching up and removing her hat, revealing long silver hair—the girl could not decide whether it was from age or not—which was neatly pinned up in a bun. "I've come to discuss two things: firstly, the country of Avarose is increasing their demand for E132. Can we meet this?"

"Well, we would need more blemished to do so."

The Oracle drummed her fingers against the top of her thigh. She sucked in a breath through her teeth. "I will have to apply to Sominium. The beastmasters will be displeased."

"Is it wise to supply more E132 to the Avarosans?"

"Many families in Railesson have deep roots in Avarose. So what else can we do? And The Conqueror is always ready to find fault with Magia." The Oracle crossed her legs, propping an elbow on the table and resting her cheek on a closed fist. "Still, tensions are high between Gershom and Avarose and we don't want to send too much E132 to Avarose if that muddies our work with Gershom."

Simeon's face remained impassive as he inclined his head to her. "An ally of an ally." He unfolded his arms. "I can make arrangements with Wayman. We'll get in touch with the beastmasters and Gershom will be prioritised over Avarose."

The Oracle gave a small smile and nod, twirling her hat in her hands. "Secondly, I've come for the item I requested a spell ago," she murmured, placing her hat in her lap. "It's as I feared. In a moment of insanity, Arche attempted to remove her gifts."

Simeon straightened in his seat. "Was she successful?"

"Nearly. She took one out, but we were able to restrain her before she got to the other. She's in a dark containment room under security until she receives a replacement. That will be better for her. The things that poor child has had to see," said The Oracle mournfully, shaking her head. "I can understand why she wanted to get rid of it."

"Well, I'm glad that I can supply you with a replacement."

The Oracle sniffed imperiously and nodded. "I suppose I should thank you."

Simeon forced a smile.

"My girls' gifts are the envy of Tempus. I will do anything to keep them safe from that man," said The Oracle, her eyes gleaming brightly as she swelled with pride.

Heart beating wildly, curiosity got the better of the girl. "Are you talking about Agnus?" she piped up, earning the stares of both The Oracle and the Colonel.

The Oracle's eyes grew soft at the sight of the girl, yet the Colonel's turned cold.

"Is this the girl you spoke of?" she asked gently, her voice wavering. A strange measure of affection radiated from her.

The Colonel said nothing, his face stony.

The Oracle gestured for the girl to approach and once the girl reached her side, The Oracle stroked her chestnut-coloured hair with delicate and trembling fingers.

"You were quite right when you said she resembled Arche. The hair colour is the only difference," she said quietly, her hand resting on the girl's head. "Aren't you a beautiful child?" Her voice was like a reverent whisper as she beamed at the confused girl. "You look the same age as my girls too."

She glanced at the Colonel, her expression twisted with pain. "Is it hers then?"

Simeon merely nodded yet it was enough to make the woman upset.

"I'm so sorry my dear," she whispered when she turned back to the girl, lightly touching the side of her face. "I must make amends. Lamina, come here."

The ox shifted to The Oracle's side. "Yes ma'am," he grunted, his voice deep and gravelly. He stared openly at the girl again.

"Look at this poor child!" cried The Oracle. "She's so thin! Honestly Simeon, don't you ever learn?"

The flash of anger diffused when her gaze fell on the girl's stump of a left arm. She gasped and seized the healed flesh, eyes burning into it as if willing it to return to normal. Despite The Oracle's stare, it remained the way it was and she erupted into tears.

"Oh no…Would Arche do something like this? My poor girl isn't right in the head because of the things she has to see! Oh, oh, oh!" blubbered The Oracle, yanking a handkerchief from under the sleeve of her dress and blowing her nose loudly.

The girl looked away, embarrassed by The Oracle's tears. After all, she had long grown accustomed to having only one hand and after a spell of having one eye, she accepted that too. You wouldn't survive in Magia with incessant blubbering.

"Lamina!" howled The Oracle, hurriedly dabbing at her eyes with the clean corner of her handkerchief and the girl was convinced the lady herself wasn't quite right in the head. "You must remain behind!"

Simeon nearly fell out of his seat trying to jump up. "That won't be necessary!"

The lady whipped her head in Simeon's direction. "This child needs care! I can't look at her without thinking about my girls. Lamina will stay behind to look after her until I return and I am determined to see her healthier than any miserable wretch in Magia!" she bellowed, stunning the Colonel. "Do not test me."

The girl swore she saw The Oracle's eyes briefly flash to an eerie red hue.

The Colonel stared, at a loss for words and his fingers twitched near the hilt of his blade.

Fawning over the girl again, The Oracle's face brightened with a perfect white smile. "Lamina is a highly skilled chef and an excellent guardian. He'll take good care of you until I return," she explained kindly, resuming her stroking of the girl's hair.

Unable to grasp the lady's unusual kindness, the girl simply nodded. Her own feelings were tumultuous and she pressed a firm lid over them as Simeon glared over the lady's head. "Thank you, ma'am."

"Please, at least call me Mrs Maremortum." The Oracle smiled softly and pulled away to look at the ox, Lamina. "Take the girl with you to The Lost Languages. There is a kitchen there. If the officers ask, give them this."

Mrs Maremortum tossed Lamina two vials of what appeared to be blood. "The danyekza will identify the blood as mine. They'll allow you entrance for two weeks."

Lamina nodded mutely and turned to the girl, gesturing for her to follow him.

"What about your journey back to Nyx?" asked Simeon through clenched teeth, pinching the bridge of his nose.

Mrs Maremortum turned to him, laughing. "Nyx isn't that far. Lamina escorts me as a pretence. I am perfectly capable of looking after myself."

The girl glanced back at Mrs Maremortum who smiled at her reassuringly.

"Lamina is just going to make you something to eat." She waved farewell as Lamina closed the door behind them.

The old ox peered closely at the girl. Then, with a grunt, he turned and wordlessly began to lead the way to The Lost Languages with such confidence that the girl was sure he had been to Magia many times before.

Following the familiar paved path to the large tower, the girl wondered about the generosity of Mrs Maremortum; extending from her love for her child, Arche. Self-consciously she touched her short brown locks, matted from sweat and coated in a film of dust from the mine she had been working in earlier that day.

She was in her eighth team cycle and had grown accustomed to the idea that she would remain forever in Magia. As long as she didn't think too deeply, this idea didn't frighten her. If she ever fell into despair, she recalled the idea of a harlequin which had come to be a secret pleasure of hers—to dream about the world beyond the mountains and mines of Magia and perhaps encountering one of those adults who had chosen to entertain others at their own expense.

The idea of Libertas comforted her and she reached The Lost Languages with a small smile playing on her lips, unaware of the quiet observation of the ox escorting her.

In a short amount of time, Lamina threw together a light meal and in less time than that, the meal vanished.

Much to Lamina's chagrin, the girl polished the plate clean with her tongue. He clicked his own reproachfully, reminding himself that manners were not a priority in such a place.

Placing the empty plate down, the girl gave a shy dimpled smile, food clinging to the corners of her mouth. "Thank you very much, Mr Lamina."

Lamina simply nodded, puzzled by the strangely endearing nature of the child. She was not as he expected her to be. In fact, he had not expected 'Agnus' Curse' to be remotely optimistic considering the length of time she had spent in Magia. He had often imagined her dead or driven to the brink of insanity from overexposure at least.

Yet here she was. Harmed, yet still capable of genuine gratitude.

Shaking his large horned head, Lamina grabbed the girl's empty plate and dumped it unceremoniously in the kitchen sink, his hooves tapping loudly across the tiled floor. "Give those rotten Magian folk something to do," he grumbled before bustling back over to the table where she patiently sat, smile still in place. He sat down with a loud sigh and scratched his chin awkwardly. "Your hair's quite short, young mistress."

Her hand shot up to her filthy hair. "It never grows…" she mumbled, lowering her gaze, face burning fiercely. "I'm not sure why…"

Lamina nodded slowly, his brow knotted. "Are you still hungry?"

The girl's face brightened, her embarrassment evaporating. "No, that meal was more than enough. Thank you very much, Mr Lamina. And you don't need to call me 'young mistress'."

Lamina grunted and waved his hand like he was swatting away a fly. "It's better if I call you young mistress. You don't have a name, do you?"

The girl shook her head, nonplussed.

Lamina grimaced at the response but nodded his head at the sink with her plate. "You licked it clean. Are you sure you don't need anymore, young mistress?"

"I'm sure. I might be sick if I eat too much."

Again, Lamina nodded slowly. Shaking his head with a growl, he rose and ushered the girl to follow suit. "We'd best be returning to Simeon's office," he muttered, almost smiling to himself when the girl quirked her head at his use of Simeon's name without the title.

With what he knew, Lamina held no respect for any Magian.

Silence enveloped the pair during the walk back to the Colonel's office. The girl didn't mind; she found Lamina's company pleasant despite his apparent disinterest in lengthy conversations.

On reaching the office, he politely held the door open for the girl and she marched sedately through.

Jumping up from his chair, the Colonel glanced suspiciously at Lamina before focusing on the girl. "The Major General wishes to discuss some matters with me, so I'll be out for a while," he explained rapidly, striding towards the office door.

The girl nodded, tension seeping out of her body as the Colonel passed.

She approached the Colonel's desk, her brow furrowed. The jar with her eye had vanished.

"0792, there is definitely a change in you."

Simeon lingered in the doorway, arms folded over his chest as he leaned casually against the door frame, his eyes scrutinising the girl.

The girl merely nodded, eye still fixed on his desk as her insides squirmed. From the corner of her eye, Lamina glanced between her and Simeon. Her stomach clenched tightly. Was he just going to watch?

She heard Simeon pace towards her. Her skin crawled as she sensed his eyes roaming over her body. *Just die,* she thought. *Better yet, let me die.*

"I am certain that there is a change in you," breathed Simeon, fingertips brushing the girl's cheek.

She shivered and inched back, averting her eye. "You've been saying that a lot lately, Colonel." She internally grimaced as she recalled the Colonel's odd mood the past month.

The ox cleared his throat loudly.

As Simeon pulled away, the girl let out the breath she had been holding and peered up to see Lamina glaring at the Colonel.

"Ah, I understand that you've been The Oracle's escort for the past two spells. You must have been to Magia *many* times then." Simeon lazily strolled towards Lamina.

The old ox narrowed his eyes further and nodded.

"Well then," said the Colonel, hands clasped behind his back as he stood tall, "you would understand the circumstances of E132 users."

Lamina studied the Colonel before replying stiffly, "I do know the laws governing Magia, Simeon, and they do not permit females of age to reside here due to the risks of overexposure and the side effects of it."

The smile fell from the Colonel's face. Rattled, he coughed and turned away.

The girl's eye widened upon seeing Simeon's face drained of colour.

Lamina's face hardened. He rounded on Simeon, pacing around to force himself into the Colonel's line of sight. "Don't delude yourself. Keeping this child here will not save you. She may be of age soon, but there is no reversing the effects of overexposure for you."

Simeon opened his mouth but only an odd noise escaped and he promptly shut it again. He began to shake, forehead breaking out into a sweat and fingers flexing, as if he were struggling to contain a maddening urge to launch himself at the ox.

He cleared his throat, determined to speak. "The Oracle will return in two weeks. She has asked me to inform you—," here he paused to take a deep breath as if it pained him to speak to Lamina, "—that you are to tend to the girl's needs until she returns." He made a face as if a bad taste filled his mouth.

Lamina inclined his head to the Colonel. "I shall do as the mistress wishes."

Simeon nodded stiffly for a while, avoiding Lamina's gaze. Abruptly, he turned on his heel and stormed to the door and the girl watched after his retreating back, delightfully alarmed.

The door snapped shut behind him and Lamina snorted.

"Cowardly, I say," grumbled the old ox, shuffling over to the sofa and plopping down into it. "He's overexposed. So young and yet he's already lost his grip on reality." He shook his head, disgruntled.

The girl was unsure how to respond—she had never seen the Colonel so shaken. She felt an uncontrollable urge to grin but instead gave herself a scolding frown, mentally chiding herself.

She shook her head to clear it and strode to the chair that Mrs Maremortum had previously occupied. A thought suddenly seized her and the girl perked up, beaming as she eagerly sat. "Lamina, have you ever seen a harlequin?"

The ox shook his shaggy head and the girl slouched back into her chair, deflated.

"What's the fuss about?"

"I thought that I'd like to see one. They entertain people and make them smile—well, that's what I've heard…" The girl lowered her eye to the floor. "If I ever saw them…" Her words trailed off and the next words stuck in her throat. *That would mean that I am free.* She gnawed on her bottom lip and shook her head vigorously. "You probably just think it's silly to smile about a harlequin. I don't. I wouldn't mind smiling over anything that proved I'm free."

Lamina ran his hairy hand along his chin. "Who told you about harlequins?"

"Colonel Simeon."

Shaking his head, the old ox rested his elbows on his knees, teeth bared in disgust. "You ought to be careful of that man, young mistress. He may be right about harlequins—odd folk in my opinion, and Avarosan at that. But, regarding Simeon, I wouldn't simply believe every word he says."

"I don't."

Lamina rubbed his chin more thoughtfully, studying the girl. "Do you know why he's so interested in you changing?"

The girl paused to think before shaking her head.

"Do you know why children are never born here in Magia? Do you know why they are bought from beastmasters outside of Magia?"

Once again, the girl shook her head, eyebrows meeting together. "I thought that was normal…"

The Colonel's claim that he had brought her in from outside of Magia rose to the forefront of her mind. Her gaze lowered to the thick carpet beneath her bare dirty feet, mind reeling. "Why are children never born here?"

"There's so little that you know about this cursed place, young mistress," explained Lamina, his voice low. He stared at her eye-patch, his mouth drawing down into a frown. "Young mistress, who gave you that?"

The girl's head shot up. "Oh, Colonel Simeon did. Why?"

Lamina leapt to his feet. "Get rid of it!"

"What?"

"Quickly, young mistress!" The ox hastily grabbed the girl's wrist and wrenched her up. He dragged her to the door as he ran.

The girl almost tripped over her own feet. "What are you doing?"

"Agnus said that I would find you eventually and my belief was not in vain!"

"Agnus?" repeated the girl, dazed. "You've met Agnus?"

Lamina nodded, his hand squeezing the girl's as they sped across the paved pathway leading away from the Colonel's office. "When he returned from Magia, four spells ago—"

"Magia? He was *here*? Four spells ago?"

"Yes—but we must be careful and remove your eye-patch! We're not safe while you wear it!"

Heart pounding, the girl dug her heels into the ground and pulled back as hard as she could, forcing Lamina to stop. "What do you mean?"

Lamina slid his hand out of the girl's. "I know it's a strange request, but if you truly want to be free, trust me. No. Trust Agnus."

The girl frowned. She hadn't liked the eye-patch and Lamina treated her better than anyone she had ever known. With a shrug, she reached up to undo the knot the Colonel had tied. Searing pain shot through her fingertips and she flinched, pulling her hand back like it'd been burnt.

"Take out a strand of your hair!"

"What?"

"Just do it!"

The girl hurriedly ripped a few hairs from her head and stared at them, convinced that Lamina was losing his mind. However, before her eye the hairs she had collected began to thicken, growing in length. Three strands of hair wormed across her hand and wove themselves together before the chestnut colour faded into a muted silver, shining in the light. The hue reminded the girl of Mrs Maremortum's hair.

Lamina cleared his throat awkwardly. "It's thread. That's why it has never grown."

"My...my hair is thread?"

"I don't understand much beyond that...it's better if you find Agnus and ask him yourself. For now, weave the thread through the strings of the eye-patch and use it to cut it."

Brow furrowed, the girl looped the thread around the strings of the eye-patch. Gripping the ends of the thread, she pulled it taut and watched as the material slid through the strings. The eye-patch dropped to the floor and a low hiss issued from a pulsating velvet glow within the eye-patch; the light of a E132 shard in communication with another. Without a word, Lamina stomped on the eye-patch, velvet light extinguished.

The girl stared incredulously at the spot where the trampled eye-patch lay, speechless. In her right eye, she saw Lamina standing before her. But in her left, she saw *him*.

He was there. Right in front of her. She recognised him from her recurring dream. Although she had never seen his face before, his name rang clear through her mind and tears sprang into her eye.

"Agnus."

Relief, excitement and hope flooded her senses.

Thousands of thoughts raced through her mind. Was he right there with her? Could he hear her?

"Agnus," she called, chewing her bottom lip.

His lips moved silently.

"What? I can't hear you, Agnus." She closed her right eye, focusing solely on what she could only see with her left. "Agnus? What are you trying to say?"

"Young mistress, listen to me." The girl felt Lamina's hand close around her arm. "You can see him through your left eye. However, he cannot see you and he cannot hear you. Nor can you hear him. He is somewhere else."

"I can see him through my left eye?" The girl opened her right eye but continued to watch Agnus intently. Her heart throbbed painfully.

She was so close to the man who she believed could free her from the hold of the Colonel, but she could not reach him at all.

"Agnus." She clutched her chest, despairing heart threatening to burst from its cage. "If you can hear me—if you can…help. Help me, please."

A bright light erupted from beneath the hand on her chest and alarmed, the girl realised with horror that there was something solid pressing up against it. Terrified, she grabbed hold of the item, ripping it out of her chest and just as quickly dropping it. Frantically examining herself, the girl's hands ran back and forth over the illuminated part of her chest. Despite the alarming suddenness of the light, the girl exhaled loudly with relief when there was no wound or blood.

Her eye darted to Lamina who had leapt forward and plunged his hand into the light, yanking the object up. The girl's eye widened, transfixed by the gleam of metal triumphantly held up in Lamina's hand.

"Wh-what is it?" The girl's voice trembled in both excitement and fascination as the light from her chest faded away.

Turning to her, Lamina grinned widely, eyes sparkling. "The sword of Agnus, *Spiritus*. Sharper than any double-edged sword…He definitely heard you."

Spiritus shone a bright white like a steadfast beacon that the girl felt drawn to. Unable to look away, she inched forward and its light embraced her, filling her with warmth.

Something caught her eye and closely studying the light that encircled her, she realised that it was formed by endless lines of minuscule words—none of which looked anything like the characters from the books Simeon read.

She was bewildered but the thought that the sword was Agnus' made her heart soar.

Lamina wordlessly held out the blade to the girl and, with some trepidation, she took the sword in her right hand, expecting it to be too heavy to hold. Yet it was as light as a feather and the girl marvelled at its weight and beauty.

"Agnus said that he would send an aid to you—and I'm glad that I'm here to witness this. I've been told that there is a phrase that unleashes the true power of the sword," explained Lamina, fixated on the splendour of Spiritus.

"A phrase?" the girl echoed, running her hand cautiously and gingerly along the blade. It was sharp, yet for some reason it did not harm her.

Lamina's shaggy head bobbed up and down. "Agnus said, that you would make one 'from the heart'."

The girl's hearth thumped in her ears, a frown marring her face as she racked her brain for a phrase that somehow linked to the majestic sword. "Are you sure that Agnus wanted *me* to make a phrase?" She turned her questioning stare to Lamina.

"Agnus always means what he says—I've learnt to trust his words," said

Lamina, his voice firm. "Again, he said that you would make a phrase that comes from your heart."

The girl continued to frown, uncertainty consuming her. What kind of phrase would be worthy of Agnus' weapon? Certainly nothing she could come up with.

The crunching of rocks underfoot made the girl jump and she spun around to face a marching group of officers led by a livid Simeon, his eyes flashing dangerously.

"It seems that you realised the use of the eye-patch," the Colonel said icily, glaring at the old ox. His narrowed eyes flickered to the girl and she promptly dropped Spiritus, her heart hammering in her chest.

"I can't do it, Lamina…" whispered the girl, pressing her hand to her chest as her breath quickened.

The light emitted from Spiritus grew dull.

Lamina growled viciously and stooped to pick up the fallen blade. "I believe," he muttered through gritted teeth, gripping the sword hilt tightly.

Spiritus exuded a brilliant light, startling the Colonel.

"I'm sure you've heard tales of Agnus' armour, Simeon," grunted the ox, returning the Colonel's glare evenly. "Even you can no longer deny Agnus."

The Colonel's eye began to twitch and his lips pulled back in a sneer. "Deny Agnus? He cannot have this girl. No, no. Return the girl to me, Lamina," he urged in a chillingly calm voice, his eyes revealing that he was anything but.

Lamina squared his shoulders and stepped in front of the girl, shielding her as she tried to rein in panicky breaths. "Heed my warning, Simeon." He brandished Spiritus. "The young mistress will return to Agnus."

At the ox's words, Simeon's eyes grew frighteningly wide and a vein throbbed visibly in his forehead. "No, I'm the one who raised and protected her." He held his hand out, his jaw clenched tightly. "Return the girl to me, *dumb* beast."

Nostrils flaring wide, Lamina roared furiously. "Proud human! Don't look down on me when you rely so heavily on that twisted stone for magick! Fool! You've thrown away so much for such evil! The child belongs to Agnus and it's where she'll go!"

Simeon let out a howl of rage and, even while sheathed, his blade appeared ablaze, a fearsome blood-red hue, stark against the black canvas of the sky. "If I can't have her, no one can—not even Agnus!"

All about him, the weapons of Element 132 oscillated in the grips of the officers following Simeon.

To the horror of the girl, scarlet weapons twisted out of their users' grips and blood splashed in the air. She flinched, turning away as an officer was pierced through the chest with his own sabre.

This ruthless brutality, the slaughtering of all these officers, made Simeon's past crimes pale in comparison.

"Young mistress!" cried Lamina, drawing the girl's attention. "You must wield Agnus' sword! Agnus said that only you can make the phrase that unleashes the weapon's true power!"

The girl's mouth fell open and she struggled to find words to express the terror she felt was threatening to swallow her whole. How could she possibly raise a sword against the Colonel without him killing her? Or without her wanting to kill him?

Focusing desperately on the vision of her left eye, she realised far too late that Agnus had vanished, leaving her eye staring at a padded white wall.

She was alone again.

"I can't," she whispered, tears welling in her eye. She glanced at the sword blanketed in lit words and shook her head. "I can't."

Lamina's face fell. For a moment, he seemed to hesitate. He looked nervously back at Simeon who had begun to draw the Element 132 out of the fallen officers and quickly turned back to the girl. "Young mistress," he began quietly, "do you wish to see a harlequin one day?"

The girl looked up. "Could I really?"

The old ox smiled warmly, his voice brimming with confidence. "Anything is possible with Agnus Dayton. Trust him."

Biting her lip, the girl reached out with trembling fingers and grabbed the hilt of the sword.

Striding forward, his face a mask of fury, Simeon tore the E132 sabre from the chest of the fallen officer and in his grasp it emitted a harsh scarlet light, morphing into another menacing blade.

The young girl swallowed nervously, her palms sweaty.

"Have faith in the sword, young mistress!" urged Lamina, as Simeon stalked towards the two. "Agnus said the key to the weapon's strength is faith! You need to believe more than ever now! Believe young mistress! Believe! Shout the command now!"

Slowly, the girl's trembling stopped and she felt a strange calm sweep over her. In this single moment her mind flashed with countless thoughts.

She thought about Agnus.

She thought about the spells of suffering in Magia. She thought about the Colonel and all the nights she had spent crying. She thought about all the days she spent deep in the mines, hacking away at the walls to retrieve the E132—the stones drenched in the blood of her friends.

And then she thought about freedom. She thought about what she had planned to do when she was finally free.

And she believed.

The youth closed her eye and took a deep shuddering breath. She lifted Spiritus, holding it vertically before her face as she muttered, "Libertas Spiritus."

From Agnus' sword, a brilliant light burst forth and a veil of runic writing enshrouded the girl and the old ox like a delicate illuminated cloak.

Simeon raised both of his blades and slashed effortlessly at the cloak of words, a look of pure elation on his face as if he believed that he had already won.

His sword, however, hadn't scratched the barrier enveloping the girl and Lamina. His face contorted to furious disbelief.

The runes swirled around both the girl and Lamina and, at regular intervals, they touched the girl and moved through her. Every time this occurred, the girl's resolve strengthened and the impact of the runes' hold on her was apparent: the fear that had previously consumed her evaporated and her limbs were filled with an energy and strength that she suspected was not her own. It was as though another's spirit had taken hold of hers.

Her body shifted, pulled into a stance by Spiritus, and a light-blue glow filled her eye as she stared the Colonel down.

In a blind fit of rage, Simeon launched himself at the pair, beating his scarlet swords against the protective mist surrounding them. The attacks dealt no damage to the brightly lit words that sleepily rotated around the girl and the ox; an unbreakable force-field.

"Mr Lamina." The girl took a deep breath to steady herself. "I'm scared. Really scared. Please, fight by my side. I promise to honour Agnus with Spiritus."

The old ox nodded, clapping the girl on the shoulder. "Can you do this?"

"Spiritus can."

Simeon's insides writhed with anger at her self-assured tone. "What makes you think that you can escape me, girl? You think just because you have Agnus' sword that you have a chance of defeating me?"

The girl was silent, coolly returning Simeon's piercing gaze which only succeeded in infuriating him further. Wordlessly, she raised Spiritus high into the air and at once the force-field surrounding her and Lamina faded away, pushing Simeon back and he staggered to remain on his feet.

"Have faith, young mistress!" Lamina shouted over his shoulder, launching himself, horns forward, at the guards who raced out from the exit in the stone walls—the outpost station that Agnus had left the girl in four spells ago.

The Colonel moved to chase Lamina but Spiritus pulled the girl and she swiftly blocked his way. Simeon let out an aggravated cry, lashing out at the girl with both his blades which Spiritus fluidly blocked.

At this, Simeon's eyes seemed to bulge in their sockets as if trying to comprehend the girl's newfound strength—it was simply impossible. And yet, here she stood, Spiritus luminescent in her grip, overflowing with determination and two other feelings she grappled with as she faced Simeon.

The words surrounding her grew more vibrant. "This is the end, Colonel Simeon," said a voice that was not her own.

As the illuminated Spiritus began to slice effortlessly through the blades of E132, Simeon's face twisted into angry realisation.

Pity and revulsion. Those were the emotions he saw in her glowing blue eye.

Spiritus cut the two blades in half and continued to arc forward, its tip brushing across the Colonel's chest, wounding him lightly. The girl gritted her teeth, gripping Spiritus tightly and fighting against the spirit within her. It would not let her push the sword further. She could not plunge it into this hateful man despite the spells of suffering he'd put her through.

Shaking her head furiously, the girl ground her teeth. How could she think like this, even now with Spiritus staying her hand?

The Colonel gave a feral roar and raised his hands, eyes flashing red. The other officers' weapons tore out of their bodies and flew into his waiting hands. He raced forward, swinging blindly at the girl who found herself yanked into different dodges.

Spiritus drew the girl's sword arm up into the air and pointed its blade downwards to the ground where it was slammed down, piercing the earth deeply. A shockwave of light and words radiated from the area, knocking the wind out of Simeon as he was flung back.

"Goodbye, Colonel," breathed the girl shakily, a look of disdain-filled pity on her face as she looked down at the fallen officer, the light-blue glow fading from her eye.

She drew Agnus' sword out from the ground and turned, prepared to follow Lamina.

Simeon rolled onto his front, gasping for air. He reached for his broken weapons but found that they had melted into the pure white substance he had seen four spells ago when Agnus had left the outpost station of Magia.

"0792!" he roared, his teeth chattering. "0792!"

The young girl didn't respond. Nor did she turn back. Her heart felt light, the idea of freedom growing with each step she took away from the Colonel. And she knew this time that someone had heard her cries.

Spiritus continued to shine in her hand as she entered the outpost station where Lamina greeted her with a grin. Together they walked to the station door where the girl stood with a smile she could not erase, the sound of grinding stone filling her ears and a view of the outside world in her grey eye.

"Let's find Agnus," Lamina said, stepping out into the humid night air.

The girl nodded eagerly, smile still in place as she took her first shaky step out of Magia.

One commands you to live as one who has been pulled out of the clutches of Hades. Like one rescued from the darkness of Death, you are to live as though you have been gifted with life undeserved.

- Lines from the *Seers of Paegaelai, Scriptura.* Translated by C. Yelnorin

6

Sweat dripped off the girl's chin onto the dusty plains below her bare feet. Her filthy, ragged clothing was plastered to her body like a layer of unwanted skin. Still, she struggled along the terrain, following closely behind Lamina who strode energetically despite his age.

Fatigue had settled deep into her muscles and Lamina happily carried Spiritus for her, their sole source of light through the thick, dense darkness that surrounded them.

Despite this, the girl's spirits seemed high with Lamina's hand around hers, gently pulling her along.

"Where are we headed?" she gasped, half dependent on Lamina to drag her across the plains. She squinted, straining to see far into the distance.

"Lacuna." Lamina held Spiritus high above their heads, its light a shield radiating about them. "Let's hope that once we reach Lacuna, Agnus will also be there."

"What do you mean?"

"Well…considering that you saw him with your left eye, it means that he's where that is. And that place would be Nyx."

The girl's face scrunched up, her brow furrowed. "Isn't that where Mrs Maremortum is from?"

"That's right. It's about less than an hour's travel from Magia." Lamina unconsciously squeezed her hand, expression grim. "Nyx is not a safe place for Agnus. Mrs Maremortum has set up additional security measures against him—she wants him dead. I can't understand why he would be there."

The girl's stomach dropped. "She wants him dead?" Wishing death on another was something only awful people did. She thought of her struggle against Spiritus—her desire to kill Simeon had almost consumed all reason within her. She bit her lip. Wasn't Mrs Maremortum a kinder and better person than her?

"Yes. She loathes him because she's fiercely protective of her daughters—or perhaps it's more correct to describe her as obsessive with a degree of overexposure," explained Lamina, shaking his head. "She came to Magia tonight to take your eye for her daughter."

At these words, a sense of dread possessed the girl. "My eye?"

The old ox sighed, hesitant. Shaking his head, he continued, "Yes, she is the one who asked the Colonel for a replacement eye for her daughter, Arche."

The girl's heart sank and she fell silent. Mrs Maremortum was no better than her.

Lamina shot a guilty glance at the girl and cleared his throat. "She hails her children as 'gifted'. Yet, her children are nothing but *cursed*."

A shiver ran down the girl's spine despite the heat, snapping her out of her thoughts. "What do you mean by that, Mr Lamina?"

"The spell those children were born was a cursed one. In that spell, about eleven spells ago, there was a great famine throughout Tempus and war broke out. Many died. No animal was born or hatched. No shoots sprang up from the earth. Not a single child was born except for Mrs Maremortum's twins.

"In Lacuna, the bearer of," Lamina paused, shuddering, "Mors Mortis announced that spell was marked as the arrival of the one who would work with him."

The girl tilted her head quizzically to the side. "The bearer of Mors Mortis?"

"Death," Lamina said gravely as the dusty terrain around them began to change the further they travelled. "There's an old prophecy that tells of the birth of Death and that after him follows Hades. The prophecy states that a fourth of the earth is theirs to destroy—something like that would destroy Tempus! Yet instead of Mrs Maremortum giving birth to one child, she gave birth to twins, two monsters to deal with instead of one." Lamina fell into a pensive silence.

Pondering on his words for a moment, the girl piped up, "The bearer of Mors Mortis—," at the crinkling of Lamina's nose, the girl corrected herself, "—I mean, Death—does he live in Lacuna now?"

Lamina shrugged. "No one knows where he truly resides. They say he travels throughout the land of Tempus claiming countless souls each spell. In some lands, they call him The Reaper and they believe that he cannot be seen unless you are on the brink of death and he appears to finish you off."

The girl swallowed thickly, the fine hairs along her arms standing on their ends. She glanced over her shoulder but could only see the deep black of the night behind her. Unconsciously she gripped Lamina's hand tightly and drew closer to him.

While the girl's thoughts were scattered by newborn fears, Lamina looked back at her, his expression guarded.

An unusual feeling of pity rose in the old ox's heart. He was not accustomed to dealing with children outside of businesses but had seen enough to understand that the land of Tempus was far too harsh for most children. A world where they weren't permitted to do anything but behave as adults. He pondered upon the ancient stories his grandfather would tell him: of a time when the world's throne was occupied by righteous kings and children were loved as gifts from Pater.

Out of his quiet reverie, Lamina noticed the girl's laboured breathing. Mentally berating himself, he cleared his throat uneasily. "We'll walk a little while more and then we'll take a break. We've walked quite a distance—there's some small landforms now—"

"Mr Lamina," interrupted the young girl, her eye staring off into the distance, "were you in Lacuna when Death appeared to announce the birth of Arche and her sister?"

Lamina shook his head. "Thank goodness for that! They say that those who had seen him were cursed!"

"Cursed?" repeated the girl, her forehead damp from perspiration. "Like the Maremortums?"

"No, not as terrible and fearsome...I know of an unfortunate lad who was rendered blind."

"Were they all blinded because they saw Death? Or was it just that person...? Who was that person?"

Lamina gave a one-shouldered shrug. "I'm not sure. There were quite a few people who claimed to be cursed..."

He broke off when the girl stumbled into him and he steadied her by grabbing her shoulder. Brow furrowed, he released the girl's shoulder and touched her forehead lightly. "How are you feeling?"

"Someone is moving my left eye—a hand has it!" The girl trembled uncontrollably, her eye wide with terror.

"You can still see everything with your left eye?"

The girl nodded feebly against the palm of Lamina's hand, her face paling while she swayed lightly on the spot. "It's taking a lot of concentration…" she murmured, eyelid drooping, "to be here."

"To be here?"

She nodded again, closing her right eye. "There's a glowing scarlet crystal in that other hand…it's moving away…and now…now, there's only darkness…" Sweat streamed down her face.

Lamina groaned. He felt like a fool.

"We must stop here, young mistress. Your temperature is rising!" he urged, anxiety lacing his words.

He pulled the girl along behind him to a patch of dead grass near a collection of small rocks where he made her sit. Sitting beside her, he heaved a sigh. "I'm sorry, young mistress," he mumbled somewhat embarrassed, "The travel conditions have not been ideal. This open resting place isn't any better. There is some grass here, however. Looks like we're leaving the grounds ruined by overexposure. We'll reach The Mare soon."

"What about my eye, Mr Lamina?"

"Best not to worry about it until we see Agnus."

"How can I not worry about it!"

Taken aback by the girl's snappy response, Lamina crossed his arms over his chest. "I could give you a variety of lies to soothe your fears momentarily, but the truth is that only Agnus can provide the answers to many of your questions," he growled. "If you want real answers, you will wait to talk to Agnus. I won't lie to you now."

There was a frustrated beat before the girl nodded begrudgingly and wordlessly laid her head against Lamina's shoulder. After a breath, she bolted upright, shaking. "I'm sorry, Mr Lamina! I didn't mean to! I'm just so tired!"

Lamina gave a lop-sided grin. "It's okay young mistress. We all get tired. We all must learn how to manage that better. But let's get you feeling better before meeting Agnus, okay?"

The girl smiled half-heartedly, inching closer to Lamina and laying her head back down on his shoulder. "I really am… free," she mumbled weakly.

The low drone of the few bugs flitting about in the humid air filled the silence that fell between them. For a moment the girl seemed to be lulled to sleep by the monotonous buzzing.

"Mr Lamina?"

"Mm-hm?"

"For a while, I didn't even know who Agnus was. My friend told me about him before he died. And once I heard about him, I wasn't sure if someone like him really cared about a child like me."

Lamina stared into the pitch-black darkness ahead, still as the girl laid against him, her voice small and frail in the muggy night air.

"You told me to believe in him. And I do. I do. I dreamed of him for spells without realising who he was. So, why me?"

The old ox heaved a heavy sigh, momentarily shifting the tired girl. "Listen young mistress," he murmured, picking at the frayed hem of his tunic. "Four spells ago—where do I start?"

Lamina mumbled a prayer for wisdom under his breath.

"Listen," he said again, clearing his throat loudly. "It's a difficult feat carrying a person all the way to Magia."

The words shook the girl wide awake. "What do you mean?"

"Agnus carried you on his back all the way to Magia from Lacuna—it's not an easy task and the journey was, without a doubt, long and gruelling," Lamina continued but the girl's expression had grown distant.

"Four spells ago. I was with him four spells ago…and he left me in Magia?"

Lamina felt his own face falling at the girl's despondent one. "Look, young mistress." Placing Spiritus down on the ground, he reached deep into the pockets of his worn pants, drawing out five small pieces of silver thread and held it out.

"What is it?"

"Your hair."

The young girl reached forward, running her fingers over the pieces of thread. She shook her head, face scrunched up. Her voice was a strangled whisper, "Why does this matter? Why should I care about this when he left me in Magia!"

"Agnus gave them to me before he headed off to Magia with you," Lamina explained, voice soft and eyes pleading. "Originally, it was a lock of your brown hair, and I wasn't aware of it at the time, but it seems that the closer I came to finding you, the more it changed into silver thread. Now, it's completely morphed, but that's not the important part."

Lamina straightened up beside his young companion and took her hand in his, pressing the pieces of thread into hers and closing her fingers over them. "The method of payment in Lacuna is to surrender something of value. Something that can identify who you are. Agnus gave me this. That man, he truly cares about you, don't ever doubt that."

The girl's eye glistened with tears as she stared at the pieces of silver thread glinting in the light of Spiritus. Her lips still twisted with conflicting emotions.

"The first thing he told me when he returned from Magia four spells ago was to trust in him. The second thing was that he needed me to be there for you. I offered my services to the beastmasters of Lacuna following Agnus' instructions and for two spells, I was stationed as a worker in the Kingdom of Sominium. One day, the beastmasters explained that a woman had arrived requesting an escort for her travels. She refused to hire a child and demanded anyone older and willing. That woman was Mrs Maremortum."

Silence filled the night air, the droning buzz of the insects louder than ever.

The girl thumbed the silver thread, her face reflecting the embarrassment and shame she felt at her outburst. Still, her eyebrows knitted together and she pressed her hand against her heart.

"Why Magia…?" her wavering voice still asked and Lamina could see the turmoil raging in her eye.

Lamina breathed deeply through his large nostrils, staring contemplatively at the dust below his hooves which stirred gently from his nervous movements.

"I don't know," he answered honestly. "I can't explain why he left you at Magia but I can tell you this, young mistress: there is *always* a reason."

"A reason for what?"

The old ox shrugged unconvincingly. "It's just like what I said about your eye, young mistress. It's best not to worry about that until you finally see Agnus. Only he has the answers to your questions. So, for now rest, young mistress. Soon, we will be heading to The Mare and from there, crossing over and heading towards Lacuna."

The girl sighed but nodded reluctantly. She laid her head against Lamina's shoulder, her thin body sagging against his side. Squeezing her eyes shut she hoped the tempest of feelings within her would die down and that sleep would come.

To her surprise, she grew drowsy quickly and managed to murmur a "thanks" before drifting off.

Fatigue washed her ashore a dreamless landscape of pure white.

Head pounding and sweat streaking down her face, the young girl bolted upright, breaths ragged and harsh.

She could not recall what had disturbed her sleep, but she felt Lamina shift beside her, his body tense and Spiritus held aloft to illuminate the space around them.

"Lamina?" she called tentatively, her slowly adjusting eye sweeping across the dark expanse.

A chilling screech filled the air.

The hairs on the back of the girl's neck stood on end.

Lamina's hand shot out, seizing the girl's hand. "No…how could they release them just for us…" He jumped to his feet, yanking the girl up with him. "Run."

In a flash, the pair were racing across the plain, Lamina with renewed vigour and the girl with all that was left in her.

"What is it?" she puffed, scrawny legs pumping beneath her to keep up.

Several shrieks pierced the stillness of the night and the panic that radiated off the old ox seeped into the girl. Despite not knowing what was behind them, fear drove her forward.

In her desperation, she lost her footing and tumbled to the ground. Pushing herself up onto her knees, she inhaled a mouthful of dust and a coughing fit wracked her body.

The tormented screams that echoed across the plains steadily grew louder.

A putrid smell assaulted the girl's nose and her coughing turned to gagging.

Strong hands hooked under her armpits, hauling her up onto her feet. "We have to move quickly, young mistress!" grunted Lamina. He let her go momentarily, ducking to pick up Spiritus from where he had placed it on the ground. "We're so close to The Mare now. Can you hear the flowing water, young mistress?"

Head reeling from the overpowering stench that grew stronger with each passing second, the girl gasped, her eye watering. "Wh-what is that smell?" she coughed.

Lamina swallowed thickly, tightening his hold on Spiritus. "Quickly, young mistress." He grabbed the girl's hand again and raced away from the screeches that chased them.

The light of the blood-red moon was no comfort for the two companions running across the plains. They flew past small withered and twisted trees, shrubs and other frail greenery. The few trees they passed gradually became taller, their branches willowy and thick. The bushes that sprung up about them now bore lush green leaves. Somewhere ahead, the sound of trickling water beckoned the two companions, urging them forward.

The young girl's lungs burned for air and beneath her small frame, her legs screamed. The rancid smell that pursued her and Lamina continued to unsettle her stomach and her head throbbed as they pounded through the grass that cut her aching feet.

The hair-raising cries of their pursuers seemed closer than before, ringing mercilessly in her ears.

A strange idea entered her mind and she thought that what she could hear were the despairing cries of agonised women.

The old ox's grip tightened on her hand. "We're nearly at The Mare!" he shouted over the piercing screams, sounding closer than before.

They ran out into a clearing, the sight of a small wooden dock and an awaiting boat and boatman relieving the young girl.

Maremortum!

The vicious screeching in her head caused the girl to jump with fright and the smooth, yet scaly skin of a long, thin animal wrapped around her ankle. The animal hissed, pulling her leg out from under her and she fell with a loud cry, hand wrenched from Lamina's as countless writhing snakes coiled around her body dragging her back towards the screeches.

"M-Mr Lamina!" gasped the girl, struggling against her bonds, head filled with the taunts of otherworldly voices.

Maremortum! Maremortum!

A terrifying thought possessed her. The Maremortum twins—Hades— were coming for her.

In front of her eye, the hunched figure of a screeching being approached and the girl's heart stopped, her mind failing her.

From what she could tell, the limping figure was a woman—or the remains of one. It wore tatters of what once would have been fine clothing and its flesh reeked of decay and rot. The fur trimmed coat the creature wore failed to cover a large, rounded belly where countless veins pulsed rhythmically, the translucent skin revealing the deformed shape of something no one would dare call a child.

At the sight of the malformed creature in the being's belly, bile rose into the back of the girl's throat and tears stung her eye. She coughed violently, sick spluttering the floor which she was then dragged through by the snakes, the vomit smearing into her hair and onto the side of her face.

Around the waist of the being hung a belt of writhing snakes, some of which had detached themselves to wrap around the young girl and pull her closer towards the deformed being, its eyes covered by aged bandages crusted with blood. The corners of its mouth had been noticeably extended and sewn haphazardly together again, the threads stretching each time the being opened its mouth to scream.

From behind the disfigured woman, several more appeared, limping hungrily forward, their mouths slowly stretching to their full extent and the small creatures, in the bellies of some of the beings, writhed in horrific joy.

"GET AWAY FROM HER!" Lamina bellowed, repelling some of the hideous beings that swarmed around him with Spiritus. "YOUNG MISTRESS!" He slashed at the snakes that leapt at him, severing their heads.

All about them, the inhumanely bent women crept and the hisses of hundreds of snakes filled the young girl's head as the beings touched her face, her hair and her body, their screams numbing her completely.

MAREMORTUM!

A cracking sound like thunder filled the air and the women before the girl howled angrily, two of them falling lifelessly onto the girl, smothering her.

Lamina spun around, slack-jawed, trying to discern where the sound had erupted from.

"Greetings, ladies!" sang a deep, mellow voice. "You seem to be lost. Who let you out of your cages?"

There was another round of thunder, eliciting more shrieks as a few more headless figures fell with a thump.

Smoke rose from the barrels of two guns, held up by a young man with long, grey hair, whose dark slanted eyes glinted with mirth.

The snakes hissed venomously at him and several beings launched themselves at him. Shooting each of them in the head left foul-smelling blood spurting from the bullet wounds as they fell gracelessly to the ground.

"Ladies, ladies! One at a time, please," he chided with a grin, spinning his guns around to empty the chambers and slotting more bullets in. The grin faded from his face, replaced with a solemn expression. "I'm sorry that I can't truly put you to rest."

The head of the nearest creature was blown clean off and the man twisted around, feet dancing beneath him and arms swinging gracefully about, fingers rapidly pulling the triggers of his guns.

With the beings distracted, Lamina sliced through a few of them to reach the fallen girl, lugging the limp figures—their flesh steadily regrowing with a scarlet glow—off her and pulling her back up to her feet. She sagged weakly against him, the sweat and sick mingled in the locks of her hair, brushed against the ox's tunic. In the scuffle, her temperature had continued to rise.

"Are they human?" the girl shakily whispered, legs threatening to crumble beneath her.

Lamina secured an arm around her and slung her left stump over his shoulder.

"They were. Once." Gritting his teeth, the ox began a cautious trot towards the dock where the boat awaited them, his heart pounding.

Noticing their movement, the gunslinger turned his gunfire towards the monsters near them, clearing the path to the boat which he also edged towards, occasionally turning one gun on the beings charging near the riverbed. Chambers emptied, bullets loaded, fired.

Lamina chanced a glance at the gunslinger.

Despite being surrounded by the deformed creatures, the man remained untouched as he wove through the horde, guns whirling. His eyes darted back and forth and at moments it seemed like an invisible force stemmed forth from them, pushing back and cutting down the enemies that his bullets didn't penetrate.

Reaching the dock, Lamina tore his eyes away from the gunslinger and sat the girl gingerly in the boat with the beggar dressed in a grey vest.

"Three passengers?" asked the gap-toothed beggar, grabbing the boat oars. "Three items of payment, please."

"What?" growled Lamina, the boat rocking slightly.

The girl clung to Lamina in a daze. "Three?"

"Here you go!" The long-haired gunslinger tossed the beggar a small leather pouch and leapt into the boat. It rocked precariously. He turned back towards the screeching beings and reloaded his guns. "Pay the boatman! I'm running out of bullets!"

Lamina glanced reproachfully at the man's back. Glimpsing the horde darting towards them, the ox stuffed his hand hurriedly into his pocket and tossed the beggar two shiny beads.

"Thank you," the beggar said curtly, his lips pursed at the beads in his hand.

"Seer Joseph, row us out of here!" shouted Lamina desperately.

The seer wagged his index finger. "No. The girl has not paid."

"I gave you two precious beads!"

"Yes, that was *your* payment. Those are of no value to the girl and her identity." A sliver of runes rose from Joseph's lips, fading into the darkness. "Now, the girl must pay."

Lamina's jaw dropped. "She can't! She doesn't have anything to give!"

"Then she can stay behind," replied Joseph coldly. "No payment, no ride."

The ox clenched the grip of Spiritus. "Why you—"

"Mr Joseph," wheezed the young girl, suppressing the urge to be sick. "That vest is Agnus', isn't it?"

The seer studied her. "Yes."

The girl nodded slowly. She had seen that vest countless times. "Mr Joseph, all I can offer for payment is this."

Turning to Lamina, the girl took Spiritus from him, his eyes searching her face uncertainly. Wordlessly, she poured her belief into the blade and cut off a few strands of hair, allowing it to collect on the boat's deck where they wove themselves neatly together, forming a long piece of silver thread. Picking the thread up, she looped it carefully around her arm and dug into her flesh. Blood seeped onto the boat deck.

"Young mistress!" cried Lamina, pressing a firm hand on the girl's wound. "*You silly girl!* Utterly reckless! Thoughtless! You should have just parted with that hair!"

"Ah. I'm sorry, my head is spinning…"

The blood dissolved into the floor of the boat and once it vanished,

Joseph nodded his head at the girl. "Payment received." Gripping the oars of the boat and, despite the thinness of his arms, he rowed effortlessly away from the dock.

"Well!" exclaimed the long-haired man, slotting his guns in the holsters on his waist. He dropped into a seat and waved happily at the screeching malformed creatures. "Farewell ladies! You can eat some more Old World technology another time!"

The beings continued to shriek, writhing along the banks of the river, the sewing at the corners of their mouths stretched to their limit. Those that had fallen had clambered to their feet, twisted necks ending in muscle tendrils, growing to reform their heads, haloed in scarlet light.

"Who are they?" rasped the girl, staggering back into a seat as the boat rocked to and fro, her stomach turning uncomfortably.

The grey-haired gunslinger turned to the girl and his cold eyes roamed over her petite figure, scrutinising the ratty cloth for a dress that hung from her bony shoulders. He tilted his head and flashed a wide toothy smile. "I didn't know there were three Maremortums…or could you be Arche?"

With the sway of the boat, Lamina put a protective arm around the young girl and glared at the gunslinger. "She's *not* Arche."

The gunslinger pursed his lips and bowed stiffly to the young girl. "Please excuse me, young miss. You look awfully like the young Maremortum."

The girl wiped sweat from the side of her face. "Have you met her before?"

"Arche?"

She nodded.

The gunslinger ran a hand along his bristly jaw, steadily returning the girl's gaze. "Not personally."

The girl shook her head sluggishly, her words slurred. "Sorry…who are you guys?"

The man surveyed the girl for a moment. "Shigure," he answered slowly, drawing himself up to his full height.

Lamina choked as he took a breath. "Isn't that the name of The Conqueror's war advisor?"

Shigure merely smiled and shrugged. "So they say." As Lamina attempted to collect his thoughts, Shigure turned back to the girl, his eyes glinting. "And what is your name, miss?"

"I don't have one." After a beat, a memory resurfaced in the girl's foggy brain. She choked out a mirthless laugh. "You can call me, Ridley."

Shigure's brow twitched and the corners of his mouth tightened. But he shrugged, running a hand through his long, thick hair and sighed. "You can relax, oldie." He shot a look at Lamina, stretching his arms out. "I'm not your enemy here. Why do you think I helped you escape those Tophets? Any person claiming complete allegiance to the New World is no friend of mine."

"Oldie?" barked the old ox, nostrils flaring. "My name is Lamina!"

Shigure rolled his eyes and waved his hand dismissively. "Yes, yes."

"Tophets?" repeated the girl blankly, hand on Lamina's arm to steady herself, her face flushed red with fever. "They're of what world?"

"Tophets. The things chasing you. They were Tophets. Those ones were from Magia, which is of the New World," Shigure explained with a sigh. He readjusted, folding his long cloak beneath himself. An impish smile crossed his unshaven face. "Judging from your appearance, you've just come from there."

The girl jumped out of her seat, falling backwards.

Lamina and Shigure instinctively leapt up and grabbed one of her arms, pulling her back in before she fell overboard.

"Be careful!" shouted Joseph. "If you fall in, I can't help you."

Lamina shot him a grimace as they pulled her back onto her seat.

The seer returned his look evenly. "My only duty is to ensure these waters are not disturbed by humans or beasts outside of this boat. I have no desire to involve myself in anything outside of that."

"Don't let us distract you, Seer Joseph. I love a single-minded individual," Shigure said with a wink, earning a scowl from Joseph. "We won't let her fall in—though she's running quite a temperature." He laid a light hand against her forehead. Digging into his pocket, he drew out a small sheet of faded paper and opened it, eyes scanning it quickly.

Lamina's eyebrows shot up questioningly.

"Ah, I see, I see," Shigure muttered under his breath. He carefully refolded the paper and slipped it back into his coat pocket. "She'll be okay."

Lamina grunted lowly, dabbing the girl's glistening forehead before sitting back, returning his gaze to Shigure.

His dark, slanted eyes were studying Agnus' sword laid across Lamina's lap before they flitted up to meet Lamina's. "That is quite a sword you have on you." A fathomless smile crossed his lips. "Where did you come across such a jewel?"

Lamina's hands dropped to the sword protectively.

The smile on Shigure's face broadened.

"Mr Shigure," the girl said in a breathy voice, shaking her aching head to clear it. "You said, that the Tophets were from Magia."

"Yes, they're tracking creatures," sighed Shigure, twiddling his thumbs. "Think of them as dogs."

"Dogs?"

"Yes. Animals that track scents. Except Tophets track only one sort of scent." Shigure's pupils dilated, an unsettling smile crossing his face. "The scent of children."

The girl unconsciously gripped Lamina's arm, her ears still ringing with the distant wails of the Magian horrors they had fled from.

Lamina's large hand patted her matted hair comfortingly, brushing out some of the sick still clinging there. "Magia was once a great military base situated at the bottom of the mountains," Lamina explained while looking out at The Mare's tranquil water. "Carved within the walls of the mountains was once a great town, its inhabitants guarded by the militia below. It was an impenetrable fortress."

Lamina's expression grew dark. "But the people began to commit horrendous acts. Children were born for the sole purpose of forcing them to carve away at the town walls. Parents sought the blood of their children for the sake of a scarlet jewel."

"I thought," interrupted the girl, fear driving her to sit closer to the ox, "that children couldn't be born in Magia."

"Magians are not able to have children," chimed in Shigure. "Not after the curse Agnus placed upon them."

"Agnus did what?"

Shigure glanced at the girl, eyebrow twitching. "It's too long of a story to tell," he said dismissively, his gaze returning to the approaching dock in the distance. "And do you really not know *anything* of this world, *Ridley*?"

Heat rose into the girl's cheeks and she looked down at her lap.

Lamina shifted forward in his seat, a growl rumbling in his chest as he stared at Shigure. He turned to the girl, a gentle smile softening his features. "Many spells before the sun's death, Agnus travelled to Magia. He cursed their people because of the terrible things they were doing. Because of this, Agnus declared that no child would come from Magia ever again.

"No one knows how, but what he said came true. Not a single child has been born there since. Even women who were expecting at the time of Agnus' declaration—their bodies froze in time. The Magians were driven to desperation and overexposure urged them to resort to horrific experiments upon themselves in attempts to reverse Agnus' curse."

The girl's mind drifted back to the grimy, bloodstained room where the Colonel had taken her eye out and a shiver shot through her. She wondered if such experiments had been conducted there.

"So…those creatures. They were real women?"

Shigure flicked a bug lazily off his arm. "What remained of them. Driven to insanity from overexposure and the inability to have children, they injected themselves with a liquefied form of Element 132. What resulted wasn't death but something far worse. Those beings who are forever looking for what they cannot have. It's been 22 spells since Agnus' curse and the only thing driving the Tophets is the Element 132 that continues to run through their veins."

A thought in the girl's mind clicked. "*Agnus' Curse?*"

The old ox turned to her. "The curse he had placed upon them. The Magians would have been fuming at Agnus' insolence: placing a child under their care. What better way to remind them of their terrible deeds?"

The question of why still echoed in the girls' head but she bitterly bit it down, remembering Lamina's words earlier.

"You're fortunate that I was heading in the same direction." Shigure flexed his fingers, bored.

"Where are you headed to?" Lamina asked, eyes narrowed.

"I have some business past The Mare with my Master," said Shigure, his tone of finality as he looked away.

Silent, the girl sat back, attempting to process everything. Her lips pressed together in a firm hard line.

"Mr Shigure, you've told me about yourself, and now I know more about Magia, but…" the girl trailed off, her brow knotted. "I asked you to both introduce yourselves, so why hasn't your friend spoken?"

Both Shigure and Lamina sat up straighter, the latter shooting a disconcerted look at the girl.

Joseph's lips formed a hard, thin line but he said nothing, lowering his gaze to the oars he gripped, his knuckles turning white.

With a glance at Joseph, Lamina shook his head. "Young mistress, Shigure is alone. There is no one else on the boat besides Shigure, Joseph, you and I."

"No, there's five people here! Who's that young man?" demanded the girl, jabbing a finger at the space beside Shigure. "I'm not making it up! There's a boy in a suit—older than me—with white hair. He hasn't said a word this entire time and he helped Mr Shigure fight off the Tophets! Didn't you see?"

Lamina shot an alarmed look at the girl, his face pale. "Young mistress, there is *no one* there."

"There is! Can't you see—," the words died on the girl's lips, her breath hitching in her throat. A lump of words collected there and she struggled to swallow it down as the young man only she could see turned his haunting fiery-coloured eyes to her and rose, towering over her.

Pupil-less eyes bore deep into hers, shocking the girl into a petrified silence.

A cold, hollow voice in her head rang above a frightful hum that filled the girl's ears.

You are the Third, the voice whispered in the young girl's mind, its owner taking a step lightly towards her, eyes fixed to hers and mouth slowly opening

to speak:
    "Young Maremortum, I am Death."

Let all look to the desolation of Thurim and its people and rise against
the wickedness of this age.
Let all walk through the ashes of Kaiern and its people and turn away
from any contrivances to act outside of One's will.

- Lines from *The Wisdom of Aurelius, Scriptura.* Translated by T.
Lowenthal

7

The world seemed to shatter, the girl's ears ringing as the pieces covered her like the fine dust of a dream, its meaning elusive to the very end.

"Death?" she whispered, throat closing up.

At her words, Lamina grabbed her hand and shook his head mutely, eyes wide with terror.

The girl gripped Lamina's hand tightly but was unable to tear her eye away from the young man standing over her.

Death tilted his youthful head to the side, face a blank canvas. "Are you afraid, young Maremortum?"

Lips trembling, the girl parted them to speak, but no words came.

"There's nothing to fear, young Maremortum."

The girl shook her head slowly. "Please," she murmured, voice trembling, "I haven't—"

The fiery-eyed young man moved with a level of grace that the girl would not have associated with Death. Reaching into his pocket, he drew out a small piece of white material attached to the ends of two strings and held it out to the girl. "There's nothing to fear. Master clearly stated that today would not be your time, even if you saw me. It's merely proof that you're the Third."

He paused and continued after some thought, "Besides, Hades did not mention you on the list."

Heart hammering painfully fast against her ribcage, the girl scarcely dared to breathe as she shrank away from The Reaper. "Not my time?"

Death steadily returned her faltering gaze. "No."

Exhaling, relief washed over the girl and tears welled in her eye. She hiccoughed, alarm flaring within her. "I'll be cursed!"

The Reaper drew himself up to his full height. "I *am* the curse. That you can *see* me is a curse in itself. All creatures deserve to see me. One day, every creature that my Master has placed under *our* care will."

"*Our?*"

"What is he saying, young mistress?"

Fixated on Death, the girl continued as if Lamina had not spoken. "What do you mean by 'our care'?"

"Hades and I," he answered, gaze unnervingly direct, "the lives of many in Tempus are under our care."

Gulping, the girl opened her mouth, her words slow and uncertain. "Am I one of those people?"

Death didn't answer and instead tossed the item he held into the girl's lap. "It's an eye-patch," he explained when she picked it up cautiously. "Master said you would need it later."

A look of bewilderment crossed the girl's face and she stared at the eye-patch with mistrust. "Your Master?"

"You should consider yourself fortunate!" laughed Shigure, yet his eyes were mirthless. "The Master of Death has spared you!"

Lamina gaped at the gunslinger, indignant. "You can see him too?"

A wide grin spread across Shigure's lips. "Why are you two so serious? Sit down, Hitori."

To the girl's surprise, The Reaper reclaimed his seat. Silence followed until the boat slowed to a halt, easing up to the simple wooden dock on the riverside.

"This is it," sang Shigure, languid as he rose. He turned to the girl and Lamina, bowing with a smirk. "It was a pleasure meeting you both." He nodded to Joseph who grimaced. "Let's go, Hitori."

With equal elegance and grace, Shigure and Hitori alighted from the boat, the former thanking Joseph.

Lamina shot up, rocking the boat. "Do we share the same destination?"

The gunslinger paused.

"What? Do you wish to follow a man whose very shadow is Death itself?" Shigure turned back to Lamina with a cold smile, amused. "Like I said, we are heading out to meet our Master."

The old ox clambered onto the dock with a quick thanks to Joseph. He reached back to hoist the girl out and Joseph gave a short wave in farewell.

"We are travelling to Lacuna," puffed Lamina, grimacing as his muscles ached dully. "And I'm curious about this master of yours."

"Oh please, do come along and bother us with your endless questions," sighed Shigure, rolling his eyes as the ox and girl fell into step with him. "I'm not interested in answering any more questions. But you're free to follow if that's what you really want!" He turned away, laughing humourlessly.

"It's safer travelling in a group," insisted Lamina, quietly taking the girl's hand, noting her tired eye and the unsteadiness of her feet.

A derisive snort issued from Shigure but he marched on without another word.

A few paces away from the dock, Lamina gestured to Spiritus and explained to the girl that it was best not to draw any sort of unpleasant attention to themselves.

Nodding imperceptibly, the girl wordlessly took the sword from a puzzled Lamina and pushed the tip of it against her chest.

Horror-stricken, Lamina leapt forward to grab Spiritus, but it began to dissipate as the girl pushed it further into her body. Grains like sand swirled around runes that were pulled into her body.

Lamina blinked, seizing the girl's shoulders. "How did you do that?"

The girl stared back at him, dazed and feverish. "I don't know, it just occurred to me that it would work."

"Strange," remarked Lamina, brow furrowed, "but effective."

Pleased with the outcome, Lamina and the girl chased after Shigure who flatly refused to wait for them.

The unusual group trekked through a long grassy field, Hitori leading the way. Mud from recent rain squelched under the girl's feet and slipped in between her toes. It was oddly liberating. The sensation of mud and grass sticking to her feet. The lightness of the air. The land beyond the overexposed was wondrously different.

Taking a deep breath and forgetting her fever, the girl's hand slipped out of Lamina's, earning a worried glance that vaporised at her expression. The old ox smiled and looked ahead, allowing the girl to slow down and soak in her surroundings.

Gazing about herself in wonder, greenery filled her vision and the soothing music of the birds twittering in the trees awed her. With each step, joy welled within her and she could not help recalling her hope of discovering the world beyond Magia. The freedom she had long dreamed of. She swiped a stray tear and shook her head.

Beyond the hilly grasslands, the girl spotted iron-wrought gates rising in the distance, illuminated by objects resembling the torches at Magia. Squinting as she approached, she realised that though they resembled torches, they needed no fire to shine brilliantly in the dark. She turned a quizzical eye to Lamina.

"Electricity," he said with a hint of pride, pointing at the orbs of light attached to the top of a tall metal pole. "They're street-lamps. We use electricity here because Lacuna is part of the Old World. Liberian scientists say electricity interferes with E132's effectiveness. So, the people here don't live under the spell of E132."

From the hilltop, the girl breathed deeply, drinking in every inch of the town she glimpsed between the bars of the iron fence. Her eye shone as it flitted about. "This is Lacuna?"

The fence raced along the outskirts of the town and Lacuna stretched across the horizon like a giant quilt, covering a large area of the grassy terrain. Uniquely shaped buildings of various sizes sat snugly together within the gates accompanied by the smog of smoke that rose slovenly from chimneys.

Along the streets that wound through the entire town, street-lamps stood tall above the occupants of Lacuna, dressed similarly to Lamina — vests, coats, and brightly coloured billowy dresses on many of the women. The pathways were filled with crowds of people and beasts. Stalls were parked on the sides of the brick paved streets and were decked with foods, mechanical devices, jewellery and a wealth of goods that the girl could've only dreamed of. A few unblemished children roamed about, chasing the tails of their masters through the crowded streets.

Swallowing nervously, she wondered how easily she would be swept away by the current of the streets.

Reaching the iron-wrought gates, the girl realised how tiny she was in comparison to it; it stood well above Lamina who towered over all in the group.

Front and centre of the gate, a metallic lion stood majestically, its lips pulled back to reveal its teeth in a fierce snarl. Upon its maned head sat a finely crafted crown with numerous shimmering jewels. Beneath its paws lay a trampled snake, its head crushed.

Busy scrutinising the figurehead, the girl snapped back to attention when Lamina approached a man who stood as the lone guard at the gates.

"You're still here then, Matthew?" a beaming Lamina asked.

The man had long, black hair tied neatly back into a ponytail which bobbed up and down when he nodded. "I'm stationed here until tomorrow and then I'll be crossing The Mare to sort out a few matters with Uriel." Matthew's face was grave yet the lights from the street-lamps danced in his blue eyes.

"You're headed to Hinnom? What about Bek?"

Matthew gave a one-shouldered shrug. "Bekah will be fine. And I'm sure I'll be permitted to return home after all my duties to The Conqueror are complete." Trailing off, he cocked an eyebrow and nodded at Shigure who merely smiled. "Interesting companions you have, Lamina."

Lamina quietly groaned, scratching his head furiously. "So, he *is* the war advisor then? I should've known…guns are a rarity since The Conqueror took the throne."

"Didn't Meiko tell you about him?" Matthew sighed as Lamina shook his head. He leaned closer, lowering his voice further, "Let's talk another time."

With that, he called over his shoulder for the gate to be opened. The crunch of unseen gears and cogs filled the air and he gestured to the wide opening into the town, bowing in welcome.

"Thank you, Matthew." Lamina smiled, clapping the man on the shoulder. "I wish you all the best with your duties."

"And you with yours."

"Say hi to that young lady of yours."

"Don't be an idiot."

Their voices faded as the girl jogged forward to the closest footpath, stopping directly under the light of one of the street-lamps. She spun slowly, sparkling eye studying the bustling town.

People and beasts swerved around her, some shooting a look of annoyance at her. A woman wearing a monocle shuffling through lenses whispered into the ear of a metal-jawed man she linked arms with. A beastmaster further down the street stared, his mouth pressed together in a thin disapproving line.

A finely dressed man swept past in a long cloak, his slave boy following close behind and bumping into the girl.

"Sorr—"

The boy stopped, looked the girl up and down before turning away and continuing along the path.

The girl's brows creased together as she stared after his retreating figure, confused thoughts interrupted when Shigure brushed past her.

"Ahh," Shigure murmured, pausing in the middle of the road and obstructing traffic as he stretched his arms out widely. He breathed in deeply, eyes blissfully closed while passers-by glared murderously at him. "Smell that? The perfume known as coal fumes."

"Please refrain from making idiotic remarks," said Lamina dryly, drawing the girl to himself, out of the way of people pushing past to enter a nearby store.

Surprised and thankful, the girl clung to Lamina. "It's really busy here!"

"Well, it *is* market day," the ox explained, weaving his way through the crowd with the girl held close. "The streets aren't usually this crammed otherwise."

Beside them, the girl noticed Hitori slipping through the crowds of people as expertly as Lamina yet his movements were silent and ghost-like and his expression vacant and cold. The fine hairs along the girl's arm stood on end.

Around the street corner, the crowd thinned with no stalls sitting along the paths. A sigh of relief escaped the girl and she let go of Lamina, eager to explore. Before she could take more than a step away, a small, strangled gasp came from behind her.

"Master!" shouted Shigure, nearly bowling the girl over as he ran past. "Master!" he yelled, catching up to Hitori who was already hurrying towards a man walking in their direction.

The man looked up, not at the duo racing towards him, but at the girl. Slowly, he removed the black top-hat from his head, striding past the two trying to grab his attention, eyes addressing the girl only.

The girl felt her knees buckling beneath her and her breath hitched in her throat. She knew this man.

"Master!" cried Shigure, stopping in front of the older man.

"Shigure," replied the man pleasantly, turning away from the girl. "Why have you—"

"Agnus!"

The man paused, turning back to the girl. Although his appearance was unlike the clean and handsome Simeon's—his hair was wild and a dark shaggy mane of a beard covered his face—the aura he exuded was inexplicably warm and kind.

At her expectant stare, Agnus smiled fondly, eyes soft. "You have grown, my child."

Tears welled up in the girl's eye and she clenched fistfuls of her dirty dress, swallowing thickly. A tumultuous wave of conflicting emotions crashed over her and she bowed her head.

Unable to see the tormented expression on her face, Lamina affectionately patted the girl's matted hair.

Looking up, Lamina returned Agnus' smile, his chest swelling.

"Lamina, you have done well. But first," Agnus turned expectantly to Shigure and Hitori, "what has made you seek me out?"

The impassive mask of the white-haired young man fell and he shuffled forward. "Master," Hitori stammered, trembling visibly. "If you allow it, I wish to go with you, please."

Much to the girl's surprise, Hitori sank to his knees, head bowed low.

"Only if you allow it, Master."

Agnus turned to him decisively. "Then I do not allow it."

The girl glanced from Agnus to Hitori and she could almost picture the young man's heart falling to rest on the floor below him. Frozen in place, his eyes lost their fiery appearance, melting to a soft caramel hue. Strangely, even though she could not fully comprehend why, she felt sympathy for Death. He looked like another lost child like her.

"You have a duty to remain loyal to the task at hand," explained Agnus. "You cannot forget that, Hazael."

The Reaper winced like he had been dealt a terrible blow. "Please Master, call me Hitori. I do not deserve the name you bestowed on me," he murmured to the floor.

"Is your birth name ill-suited now, Hazael? Does its meaning no longer ring any truth?"

Hitori fell silent, head still bowed low.

"Are your eyes no longer those of One's?"

"Master, if I may speak." Shigure knelt before the older man, voice wavering with uncertainty. "We have travelled from Shin'en Kiryuu to see you. Please, don't turn him away, Master."

"Do not speak to me about matters of turning away, Shigure. I am not turning him away. It is he who is turning away from his duty," Agnus replied sharply, gaze stern. "You forget that I have given each of you something to ease the burden of your tasks. These you must rely on and use to their fullest extent."

Hitori raised his head and the girl was stunned as faded pupils appeared in his eyes, slowly darkening with each despairing word he spoke. "Master, the task is too difficult to bear. Where will I gather the strength to—?" He fell silent, unable to voice the words stuck in his throat.

Eyes softening, Agnus reached out to the kneeling men. "As long as your journey runs, I will lend you all the strength you need."

With those words, Hitori and Shigure grasped Agnus' hands and were pulled to their feet.

"Remember my words: do not turn back. I will wait for you at the end of these trials," said Agnus, his voice strong and clear.

The pupils that had begun to appear in Hitori's eyes faded away and his stare was once again blank glowing embers. "Will the whole armour be useable then?" he asked, eyes fixed intently on Agnus.

"Well, we've seen proof of that already," chimed in Shigure.

Agnus smiled at the pair, squeezing their hands before releasing them. "Shigure." He scanned the grey-haired man's figure. "Where have you placed the sword I gave you?"

"…I like my guns." sulked Shigure, pouting.

"Take it with you at the very least. I will call on your swordsmanship another time."

"Yes, Master." Shigure paused for a moment. "Master, can't Hitori go with you?"

Agnus studied the two before him. "There are things in the future that must come to pass. Knowing this, you cannot stray from your paths." He looked pointedly at Hitori, who bowed lowly. Agnus stepped towards him, placing a hand gently on his head, dark eyes warm. "Do not forget. I am here."

Hitori held Agnus' gaze, his face unreadable. "Thank you, Master, I won't forget," he vowed solemnly, removing Agnus' hand from his head and pressing his forehead against the top of it. "I won't forget."

The girl sneaked a look at Lamina who smiled broadly at her, ruffling her hair affectionately before turning back to the scene before them and clearing his throat, earning the attention of the others.

"If I may intrude," his voice rumbled loudly, eyes twinkling. "Here is the young mistress you sent for, Agnus."

The girl grabbed the hem of Lamina's shirt, face a brighter red despite her fever. She hadn't gathered her thoughts or feelings. How would she speak to Agnus—this man who had both given her hope and left her in place that almost robbed her of it.

"What are you doing, young mistress? Let Agnus have a proper look at you!" Lamina pulled his arm away, nudging the young girl forward.

Silently, she wished she could dissolve into liquid, collecting into a puddle at Lamina's feet and hopefully being absorbed into the bricks beneath her dirty feet. What could she say to this man of immense power? The one Ridley wanted to run to and Magians feared. She gripped a handful of her tattered dress and wrung it mercilessly, eye fixed on the floor.

Just as she parted her lips to speak, Shigure interrupted. "Ah! That's right!" Sauntering up to the girl, Shigure patted her lightly on the head, smirking. "I do believe that you owe me a payment."

The girl gaped at him, feeling her eyebrow twitch. "For what?"

"For saving your life!"

"What's this?" growled Lamina and the girl swore that steam blew out of his nostrils. "What's this payment you seek, swindler?"

"Hey now—"

The girl glimpsed a hand reaching towards her and she turned, eye widening at the sight of Agnus smiling fondly as he placed his hand on her head. Her temperature faded completely and the feverish fog cleared from her mind.

Agnus leaned down and kissed the top of her head, the tip of his beard tickling her forehead as he murmured softly, "Hello, my child." He straightened up, eyes still on the girl. "What did you say to use the sword?"

The girl swallowed nervously and licked her dry, cracked lips. "Libertas."

Agnus continued to smile kindly at her. "You will request nothing more of this child, Shigure."

Shigure grinned broadly, bowing. "Sorry, Master."

"We'll be returning to our duties, Master," stated Hitori, eliciting a loud groan from his grey-haired companion. "The Conqueror is sure to call on Shigure's assistance again."

"But our duties are all the way in Gershom!" wailed Shigure, flinging his hands despairingly into the air. "And I didn't even get to see any of the beauties here!"

"Shigure," said Agnus sternly, like a father would to a child.

"I'll keep him in line, Master."

"What do you mean by that, Hitori? I'm not the type to cause trouble!"

"Thank you, Hazael," said Agnus. He wordlessly removed his hand from the girl's head and slipped it into his pocket, drawing out a slip of paper that he held out to Death. "You must take this with you."

Taking the paper, Hitori looked at it with apparent disinterest.

Shigure peered curiously over the young man's shoulder, a frown marring his face. "A number?"

Silently pocketing it, Hitori thanked Agnus and turned to Shigure with a nod. "Let's go."

"I didn't know you owned a telephone, Master!" exclaimed Shigure as Hitori pulled away from the group. "It would have saved us the trouble travelling all the way down here."

"I don't," replied Agnus smilingly, waving farewell.

"Huh—Hitori! Wait for me!" cried Shigure, noticing that his companion had already begun to turn the corner of the street. He spun around, bowing quickly to Agnus. "Until we next meet, Master!" He sped past several people, diving into the crowds to catch up to the silent Reaper.

After watching the scampering figure of Shigure disappear with a bemused look, Agnus turned back to the girl and Lamina, his face solemn. "It has been a long time." He donned his top-hat gravely.

"Agnus," began the girl fretfully but the older man held his hand up to interrupt her.

"I am sorry my child. I'm afraid there are things that I must take care of."

Disappointment arose in the girl, his words crushing her hopes in their entirety. "You're going?" she whispered through clenched teeth, barely aware of Lamina's hand lightly touching her arm. Mangled accusations rushed to the back of her throat. Hands balling into fists, her shoulders trembled—with

90

anger or fear, she did not know.

Agnus studied her face momentarily. "I must my child. That is why we cannot waste a single moment. Will you both accompany me?"

"Accompany you?" spluttered Lamina, surprised.

The girl glanced from the old ox to Agnus, her heart fluttering with the excitement of adventure and the uncertainty of wavering faith. *Was life worth living?* Hope continued to flower in her chest and she fixed Agnus with a look of curiosity. Could she really find something worth believing in here?

"To where Agnus?"

Folding back the cuffs of his coat, Agnus looked up grimly. "The resting place of the Kings of Old. Initium."

A silver-haired man awoke with a start in a tangled heap, his forehead damp with sweat and his linen sheets knotted uncomfortably around his legs. Slowly, he sat up and disentangled himself. Swinging his legs neatly over the side of his bed, he ran a shaky hand over his face.

The drowsy voice of Mrs Maremortum rose from under the other half of the bed sheet: "Are you okay, sweetheart?"

Turning his head in her direction, the man mumbled a "yes", hoping that he convinced her more than he did himself. Rising, he excused himself and felt his way to the bathroom, mind racing with the thoughts of the man from his dream.

I long for days
Where the sun's gentle warmth
Reminds me of my childhood beliefs:
A life of my own
One who answers prayers

- Lines from the *Laments of Lerielle, Scriptura.* Translated by J. Talis

8

At the furthest side of a large torch-lit ornamental room, the grotesque figures of Tophets writhed behind the iron bars of cages. A cacophony of shrieks rose from their throats as they clawed through the gaps of their prisons, desperate to chase the scent of innocent blood that pervaded the air of Magia.

Before the caged Tophets stood a long, white marble table, the lengths of which were occupied by many uniformed officers. A heated discussion resounded off the room's polished rock walls.

Amongst the huddled figures around the table sat a quiet Colonel, his expression contemplative. His hand rested lightly on a healing wound that, thankfully, lay hidden beneath his navy-blue coat.

Two seats to his left, spit sprayed from the mouth of the Major General: "We cannot let his curse return to his hands! What a laughingstock we'll become if we allow him to reclaim her—"

In between Tres and Simeon, the small Brigadier with a mousy brown bob spoke up, her booming voice betraying her appearance, "How do you propose we intervene? Wasn't it your error in judgement that brought about this issue?"

A vein throbbed in the Major-General's temple. "I'll be generous with you Brigadier and ignore your accusation if you allow me to finish enlightening you on the gravity of our situation and how we may escape it—"

"It's probably too late to prevent that," cut in Simeon. He absentmindedly flicked the cup of water on a coaster before him, the ice cubes within chinking gently together. "The Tophets were empty-handed when we retrieved them. So, my charge, and the beast accompanying her, crossed The Mare successfully." The ice cubes chinked again.

"You can't be sure of that," mumbled an officer from across the table.

"Please, speak louder Major Casdaine. People may be unable to hear you," Simeon said loudly, appearing composed yet his tone was icy.

The fair-haired Major shrunk a little in his chair, averting his eyes.

Flicking the cup of water in front of him once more, Simeon shifted in his seat and straightened. "Considering the circumstances, I believe my charge would have met back up with Agnus at Lacuna—"

"What makes you think he's there?" grumbled Major General Tres, eyes glinting angrily.

Simeon's chest heaved from the deep sigh that blew through his gritted teeth. "The last place that Agnus was noted to have been in was Lacuna. I've looked into the background of the beast, Lamina, and found that he owns an old café in the market district of that town. And let's not forget," continued Simeon, lacing his fingers together, "that the town Agnus first took the girl to, as the rumours go, was Lacuna."

The Major General opened his mouth to reply but found no words and flustered, he promptly closed it, nostrils flaring.

Dressed in a modified version of the Magian officer's uniform—with white lacey cuffs and gold trimmed shoulders and collar—, the silver-haired Mrs Maremortum scrunched her face up, lips pursed thoughtfully. "I hired Lamina in Nyx. If what you say is true, what could have brought him there?"

"I don't know. What I *do* know is your leaving him in Magia resulted in my girl escaping," Simeon replied with a sneer.

Mrs Maremortum's eyes narrowed into slits. "You're pinning the blame solely on me?"

"Obviously."

The silver-haired beauty slammed her fist on the table, eyes flashing red.

Simeon tilted his head back as he looked down at her, challenging her silently with a smirk.

The Brigadier drummed her nail-bitten fingers on the table, her expression stern. "Were you not in charge of this girl, Colonel?"

Simeon's jaw clenched. "Yes, Brigadier."

"If the General is supportive of my thoughts, I expect that you'll make up for the loss of her then?"

"By any means necessary."

"I will hold you to those words." The Brigadier folded her arms calmly over her chest, her eyes half-lidded as if contemplating sleep. "Regardless, your deduction is correct. The Conqueror's war advisor was caught in a battle with the Tophets on his return to Sominium."

The Major General's head jerked in The Brigadier's direction. "Didn't he leave Magia after arriving through Shin'en Kiryuu's teleportation sigil? How could he have been caught up in the horde of Tophets?"

"Yes, the timing is strange. Almost as though he lingered in the area," sighed the Brigadier, biting her thumbnail. "Unfortunately, publicly questioning the motives of The Conqueror's war advisor would not be wise. We are already viewed unfavourably by The Conqueror, especially now that we have received a request to not use Tophets without permission. It would do us some good to acquiesce to this request and relieve some pressure from the Sominium throne."

Simeon flinched at the words 'Sominium throne' and mentally scolded himself when the Brigadier's half-lidded eyes flickered towards him. "I agree with you, Brigadier," he chimed in. "The Conqueror has proposed sending Sominium soldiers to help reinforce the protection around the teleportation sigil. Let's broker some peace with him through accepting this proposal and agree to seek permission to use Tophets from now on."

The Brigadier closed her eyes and nodded. "I support that idea. But let's return to the original purpose of this meeting: the girl and Agnus' plans for her."

Smirking inwardly, Simeon returned his attention to Mrs Maremortum. "I think it goes without saying, Oracle, that the best course of action would be to wait until word comes out that Agnus is on the move. Once that happens, we'll send in the right people to apprehend the group and bring them in. What do you say?"

"There is logic behind your words, Colonel," replied Mrs Maremortum, smiling politely. "But I can't give the command myself. The order must be given by the Marshal of Magia. And anyway, we still haven't decided what is to become of Agnus' Curse."

Simeon's face was devoid of emotion. "Then what does the Marshal wish for my charge?"

Smile fixed in place, Mrs Maremortum tilted her head to the side. "I know that you're quite fond of the girl, but as acting General, I request that you part with your last souvenir for the Marshal to examine."

A muscle twitched in Simeon's cheek.

There was a beat before Mrs Maremortum tapped her well-manicured, grey painted fingernails on the marble tabletop, her smile morphing into a frown. "It's no matter," she began, lips pressed thinly together. "If you don't wish to part with it then—"

The Colonel sighed loudly, placing his hands down firmly on the tabletop. "I thought it would come to this, so I brought it myself for the Marshal to see."

At his nod, the officers stationed at the door signalled for two more to enter the room.

Mrs Maremortum watched the two marching officers, curling her lip at the cloth-covered item they carried into the room. "You were always so sentimental. Even with our dear mother."

"I will bear many things," said the Colonel, his tone icy, "even the scandal of your twins. But I won't have you speak about our relation."

Mrs Maremortum leaned forward in her seat, voice low and threatening, "And I won't have you blaming me for this."

"Enough," spoke the figure seated at the head of the table.

The entire table's occupants turned, focus now on the Marshal of Magia who raised her hand, motioning for the two officers to approach.

"Bring it to me."

Simeon sensed the fear radiating off the officers as they marched towards the Marshal. They stopped beside her seat and she reached up with her small youthful hand, pulling the purple cloth off.

Beneath it was a large jar filled with yellow fluid and housed within it was a child's arm.

Perspiration dripped down the officers' foreheads and the Marshal glanced up at them, apathetic.

"Fear not. You won't be cursed. That's Death's role, not mine," she explained, calmly grabbing the jar with both hands. "No. I do not curse. I simply know your worth."

The officers gulped as the young Lachesis Maremortum looked up at them with piercing scarlet eyes. Eyes that rivalled the polished surface of Element 132. Her wavy long hair, silver like her mother's, ran down her back in a neat braid while sections of the top half had been cut short. A small silver-haired ragdoll, resembling her in appearance, perched on her lap.

Placing a hand on the lid of the jar, she turned it with a surprising amount of strength that her small body didn't display. Her eyes, however, continued to address the nervous officers. "And your worth," she said, voice ringing as her eyes bore into their very beings, "determines your end."

There was a pop as the jar opened and Lachesis set the lid on the table. Reaching in, she removed the arm and sat it next to the jar.

"Is this Agnus' girl?" she asked, picking the arm back up to examine it closely. There was a slight, yet unmistakable tremor in her voice when she spoke his name.

Mrs Maremortum glanced at her daughter before peering down at the arm that Lachesis rotated in her hands. "Yes. I saw her for myself..." She paused, eyes suddenly distant. "She looked...she looked like your sister, Arche..."

Lachesis silently sniffed the arm, appearing as if she had not heard her mother, and ran her fingertips along it. She prodded different parts of the arm. "You've had this in your possession since the girl first arrived in Magia?"

The Colonel's lips were pressed firmly together whilst watching Lachesis study the arm, his eyes narrowed. He nodded when she glanced up at him, yet his eyes remained cold.

Without warning, Lachesis bit into the arm, ripping off a piece of preserved flesh. After rolling the flesh in her mouth a few times, she spat it out, covering her eyes and lurching forward in her seat as if she was about to vomit.

"What is it, sweetheart?" Mrs Maremortum reached for her daughter and wrapped an arm around her. "What is it? Are you okay?"

Lachesis straightened suddenly and her mother jumped back in surprise. She swept the ragdoll up into her arms, holding it close while her wide eyes darted about. "Interesting."

Some at the table exchanged uncertain glances.

Lachesis rose from her seat. "Bring him here. I want to see him with my own eyes and see his worth."

"Bring him here?" repeated Tres, thunderstruck. "I presume you mean Agnus? What makes you say, 'bring him here' like it's that simple?"

"If this is all he is capable of, how did we lose The War of Sominium?" Lachesis' voice was soft as if she were speaking to her doll. Her gaze turned to fix on Tres and she lowered her doll to the table. "We should not fear him until I know his worth."

Picking the arm back up, Lachesis ran a hand along it before gripping each end and snapping it. Dropping the broken arm to the floor, she continued, "the War should have been ours."

Murmurs of agreement arose from some at the table, yet the Colonel remained tight-lipped, eyes on the broken arm.

"We will send out an advance guard to retrieve him," announced Lachesis, rousing a chorus of assent around the table. She raised her hand in a silencing gesture and the room fell silent. "Colonel Van de Berg."

Simeon looked up at Lachesis, his face a blank canvas again. "Yes, Miss Maremortum?"

"Once retrieved, the little doll will be yours." The scarlet-eyed youth gestured to the broken limb at her feet. "You will have the honour of crushing her yourself."

Apathetic, the Colonel placed a hand on his chest and bowed to the young Maremortum. "I will do my best."

"Spin around, young mistress."

A bright blush bloomed across the girl's face and she twirled around awkwardly in a new pair of baggy green pants, barely held up by a leather belt set to the tightest possible hole. Instead of her old and ragged clothing from Magia, she wore a loose cream blouse that billowed out like a small dress, covering the top half of her pants where her new eye-patch was tucked neatly away in one of the pockets. A small selection of other clothes hung over Lamina's arm which he insisted he could carry in a backpack.

Having taken a shower over at the public baths, the girl appeared well groomed thanks also to her new attire and Lamina's dedicated combing of her hair.

Unaccustomed to her newly purchased socks and leather boots, the girl nearly tripped over her own feet while spinning, her cheeks turning a shade darker.

"That will be fine." Agnus rose from his seat to thank the thin-lipped shopkeeper.

"Sure, sure," grumbled the old toothless woman, limping over to the counter and muttering lowly, "makin' me give fine clothin' do blemished, *honesdly*. Wha' is da worl' comin' do?"

"Too bad there's nothing really in your size," Lamina muttered to the girl as they approached the counter with Agnus. "We got you the smallest sizes available, you're just so small and thin though."

"Sorry."

"Hey, nothing to apologise for!" laughed Lamina, ruffling the girl's hair. "It's not your fault. At least you have something more suitable to travel in now. Soon enough we'll have you filling those clothes out after some good food!"

The shopkeeper cleared her throat, shooting Lamina and the girl a dry look. "Dose clothes are a lil' pricey. 'Ope yer willin' do 'ave da lil' miss pay up, Daydon." She held her hand out, thin nose high in the air. "I don' normally go ou' o' my way do 'elp da blemished."

The look on the girl's face seemed to rile the lady who wagged her finger at her, nostrils flaring. "Dose who do nod work shall nod ead! And blemished 'ave no business bein' well clothe'!"

Agnus studied the woman's face in the silence that followed. His eyes slid to the girl and a small smile flitted across his face at her clenched fist.

Just as the shopkeeper drew a breath to berate the girl again, she spoke, her voice unmistakably clear and calm. "As you say, I'm blemished. We work so hard, we die." She steadily returned the startled older woman's gaze. The faces of her mining friends sat in the forefront of her mind as she continued bitterly, "So, I do know the meaning of hard work."

At a loss for words, the woman huffed, a vein visibly throbbing in her temple. "I've never been so poorly spoken do by a child! Mr Daydon, da girl musd pay for da clothes an' leave!"

Agnus wrapped a protective arm around the girl, his gaze hard when he regarded the shopkeeper. "The price of the clothing is high?"

"Ye be' id is!"

Nodding, Agnus smiled. "The girl's name shall be more than enough."

All eyes turned to Agnus and the girl felt herself tremble unexpectedly, her heart racing as she studied his face. His eyes sparkled. What was he talking about?

"'Er name? Enough fo' a bag full o' *my* clothin'? Daydon, 'ow dare ye insuld me!" The lady's eyes flashed angrily. "Wha' do ye dake me for? 'Er name 'as no value!"

"Oh, but it does." Agnus released the girl and planted his hands firmly on the counter, his eyes boring into the shopkeeper's. "You see, her name is very special because she does not yet know the name I gave her."

Lamina and the girl exchanged looks of confusion.

"Wai', ye mean to say da' dis child doesn' even know 'er own name? Da name da' Agnus Daydon 'imself gave 'er?"

"Yes."

The old woman picked at the long grey hairs on her chin, mumbling to herself. "Fine." She slapped her hand against the countertop. "Give me da lil' miss' name."

Agnus smiled, reflected lights dancing in his dark eyes. "Terra."

At the utterance of her name, an acrid taste filled the girl's mouth and her tongue throbbed as if it had been seared. "A-Agnus!" she choked, the inside of her mouth stinging.

Lamina gripped his throat, eyes watering and mouth spluttering, "What's happening?"

Words filled Terra's head—a language she could not understand in the old lady's voice:

Iiryonyomuul Yiellmaekiel nakchaell Taumjiellnak.

Floating letters materialized before Agnus and the old woman and 'T E R R A' burned like bright embers etched into the air. A gust of wind circled the letters, gathering them in a small bunch before the woman closed her fist over it, the light from the glowing characters vanishing.

"I 'ave received dis name and in accordance with da laws da' govern da land o' Dempus, I shall be da Keeper o' dis name 'dil Death claims me or da nam'd." The woman pressed her closed fist to her brow.

From the small gaps between her fingers, the light from the letters seeped out, swirling up and collecting like a rotating mass of diamond dust. Most of the mass divided and dispersed, racing into the foreheads of both Agnus and the old woman, illuminating their temples briefly before that light too was completely absorbed.

A small amount of the light remained in the air, splitting neatly into two as the woman continued to chant.

"As dere are doo who 'ave witness'd, dere are doo addidional pardakers o' da knowledge. May deir dongues be bound dil my passing or da' o' da nam'd."

The last of the light slipped through the air into Lamina and Terra's foreheads and the grey-eyed girl winced at the sudden burst of energy that was channelled into her mind, accompanied by the sphere of light that glowed beneath the skin of her temple. The energy abruptly vanished along with the light and Terra pressed one hand against her head and the other to her mouth where her tongue continued to throb.

"What was that Agnus?" barked Lamina, his voice hoarse.

Agnus inclined his head to the old shopkeeper, smiling. "Thank you, Mathelda." He motioned for Terra and Lamina to follow him out of the store.

"Agnus!" hissed Lamina, trying to catch Agnus' attention.

"Da paymend 'ave lefd me owin' ye," called the old woman from her counter, "bu' don' brin' dis Derra nexd dime."

The door snapped shut behind the trio, and Lamina turned on Agnus.

"What was that?" he asked, barring the way. "I glimpsed my tongue reflected on the glass countertop. There is a mark!" he cried, opening his mouth to show the large 'X' that appeared to have been seared on the base of his tongue.

Terra pressed her fingers to her lips, certain that the same mark was on her tongue too.

"What is it, Agnus?" demanded Lamina. "Please tell us!"

Peering over at Terra, Agnus sighed. "In order to pay for the clothing, I offered Terra's name."

"My name…" Clenching her fists, Terra opened her mouth and choked, hand flying to her throat as if something were stuck. A sudden scream tore from her throat and pain surged through her entire mouth.

"Terra, Terra…" hushed Agnus, placing a gentle hand on her head, eyes filled with concern. "You must not attempt to say your name. Nor should you Lamina," he instructed, moving to pull Terra into an embrace.

The sound of Terra slapping Agnus' hands away echoed in the quiet. "H-how could you?" Tears spilled from Terra's eye as she glared at the older man. "You let someone take *this* away from me too?"

Agnus' gaze was steady. "Yes."

With a howl of frustration, Terra threw a fist at Agnus, screeching when he easily caught her wrist.

"My child, your life is not your own."

"How could you say that after giving my name away!"

Wrestling against his hands, more tears fell from Terra's eye. It was futile. Without the strength of Spiritus, she was still that weak girl struggling against Simeon in the mines.

"Your name," Agnus continued, addressing Terra who looked up at him tearfully, "does not belong to you for now. It was given as payment to Mathelda until her passing or your own. I am sorry for that payment my dear child, but I am sure that Lamina has explained the currency situation of this world. It is difficult when there is nothing to give. That is why people are allowed to pay with their names. But do not fear, your name is safe," he explained as Terra slumped, face hidden behind her hair.

"How can I know that? How can I trust that awful lady? Won't she tell my name to others?"

"She cannot. Names have a special treatment in Currency Law. And despite her cruel manner, she would not do that, even if she could." Agnus released Terra's arms and rose, looking down at her despondent form. "Regardless, you both must remember that the binding on you means you cannot even mention the restriction to others."

"And this journey, Agnus?" interrupted Lamina, hand resting heavily on Terra's bowed head.

"Are you prepared to follow me? Prepared for losses and hardships? If yes, know that there will be no turning back."

Lamina shifted, straightening. "Agnus, I have seen the results of believing in your words for spells. I will go wherever you lead me. Lead on."

"And you, my child?"

Terra did not move.

"If you wish to stay behind, you may. But I will depart. There are things that must be set in motion."

Terra flinched like she had been struck. "You're going to leave me? Again?"

"That is your choice."

Where would she go? Where could she go? She felt her heart shrivel even as Spiritus burned within her chest.

"Follow me, Terra and I will give you reason for that hope that burns within you."

Terra raised her wet eye to Agnus' earnest gaze. His eyes seemed to challenge her. Gripping her stump arm tightly, Terra sobbed, recalling the dark nights in Magia where the flower of baseless hope kept her alive. Somehow, he knew about this. "Fine." *Give me something to believe in.* She glared desperately at Agnus. "Take me to Initium."

I grow weary in my old age. I long for the depths of The Mare and the call of One. Let the world ring with the flung open doors of Praeter Tempus. I long to reawaken with a body that no longer grieves me. But for now, let me sink into the deep and sleep.

- Lines from *Laments of Lerielle, Scriptura.* Translated by J. Talis

9

With the conclusion of the meeting, Lachesis dismissed the officers and watched as they all slowly dispersed from the room. Movement from the corner of her eye made her turn to address her mother.

Lachesis' small hand clasped her mother's, stopping the latter in her tracks. "Mama."

Overcome by a surge of love, Mrs Maremortum could only give a small nod and a faint, "Yes, dear?"

"Should the Colonel hesitate, you must kill the doll."

Lachesis felt her mother stiffen at her words. Mentally tutting, Lachesis raised her steady gaze to see her mother was averting hers. The young girl pressed her mother's hand with both of her own, finally drawing her attention. "Left to her own devices, the girl will become a threat to Arche and I." She allowed her voice to waver, her eyes pleading but dry. "We're your real daughters, remember that."

Mrs Maremortum flinched and slipped her hand out of Lachesis'. "Sweetheart," she spoke up after a beat, her stomach writhing. "You and

Arche are my only children."

"Of course," replied Lachesis, relaxed. "It is as Pater willed."

Lowering her gaze again, Mrs Maremortum turned away, tight-lipped but convicted.

"Where is Initium?" Terra asked Lamina as he passed her a piece of cracker to nibble on. Thanking him, she bit gratefully into it, crumbs falling from the corners of her mouth.

Lamina politely wiped crumbs from around his mouth: "Up at the very heavenward part of Railesson—past the barren land of Attero."

"Heavenward?"

"Sorry. The old compass term for north."

"Okay. And Attero?"

"The place of my ancestors." Lamina puffed out his chest. "Of course, it no longer exists but that's another tale. Now, Initium is as Agnus mentioned earlier: the resting place of the Kings of Old. In fact, some say it was also the old temple of worship and that it once connected Tempus to Praeter Tempus when all the lands were one." He paused and finished with a mumble: "I don't know too much more about it though."

The final admittance left a sheepish grin on Lamina's face and Terra smiled, patting his arm.

Lamina glanced nervously at Agnus' back. "They say that the inner throne room of the Old Kingdom cannot be opened. The doors are sealed by the sole guardian that lingers within it," whispered Lamina, as if hoping that Agnus would not hear the story. "They say it will not open until One removes a bone from the guardian and joins him to another."

"Joins?"

"Some suggest in marriage."

Terra tilted her head. "That's a strange rumour."

"They also say that the few survivors of the destruction of Attero dwell inside the walls of Initium," Agnus added loudly over his shoulder, causing both Lamina and Terra to jump. "What we should be doing is being discerning about what we hear people say."

After a tense moment of silence, Terra whispered to Lamina, wary that Agnus was listening, "Where do all these rumours come from anyway?"

Lamina gave a look of surprise. "Don't you know?" he asked. "Haven't you heard of Sominium?"

Nonplussed, Terra shook her head.

The old ox made a face. "How could you not have heard of Sominium? The Kingdom of Sominium? Daniel Sominium? Any of them ringing a bell?"

Again, Terra shook her head.

"Well, it *is* before your time."

Terra fought the urge to roll her eyes. "I didn't really have the opportunity to study." She tried to keep a straight face as she continued, "Unless learning how to avoid the Colonel's wrath counts."

Lamina peered closely at her, the corner of his mouth lifting into a grin. "I didn't know you had such cheek."

"Sorry. So, can you teach me about Sominium?"

Lamina stroked his chin thoughtfully. "There was a great long war over the throne in the capital of Railesson. The capital is now known as Sominium because the war ended with the Sominium family successfully claiming the throne."

"A war?"

"Large scale fights involving lots of people."

"Over a throne?"

"Not just any throne. *The* throne. In ancient Pateran prophecies, it's known as the throne on which the true king will sit. This king will restore Paradise and bring eternal peace. Other historical faiths have their own beliefs regarding the throne, but all of them agree on the significance of it..."

Terra scrunched her face up in confusion and Lamina shot her a sympathetic look.

"There's a lot you wouldn't have learnt as a blemished in Magia. There's no rush. You can learn at your own pace," the ox said with a warm smile.

Cheeks flushed in appreciation, Terra couldn't help but mirror Lamina's smile. Looking ahead, she watched as Agnus stopped to survey the land, eyes narrowed. In his hand he held an electric lantern which creaked with each gust of wind that swept across the land.

"We will travel until we reach the borders of Attero where we will set up camp and scout the area before entering it. Terra, keep Spiritus ready at all times," instructed Agnus, peering at the young brunette meaningfully.

Terra pursed her lips, an eyebrow twitching. She pressed her fingertips on the centre of her chest and imagined the hilt of Agnus' sword lying dormant there. "It's here. Ready to be summoned."

"Yes, it is," replied Agnus gently, "but it is not the physical preparation that determines the strength of the sword."

The youth tilted her head, brows drawing tightly together. "Are you talking about faith? That's what Lamina told me when I first used Spiritus."

Agnus nodded, briskly following the pathway weaving through the fields of grass. "Faith is the key my child," he said, eyes continually scanning the terrain about them. "We mustn't be deceived by our own capabilities and deeds. But even with the tiniest degree of faith you can summon some strength from the sword. Pour all of your faith in it and mountains will topple with a swing."

Terra fell silent, an ounce of doubt growing within her. Agnus seemed to have a lot of strange ideas.

They walked tirelessly, commenting on different topics that arose. During these conversations, Terra was sometimes prompted to speak by a question from either Lamina or Agnus, but she preferred to walk quietly, listening carefully to their words mingling with the sounds of the wind and the small animals scuttling in the greenery about them.

Her wide eye drank in every patch of grass, leaf, insect and bird around them. At one point, she observed a bird feeding its young, squawking hungrily in a tidy nest. She admired this attentive parenting; the young bird was not abandoned.

The cold fingers of loneliness crept up her neck and Terra forced the memory down, turning sharply away.

Like the journey to Lacuna, there was plenty for her to take in and she inhaled the fresh air deeply; the heavy and humid Magian air seemed but a distant memory.

Terra grew fascinated with all of the ground within a small radius of Agnus which seemed to temporarily bloom and flourish; flower heads opened their petals, following his passing like they might for the sun and the grass became lush and green, singing a melody that Terra thought she could hear. She was unable to tear her eye away from the mystifying sight.

They walked endlessly, pausing only to eat—simple meals that Terra would've been glad for during her time in Magia—the day wearing on yet the wondrous landscape was unchanging.

Unlike south of The Mare, the land did not gradually morph into the barren wasteland that Terra anticipated. For most of their travel, the land remained quite green and budding flowers lined the pathway further along. Terra bent to skim the tops of the flower heads, humming lightly to herself.

"We will be stopping soon," announced Agnus, pointing out the dimming light of the artificial sun as it descended.

Shading her eye, Terra looked up the hilly pathway they were following. "Are we nearly there?"

"You will know," replied Agnus mysteriously, a small smile on his face.

Terra's brow furrowed but she followed quietly, filled with doubt. Her eye slowly widened as they mounted the hill.

At the foot of the slope, the lush green grass and swaying trees ended abruptly and Terra's eye roamed over the barren wasteland beyond it, check-marked with countless craters.

Her jaw dropped. "That's Attero?"

"Yes," answered Agnus, his gaze suddenly distant.

Lamina gave a small grunt, his dark eyes fixed on the pockmarked plains. "It was once a grand place."

"Indeed," remarked Agnus, stopping in his tracks. Terra and Lamina quickly came to a halt beside him and he turned to them with a smile. "We will rest here for the night."

On the cold grass, Terra laid between Agnus and Lamina, both asleep with their backs to her. She tried to keep warm under Agnus' jacket, determined to not complain. Staring up at the blood-red moon, her hand gently massaged the scarred end of her left arm.

She wondered how many nights she had spent staring up at the same moon at the top of the hill leading to the Colonel's office, wondering if her existence meant anything at all. She hoped following Agnus would give her the answers she needed—because she planned to judge for herself whether this man was great or not.

Slowly, her eye grew heavy with sleep and she dreamt of her and an enthused Agnus applauding Lamina prancing across a stage, dressed as a harlequin for the night. The room roared with laughter and the faceless crowd cheered as Lamina pirouetted across the stage, landing gracefully on his hooves.

To the left of her came a loud resounding crash yet Terra continued to stare at the dancing harlequin Lamina, dread filling her.

Don't turn. Don't look.

"Mr Lamina!" Terra cried, fear gripping her entire being as the old ox stumbled off the stage, body limp. "MR LAMINA!"

"Terra!" shouted Lamina, shaking the youth from her dream-state and scooping her up into his arms. He launched himself at a nearby bush, tumbling into it and causing the girl to squeal. "We're under attack! Quick, Terra! Draw Spiritus and we'll help Agnus!"

Adrenaline pulsing through her veins, Terra nodded, determination etched on her face. Until she had a reason for her hope, she would help Agnus.

They jumped up over the bush, eyes greeted by the sight of Agnus skilfully skidding under the swinging sword of an assailant.

A silver-haired blur darted away, tossing long red needles in the process and forcing Agnus further back. As Agnus dodged the shards, the rushing figure leapt into the nearby trees.

"Terra!" Agnus dove to the left as the shards flew back. "Terra, take arms!"

A wave of electricity jolted through her numb body and Terra wrenched out Spiritus when an agonised yelp issued from Lamina. She whipped around, sword barely out of her when her wide and terrified eye glimpsed the silver blur passing over Lamina's bloody and fallen body.

"Mr Lamina!" Horror and dread gripped Terra as the person landed in front of her.

A pale hand seized Terra's chin and her blood turned cold as her eye met with milky-hued ones.

"Are you the Arche duplicate?" asked the man hunched over before her, his long silver hair falling forward over his shoulders. On his tongue, a small sparkle of solid scarlet rolled about.

For a moment, fear consumed Terra rooting her to the spot. Her body quivered under eyes that did not seem to perceive her at all.

The man appeared to slowly pull back his sword arm as her mind raced.

How had he crept up to Lamina with such ease and speed? Beads of sweat trickled down Terra's brow and, at the thought of Lamina, her eye flickered towards his fallen body and anger rapidly surged through her.

"Mr Lamina!" She swung Spiritus and their swords clanged together, forcing the man to jump back. "Mr Lamina—are you okay?" She desperately thrusted Agnus' sword at the man and he swiftly blocked it.

In the silence, the man chewed the red shard in his mouth and brought his left elbow around, slamming it into the side of Terra's face.

She staggered back, gasping and spitting. Wiping bloody saliva away with the back of her hand, Terra's vision blurred with the blow but her eye darted again to Lamina's fallen figure. "MR LAMINA!"

Spiritus ripped Terra from where she stood, throwing her to the ground and the man's blade sliced through the air where she had been. Teeth cracking against the E132 in his mouth, the man shifted forward, relentless as he plunged the sword down towards the fallen Terra.

The earth beneath the man's feet shot up, almost sending him spiralling to the ground but he instinctively leapt away, aware of Agnus in the distance who stood with a hand raised. Grunting, the man jumped as the earth opened below him, a ravenous maw that chased him as he raced, light-footed across the plains. Dropping quickly into a squat, the man bounded up high from the plains just as another yawning hole tore open beneath him. He soared through the air towards Agnus, bringing his sword down in a slash.

Agnus dropped to his hands and knees and spun quickly away, rolling into the dust and flipping easily back onto his feet, hand rising and closing into a fist.

Earthen walls shot up around the man and he whipped his head towards Agnus, his eyes briefly flashing red as he spat a red, needle-like shard at Agnus before the walls closed him in.

Reflexively, Agnus caught the shard and it buried deep into his palm, piercing through to the other side, stopping centimetres before his eye.

"Agnus!"

"Pay me no heed, my child—tend to Lamina!" ordered Agnus as the shard bubbled black and melted into a pure white substance, dripping to the ground and leaving a hole in the centre of his hand.

Obediently, Terra raced to Lamina's side, stooping to the ground beside him, Spiritus dissipating back into her body. "Mr Lamina!" Unbidden tears sprang into her eye. A deep gash ran along his back and the blood pooled around his body. "Mr Lamina!"

Footsteps pounded on the ground behind Terra and Agnus stopped before the ox's body, kneeling to take a hold of his arm. He had made a crude bandage for his hand with a handkerchief.

"Lamina, my friend." Agnus slipped his uninjured hand under the ox's chest. "I'm going to lift you up. We still have a long way to go and I will support you the rest of the way, but you *must* hold on my friend."

A small groan escaped Lamina and Terra breathed a tiny sigh of relief.

With steel nerves, Agnus peered gravely at the youth before him. "Terra, you must lead the way. Survey the land. Ensure the path we take is safe. We must reach Initium quickly. Lamina is losing too much blood." He then shifted Lamina into position to lean on his shoulder before, with some tremulous effort, standing.

Scurrying several metres ahead, Terra scanned the land, stumbling over rocks and slipping into craters in her rush. For some reason, she found herself staring at particular areas of the barren plains of Attero, an unusual feeling descending upon her.

"Quickly, my child! I have only temporarily locked our assailant in the earth. We have no time to spare," he urged, his right arm supporting Lamina and his left hand holding the electric lantern. A gust of wind billowed across the land and Agnus clumsily clung to his top hat with the back of his hand.

Caught in her curious survey of the wasteland, Terra fixed her eye back ahead. "I'm sorry... it's just—I feel as if I've seen this place before. This place—Attero—it seems so familiar. But I've never travelled this far in Railesson." She shook her head to clear it and slapped her hands against the sides of her face. This was not the time, she must keep moving.

The old ox at Agnus' side groaned, blood trailing behind them. "Agnus, leave me. I won't make it to the Old Kingdom."

"Lamina, old friend." Agnus gave a strained smile. "We are nearly there. Do not give up so soon."

Terra shot several nervous glances at Lamina, concern gnawing away at her. Desperately she searched for any sign of the Old Kingdom known as Initium, but to no avail.

Seconds trickled into minutes.

Minutes turned into an hour.

The artificial sun glared brightly overhead, and Terra, having walked ahead a little further, looked back at her two companions. Agnus appeared to struggle under the sheer weight of the old ox, yet he remained quiet, an expression of determination clear on his face. Lamina's shoulder sagged, his legs barely moving below him. Patches of blood marked the sand below the two.

Staring ahead again, Terra fervently hoped that her dream was not a premonition and that they would soon stumble upon the Old Kingdom.

Tears filled her eye and her legs shook as she pushed herself to continue walking, to keep searching.

A memory of her friends talking about prayer came to mind and, in her desperation, she called out to the Ezer that her friend had spoken of.

Please, she begged in her mind, raising her eye to the dark canvas looming above. *Please, don't take Mr Lamina away.*

"Terra!" cried Agnus, breaking her train of thought. "Look ahead!"

Lowering her eye to the land extending before her, Terra glimpsed a small shape on the horizon: an old, grey and worn building. As they approached, Terra's eye barely ran over some of the broken pillars before she noted the long flight of half-destroyed stairs leading to the entrance. Despite the daunting number of stairs, joy and hope filled her and she scurried back to her companions, eagerly taking Lamina's weight from his other side.

"We'll get there quicker this way!" she insisted, ignoring the incredible weight that now laid across her shoulders.

The trio inched across the gap between them and their destination, sweat drenching the foreheads of both Agnus and Terra. Trembling under the old ox's arm, Terra's thin legs threatened to soon give way beneath her.

Taking deep shuddering breaths, Terra mentally vowed to not let Mr Lamina down again—she couldn't help but blame herself for the deep gash that ran across his back. She lifted her chin, mouth forming a thin, hard line.

Close to her ear, Lamina let out a deep guttural groan, surprising Terra who nearly stumbled.

"Will I die, Agnus?" rasped Lamina, breathing harshly.

"Do you believe that you will?"

Without hesitation, Lamina shook his weary head. "No. I believe in you, Agnus."

Tears filled Terra's eye and her heart trembled at the hope he had.

Agnus smiled with tired reassurance. "Then hold on, my friend. You will see the glory beyond Initium."

With those words, Agnus and Terra supported Lamina through the last of the destroyed plains of Attero, reaching the stairs of Initium.

A weak heart is a poor foundation. A man with such a heart will crumble under any strain. Raise me up, One. Send your Ezer. I long to stand strong again.

- Lines from *Writings of the Kings of Old, Scriptura*. Translated by C. Yelnorin

10

It was with staggering effort that Agnus and Terra hoisted Lamina up onto the staircase leading to the Old Kingdom.

Terra climbed cautiously, fearful of the old stairs crumbling beneath their feet. Breathing was laborious and the stairs stretched on in front of her eye. Still, she sucked in deep breaths through her gritted teeth, determined to stagger up to the doors of the dilapidated building.

Focusing on one stair at a time, she ignored those that rose above their heads. Stair after stair, they heaved the old ox up, legs trembling beneath his weight and leaving Terra gasping desperately for air, sweat trickling down her jaw.

Lamina's breaths were shallow and raspy. Agnus continued to murmur assurances to him.

At the very top of the stairs, Terra's legs gave way and she planted her palm onto the ground to prevent herself from completely collapsing.

Lamina let out a low groan as Agnus strained to keep him from falling with Terra. Shifting his weight to his other foot, Agnus slowly lowered the old ox down to where Terra crouched and carefully placed him against her.

Terra wrapped her arms securely around the old ox, his long shaggy mane tickling her chin. "It's okay, Mr Lamina," she said quietly, watching Agnus approach the door to the temple. Her eye darted down to the warm red liquid that dripped onto her leg, images of her friends flashed in her mind. "It's okay…"

Heart beating erratically, a strange and unwelcome hollowness filled Terra as she stared listlessly at the door barring their entry. Willing the hollow feeling to subside, she laid her cheek against the ox's broad shoulder, listening to Agnus murmur softly to the door before him, her eye following the slow movement of his hand along the door frame.

Dust fell off the hinges of the old stone doors and Agnus hurried back to Lamina's side, helping Terra heave him back up to lean on their shoulders. They staggered towards the door and a final whisper from Agnus, in a tongue Terra couldn't understand, pushed it open with an unknown force, allowing the trio to struggle across the threshold into the room beyond.

Despite the old and weathered appearance of Initium on the outside, the bare stone walls within were polished and smooth, painted a creamy white. Tall pillars supported the high concave ceiling that was covered in elaborately carved designs; symbols and words that Terra could not decipher. At the far end of the room were two heavy doors that were almost as tall as the ceiling itself.

Her attention returned to Agnus who directed her to one of the pillars which they gingerly sat Lamina against. A trail of blood followed them and Terra knelt anxiously beside Lamina, clasping his hand in both of hers as Agnus drew away.

"What are we going to do Agnus?" Terra whispered, eye fixed on Lamina whose eyes remained closed.

Silence followed and Terra glanced over her shoulder to find Agnus pacing towards the middle of the room. "Agnus?"

Gently putting Lamina's hand down, Terra rose, eye following Agnus and past him to the object he approached.

On a stone table at the centre of the room lay a young man. He seemed to blend into his surroundings, his hair a shocking white and skin a deathly pale colour. His eyes were closed in what Terra thought to be sleep and she soon found herself trailing closely behind Agnus, noting the young man's light-coloured lashes that curled against his cheeks. He looked only a little older than her.

The stone table the young man laid upon sat in the middle of a circle of runic writing engraved into the ground—the characters appeared to be the very same that was on the ceiling and bore a striking similarity to the runes that surrounded Spiritus.

She continued to watch curiously until Agnus came to a halt before the young man's sleeping form and her fear for Lamina surged to the forefront of her mind. "Agnus, what are we going to do?" she asked more impatiently, glancing back at Lamina's unmoving form. Her heart squeezed tightly. "Ag—!"

Terra's words died on her lips when Agnus signalled for silence.

He raised his index finger and pressed the tip of it heavily against the ribcage of the young man. Pressing hard on the youth's pale skin, he traced his finger along the side of his ribs. The layers of skin and muscle beneath his fingertip separated in a clean slit, revealing the bones beneath.

"Agnus—!" gasped Terra, eye fixed on the incision. She opened her mouth again but was at a loss for words when Agnus slid his hand into the young man's body and a crack issued from his ribs.

Agnus carefully withdrew his hand—not a single drop of blood covered it—and between his index finger and thumb he held a long and pale object that stopped Terra's heart.

A rib bone.

"Agnus, what are you doing?" cried Terra, horrified when Agnus ran his hand along the incision on the young man's body.

The severed ends of muscle and skin layers neatly drew themselves together, closing up the body. There was no blood at all, yet Terra noted the sudden movement of the young man's chest as it began to rise and fall. A hint of pink coloured his cheeks.

The circle of runes beneath their feet glowed momentarily and Terra's heart did not feel at ease.

Agnus stepped back from the young man and turned to the alarmed girl behind him. "Terra, hold your left arm out." Agnus pointed the rib bone towards her.

Shock and horror possessed Terra at the sight of Agnus holding the bone out to her. For a second, she wondered what had happened in the last few minutes to make him act in such a way. For a minute she hesitated, uncertainty consuming her.

Spiritus weighed heavily in her being, a form both physical and not, pulsing under her skin; a reminder to her.

The thought dawned on her: did she still doubt him? Was this not the man who Lamina believed would save his life? Whose sword had enabled her escape? The man that Lamina had spoken grandly of while showing the sliver of thread that was her hair that Agnus had given?

Uncertainty gnawing at her, she looked up, catching Agnus' eye and her heart swelled with emotion at the soft and understanding expression on his face.

'I will give you reason for the hope that burns within you.'

Taking a deep breath, Terra stretched out her stump of an arm, eye holding Agnus'. *I'll put my trust in you*, her gaze said and smiling with gratitude, Agnus leaned forward, the tip of the bone meeting the end of her arm.

Inhaling deeply through his nose, Agnus murmured something under his breath and a bright light grew from the point where the rib bone and Terra's arm met, slowly growing and encircling the entire end of her arm.

The image of a blood-stained doll flashed within Terra's mind and for a moment she felt her stomach shift as if to empty itself and her body felt weightless.

Before her eye, the bone began to fuse together with her arm, the cells of the bone dividing rapidly and differentiating; muscle and skin began to form with arteries, veins and capillaries weaving through the growing layers.

The light surrounding the developing flesh and bones grew brighter until Terra was forced to tear her eye away from the sight before it slowly faded away. An unfamiliar weight sat at the end of her arm and turning back, Terra found herself speechless at the sight of her newly reformed arm.

She blinked several times, attempting to determine whether this was a dream or not. Mouth agape, she flexed the fingers on her left hand, turned it over and back, over and back and over again. The part of her arm that had been formed from the young man's bone was a sickly pale, yet she found it still sinewy and strong for she was comfortable enough to reach in and draw out Spiritus with ease before returning it.

Excitedly, Terra turned to show her arm to Lamina but her words died on her lips. He lay very still against the pillar. "Mr Lamina?" She took several shaky steps towards him.

"Who interrupts my sleep?"

The crisp and cold tone caused Terra to jump. She and Agnus looked back to the centre of the room, their eyes greeted by the sight of the young man sitting upright on the stone table. His hazel eyes passed over Terra to focus on Agnus who smiled pleasantly at him.

"Did we wake you?"

The young man swung his legs over the side of the table and placed his feet on the ground. "If you were listening, you would know the answer to that," he answered curtly, his two hands holding onto the table as he stood. His legs trembled slightly as if he had not used them to stand in a long time.

"Why were you sleeping here?"

The young man slowly drew his hands away from the stone when his legs stopped shaking. Lifting his chin, he folded his arms over his chest, nose in the air and lips pressed thinly together. "I am the guardian of this place. I have been awaiting Agnus' return."

Smiling to himself, Agnus gave a short bow and removed his hat in one fluid movement. "That would be me."

The young man's eyebrows shot up into his hair and almost disappeared. Regaining his composure, he narrowed his eyes, lips pursed again. Eyes roaming over the people before him, his gaze rested on Lamina's unmoving form against the pillar. His cold eyes flickered back to Agnus. "If you're really Agnus Dayton, why didn't you save your friend?"

Voice caught in her throat, Terra dashed to Lamina and dropped beside him. "Mr Lamina?" Her voice was barely above a whisper. Again, her friends' lifeless bodies swam before her vision. Tears brimmed in Terra's eye and a warm arm wrapped around her shoulders, pulling her back.

"It's okay, my child."

"It's not! How could you say that?" Terra twisted around to shove Agnus away.

He caught her hands and gently pressed them with his own. "He is not dead."

Mouth twisting and mind buzzing, a numb Terra allowed Agnus to pull her back.

He approached the unmoving Lamina, his mouth set into a thin line. "Watch carefully, Adam."

The young man twitched. "How did you know my—?"

His sentence trailed off as Agnus took the ox's hand. Closing his eyes, Agnus laid his free hand against Lamina's chest and inhaled sharply, his hand aglow. After a moment, the light faded away and Agnus opened his eyes. He squeezed Lamina's hand gently. "Old friend, why do you rest?"

Terra held her breath. Adam snorted derisively when nothing happened.

Suddenly, Lamina's hand squeezed Agnus' and he shifted his body away from the pillar with a sharp intake of breath. "Agnus, is this Initium?" He gawked at the marble interior, peering about himself energetically.

"Mr Lamina!" Terra rushed to the old ox's side, sobbing. She flung her arms around him, relief and joy flooding her. "You're okay now!"

Lamina laughed, hugging the girl back and kissing the top of her head. "Thank you for helping me." He grinned as Terra pulled back with a teary smile. The old ox's grin faded when he noticed her left arm and he did a double-take. "Young mistress, your arm has returned!"

"Yes! Agnus did it!" Terra held her arm out for the ox to examine. "He made it from that man's rib."

"My rib?" repeated Adam, a strange look passing over his face. He turned to Agnus, his mouth falling open as the older man gave him an amused smile.

Falling on one knee, Adam bowed his head, one hand pressed solemnly to his chest. "My Lord! Forgive me, you have aged much since we last spoke!"

Agnus approached him and placed a hand lightly on his shoulder, prompting Adam to look up at him. "Yes, you have been asleep since that time. And what of the Temple?"

"I've done as you instructed. I did not allow the enemy to gain access to the Temple."

"You have done well, Adam."

Adam smiled and raised his eyes to Terra and Lamina who still had their arms around one another. "Are these your followers?"

"They are my friends," Agnus answered, eyes soft with fondness. He turned to both Lamina and Terra, gesturing for them to rise. "Please introduce yourselves to Adam."

"Hello Adam," greeted the ox, nodding stiffly, "my name is Lamina."

"It's a pleasure to meet a descendant of the inhabitants of Attero," replied Adam, giving an equally stilted bow. "It is unfortunate what happened to many of your kin…"

The old ox shrugged. "The prophecies of old foretold of such an event. Thankfully my grandfather was wise enough to heed those warnings and my family fled to Lacuna," he explained lightly, scrutinising Adam the whole while.

Straining a smile, Adam turned his eyes to Terra as she pulled away from Lamina, her fingers still resting on his arm.

Lamina gave Terra a not-so subtle nudge while looking askance at Adam. "Young mistress, is this the young man whose rib turned into your new arm?" he whispered out of the corner of his mouth.

Threading her fingers through his shaggy mane, Terra drew herself closer to Lamina, unable to wipe the smile from her face. He was alive. Agnus saved him. "Yes," she replied promptly after Lamina glanced down at her. "Agnus took his rib out while he was asleep and joined it to my arm."

"What is your name?" Adam asked suddenly, making Terra jump.

"Um." Terra was unsure of how to reply.

Lamina's eyes narrowed in distrust. "Her name might as well be *Ridley* to you."

Adam regarded the old ox coolly. After a moment, he shrugged his shoulders. "Ridley is fine by me. Do *you* mind, Miss Ridley?"

Terra blinked, a frown marring her face as she thought about the brand on her tongue. "Well…if you want to call me that. I guess it's fine."

Deflated, Adam's shoulders sagged and he shot a glance at Agnus who merely smiled at him.

"Adam, I will open these doors. You must retrieve the armour within."

Without waiting for a reply, Agnus gestured to the door and with a murmur of that foreign language—which reminded Terra of what she heard in Mathelda's shop—and a flick of his wrist it opened, a rush of cool air escaping from the next room. "Once that is complete, we will depart from here. We must prepare for the storm, and work until all of the prophecies come to fulfilment and time itself draws to a close."

With a better grasp of Agnus' statement than Terra and Lamina, Adam obediently swept out of the room and disappeared into the next.

"Well, with Adam busy, I must say that I am very sorry that this day started off so terribly," murmured Agnus, shooting a meaningful look at Lamina before turning his gaze to Terra. "But we can hope to make this birthday of yours a little better now."

Terra nodded without comprehending. "That's okay...I mean...my birthday...?" she repeated, drawing a blank on the word. "Is that...something important...?"

"IMPORTANT?" bellowed Lamina, a look of disbelief on his face. "Good grief! Important? Of course it's important—what, have you never celebrated a birthday or known anyone to have done so?"

Terra racked her brain for any memory that related to the unfamiliar concept, yet none came and she shook her head wordlessly.

Lamina opened his mouth to make a remark before seeming to remember something and promptly closing it. "Ah... that would be about right..." he muttered to himself sheepishly, glancing at Agnus who merely nodded.

A smile lit Agnus' face as he approached Terra. "A birthday is what the name suggests—a celebration that commemorates the day of your birth." Agnus stopped in front of Terra and dug into a pocket within his jacket. "On this very day, the third day of the fourth month, a girl came into existence. And her name was Terra." He slipped a gold chain around Terra's neck and carefully clipped the clasp in place. "This is for you." He beamed at her.

Speechless, Terra looked down at the golden arch that dangled on the end of the chain. "For...me?" Her eye shimmered as she studied the item.

"Yes."

"What is it?" Terra lightly traced the arch with her fingertips.

"A bridge," explained Agnus, eyes twinkling. "I made it myself."

"You made this Agnus?"

"Indeed."

Heart trembling, Terra mirrored his smile, dimples appearing in her cheeks. "Thank you..." He had already given her so much today.

"And here," declared Lamina, stepping towards the girl, "is *my* gift!" He thrust a silver ring under Terra's nose.

"A ring? Surely not a betrothal ring, Lamina?" teased Agnus, grinning broadly.

"WHAT? Of course not!" It appeared as if steam would blow out from Lamina's nostrils at any moment. "It's a friendship token! I have one for all three of us. Made it one day while working as a smithy in Sominium and kept it on me ever since…well, it wasn't really a friendship token in the beginning but I just thought that…one day it might be nice to give as a gift when you came of age…though I guess it's good enough for now too…"

Terra stared blankly at the ring in Lamina's hand, barely taking in any of his flustered mumblings. "A friendship token?"

Lamina made an embarrassed expression and shoved the ring into her hands. "We're friends—aren't we?"

Terra's heart pounded in her chest. She parted her trembling lips, almost too thrilled to utter a word. "Y-yes!" Tears sprang up in her eye. As Lamina slipped the ring onto the middle finger of her right hand, Terra tried to blink her tears away. She swallowed thickly and her voice wavered as she asked: "Mr Lamina and Agnus are my friends?"

Lamina's face broke out into a grin. "Of course!"

"Always," agreed Agnus, soft smile never leaving his face.

Tears slid down Terra's cheeks. "I'm sorry," she whispered, hiding behind her hands. In Magia, Simeon would sneer and lash out in such a moment of vulnerability. "I'm sorry…" Why was she crying? She had never felt this way before. It was as if she had been gifted more good than she ever deserved. But why didn't she deserve it? Was she allowed this moment of joy?

Hands gently peeled hers away and Agnus and Lamina wordlessly hugged her. A mixture of emotions left Terra sobbing and laughing as her friends held her tightly. She had never shed tears that mingled with such joy before. Whatever this storm of emotions was, for once in her life, she was happy to be alive.

"Are we celebrating something…?"

Terra jumped away at Adam's voice and scrubbed her face on her sleeve.

"It's the young mistress' birthday." Lamina donned his own silver ring and handed Agnus his which he slipped onto his uninjured hand.

Adam blinked. "Happy birthday. I'm sorry that I do not have something to offer you—especially if you're now of age."

At the words 'of age', Simeon's face flashed in Terra's mind. She gulped, pushing the thought away.

"She will be of age *next* spell."

"Of age for what?" Terra's voice sounded oddly small in her ears.

"Of age to marry," explained Adam, earning a dirty look from Lamina. "Once children turn thirteen, they are considered adults and have a coming of age ceremony in Sominium to commemorate this event."

There was a pause where Adam closed his eyes, appearing deep in thought. Terra's heart leapt as his eyes snapped open, revealing that they had assumed an ethereal light blue hue. As abruptly as his eyes had begun to glow, letters and symbols burst from his body and Terra was reminded of the words that circled Spiritus.

"But for you, the path you shall walk will be perilous," he stated, voice otherworldly. "Before your eye, a great city shall fall, and at your feet it shall crumble."

Adam closed his eyes and took a deep shuddering breath. The letters and symbols that circled him faded away. Opening his eyes again, he smiled pleasantly at Terra who stared at him, stunned.

Mouth hanging open, Lamina glanced from Adam to Agnus. "Was that a Pateran prophecy...?"

Agnus stepped forward. "Friends, this is why Adam will travel with us. He will accompany us to the outskirts of Magia. There we will deliver a message to its inhabitants."

"A message?" repeated Terra. "To Magia?"

Nodding, Agnus gave a tight smile. "It is a task that I've chosen Adam to complete."

"Can we rest, Agnus?" asked Lamina, laying a hand on Terra's shoulder. "The young mistress looks exhausted..."

Agnus shook his head. "Lamina, my friend, there is too much to do. We must make tracks now—Levi will have escaped and will surely warn Magia of our location. There are events that *must* come to pass and Magia must be given a chance turn away from what they are doing."

Adam turned to Agnus. "A Maremortum pursued you?"

"Yes."

Tilting his head to the side, Adam's expression was contemplative, yet he said no more regarding this, instead agreeing with Agnus' proposal to leave Initium immediately.

"We cannot allow Magia to catch wind of our journey."

The old ox nodded slowly and stroked his chin. "Their military force has dwindled greatly in power since the Sominiums claimed the Kingdom's throne. But you're right...they should not be taken lightly."

Despite the fear that made her heart tremble at the idea of returning to Magia, Terra held her newly reformed arm and glanced at her ring and necklace. She bit her lip and stuck her chin out, appearing braver than she felt. "Well then," she said, drawing the attention of the others. She smiled broadly, hope strengthening her even as her voice wavered, "Lead on, Agnus."

My enemies have grown fat from my suffering. Their tongues lap at my wounds, their fingers pick at my flesh and their teeth gnaw on my bones. How long will I lie in the valley of your wrath? Remember me One and send your Ezer.

- Lines from *Laments of Lerielle, Scriptura*. Translated by J. Talis

11

The polished shop sign hanging in the front window of a brick duplex building caught the light of the artificial sun, its painted words gleaming:

Issa's Babylonian Slave Traders
The city's finest traders and beastmasters at your service!
Babylonian children now in stock!

A varied assortment of shops lined the streets of Babylonia; both old and new businesses but their size and grandeur dulled when compared to those in Lacuna. The heavy scent of spices and perfumes was everywhere, overwhelming any unprepared traveller, but Simeon had long grown accustomed to the smells over the spells.

Dressed in a dark linen shirt and slacks, a stark contrast from his Magian uniform, Simeon followed a paved pathway down toward the tall brick tower at the centre of the city. His eyes peered out from a gap between the dark strips of cloth wrapped around his head. He blended in with the few other travellers he passed along the brick roads. It pleased him that not a single resident of the city had bothered to glance in his direction. He was just another faceless stranger. Perhaps he was a tourist, making a stop before heading to the eastern city, Lacuna. Or an Old World zealot determined to trek the dismal remains of Attero—revering the destruction with such ill fervour that Simeon believed Pater would feel sick.

Continuing along the road, he passed by vendors of trinkets and souvenirs, eyes glossing over the flashes of gold and gleaming of jewels. Food and beverage stalls were a little further away and though interested by the sweets on offer, Simeon marched on, focused on the tower that loomed in front of him.

It stood high above the rest of the city, a monument formed by brick, mortar, bitumen, blood and sweat. The tower bore a striking resemblance to Magia's own and Simeon half-smiled at this fact. It was difficult not to admire the work of the Babylonian slaves.

At the bottom of the tower, Simeon spotted a familiar building and hastened to a trot.

A little way down by the roadside, an old, bearded man sat beside a bony woman. A thin baby howled in her lap. The woman stared despondently at the road, not once glancing at the baby. At Simeon's approach, however, the old man bounded to his feet, hands cupped together in front of him.

Simeon halted, peering over the man's shoulder at the woman. "What's wrong with her?"

"My daughter has no milk to feed her son...she has decided to give up...we have no items to offer, no societal possessions either..." he said, his voice wavering. "And if we continue to bleed ourselves to pay for things, we'll surely die before this child even reaches an age when beastmasters can take him... please sir, if you could help us so that this child may live..."

The Colonel snorted. "You want this child to live so that it may grow up to become a slave?" he laughed, yet there was no mirth reflected in his eyes. "Why not just let him die now?"

The man's eyes hardened. "I cannot let my grandson follow the path of Death that his father tread."

"And you think that his life will be better when he's enslaved in some godforsaken city in Tempus?"

There was no response from the man. His eyes had begun to water and his chapped lips trembled at the truth behind the Colonel's words. But despite his tears, he continued to hold his shaking hands out. "Who are you to say that a life is not worth living?" he whispered. "Who are you to judge that his life will be worthless?"

The heavy silence that stretched between the pair was broken by the wailing of the baby.

Thrusting his hand deep into his pant pocket, Simeon withdrew a vial of blood and tossed it at the man before proceeding along the road. "I drained some blood this morning for my own purchasing purposes. But it won't last long in the heat."

"Thank you, sir!" came the tremulous call from behind him. "Thank you so much!"

The Magian did not look back and continued along his way to the large ornate building at the foot of the city's tower. The artificial sun was beginning to sink.

Permitted entry by the guards at the front, Simeon slipped into the candle-lit room beyond and the heady smell of perfume and incense filled his nose as he ducked under the deep crimson drapes running along the edges of the room.

In the centre of the room, two small boys tended to a figure that lay across a chaise longue. Its colour matched the drapes and the fingernails of the slender figure who rose at Simeon's entry.

With a tug at the end of the cloth around his head, Simeon unravelled the material, grinning at the woman sitting up on the longue.

"Simeon," gasped the woman, dark dreadlocks falling over her shoulders as she stood up with a hand from the boy closest to her. "I was not expecting your arrival so soon," she exclaimed, breathless when she reached the Colonel.

After a moment to catch her breath, excitement lighting her eyes, she snapped her fingers. One of the boys, the youngest in appearance, scurried to her side with his attention fixed on the goblet he carried with the utmost care. He placed it delicately into the woman's expectant hand.

"Well, Simeon?" drawled the woman, bringing the gem-encrusted cup up under the Magian's nose. "Will you drink from it this time?"

Icy blue eyes locked with bi-coloured ones and the woman scarcely dared to breathe, a flush visibly spreading up her neck.

"Your offer is kind Tiamat, but I cannot accept it," murmured Simeon with a smirk, bowing courteously. "I am not certain that it will resolve my current circumstance."

The Babylonian leader gave a coy smile and continued to hold the cup out to the younger man. "Your beloved sister overcame the infertility E132 causes. I'm sure you too are eager to try anything to break the curse on all Magian citizens…" she whispered, her free arm snaking around the Colonel's waist as she pressed herself against him.

Simeon shook himself out of her grasp and laughed at her crestfallen expression. "Your attentions are always much appreciated but you know that I can't return such interest."

Tiamat pursed her lips. "I do hope you change your mind about that matter, Simeon. It would be quite advantageous for you if you did. And besides, it would be far too difficult for a man like you to pluck a fresh flower."

"Well, that's debatable…but on a different note, why don't you come and see Magia sometime soon?" The Colonel dropped down into a nearby chair, gesturing for Tiamat to return to hers. "You might be surprised by the new leadership…the Maremortum girl is quite interesting."

"The eldest?" asked Tiamat, her expression devoid of interest as she flung herself back onto the chaise longue.

"No, the youngest. She knows exactly what she wants."

A smirk spread Tiamat's lips. "Is she anything like *your* little doll?"

Simeon fell silent. Reclining in his chair, he held Tiamat's gaze. "*My* little doll? She has been far less fortunate and yet…she's more resilient than the younger Maremortum."

"So, you were dearly fond of her then," observed Tiamat with a coy smile, clapping her hands together.

One of the boys shuffled forward and crouched to reach beneath the side table. He pulled out a white teapot, its round sides decorated with a shimmering azure dragon, and placed it carefully on the table beside a bowl of green grapes. Stooping down again, he withdrew matching cups and saucers from below the table and set them on the top. He proceeded to take the pot and pour tea into a cup, steam unfurling from the mouth of the dragon.

"Well, is that true?" asked Tiamat once Simeon accepted the cup from the boy.

"Is what true?"

"That you were terribly fond of her."

Head tilted to the side, a smirk played about Simeon's lips. "Does that upset you?"

"No," sniffed Tiamat, "You've never shown as much interest nor were as fond of the Maremortum girls."

A harsh laugh escaped Simeon's lips. "Arche bears similarities with the girl. She spent all her childhood in fear and terror. She is meek and humble. Lachesis on the other hand…" Simeon paused, pensive. "I was never too fond of Lachesis," reflected Simeon, smile still in place. "She was always such a cruel sister."

Tiamat sat up and batted her eyelashes, an amused smile tugging at the corners of her lips. "You don't like cruel sisters, do you?" she asked, her voice a delighted squeal.

Simeon's smile remained. "Children are terrors, aren't they?"

Tiamat matched his smile, her voice a purr when she reasoned: "Of course. That's why we must treat them as cruelly as possible." Her smile appeared more twisted and sinister. "It's the only way that they'll learn. And that *is* the most important thing. That they learn their place in the world." She scooted back in her seat, rotating her wrist and swirling the gold liquid within the goblet. "Once they learn their place in the world, then you can control them completely. Bondage and despair are what they become accustomed to and once they realise that there is no escape from their fate, they will not attempt to flee from it." She leaned forward and plucked a grape from the bowl on the side table, popping it into her mouth. "You see, when there is no hope, they cannot place their faith in something as whimsical as a saviour that will break them free from the binds that hold them to their life of slavery. All they can hope for is a quick and painless death. That is the only thing they can place their faith in for freeing them from their miserable lives. Death is their only comfort."

Simeon listened silently, sipping calmly at his tea. Placing his cup back down, he smiled at Tiamat. "It seems that, if you had siblings, you would be a cruel sister."

Smile faltering, Tiamat studied the Colonel critically. A moment passed and the older woman's eyes glittered suddenly with mirth, smile hitched back on. "Is that why you rarely turn up on my doorstep nowadays?" she teased.

"I'm simply making an observation," replied Simeon, hands upturned to emphasise innocence.

Tiamat leaned forward on the longue, beaming at the Colonel. "That's why you are my favourite out of the Maremortums."

"I'm a Van de Berg," corrected Simeon, his tone low in warning. "You'd do well to remember that, Tiamat."

Rather than alarmed by his abrupt anger, the older woman threw her head back and gave a laugh like a harsh bark. "Oh, I *have* remembered, never fear my dear Colonel," she purred with a smug look. "I'm merely keeping you on your toes."

"What ever for?"

"Knowing people's allegiances matters."

"And where is your allegiance?"

"I fully support The Conqueror's vision for the New World." Tiamat sighed dreamily, fluttering her lashes with a gentle eyeroll as her tongue ran along her upper lip. "Children truly are the foundation for the New World—

once they know their place within it, of course. They will pour life into the veins of this world and we will all help to nurture and restore it.

The Colonel's eyes glimmered in the light. "That, we can agree on."

A broad smile crossed Tiamat's face. Leaning back, she clapped her hands together and one of the boys ran to her side.

Simeon noted the black collar that peeped up above the high collar of the boy's shirt.

"Go and prepare the guest room for the Colonel," she instructed the boy. He scurried away and Tiamat returned her attention to Simeon, smiling broadly. "You must stay for the night my dear. You know that night-time travel is not recommended in Babylonia."

"Thank you," he murmured, nodding his head.

"You brought officers too, didn't you? Where did you station them?"

"In a house nearby. They will send word to me here once Levi returns."

Eyebrows raised so high that they had the potential to be lost in her hairline, Tiamat's bi-coloured eyes glittered with amusement. "So, all of the Maremortums travelled here then?" she asked, her voice oddly high.

"Not all. But don't worry, we'll be departing once Levi and The Oracle return. Thank you for your hospitality. You are most kind to me." Simeon bowed politely.

Tiamat's brown and green eyes shone. "I'm always happy to have you," she said pointedly. "In fact, I wish you would come and see me more often."

The Colonel assumed this was his cue to leave and was relieved by the return of the boy who had exited earlier.

"If you follow the boy, he will lead you to your room," said Tiamat, laying back on the chaise longue and stretching her legs out.

The boy said nothing as Simeon followed him out of the room. He zipped down the carpeted hallways, Simeon close behind, coming to an abrupt halt by a cream-coloured door. Opening the door, he stood back to allow room for the Colonel to pass, motioning for Simeon to enter.

The decoration of the room bore similarities to the one Simeon had met Tiamat in; it was lavished with red velvet curtains along the edges and in the nearest corner, a chaise longue. On the furthest wall was a large window with a padded seat covered in plush golden cushions. The fading light from the window spilled into the room onto a four-poster bed, covered in quilts and pillows embroidered with swirling Avarosan patterns of the finest needlework.

Nodding approvingly, Simeon glanced over his shoulder at the boy. "You may leave now. Thank Tiamat for the room."

The boy bowed and closed the door as he stepped out.

Simeon kicked his boots off and strode to the bed, sliding his hand along the wooden posts as he passed them. Collapsing face first onto the bed, he inhaled the cinnamon scent of the sheets and rolled over, flopping onto his back, staring up at the canopy of the four-poster bed.

A drop of blood fell from the young boy's chin. "Mo...ther..." he whimpered, hand filled with the scarlet-coloured element, oozing through his fingertips and down towards the twisted form of a woman. "Mother..."

Secluded in his room, Simeon laid sprawled across his bed, eyes slowly opening from sleep. He shifted up into a sitting position and rested his head in his hands.

There was a loud rap of knuckles against the guest room door and without looking up, Simeon bid the person to enter.

A young cadet stepped into the room, clicking his heels together and saluting the Colonel. "There is a message for you on the communicator, sir. It's from The Oracle."

The Colonel sighed, leaning back into the headboard of the bed, his icy-blue eyes studying the cadet wearily. "What is it?"

"She said that she and the Lieutenant-General are close to Babylonia and to deliver this message to you with her exact words: '*We have found your doll*'."

Simeon leapt to his feet, eyes alert and irate with excitement. "Did she state their current location and where they are headed?"

The cadet nodded. "The Lieutenant-General said that there is nothing truly for them to do at Attero and informed us that he believes that they will be returning to Lacuna."

"Bargain with a beastmaster for a horse," he ordered, tossing a lump at the cadet.

The young man glanced down at the object in his hand, confused. From what he could tell, it was the crushed remains of a discarded eye-patch. "Colonel? What's this for?"

"Payment for the horse." Simeon pulled his boots on. "Transport is a major deal in Tempus and the beastmasters won't so much as look at any offerings of blood exchanges. Once we have the horse, we can cut off the girl and Agnus. They won't have gained enough ground to exit Attero and enter the land around Lacuna. We can intercept them before they make it there."

He touched his hand to the blade sheathed at his waist and the scarlet element seemed to oscillate with anticipation. "Mother," he murmured quietly to himself, a cruel smile twisting his lips, "it seems that I cannot be any more grateful for this E132 you've given me and the gift you awoke in my veins."

With that, he strode past the cadet who followed him, the face of his runaway slave imprinted within his mind and his sword thirsty for blood.

The newly formed group of four puffed across the plains and in the distance, Terra recognised the large broken lump of earth; the prison that had entrapped the Maremortum. "He already escaped!" she gasped, continuing to sprint after the faster figures of Agnus and Adam who easily led the pack. She felt a stitch building up in her side.

Lamina glanced down at the girl who clamped her hand over her side, teeth gritted. "Young mistress, if you're tired, I can carry you on my shoulders."

The young girl smiled kindly at the old ox. "Thanks Lamina. I'm just getting a bit sore in my side."

Adam slowed down considerably, his hand outstretched to Terra. "I'll carry you instead if you're tired," he offered. "It's better if you're free to fight, Lamina," he responded to the incredulous expression on the old ox's face.

Terra automatically turned down his offer, more comfortable with being carried by Lamina than this young man she hardly knew. "I think it would be easier if Lamina carried me," she said staunchly. "Besides, it's only a little sore. I'll just keep running and get over it."

The young man said nothing and sped back up, returning to the same pace at which Agnus ran.

They raced without stopping across the endless expanse of the plains, dodging craters and potholes along the way. By this time, Terra was drenched in sweat and had slowed her pace significantly, the stitch burning painfully in her side. Her breaths became short, and ragged; body too weak and unaccustomed to long distances. "La-Lamin—" she rasped, hand weakly reaching out to the ox.

Lamina quickly grabbed her by the waist and lifted her onto his shoulders. "Hold on tight!"

Terra feebly leaned over and grabbed the horns on his head. "Thanks, Lamina," she gasped, trying to ignore the tightening pain in her ribs. Resisting the temptation to lay her head down on the mass of hair on Lamina's head,

Terra shook herself awake, keeping an eye on the horizon. "I think I can see green in the distance! It's not too far away now!"

Something in the distance by the trees caught her eye and Terra squinted, a deep frown marring her face.

"Everyone!" yelled Agnus.

Lamina cracked his knuckles and Terra drew out Spiritus, her other hand continuing to tightly grip the ox's horn.

At the very edge of the plains stood three familiar figures with weapons drawn. Simeon held his blood-red blade before him and Mrs Maremortum's hand squeezed the blind Maremortum's shoulder. His clothes were still covered in dust from the earth prison Agnus had created for him.

Terra's lips pressed together. Did she have to fight Mrs Maremortum too? "Lamina, I'll get down here."

Spiritus shone with the light of the miniscule words surrounding the blade and the Element 132 in the hands of their opponents glowed a sinister blood-red like the moon that hung high above them in the black sky.

Rolling back the sleeves of his suit jacket, Agnus grimaced at the Magians approaching. "It was not wise for you three to come here," he said, buttoning back the cuffs of his shirt. A gust of wind began to gather around his feet, swaying the grass that grew beneath them and kicking up the dust around the unusual patch of green. "Turn back now and take my warning with you to the rest of Magia: Magia must pay for the crimes it has committed."

"We don't intend to flee nor do we wish to listen to your nonsense, Agnus," jeered the silver-haired man.

Agnus sighed. "If you do not wish to heed my words, that is your choice. But when the end of your time descends upon you, do not claim that I did not warn you. As the old of Magia were forced to learn firsthand."

"Mrs Maremortum!"

The silver-haired woman swallowed visibly. She clenched her teeth, avoiding Terra's pleading gaze. "Shut up, you doll!" She whipped out several shards of E132 and flung them at the four companions.

"Libertas Spiritus!"

A large forcefield of words cloaked the four with Terra standing tall in the centre, Spiritus pressed into the ground. She returned Mrs Maremortum's glare with a look of sadness.

"Terra, you take Adam with you and try to get ahead! Lamina and I will deal with these three and catch up to you!" instructed Agnus as he lifted his hands together slowly. The earth began to rumble and walls shot up around Simeon and the Maremortums.

"Come on Adam!" Terra grabbed the young man's hand and raced away from the battle, the veil of words returning to their circling of Spiritus' blade.

She didn't want to leave, but she wanted to start trusting in Agnus.

There was a guttural roar from behind them and Terra glimpsed Simeon leaping up over the earth walls Agnus had created, propelled by E132. He summoned the levitating scarlet platform from under his feet to his hands and it separated, morphing into six different blades; he held a gladius in one hand and a scimitar in the other with the four remaining swords hovering behind him in the air. His eyes had assumed a chilling red hue.

With a snarl, he hurled the gladius at Terra and Adam.

The two companions leapt to the side, avoiding the hurtling sword but Simeon flicked his wrist back and it swung around, flying back towards the two. They tore their hands apart and threw themselves away from each other, dodging the blade once again.

Adam scrambled to his feet. "Manipulating Element 132 with such ease...Are you a Maremortum?"

"That's none of your business," snarled Simeon, catching the returning gladius. He launched himself at Adam, thrusting both swords at him rapidly, his movements like a madman's.

Clambering onto her grazed knees, Terra watched as Adam twisted and turned, ducked and weaved, slipped and slid past each thrust of Simeon's blades, brows knotted in concentration and skin faintly glowing a light blue.

"To have such a compatibility with the Element 132..." Adam gasped as he dodged several more slashes, runic slivers escaping his lips. Sweat dewed on his forehead and a weary smile appeared on his face. "You must have the blood of Vei in you."

Jaw clenching, Simeon swung out wide, forcing Adam to jump back to a safer distance as the sword nicked his leg. "You don't know anything!" growled Simeon, rushing at Adam.

Adam sidestepped the initial blade, grimacing as the other ripped deep into his arm. With clenched teeth, Adam grabbed Simeon's left arm. "No, *you* don't know anything, Simeon Van de Berg." He felt the Colonel stiffen. Adam's eyes flashed light blue and his voice softened. "No, that's not right." He took a breath and cocked his head, as if listening to something. "I should call you Simeon Railesson, shouldn't I?"

With a furious roar, Simeon tore his arm away from Adam's grip and slashed wildly at him. "WHERE DID YOU GET THAT NAME FROM?" he bellowed, eyes turning a vivid blood-red.

"Adam!"

Darting forward, Terra parried the blows directed at the young man while he slipped back to a safer distance and tore a piece of cloth from his shirt to wound around his arm. She miscalculated a block, resulting in a cut along her own forearm and a shallow one across her cheek.

Simeon's slashes were relentless and Terra had to mentally steel herself, focusing solely on the sword in her hands that guided her movements. Occasionally she misjudged and Simeon's blades licked different parts of her arms or legs, but Spiritus held its ground even as her arms grew weary. It cleaved through the scimitar and it bubbled black before dispersing as white liquid through the air but Simeon was already summoning one of the swords behind him and a katana leapt into his free hand.

A few metres away, Lamina rolled into the dust as Mr Maremortum dodged his punch. Pushing himself back up with a grunt of effort, Lamina charged again at the silver-haired man, swinging at him yet missing each time. "Y'know, I really owe you for earlier today," said Lamina, jumping back when the Maremortum swung his sword out at the old ox. "But looks like it will be harder than I thought. For a man who's blind, you sure move as if you *can* see."

"I see with all my other senses," he replied, voice dull. His teeth audibly cracked against what Lamina glimpsed to be a fragment of scarlet. He held his sword straight before him with one hand, placing his other hand behind his back. "Now, let's see. Which way of seeing is better? Mine or yours?"

He kicked dust into Lamina's eyes, causing the ox to stumble back, rubbing at his eyes. He dashed forward, his blade pointed at Lamina's heart.

The earth beneath his feet disrupted his movement, jutting up and forcing him to flip backwards.

In mid-air while dodging Mrs Maremortum's attacks, Agnus had flicked his wrist up, forcing the earth out of its place. "Lamina's already suffered enough at your hand," he said as he landed on the dust, grass springing up beneath his feet. "And Terra should not endure that again."

Mrs Maremortum sneered. "What a fitting name you gave that doll. T—" She convulsed, gripping her throat as her mouth foamed.

Agnus' face darkened as he turned to her. "You don't have permission to say that name."

Spitting and cackling, Mrs Maremortum wiped her mouth on the back of her sleeve, veins throbbing in her temple. "She's already sold her name?" She threw her head back and laughed.

"You're twisted by a degree of overexposure, Dinah."

The name caused Mrs Maremortum to jump.

Agnus continued to speak softly: "That name does not suit you. Your mother was mistaken to name her children after the ancestors she was so proud of."

A muscle in Mrs Maremortum's jaw twitched. Her eyes grew hard and cold as she regarded Agnus. "Agnus Dayton." She spat as if the name were vile. "Do you know how long a doll lives for? For as long as it isn't broken."

Without turning, Mrs Maremortum slung the E132 crystal shards at Terra. "Young mistress!"

A barrier of words burst forth from Adam's body, expanding across the ground between him and Terra until it covered her also. It blocked the barrage of scarlet shards, sending them back at Mrs Maremortum who leapt back just before the E132 shards were buried in the ground at her feet. With a flick of her wrists, she forced the pieces out of the ground, drawing it back into her hands.

For the briefest of moments, the words shimmered about Adam's body like a protective body piece.

There was a vicious snarl as Lamina launched himself at Mrs Maremortum. He tried to gore her on the tips of his horns but she was yanked back against Mr Maremortum who dashed to her side.

"Thanks Adam!" grunted Terra as the boy's barrier evaporated. She sliced another E132 sword through with Spiritus, sweat dripping down her face.

Summoning the remaining sword behind him, Simeon sidestepped Spiritus' next swing and ducked under the one that followed, the tips of his hair trimmed and drifting to the floor. He swung out at her in an attempt to slow her slashes, but Spiritus danced around his blade, shining with each step its vessel took to avoid the blows he directed at her. Infuriated, Simeon slashed at her legs to stop Terra's movement, but Spiritus pulled her into a jump, drawing her knees up and then cutting through the air to force the Colonel back. The glowing letters surrounding Agnus' sword left a small cut on the bottom of Simeon's chin as he fell back.

"Why?" growled the Colonel, wiping the blood off his chin. He gripped both of his swords tightly in one hand, holding it out horizontally before him and touching the length of it with his free hand. A scarlet light emitted from the blade and its form trembled before morphing. "It doesn't make sense! Where has this power of yours come from?" he yelled, raising the newly formed two-bladed tribal execution sword above his head, prepared to charge forward.

"Your mother's voice."

Simeon halted. He turned towards the voice and stared at the characters that were aglow upon Adam's forehead as if they had been etched there.

The young man's eyes shone a deep blue, piercing through the Colonel. "It cries out to you, Colonel," he said, sending shivers down Terra's spine. "The blood of your mother that is intermingled with the Element 132. It is crying out to you with her voice. Can you not hear it?" The markings on his forehead faded and his eyes returned to their normal hazel hue.

Grip slackening on the execution sword, Simeon stared at Adam, eyes wide with shock and an underlying fear.

"That's where I got your name from," said Adam with a mysterious smile. "Your moth—"

"DON'T TALK ABOUT THAT WORTHLESS TOPHET!" roared Simeon, his entire body glowing red. With a loud cry from the Colonel, the execution sword spread into a thin armour around his body and Terra felt an unexplainable dread.

Returning Spiritus to her body, her legs trembled as Simeon's pupils and irises vanished in a flood of red and blood streamed down from the corners of his lips. "R-run," she muttered to Adam, her hairs standing on end from the tremendous power that emanated from Simeon. A terrible shriek filled the air and Terra was immediately reminded of the Tophets from Magia. She clamped her hands tightly over her ears, eye wide with horror. She knew the noise was coming from the E132 but the sheer terror and foreboding the tortured screams filled her with brought unbidden tears to her eye.

"Everyone run!" Agnus shouted darting towards the Colonel. "I need to suppress this power—now, just run!"

Adam took Terra by the shoulders, trying to shake her out of her petrified state.

She turned to him shakily, her sight blurred from the tears. "There are really people's souls trapped in those things…"

"No." Adam laid his hand gently on hers. "Merely memories. Trust me," he murmured, eyes kind. "I know."

Reassured, Terra nodded and turned to Lamina who barrelled towards them, taking her hand in his.

"Young mistress, some of your hair for Agnus please!"

Without a question, Terra yanked out a few of her hairs, wincing as they detached from her scalp. She tossed them to the wind that had gathered around her feet and watched as Agnus closed his fingers slowly over the palm of his hand, drawing the hair strands to himself. The strands quickly turned to thread in his grasp.

"Let's go!" Lamina said quickly, ushering the two to run. "Only Agnus will be able to battle with Simeon in that crazed state he's in! Now, hurry!"

"But I don't want to leave him," Terra found herself saying.

"Terra, my child. Go."

Glancing at Agnus' back, Terra gripped the bridge on her necklace so tightly, the corners dug deep into the palm of her hand. She nodded at Lamina and the trio raced away.

A motionless Mr Maremortum stared in the direction where Simeon stood. "Simeon…"

"Where are you all going?" shouted Mrs Maremortum over the screams that issued from the E132 connected to Simeon. She raised her hand, prepared to throw her crystal shards at the unarmed Agnus when the E132 trembled in her grasp. "What is—?"

All the Maremortums' E132 were pulled from them, gravitating towards Simeon whose screams had joined those of the Element 132. They fused together to create a helm and beads of sweat formed on the Maremortum's bodies at the intense heat that burst in waves from Simeon.

Agnus paced towards the screaming Simeon, eyes sad. "Simeon Railesson," he said, raising both of his hands. He took up Terra's thread in one hand and dug it into the flesh of his other arm. Blood dripped down his arm and Agnus ran his uninjured hand along it. He took another step towards Simeon, drenched in sweat from the immense heat emanating from the Element 132. He held his hand out, slick with blood. "It is not your time," he whispered before touching the helm that covered Simeon's head.

On Lerielle's return to Yiellnyorein, One showered her with mercy and
raised her up.

- Lines from *Writings of the Kings of Old, Scriptura.* Translated by C.
Yelnorin

12

Lamina led Terra and Adam past the guard at the northern gates of Lacuna,
where they made a short stop to gather supplies. "Agnus will catch up and
we'll be better prepared for travel this way," Lamina said as they paced down
the half-empty lamp-lit streets to collect some items he had stored away in a
cabinet at his old café.

After several more whispered assurances from both Lamina and Adam,
Terra slipped into a pensive silence. Not wanting to burden the other two
with her own tumultuous emotions and worries, Terra fell back into the safe
and familiar and suppressed her burgeoning feelings.

She wondered if the turmoil she felt was because of a lack of trust but
neither Lamina nor Adam made her feel that way, with the latter softly saying,
"I'm worried too. But we must trust him when he tells us to."

The café was a block or so down from Mathelda's clothing store and when
they found it, Terra's eye lit up, glad for a happy distraction.

The muggy café, lit by countless lights hanging from the ceiling, awed
Terra and she found herself gawking at the entire interior. It felt whimsical
in its modesty.

She scurried after Lamina and Adam to the store counter where a woman with wavy golden hair stood with a perfectly manicured hand on her hip and an expression of annoyance on her face.

"Look what the cat dragged in," grunted the woman through glossy lips. "I mean, literally. You're covered in dirt and sweat. Long time no see, Lamina."

Lamina gave a sheepish grin. "Sorry to have you man the café for so long, Rebekah."

The woman shrugged. "Well, it couldn't be helped. Since Kouki left, it's been a lot harder to find people to do shifts here." She rounded the counter, high-heels clacking against the wooden floorboards. Shaking back her long hair, she set her caramel eyes on Terra and Adam.

Terra felt sure she had seen those eyes before.

"Who would these equally dirt-caked birds be?" asked Rebekah, tossing a set of keys to Lamina before stepping aside to allow him access to the cabinet behind the counter.

Lamina glanced over his shoulder, brows knotted. "Well…they would be my travelling companions: Ridley and Adam," he said, nodding to each as he introduced them. There was a pause where Rebekah raised an eyebrow and the old ox cleared his throat awkwardly, keys jingling to fill the silence.

"What sort of travelling companions?" quizzed Rebekah, stalking towards the two youths before her, studying them critically.

Adam returned her gaze apathetically and Terra smiled weakly.

Rebekah looked over the two of them, her full lips pursed. "I thought you weren't into slaves."

A derisive snort issued from the cabinet which Lamina had buried his head into. "Coming from the lady who helps keep that business running," came his nasty reply, earning a cold glare from the tall beauty.

"It's a very good business," she sniffed. "Has kept bread on the table, which is more than what I can say about this café you're running."

She turned away from the two youths and walked back over to the counter, peering over Lamina's shoulder. Folding her arms across her chest, she knelt down behind the old ox and, to the surprise of both Terra and Adam, placed a hand in Lamina's mane of hair. "I can't keep running this café just because you ask me to," she said in a tone Terra could not quite pick. She gently curled a bit of his hair around her finger. "You definitely owe me for the past four spells."

Lamina glanced at her and then resumed his rummaging through the cabinet. He shook his head and mumbled something inaudible.

Rebekah laughed. "Ooh, you're so *bor-ing*, Lamina," she teased, ruffling his thick hair. She stood back up, dusted her knees off and turned away, headed for the back room of the café. "Just let me know when you're leaving, okay?" she called over her shoulder, waving.

When the back-room door clicked shut behind her, Lamina pulled his head out of the cabinet while heaving a great sigh of relief.

Adam gave a small "huh".

"So," he began, "she's in love with Lamina."

There was a loud bang behind the counter that caused Terra to jump. Lamina had hit his head on the inside of the cabinet as he stood up.

"She's just a terrible flirt, that's all!" came the growl from the cabinet. "She does that to everyone! A horrid flirt!"

Terra turned pointedly to Adam. "You've upset, Mr Lamina."

Adam inclined his head to her, the corners of his mouth twitching up. "My apologies, Miss Ridley. Though I'm inclined to believe her feelings are what's more upsetting to Lamina."

Terra bit the insides of her cheeks, trying to hold in a laugh and Adam's eyes sparkled as they exchanged grins.

By the cabinet, the old ox sighed, lightly touching the tender bump on his forehead. "Oh, it's all wrong!" Flustered, Lamina shoved the items he had retrieved from the cabinet into his pockets, hair suddenly frazzled. "Just too wrong. She can't keep working here. Honestly, what was I thinking? As soon as this is all finished, she has to go!" he muttered under his breath, combing his mane back with a shaky hand. "She just terrorises both the customers and the workers with that behaviour. It's too hard to find people to work here because of her!" He stomped towards the café exit.

"Mr Lamina?" called Terra tentatively. "Are we leaving now?"

Bustling over to the exit, Lamina glanced back at Terra and Adam and motioned for them to follow him. "We can't waste any more time here!"

"But what about telling Miss Rebekah about us leaving...?"

"She might miss you."

Terra elbowed Adam in the ribs.

Lamina shot a withering look at the young man. "For someone quite injured, you've got a mouth." He turned on his heel and sped out of the café, striding across the streets with Adam attempting to match him and Terra jogging to keep up with them.

The trio stopped by a bakery to exchange items for bread and continued onto a store with preserved and wrapped goods where Lamina traded for some food. They then traded an item for a large backpack at a bag store and Lamina filled it with the food he had gotten while also transferring Terra's clothes from the smaller bag he had. As they raced across the streets the old ox explained that the items he had traded were things the shop owners had given to him sometime in the past to dine or drink at his café.

The bag bulged with their purchases and Lamina slung it eagerly onto his back. "We'll never know how long we'll be on the road," he said with a smile, breaking off pieces of bread for all of them. "We'll be better prepared this time."

"Mr Lamina, why did you run away from the café?" she asked, mouth full of bread.

Lips pursed, Lamina's face darkened. "Women are frightful creatures," he grumbled, more to himself than to the inquisitive girl beside him.

Terra tilted her head, confused. "What do you mean by that?"

Lamina looked abashed. "Don't worry about it young mistress," he mumbled, keeping his eyes ahead.

The young girl fell silent, sensing she had made him uncomfortable. "Mr Lamina," she began again, eager to change the subject, "should we use the small bag to carry more things with us? I think Adam needs stuff for his arm too."

The old ox grinned at Terra and ruffled her hair affectionately. "We'll do that."

The trio stopped by several other stores to fill the smaller bag with items Lamina insisted would be useful for the journey, including medicinal ointment for Adam. While sorting the contents of the bag out, Terra handed the eye-patch in her pocket over, deeming it to be safer in there.

Inspecting the now heavy bag, Adam offered to carry it, explaining that it would be better for Terra to not carry extra baggage so that she could use Spiritus effectively.

"Are you sure?"

The young man smiled, zipping up the bag and slinging it onto his shoulder. "Of course."

Terra frowned at his heavily bandaged arm, freshly cleaned. "Don't push yourself."

"Alright then! Let's head off!" declared Lamina, turning around and pacing down the street.

"What will we do once we reach Magia, Mr Lamina?" asked Terra, tottering after the old ox with Adam close behind. She continued to push down any rising concern regarding Agnus.

"Whatever Agnus wills, young mistress," replied Lamina as they stopped by the southern gates and Terra was against struck by his confidence in the man. Lamina exchanged a brief word with the guard who allowed them passage and they continued their way south from there. "It seems that something is to be done at Magia and so be it—the people there must be rooted out of their foolhardiness!"

Terra fell silent, her mind straying to the children trapped in Magia. She hoped that there would be a way to free them before any more punishment was doled out to the Magians.

It was a few hours' walk along the path that led to The Mare and with each step the companions took, Terra surprised herself with how much more concerned she felt for Agnus' safety. Unconsciously, she held onto her necklace, fingers closed tightly over the bridge.

"He'll be alright," murmured Lamina, trying to allay both their fears. "He won't be beaten."

Nodding absentmindedly, Terra continued to survey the land around them, hoping that with each kilometre they covered, they would see Agnus' figure in the distance, hurrying to catch up to them.

Yet there was no sign of him anywhere.

By this time, it was well into the night, and Lamina called for Terra and Adam to stop behind some bushes under the shade of a tree where he insisted that they would rest. "It's been a long day," he explained. "And there's no use storming ahead if we've got no energy to." He reached into the bag he had been carrying and rummaged around in it. "We'll have something to eat first. Then we'll rest."

"Shall we take it in turns to keep watch, Lamina?" Adam was pulling out an electric lamp that Lamina had brought from the cabinet in his store. Examining it briefly, he rotated the knob on its side, his face illuminated as the bulb flickered on.

Lamina withdrew an assortment of wrapped food before proceeding to hand some to Adam and Terra. "We'll definitely do that. I will keep watch first and then you, Adam—"

"And me?" asked Terra, carving into a loaf of bread with a knife.

Grinning at the young girl, Lamina leaned forward and tousled her hair. "Of course," he chuckled. "Since you're the youngest here, you can keep watch after Adam. But not for too long, you need lots of rest."

"I suppose I could keep watch too then," came a voice from the bushes behind them.

Lamina leapt to his feet and Terra swiftly brandished Spiritus.

As the leaves were pushed aside, Terra lowered Spiritus and bounded to her feet, dashing to the figure. "Agnus!" she cried with delight, rushing to him. For a moment, she forgot herself and threw her arms out for a hug. Before she could pull away in embarrassment, Agnus briefly wrapped his arms around her. He pulled away, a smile lighting his bearded face.

He didn't mind at all…Even though I tried to hit him not long ago. Terra blinked away tears she hadn't realised were in her eye. "You made it!"

"I came as quickly as I could." Agnus laughed when Lamina tugged him into a rough embrace and, after pulling away, approached Adam who threw his arms around him in another fierce hug. "Now, let's not waste a moment. We will be needing some wood for a fire—Lamina, if you would be kind enough to take care of that. Then, Adam, if you could find something we could use as a flint to start the fire. In the meantime, I will set up a shelter for us with the earth."

Quick to obey, Lamina and Adam set out to complete their tasks leaving Agnus and Terra alone.

Terra stepped forward. "Is there anything you'd like for me to do?"

"You can organise the sleeping arrangements. I am certain that Lamina would've brought some sheets," instructed Agnus, his attention fixed on the earth that he drew up with hand gestures. He carefully sculpted it into a small dome and ensured that the side of the structure, that faced the bushes, remained open.

Digging through the bags and surprised with the number of items that the bags could carry, Terra found the sheets the ox had thoughtfully packed. As she laid them out, a thought occurred to her.

"Agnus…" Terra paused, hesitant. "About Colonel Simeon…did you save him…?" she asked after a beat, her eye rising to meet Agnus'. She breathed a sigh of relief when he inclined his head to her.

Agnus finished sealing the top of the dome and turned to study Terra for a moment. "You asked if I saved him despite the fact that he caused you great suffering."

Terra bit her lip. "Yes. He did, but…" She looked down at her boots, lips pressed together. "I don't know what to think. I really hated the things he did to me. It was so awful. But I…he was all I had and knew for a long time. And I…I wanted him to disappear…" Terra faltered, breathing rapidly, her chest squeezing too tight. "I'm so awful. I'm no better than him!"

Closing the distance between them, Agnus wordlessly embraced her. "I'm here. Breathe, my child. Hold on to me."

Eye squeezed shut, Terra felt her breaths quicken and her body tremble. There wasn't enough air. She gripped handfuls of Agnus' coat, her mind a cage of hurtful thoughts, both towards Simeon and herself. *I want him to die. How could I want someone else to die? Why shouldn't I want it?*

"You're safe, Terra. Hold on to me. You're safe."

Focusing on Agnus' voice, Terra clung to him as he continued to speak to her, his gentle voice a rising blockade against the storm lashing in her mind. Slowly, her breathing eased and her trembling ceased. But the dark thoughts that troubled her remained and she pulled back from Agnus, face apologetic.

"I'm sorry," she whispered, voice barely audible and eye glistening with tears. "I'm a horrible person, aren't I?"

Agnus touched her cheek lightly, his expression knowing but kind. "Why do you say that?"

"I don't want to think the way I do, but it's so hard. It's so hard..."

"Terra, be kind to yourself. Take your time. You have a heart that yearns to forgive, but it is grappling with incredibly deep hurt. And that is okay. That is normal. Let yourself heal. Only then, can you move forward, holding on to that gentle heart of yours."

Overwhelmed with thankfulness, Terra hugged Agnus again, allowing her tears to dry while he smoothed out her hair and quietly hummed a forlorn tune. After a while, Terra drew away and they sat across from each other in the domed shelter.

"So, you saved Simeon?" she pressed again.

"Yes. There are things that must come to pass. I stopped him from destroying himself."

"How?"

"My blood."

The young girl cocked her head to the side. "I'm sorry—your what?"

"My blood," repeated Agnus, mysterious smile in place. "My blood melts away the basic composition of Element 132 and nullifies the magickal properties of it."

Mind jumping back to the shard that pierced his hand earlier, Terra nodded. She couldn't fully grasp it, but it made sense enough. "So, because you did that, does that mean Simeon will be different...?" she asked, anxiety creeping into her voice.

Leaning forward in his seat, Agnus studied Terra. "His allegiance is divided between two people. The first person who showed him kindness and the person who gave him a reason to exist."

"A reason to exist?"

Agnus nodded. "Everyone desires a reason to exist. In fact, everyone *has* one," he explained. "At the centre of everyone's existence lies their reason. Often, people do not see this reason or believe that there is a need to search for a "better" reason once they learn of the one within them."

"But why?"

A small smile played on Agnus' lips. "Terra, my child, why do you exist?"

Silence fell over the pair and Terra frowned, taken aback by the fact that she could not immediately answer the question. She pondered for a moment, quietly contemplating each thought that arose in her mind. "I..." She paused, hesitant. With a shake of her head, she raised her gaze to Agnus, her expression solemn. "Those dreams I used to have of you while growing up in Magia…" she started, eye shining. "They kept me going. Despite all the times I hoped I'd die…"

A sad smile broke across Agnus' face and he stroked Terra's hair. "A reason for one's existence is the key motivation for living," he murmured, eyes brighter than before.

Terra looked down at her boots and gnawed on her bottom lip. "I believe that…" she murmured. "Because it was really hard growing up in Magia without any real reason…without anything real to believe in…it was…really…" Words failed her as she tried to swallow back her tears.

"I know," murmured Agnus, breaking the silence that had enveloped the pair.

The youth looked up to find tears in Agnus' eyes. The tears that she had been trying to hold back resurfaced.

"I know," he said, taking her hand.

The tears fell and Terra pressed Agnus' hand to her face and sobbed. "I was mad at you when I found out you were the one who put me in Magia. You gave me such hope but you had left me somewhere so hopeless." She sucked in a shaky breath, gripping Agnus' hand tightly. "Why did you leave me there?"

"I had to die."

Terra's head shot up, face screwed up in confusion and her mouth hanging wide open. "What?"

"No, that's not the point." Shaking his head, Agnus laid his other hand on top of hers, steadily holding her gaze despite the tears swimming in his eyes. "You suffered so much. And still, I will ask you to persevere. Right now, you have a truth in your heart that you cannot deny—your reason for existence. Hold onto that, my child." He took a breath and closed his eyes. "Don't allow your sufferings to overwhelm you—hold onto me. Hold onto Spiritus. You were chosen and you are loved."

Heart in her throat, Terra choked out a sob, her words incoherent and her head bobbed up and down while she frantically wiped her face and nose. She wondered if she had the strength to persevere. She had made it this far in life, but even that thought brought no comfort. And if she pushed through the pain of living, would she ever be able to forgive Simeon? She forced the thought away, her insides writhing in both anger and guilt at the idea.

"Agnus," sniffed Terra after her tears had dried. "Is my hair really thread?"

"Yes."

"Why?"

Agnus smiled, yet Terra could see sadness within his eyes. "I cannot tell you that now."

Despondent, Terra nodded and looked down at her lap. "Why does everyone call me a Maremortum?"

"I cannot tell you that for now either." Agnus squeezed Terra's hand gently, his expression pained. "These things will be revealed to you when the time comes. Until then, hold onto Spiritus and let it guide you. Do not fall from the path which it lights."

Terra's heart sank, yet she braved a smile. She forced her disappointment to the back of her mind. "Can I really trust you, Agnus?"

"That is your choice, my child. But answer this, will you continue to ignore my voice and the hope burning within you?"

Pressing a hand over her heart, Terra closed her eye. "I want to trust you. Before, I was mad at you. But you saved Lamina. You gave me an arm. This necklace too. Not to mention, Spiritus and a way to escape Magia." She took a breath and clenched her fist, smiling as she raised her eye to Agnus'. "If this is just the start, I want to know where else I will go if I follow you."

Wordlessly, Agnus stooped down and wrapped his arms around her and she hugged him back. "Do not lose your way when the time comes." His voice was so soft that Terra had almost missed what he had said.

Later that night when everyone bid each other goodnight and Terra laid down on her makeshift bed, she thought back to that moment when Agnus had hugged her and pondered on his words. Her eye gradually grew heavy with sleep. Closing her eye, Terra curled up with a blanket wound tight around her small frame. She dreamed of a room bathed in a brilliant light. In the room, it was white all around her and she drifted alone through the endless space...

In the late hours of sun down, Terra rolled over, the strange croaking squawks of nearby birds rousing her. Peering out groggily, she glimpsed a hatless Agnus sitting amongst several black birds that eagerly crowed and hopped about him. Scrunching her face up in exhausted confusion, Terra turned back over, too tired to even want to address the bizarre sight.

Travel recommenced a couple hours later, with Agnus keeping ahead to scout out the area. Moving in the light of the rising azure sun, the companions trudged along the path with solemn expressions.

Terra continued to mull over Agnus' words, missing her step every so often. On one occasion, Adam caught her wrist when her foot sank into a small hole.

"Be careful, Miss Ridley," he murmured, pulling her up, his other hand on her waist to steady her.

Quietly, Terra thanked him and they continued on their way. She trailed behind the group but was more attentive to where she stepped.

Eventually they came to a halt on The Mare riverbed and were greeted by the sight of the seer, Joseph, who was busily untying his boat from the dock, having spotted them along the path.

To Terra's surprise, Adam broke away from the group and hopped down into the boat, throwing his arms around Joseph with a small sob. "I've missed you!"

The seer smiled, and his arms tightly wound around Adam. "You're finally awake," he murmured, tears glistening in the corners of his eyes. "Praise Pater." He drew back, cupping Adam's face in his hands. "I cannot abandon my duty here. This is where I must be until the end. But you must continue to obey Agnus."

"I will."

From beside Terra, Lamina scratched his head and Terra felt he was as mystified by this exchange as she was.

Releasing Adam, Joseph turned and bowed deeply to Agnus. "You wish to travel to Magia then, my Lord?"

Agnus laid his hand on Joseph's shoulder, eyes kind. "Yes, my friend. You, unlike the others, have been faithful to your people's work."

The seer bowed lower still. "I work to serve the true heir."

"And you will be richly rewarded."

Terra raised an eyebrow but she had no time to ask any questions as everyone except Agnus—he was still owed much more for the vest he had given long ago—presented their payments for the boat trip. She parted with the washed remains of her old dress and watched the water lap at the bottom of the boat as they drifted over it, her thoughts wandering back to the conversation she had with Agnus.

Her wandering mind was drawn back by laughter. Adam spoke in hushed, but enthusiastic tones with Joseph on the ride across The Mare and Terra quietly watched his many fluctuating emotions; from sheer joy to crushing sadness.

Joseph's face had also morphed; engaged, vivacious and bright, with far less wrinkles—a far cry from his general disinterest on Terra's last trip across The Mare. He gave another hearty laugh while Adam recounted his waking and he turned to Agnus, eyes sparkling. "Well, you *have* grown far older since that time you sealed him away. If I recall correctly, you were a touch younger than Adam."

"You always find the humour in these sorts of things, Joseph," Agnus said, an amused smile lighting his face.

Adam pouted. "It was a silly mistake on my part."

"It certainly was."

"Hey!"

Huddled against Lamina, Terra noted how different Adam's demeanour was with the seer, Joseph. She had thought Adam a stern and stiff young man when he first awoke, but watching him now, she found herself glad that she was wrong in her conclusion.

Adam raised a hand to quickly brush away several stray tears. Seeming self-conscious, he glanced back at Terra and she quickly smiled, hoping it was comforting. Red tinged his cheeks, reaching to the tips of his ears and he returned a small, but embarrassed smile before turning away.

Terra decided to look out at the water, pretending not to listen. It was the only privacy she could offer him and as they continued to bob along, her own mind churned with dark fears that came to life in her eye.

Across the river, she could see the distant shapes of the Magian mountains.

Agnus laid a gentle hand on Terra's shoulder and she realised that she was trembling.

Biting her lip, Terra clasped her hands tightly together, willing the tremor to stop. She closed her eye and an image of the Colonel's angered face surfaced in her mind.

It'll be alright, she exhaled the breath she hadn't known she was holding.

Too soon, they reached the opposite bank's dock and thanked Joseph as they disembarked, with Adam lingering behind before rushing to catch up to the group.

Apprehensively, Terra followed closely behind Agnus who led the way, feeling consumed by her thoughts as they progressed along the path to Magia. It brought back memories of the last time she had run through these barren plains: chased by the malformed Tophets who relentlessly followed both her and Lamina until Shigure and Hitori had appeared. Terra had cherished her first step out of Magia, only to now return.

She took a deep, shuddering breath and clenched her fists. This time she returned without being completely suffocated by dread. Fear gnawed away at her but it had no strength to devour her.

Retracing the steps that both Terra and Lamina had made a few days earlier, the group made considerable progress during the day, only taking a couple of brief breaks. During these moments of respite, Terra would look out at the land that led to the prison she had known all of her life. She reassured herself that it was fine. Agnus was here this time. With this as a constant refrain, Terra could contain her fear as they drew closer to their destination.

Soon, they could make out the torches in brackets along the walls of the outpost station. Beyond that, the mountainous region of Magia and the tower of Lost Languages loomed above them, a frightening backdrop.

Terra took a deep breath. *It's fine.*

The old ox grunted, breaking the silence. "Agnus, what if the Maremortums decide to attack us?"

"I do not believe they will have reason to raise their hand against us again."

Lamina made a face. "What do you mean by that Agnus? Did you speak to them?"

"Indeed, I did."

At this, silence ensued and Terra wondered what Lamina thought of the matter. But there was no time to dwell on this. They were close enough to the outpost station that the Magian officer manning it stood from his seat, greeting them indifferently.

"State your name and business here."

"Agnus Dayton." Agnus raised his hand in a silencing gesture when the guard opened his mouth. "I have come to deliver a message to the Marshal of Magia."

The guard licked his lips and swallowed, unable to mask his fear. "You're not permitted entry into Magia, Agnus Dayton. By order of the Marshal of Magia, Lady Lachesis Maremortum."

Terra furrowed her brow. *Lachesis?*

"Lady?" scoffed Lamina, flaring his nostrils. At Agnus' look, he fell silent.

The guard cleared his throat. "You cannot enter."

Agnus closed his eyes, a heavy sigh escaping his lips. He stepped forward, raised his head and looked up toward the artificial Sun and the, almost indiscernible, thin scarlet beam of light that followed it to the Tower of Lost Languages. "Magia must fall."

Terra looked at the back of Agnus' head, horror-stricken, the faces of the children she shared bread with flashing through her mind. "Will people be saved?"

"If they turned from the things they are doing."

"But what about the children? Agnus, you can save all of the children in those mines…can't you?" Terra had unconsciously stepped forward. "They don't deserve to die!"

There was a beat where Agnus continued to stare at the thin scarlet beam of light that streamed up from the large E132 situated at the top of the Lost Languages.

Lamina spoke up, his voice strangled with emotions. "Agnus, do the rest deserve to die too?"

"Things must come to pass."

Blinking back tears, Terra clenched her fists, her chest feeling tight. "What?" Had she made the wrong choice to follow him?

Another moment of silence passed and even Lamina had turned anxiously to Agnus.

Yet Agnus remained silent, his back to them, appearing to be fixated on the glowing scarlet crystal.

Terra paled, her body trembling. "Agnus! Please—"

"My child," he murmured without turning. "How many more children will they sacrifice?"

Afraid of believing her ears, Terra looked down at Agnus' shoulders and noticed the slight tremble of them. She was not mistaken when she heard the wavering of his voice.

He was crying.

"How many more," he continued, his voice breaking, the tears resurfacing in Terra's eye. "How many more lives will men take before they are satisfied? Magia, because you did not listen each time I warned you, the splendour you have built for yourself in this land will spoil. For within your walls, you fed the beast and from the depths of an old king's bones he will claw through." He shook his head as if to clear it and raised his chin, squaring his shoulders. "Adam, come before me."

The white-haired young man was swift to obey, kneeling before Agnus and bowing his head.

Agnus wiped away the last of his tears and laid his hand on Adam's head. He closed his eyes and took a deep and shaky breath. "Prophesy to them. The Lady herself will come out if you use my name."

Words cloaked Adam in a brilliant light and Terra jumped at the sound of his voice.

"*People of Magia,*" boomed Adam's voice, filling Terra's head. She watched in stunned silence as he continued to speak yet his lips were unmoving. After a moment, she realised, from the expression on Lamina's face, that he too, could hear Adam's voice. The Magian soldier before them paled, his eyes wide as he stared, open-mouthed, at Adam. Terra could only guess that everyone within Magia could hear Adam within their minds too. The hair on the back of her neck stood on end as Adam continued: "*Turn away from the evil you have fed. Let all the children go or face Agnus' wrath. The land of your ancestors shall crumble around you and the earth will open up to swallow you in a final warning.*"

A shiver zipped down Terra's spine and her legs threatened to collapse beneath her. Despite her mingled emotions of fear and horror for the children in the mines, she felt a growing sense of awe.

The guard slammed his hand into the crystal hand mould near him. As stone ground against each other, the station door opened and the guard turned and tripped as he hurried away, scrambling through the doorway.

Adam's voice reverberated in Terra's head, firm and harsh. *"You continued to invite the Other and have incensed One. Was a curse not enough for your people? And so, you will be stripped bare, and naked you will fall. You will cry for help but no one will heed you."*

Gooseflesh erupted all along Terra's arms and her legs grew unsteady; so much so that she was almost convinced that the earth itself trembled below her. A beat passed and Terra realised that the earth really was shaking.

As this thought passed through her mind, a girl who appeared to be her age, stepped out of the station, the silver braid of her longer locks bouncing behind her.

Following her, armed soldiers—some that Terra recognised—marched, their eyes cold and clenched jaws set.

The young girl's scarlet eyes darted over the group stopping on Agnus. She froze, her eyes locked with his. Gritting her teeth, the girl's scarlet eyes shone as she began to draw a thin rod of red from within her wrist.

Eyes narrowing, Agnus raised his free hand towards her and the girl stilled. Without warning, her legs gave way beneath her and she collapsed in a heap.

There were cries of concern from the soldiers escorting her, but as they gathered about her small figure, another tremor zipped through the earth. The ground beneath the outpost station split open and, in a panicked frenzy, the soldiers grabbed the girl and scrambled away from the crack. Even as they ran, the earth continued to quake and its newly formed mouth grew wider, swallowing the station that had previously stood upon it and some slower officers.

Lips pressed together and eyebrows knotted, Agnus removed his hand from Adam's head. "Rise, Adam." When the young man obediently stood, Agnus turned to Terra and Lamina. "Let's go."

Terra's eye widened and she stumbled forward, the earth continuing to crack beyond the outpost station. "What about the children?"

"Their prisons will be opened." Agnus turned away and began to walk back towards the river, his expression dark. "Before the youngest Maremortum awakens, we must go."

Swallowing down a jumble of questions, Terra followed suit, jogging to keep up with Agnus' long strides. With Lamina and Adam not far behind, Terra felt an urge to turn and look back, but the focus on Agnus' face convinced her not to and instead she concentrated on maintaining her balance as the earth continued to tear itself apart behind them. The further they travelled, the less she felt the earth shift below her and eventually they reached the riverbed where Joseph greeted them.

Once they had boarded the boat and made their payments (Terra parted with more blood, upsetting Lamina—she knew now that she would never gain back any hair she removed), Agnus gestured to Joseph, his expression grave. "Should any child wish to cross here, a raven will provide a payment for them. Take the payment and allow the child to cross The Mare."

Joseph gnawed his lip. "I don't have the strength to help that many children, my Lord."

"Agnus!" Adam stepped forward. "I can help."

Shaking his head, Joseph laid a heavy hand on Adam's shoulder and squeezed it. "No, Adam, you must remain by Agnus' side."

"But—"

Joseph gave Adam a sharp look and he fell silent.

"A helper will relieve you should you be overwhelmed," assured Agnus, reaching into his pocket and pulling out a slip of paper which he handed to Joseph.

With a nod of his head, Joseph rowed to the other side of the riverbed and as the boat eased its way across, Terra finally turned to look back. But Magia was long out of view.

The door to the Maremortum's living quarters burst open. Mr Maremortum finished buttoning up his cuffs while a breathless fair-haired man stood by the door, his eyes wild.

"Is that you Lieutenant Wayman?"

"Yes, sir."

"I was waiting for a report on that rumble. What happened?"

Shoving his hand into his breast-pocket, Lieutenant Wayman yanked out a yellow-spotted handkerchief and dabbed his forehead, his lips smacking together as he struggled for words. "A-Agnus Dayton came with his Curse."

With a sneer, Mr Maremortum slung on his coat. "That *thing*?"

The handkerchief was now at Lieutenant Wayman's upper lip and there was an unmistakable tremor in his voice. "The Marshal collapsed and the earthquake destroyed the outpost station and a number of other areas. We're calculating the extent of the damage now."

"Lachesis collapsed?" Mr Maremortum rushed to the door where he paused, pensive. "So, what I heard earlier really was Agnus threatening us?"

"Yes, sir. He was accompanied by a young man we had not seen before," answered Wayman, sweat dewing on his upper lip. "But more pressingly, was that a Pateran styled prophecy? Aside from the boat beggar, I thought the line of seers fell with Lune! And now we have a prophecy promising the downfall of Magia!"

"If Agnus wants us to fall, we will fight. If it comes down to a war, so be it."

"What of the Colonel? And your wife?"

Mr Maremortum raised his right hand to his hair and threaded his fingers through. "Both are currently incapacitated. Regardless, I've already received orders from Daniel Sominium, himself." He lowered his hand and strode through the door, leaving Lieutenant Wayman to stumble after him. "Take me to Lachesis first."

We were to be One's people: the remnant that held fast to One whilst all the world fell away, lured by the wine of the Other.

- Lines from *Writings of the Kings of Old, Scriptura*. Translated by C. Yelnorin

13

The light of the artificial sun followed the four travellers as they disembarked from Joseph's boat.

While Agnus and Lamina readied to depart, slowly adjusting and slinging backpacks on, Adam clasped hands with Joseph.

"I'll be here whenever you return. But keep your eyes on your duty."

"I will, father."

Mouth dropping open, Terra tried to catch Adam's eye when he turned away from the seer. Whirling back to Joseph, their eyes met, and she stumbled into a clumsy bow. "Thank you so much for all of your help!"

Joseph's eyes softened and faint runes suddenly materialised around his body, but just as quickly vanished.

Terra blinked. Had she imagined it?

"I'm merely doing my duty," Joseph said with a warm smile. "Make sure my son does his too," he added with a wink.

"I'll try to," Terra replied in a serious tone. She paused before continuing, straight-faced, "But I'm not sure he'll listen. He's an awfully snarky man."

Joseph's eyebrows rose. "Oh?"

"Hey," came a voice near Terra's left ear.

Steeling her nerves, Terra turned, coming eye to eye with Adam, his arms folded over his chest as he stooped down to peer closely at her. "Yes?"

"Are you making fun of me?"

Terra bit the inside of her cheek, holding back a grin. "I would never."

Adam studied her, the corners of his lips twitching in that funny way; like he was resisting the urge to laugh. He pinched her left cheek and Terra couldn't hold in her laughter anymore. She needed this moment of levity.

"I'm on to you," Adam mumbled, with his cheeks tinged pink.

"As am I." Lamina fixed Adam with a protective glare and Adam rolled his eyes as Lamina towed Terra away by the arm.

After Joseph bid them farewell, Agnus led the way across the lush grass, striding through the endless field of green.

As they plodded along, Lamina scratched his chin and cleared his throat. "Agnus, this is not the way to Lacuna."

"That is because we are not returning there, my friend."

"You don't intend to head to Sominium then, do you?"

Agnus shook his head, swerving around a drooping pine branch. The tip of the branch brushed the top of his hat and new green shoots burst out along it. "There is an old town nearby where we will stay for the next few months."

Stopping dead in his tracks, Lamina turned to Agnus, his mouth agape. "Surely not to Babylonia?" His large brown eyes swept back over the fields of grass, resting on a familiar looking tower in the distance.

Confused, Terra squinted at the tower. From a distance, she wasn't sure if she was looking at The Lost Languages or not.

Noticing both of their gazes, Agnus stopped and gestured in a direction to the left of the tower, closer to them. "We're going to a town that is not indulged in itself." Turning back around, Agnus continued walking with Adam following closely behind him.

The group continued their trek through the grassy fields when what appeared to be a small stone wall came into view. As they drew closer to it, Terra realised that rather than small, the wall seemed old and collapsed with several stones knocked from their place and rubble laid strewn all along the ground around the wall. Shards of glass and pottery and other miscellaneous items littered the debris and crunched underfoot as the group approached what could've been the entry into the town.

"What…happened here…?" Terra's eye swept over the remains of the town before her.

The roofs of countless houses had caved in, their windows shattered and doors broken down. Many of the houses were charred from what could have been a fire that had blazed through the streets of the ruined city.

"When the famine ravaged the land and the war worsened for Magia, they sought aid from the cities that had not taken part in the war," explained Agnus, expression withdrawn. "This is the remains of one of the cities that refused them."

Terra's breath hitched in her throat. Her eye roamed over the wasted landscape, dismay filling her. She imagined the terror that the people would have felt as they tried to flee from their houses, only to be faced with the fiery furnace that burned outside of their doors and the malignant shine of E132 weapons. "How cruel…" she whispered. "What was this place called?"

Crouching down, Agnus brushed his hand over the earth and grabbed a handful of dirt. He watched it slip through his fingers, expression unreadable. "This place once belonged to a King of Old," he answered. "It was known as Manna." Rubbing his hands together, he cleaned the last of the dust off and quietly rose, eyes narrowing as he studied the dilapidated remains. Wordlessly, he strode through the entry of the broken city wall.

"Agnus?"

Hurrying to keep up, Lamina and Terra picked through the rubble, trailing behind Adam. Keeping Agnus in her peripheral, Terra cast her eye around the ruins, her heart sinking with each step. Abandoned homes made of old brick, walls flecked with dots of dried blood or check-marked with streaky ash patterns. Wooden doors missing or hanging on a hinge. Windows smashed, the broken glass scattered across the grimy grey paths winding through the town.

Besides the weeds peering from every crack and crevice in paths and buildings, the town was devoid of life.

But the hairs on the back of Terra's neck stood on end.

She turned her head, peering over her shoulder at the vacant houses they had passed and a shiver ripped through her. Edging closer to Lamina, Terra couldn't shake the feeling of dread that gripped her with each abandoned home they passed.

Lamina's arm wrapped securely around Terra's shoulder, pulling her closer to his side. He felt it too.

Coming to an abrupt halt, Agnus looked back at his friends, eyes twinkling at the looks on their faces. "You've all noticed then."

"Agnus, why are we here?" mumbled Lamina. "There's no one here but I feel uneasy."

Strolling over to a nearby building, Agnus, pressing his weight upon the worn wood, opened a stuck door and motioned for his companions to follow. They shuffled into the room, eyes darting about them.

Shafts of light streamed in through the open door and the broken windows, illuminating parts of the abandoned home. A fractured vase lay on its side its rotting flowery contents strewn across the floorboards. Wooden chairs stood apart from a dining table as if the occupants left in a hurry. An old, faded rug lay askew beneath the table.

With Adam's help, Agnus moved the table aside. Peeling the rug away from the floorboards, he rapped his knuckles against the floorboards in a certain rhythm.

Silence followed the knocking.

Again, Agnus beat his knuckles rhythmically against the wood, pausing with his index finger in the air for quiet.

They all waited. Terra wondered what Agnus wanted them to wait for and her thoughts drifted to all that had happened in Magia. She thought of the children, whose passage on Joseph's boat, Agnus had paid for. Her mind wandered back to the image of Agnus sitting amongst the black birds early that morning.

The light tinkling sounds of the wind—like airy musical items beating gently against each other in the breeze—interrupted her thoughts. Her eye darted about and she looked over her shoulder towards the open door. Where had the sound come from?

She had no timed to wonder as Agnus began to sing in that language Terra didn't recognise; a short and haunting melody. As the final note rang out in the air, a panel from the floor slid open and Agnus reached forward into the opening, wrenching a hidden door up to reveal an unlit passage beneath.

Terra peered down into the dark passageway, her arms covered in gooseflesh prompting her to cling more tightly to Lamina. Even as she squinted, unable to make out anything, Agnus wordlessly stepped down into the darkness. She watched as Adam made a face and followed suit. He paused and quickly turned to smile reassuringly at her before continuing his descent, his footsteps resounding with Agnus' on what seemed to be stone.

In silent agreement, Lamina edged forward, approaching the opening with Terra attached to his side, gripping handfuls of his fur. They strode into the darkness, with a small ouch issuing from Lamina who stooped down to fit through the stone tunnel.

The tunnel wound itself downward, following a long flight of stairs. For what felt like an age, there was no chatter, only the beating of feet on the stone steps and the laboured breathing of Terra who felt the events of the past couple of days catch up to her. Her initial fear of the unknown had worn away, fatigue threatening to send her tumbling down the stairs. Straining her eye in the endless darkness did not help. Mumbling about her exhaustion, Terra closed her eye and leaned against Lamina's arm, following his careful movements.

After several more steps in the dark, the familiar buzz of an electrical lantern shook Terra out of her stupor. She watched Agnus and Adam alight from the steps onto a long narrow dirt path that slowly lit up as several more lanterns flickered to life. The lanterns hung from the walls of tall mounds of packed dirt and stone, rising up on either side of the pathway. A few people lined the path, with others poking their heads out from both small and large circular openings within these mounds—it was then that Terra realised these were houses.

Agnus ushered their group along the crowded path. Several paths intersected it, leading to different areas of the underground cavern which stretched far beyond the size that Terra had initially believe it to be.

From the other end of the path, a swarthy skinned man with a heavy black beard approached them, his dark eyes narrowed and full lips pursed. His eyes swept over the four travellers and rested on Agnus. He bowed, voice velvety and low, "We are honoured to welcome you again, Agnus." He gestured to the others. "We cannot say the same for these strangers you have brought with you."

Agnus quickly raised his hand in front of Lamina when he shifted forward. "Nicholo, I ask that you extend the welcome you have given me to my friends as well. I have returned here as promised and I wish to remain here for a time with my friends."

The man named Nicholo grimaced and lowered his head. In the distance, some people exited their houses and ambled towards the group. "Agnus, all of Railesson has heard the tale of the girl you retrieved from Attero. The girl that Magia deemed your Curse." Nicholo lifted his chin again, folding his arms over his chest.

Terra felt a cold sense of foreboding when Nicholo's eyes darted to her before returning to address Agnus. Several others had joined them, crowding behind Nicholo, their murmurs of assent filling the air.

"And now you have brought her here before us. Is your desire for us to suffer as Magia has? Have we wronged Pater, my Lord?" Nicholo's tone was clipped and terse and Terra bit her lip at the rumble of disagreement rising from Lamina.

Brow knotted, Agnus pressed his lips together and narrowed his eyes. "I have not come to place a curse upon you." He peered around the underground cavern, catching the eyes of those watching, his expression hard. "I have returned in order that the prophecies of old may be fulfilled." His gaze returned to Nicholo.

Adam stepped forward, eyes shining in that otherworldly blue hue. "Magia and the fruit of the Other must fall. Those it has destroyed will be raised up to bring about its ruin again. Manna was a stalwart companion against Magia during the war with Sominium. One would call upon you to stand against them." Runic symbols dissipated from Adam's body, sweeping over everyone and sending a shiver that rippled through the crowd. His eyes faded to hazel and he glanced over at Agnus who continued to scrutinise Nicholo and the crowd.

Laying a solemn hand on his chest, Nicholo bowed low with many others following suit. "A Pateran prophecy…" He straightened awkwardly and Terra noted the slight tremor in his voice as he spoke, "Forgive me, Agnus. Trading in Taliph has been difficult as of late. How can we even hope to aid you in defeating Magia?"

"Prepare a place for me and my friends to stay." Agnus removed his top hat and reached into the inner pocket of his jacket. He drew out a handful of gold and silver circular pieces of metal and handed these over with his hat. "For the foreign trade in Taliph. A Gershomite ship will be arriving next week."

"Coins too? Thank you, Agnus." Nicholo passed the items over to a young woman behind him who gave a reverent bow to Agnus, her eyes sparkling with tears. "We are honoured to serve you, always."

Straightening his tie, Agnus squared his shoulders. "I will be leaving for now and returning later tonight. Please see that you provide for the needs of my friends." He smiled briefly to the three behind him, with Lamina spluttering for explanations. Agnus dismissed him with a wave, pressed the backpack he carried into Adam's arms and made his way back up the stairs, shouting over his shoulder, "Take good care of them, Nicholo!"

With Agnus' departure and promise to return, the lady with his top hat ushered for them to follow her to a guest home that they had prepared previously for Agnus.

Terra lingered behind Lamina's decisive movements, dawdling on the footpath. She couldn't shake the thought of the people of Manna perceiving her as a curse.

"She's safe to follow," Adam whispered to Terra breaking through her web of insecurities. "The thoughts surrounding her appear to be good."

Processing his comment left Terra at a loss for words and she shot the white-haired young man a disconcerted look. The bizarre nature of his words caused a bubble of laughter to rise behind her lips. "Are you being weird?"

Adam pressed a hand to his heart, his mouth agape. "Oh, that hurts."

Terra stifled a laugh when Lamina gave them a stern look, his glare fixed on Adam in particular. She cleared her throat, shifting her gaze ahead with a grin and hastened to keep up with Lamina, slotting Adam's unusual remark in a corner of her mind.

The lady, who introduced herself as Talia, explained that the men and women gathered before them had sworn loyalty to Agnus long ago. As they walked through the cavern, Terra's heart was warmed knowing there were people who held such strong faith in Agnus.

Talia introduced them to several people as they passed different homes and pointed out important locations to remember including the well, the in development man-made stream and the fields which were lit and warmed by machinery that Terra felt she had glimpsed in the Lacuna markets.

"Avarosan technology that we gave Agnus' blood for," explained Talia, unconsciously holding the top hat closer. "We're able to live in peace thanks to Agnus."

When they had reached the house reserved for them, Talia gave them a quick tour. It had two rooms: an open living area with basic facilities for cooking and a separate bathroom with several chamber pots for a toilet.

While Terra took note of the need to clean out the chamber pots after use, Talia lightly touched her shoulder.

"For you," whispered Talia, pressing a small, polished mirror into Terra's hand. "If you ever need time away from the men or some feminine rags, let me know."

"Rags?"

Talia nodded, smiling softly. "You'll understand."

Confused, Terra merely nodded and Talia wished them all well before leaving. Running her fingers along the metal handle of the mirror, Terra admired the decorative grooves. She had never owned one herself.

Glimpsing into its reflective surface, Terra stared. Fear and horror washed over her.

Silver streaks had started in a small segment of her hair.

In the dead of night, the tinny ringing of an old rotary wall phone echoed throughout a run-down, dingy house. The pounding of feet on wooden stairs followed the second ring and a grey-haired man bounded off onto the landing below, sliding along the floorboards and skidding to a halt before the phone. He picked up the wooden handle of the receiver, reinforced with a metal frame, and placed it to his ear.

"Hello?" There was a beat before a grin covered the man's face. "I can never hide from you, can I, Master?" The man wound the curled phone cord around his index finger. The sound of shuffling footsteps caught his attention and he smiled up at the fiery-eyed male on the stairs. "Taliph? A costly call indeed." Another pause. His grin widened. "Well, it is a long journey from

Gershom, but we've done what you asked. We'll take the next ship."

It was harder to tell morning from night in the cavern and Adam had to shake Terra to rouse her the following day. He waved her over to one of the circular holes that Terra assumed to be glassless windows. They watched Lamina's hulking form bustling about outside, singing to himself as he prepared a morning meal for them by the fireside.

Terra's face lit up as she watched the ox sing a heartening song about a man named Pater and his love. She rested her chin in her cupped hands, her elbows against the stone windowsill and a soft smile playing on her lips. How strange it was to enjoy a sense of 'home' while underground with people she'd only met over a week ago.

Beside her, Adam quietly noted the streak of silver in the unkempt section of her hair. He followed her gaze out of the window, his thoughts drifting elsewhere.

Terra waved eagerly at the sight of Agnus, winding his way up towards the house.

Lamina shouted over his shoulder to Adam and the young man scurried out to help carry in the plates of breakfast.

"We will commence your lessons in understanding Spiritus," announced Agnus after stripping off his jacket and settling onto the living area's woven mat for breakfast.

Almost fumbling the plate of eggs, Terra shook her head to clear it. "Lessons?"

"Yes." Agnus snagged an egg with some flatbread. "During which," he turned to Lamina before continuing, "I have assured Nicholo that you would assist in recruiting and preparing any able-bodied citizen for the confrontation with Magia."

Terra's head whipped back and forth while Lamina and Agnus discussed "tactics, provisions and numbers", her mind still on the idea of lessons. She numbly ate her egg and flatbread, struggling to absorb the conversation before her.

"We will certainly have allies in Lune, Sorek and Farim. They were destroyed in the war for the throne."

"Yes, whether they rally to the call or not is the issue."

Biting into his flatbread, the old ox chewed pensively. "You know which way they will go, don't you, Agnus?"

Agnus gave a small smile, holding Lamina's gaze. "You must call them regardless and say that you come in my name. If they turn you away, know it is not you they are turning away, but me."

Lamina's shoulders sagged but he nodded and then held his plate out to Adam, requesting another egg.

"What should I to do, Agnus?" asked Adam, passing the plate of eggs to Lamina.

"I need you to establish a barrier above ground for the training. One that is not visible from afar."

"Would Spiritus not be suitable for that?"

"We will be reading from it."

Nodding his head, Adam quickly swallowed the rest of his meal and left to gather water in the house pail to clean the dishes before setting up the barrier.

While Lamina prepared the civilians for battle or made visits to Taliph for recruitment, Agnus and Terra held their own training sessions each day above ground in the abandoned houses. Their training varied from day to day. Some days were spent reading the words that were wrapped around the length of Spiritus' blade. Others were filled with some light sword swinging and positioning. Still others in interpreting and understanding the meaning of the stories told from the blade's words.

"But Agnus," Terra piped up one day as the two of them pored over Spiritus. "Why must I understand the meaning of these words?"

There was a twinkle in Agnus' eyes as he raised his gaze to meet hers. "There is life in these words, my child. Once you understand that, you will learn to live by them."

Terra could only stare quizzically at Agnus but soon returned her attention to his explanation of the story he had just read to her. It was not a simple one as it connected to several of the other tales he had told but as she listened, she began to understand some of the previous stories she had heard. When placed together, the tales formed a greater picture, one which Terra could not fully comprehend now but felt that both she and Agnus were deeply connected to it somehow.

Each day, Terra rose early to complete a few tasks before resuming her training with Agnus.

It was not long before she discovered that Adam was skilful with his hands and he spent much of their time in Manna creating new clothes for the group.

Creating clothes, of course meant that he needed to take people's measurements and Lamina insisted on "keeping his eye" on Adam when it was Terra's turn to be measured, to which Adam rolled his eyes at.

"Miss Ridley, you're so thin," Adam mumbled to Terra upon taking her measurements.

A deep blush coloured Terra's cheeks. "I'm sorry!"

Adam stopped to stare at her. "It isn't something to apologise about."

"I know, I just—"

Adam looked pointedly at Terra and she promptly closed her mouth, the silence filled by the soft padding of Adam's feet as he continued to step around Terra while measuring her. Once done, Adam rolled up the measuring tape and slipped it into his pocket. "Would you like practical or pretty?"

"Practical."

Nodding, Adam scrawled onto a piece of parchment the measurements he had taken. Looking up, he grinned broadly at the girl before him, his cheeks colouring. "Well, I guess you don't need pretty, do you?"

Terra blinked.

"Your flirtations are wasted on the young mistress!" hollered Lamina from the doorway.

Adam gritted his teeth, his cheeks a few shades darker. "Go away, annoying ox!"

Chortling from the doorway, Lamina lumbered over to the pot outside to prepare lunch, calling Terra over to help.

While Lamina and Terra busily chattered away over the bubbling soup, Adam sat outside, stitching cut fabric together for Terra's new clothes.

Ladling the cooked soup into two bowls, Lamina handed them to Terra and she carefully carried them to where Adam sat near the fire. After handing him a bowl, she plopped down beside him with a contented sigh, placing her bowl down in front of her.

A thought occurred to her and, mindful not to knock over her soup, Terra leaned towards Adam. "How's your father?"

Adam screwed his face up. "I'm not sure."

"Have you visited him?"

He shook his head, averting his eyes. "I need to stay here…like he instructed me to." Biting his lip, Adam stirred his soup and fell silent, his shoulders slumped.

Heart thumping, Terra glanced over her shoulder to where Agnus and Lamina stood, deep in conversation. "Agnus."

With a smile, Agnus turned and inclined his head to her. "Yes, my child?"

Terra felt Adam's hand close over hers as if to deter her next words,

"Adam would like to visit his father."

Agnus' smile grew, his eyes glittering in amusement, and he turned his attention to Adam, whose hand was now uncomfortably tight around Terra's. "It's just as with the times he leaves Manna to purchase goods. As long as he informs Nicholo how long the barrier will be down for, he is most welcome to visit Joseph."

Terra swung back around to grin at Adam, catching his flushed cheeks and tightly pinched mouth.

"Th-thank you, Agnus," he whispered. Loosening his grip on Terra's hand, Adam's eyes slid to hers and he smiled, with his cheeks—if possible—turning a brighter red.

Terra felt her own cheeks flush when he withdrew his hand and returned to his soup. She had been too caught up in trying to help him that she hadn't given thought to how close she was to him. Lowering her head, she sat back and avoided looking at him for the rest of lunch but couldn't dislodge the image of his warm smile from her mind.

The new set of clothes that Adam finished that night became Terra's training clothes. Each morning, she changed into them and every afternoon she would change out of them and would wash them in the man-made stream.

This was followed by heating water in a small tub in a communal shack nearby and Terra found bathing to be a wonderful experience, having never regularly bathed before. Lamina was of a different persuasion, grumbling about the absence of a hot water system and the hassle of lighting a fire to heat the bath, to which Adam would dryly remark "precious".

Sometimes while Terra trained with Agnus, Lamina would hunt and gather food and, when he could head into other towns, fabrics and goods for the next few days. He was always returning with a selection of items or news about people. If training concluded early, Terra often ran down to the underground house, where the group stayed, to closely study the ox's cooking.

Whenever the artificial sun slunk down towards the horizon, Terra's training would finish with a pleased Agnus urging her to have dinner. It was during one of these evenings that a trip to the chamber pots left Terra reeling and scrambling out.

"Are you okay, young mistress?" Lamina called after her as she bolted from the house.

She made a beeline for Talia's farm and slowed down when she noticed two figures conversing there. Hovering nearby, Terra toed the dirt.

The man, whose name she remembered to be Nicholo, and Talia appeared to be arguing but laughing all the same.

Eyes shimmering with mirth, Talia turned and spotted Terra. "Oh, Ridley!" She waved an olive arm enthusiastically and Terra shuffled towards the pair.

Nicholo gave a polite nod. "Young Ridley."

"Hi, Mr Nicholo."

Elbow flying and narrowly missing Nicholo's shoulder, Talia shrieked in excitement: "Let's have Ridley over for our monthly dinner!"

"Pay attention to where you're swinging!" Nicholo scowled. "And you should be asking Cecilia that!"

"I'm sure she would love to have Ridley over!"

"I'm sorry, but when did our house become yours?"

Talia skipped forward, linking arms with Terra and dragging her along. "Let Lamina know that Terra will be with us for dinner!" she called over her shoulder.

Grimacing, Terra tried to pull away. "No, I came just to ask about something—"

"Oh!" Talia paused and leaned close, lowering her voice to a whisper. "Do you need rags?"

Heat rose into Terra's face, reaching the tips of her ears. She nodded.

Tugging harder, Talia steered them away from the farm. "Stay for dinner. I'll show you what to do beforehand."

Charging through the winding pathways, Talia barged into a house, shouting apologies to a lady she called "Cecilia" as she dragged Terra over to the bathroom.

"Coming of age can be quite exciting!" enthused Talia after laying out instructions for the young girl.

Pressing her lips together, Terra made a face and shook her head. "I don't really like it."

Talia grinned and waggled her eyebrows. "Don't you want to fill out in nice ways and catch a man's eye?" At Terra's mortified expression, Talia cackled and pressed another cloth into the young girl's hands to use for rags. "I'm just teasing you."

Pocketing the cloth, Terra paused. A deep blush covered her cheeks. "Do boys go through something similar?"

"They go through their own coming of age."

"Is it just as scary as it is for girls?"

Talia smiled gently and opened the bathroom door. "Change is scary for everyone."

Taking the seat that Cecilia pointed out to her—after several "Are you sure?"s from Terra—, a relieved Terra sat before the food laid out on the table, with Nicholo and Talia sitting opposite each other. They insisted on drawing lots for who would pray and Cecilia slammed a hand on the table.

"Don't draw lots over something like dinner prayers!" With a loud sigh, Cecilia urged everyone to close their eyes. "Pater, we thank you for this food."

"We thank you for this food!" Nicholo and Talia sang in hearty agreement.

Terra smiled, heart warmed as she watched Talia load up her plate. "I like that you guys regularly enjoy a meal together. Even though you're not family."

Scratching his jaw, Nicholo smiled, a gleam in his eyes. "Yes, well, Talia is a stray cat we leave food out for."

Talia rolled her eyes, flinging couscous at him.

"What was that for?"

"You know exactly what."

"So childish."

Cecilia let out a content sigh and stirred a lump of sugar into her tea. "A house is much warmer with banter, isn't it?" She mirrored Terra's smile.

"I'm not very good at it," Terra confessed, watching Nicholo flick the couscous back across the table. She paused, biting her lip. "It… it was safer not to act out."

Terra jumped when she felt Cecilia's callused fingers curl around her own coarse ones. Hands that understood hard work with scars that spoke of perseverance.

"My dear, you are not in that place anymore. You are safe here."

Heart thudding in her ears, Terra realised how tense her body was. She squeezed Cecilia's hand. "I'm sorry—"

"Don't be."

Terra smiled softly. Pulling away, she returned to her meal. "It's nice eating with a family."

"It's not too different from your own."

Pausing, Terra felt a flush of pleasure. She imagined Lamina and Adam arguing over the fire as they ate, Agnus chiding them after a while. "No," she whispered, heart full, "not too different."

The happy hush fell over the table, filled by the tinkling of cutlery as everyone ate.

"So, Ridley!" Cecilia said cheerily after a moment of quiet, "I heard that you'll be of age next spell."

Terra's eye widened. She swallowed down a stuck piece of meat. "Who told you that?"

"Adam." Smiling in a knowing manner, Cecilia folded her hands under her chin. "He's a sweet young man, isn't he?"

Terra choked on a bit of tomato.

Rolling her eyes at Cecilia's chuckle, Talia thumped Terra's back. "Don't kill her with your idle gossip."

"It's not gossip. It's an observation. He stopped by to mend some of our frayed clothes and took no payment for it." Cecilia nudged Nicholo. "He was a lovely man, wasn't he?"

"I suppose he had a good sense of humour."

"How is that your measurement of a man?"

Wagging his knife in the air, Nicholo tutted. "In any case, Ridley will have to survive the coming of age ceremony before she even considers marriage."

Talia continued to whack a coughing Terra. "I'm sure Ridley is overjoyed by your confidence in her."

"I-I don't want to g-go," Terra managed to wheeze out. At the questioning looks, Terra lowered her eye. "I'll tell Agnus. I don't want to go to the ceremony."

Cecelia piled some more meat onto Terra's plate. "If he wills it, it's definitely possible. But enough of this talk, we want you to enjoy your time here."

Talia rested her chin in her hands, face deadpan. "Hey, I'm here too, the marriage comment hurts me too. Do you want me to enjoy my time here or not?"

"Poor little stray cat."

"What was that, old man?"

The rest of the dinner was filled with laughter and warm conversations and Terra felt her heart soar with gratitude at how comfortable her life had become with all the new faces that had entered in it.

When Adam arrived on the doorstep to escort Terra back, all the discomfort from talking about the coming of age ceremony had dissipated.

After a moment of pleasantries, Terra hastily shoved Adam away from the front door, pushing him down the pathway.

"Miss Ridley?"

Cecilia's eyes had a wicked gleam to them. "Oh, in a hurry are you, Ridley?"

"Shush! Don't listen to anything they say to you!"

Adam sighed and shook his head, allowing Terra to steer him away. "They're teasing you, aren't they? But what does this have to do with me?"

"Shush!"

The idea of the coming of age ceremony seemed a distant and impossible thought.

Ω

After a particularly uncomfortable training day with Terra still adjusting to the changes in her body, she settled by the fire and warmed her feet while massaging her aching back. She thanked Adam as he passed her a plate of food. He had surprised the group by cooking dinner—a skill he had been learning from following Lamina around.

Terra wasn't sure if it was the strange emotions that accompanied the changes in her body, but she greatly admired Adam's simple cooking of meat, vegetables and mashed up potatoes.

"You are doing well, my child," Agnus said over the clinking of chipped plates and cups in the underground ruins. "Remember the importance of awareness. Be responsive to any changes in battle."

Scrunching her nose, Terra swallowed a bite of potatoes before speaking: "But Agnus, why am I training in this way and not training to learn real combat techniques? Wouldn't that be more helpful instead of reading about One?"

With a shake of his head, Agnus smiled. "My dear child, should there be a time that I am not with you in the flesh, what will you set your feet upon? How will you push on should you feel physically alone? For now we will continue in the feeding and training of your mind. Many battles are waged mentally and even the greatest of fighters can crumble with the slightest doubt." He took a sip from his cup of tea. "In any case, you will have another to teach you swordsmanship."

Terra had some reservations about physically training which she decided to keep to herself. "But how will this current 'training' help me beat Colonel Simeon? He's able to control all of the E132 around him!"

"If those are your concerns then there is nothing to fear." Agnus took another sip of his tea. "If you doubt me and Spiritus then of course you will be easily cut down by a man."

Frowning, Terra decided the answers weren't worth the effort and moodily shovelled food into her mouth. Agnus' words were too cryptic and confusing for her.

"His words don't make much sense to me either, young mistress," confessed Lamina that night when Terra asked if he could explain Agnus' words at dinner. "In fact," continued Lamina, his expression thoughtful, "I've never fully understood a lot of the things Agnus says."

Terra sighed. She had agreed to follow him but would she ever understand him?

Lamina cleared his throat. "What is it, young mistress?"

Sighing again, Terra shook her head. "I don't doubt Agnus. I've seen what he can do. I'm just afraid. Afraid of facing Colonel Simeon again. Here I am, reading ancient texts but...what am I supposed to do when I *do* face him again?"

Lamina inhaled deeply and squared his shoulders. He firmly planted his hands on Terra's shoulders, prompting her to look up. "If you're instructed to kill him, then kill him. Do not hesitate. Do not pity him. Follow Agnus' commands."

Terra's eye widened and the colour in her face drained away. "Ag-Agnus hasn't given me any directions for Colonel Simeon."

"But when he does, what will you do?"

Biting her lip, Terra looked down and pushed back the images of her hands slick with Simeon's blood. Her gut twisted in guilt when the word 'good' flashed through her mind.

'*Let yourself heal.*' Could she truly heal enough to overcome these dark desires?

"I," Terra hesitated, her chest beginning to tighten, "don't know..."

"Young mistress, if you doubt in that moment then you will not be able to harness the full power of Spiritus—"

"Don't you think I know that!" Terra clapped a hand over her mouth.

Lamina gave a strained smile.

"I'm sorry, Mr Lamina." Terra's eye welled with tears. "I didn't mean to snap."

"I know you didn't. How about we get some rest and you pray about things? You've got another big day of training tomorrow."

Memories of Terra's friends resurfaced. "We read about prayer today. Is it really something so important?"

"More than you think. You should try it as you come to understand the writings on Spiritus more."

That night, Terra laid awake. She tried to pray in the way the characters she had learnt about did but didn't know if her words were just incoherent muttering like Ridley had once joked about. As she tried to understand her confusion, her thoughts eventually shifted from dreading the idea of facing Colonel Simeon to what Agnus would expect of her. That night she woke from a nightmare where she was covered in the Colonel's blood.

Outside, Agnus climbed the long stairway back up to the surface, the air filled with the echoes of his footsteps against stone. Stepping up into the still night air, he kicked the rug back over the concealed entry and perched on a tired, wooden chair nearby. He waited, eyes closed against the remnant light of the sinking artificial sun.

The muted passing of the wind carried whispers of news that would set a normal man's teeth on edge but Agnus knew better than to despair. He quietly prayed in the darkness of the night. Time slipped by unnoticed beneath the scarlet grin of the moon. Ceaseless prayers filled the quiet. The blood-red moon remained unchanging, unable to convey the time that continued to creep away.

The creaking of the house door caused Agnus to look up with a smile.

Framed in the doorway and silhouetted against the light of the moon stood a man with long grey-hair that was roughly pulled back into a ponytail. The figure sauntered into the room, cloak swishing about his ankles and leaves crunching underfoot. "Master," was the man's reverent greeting, his slanted dark eyes sparkling in the slit of light from a patchy hole in the ceiling.

With a squeak of protest from the chair, Agnus stood. "Shigure, I suspect that Sominium has requested payment for the children?"

Shigure nodded, frowning. "Yes, Rebekah intercepted as many of the children she could. She's sheltering them under the guise that she'll be submitting them to the beastmasters she works with." He paused, allowing a momentary slip in his cool I. "But we think some may have been led astray. A merchant at Taliph's port reported the abrupt shipping of what he assumed to be blemished..." he trailed off, hanging his head. "Keira has promised to investigate it... I'm sorry."

Agnus nodded, his heart aching. "The monsters of this world will continue to thrive. But in the end, all will meet me." He shook his head as if to clear it. "Did you make contact with the Lowenthals in Gershom?"

"Yes. They were a most gracious host."

"And what of Hazael?"

"Departed for Nyx. As you ordered."

Sighing, Agnus closed his eyes and took a breath. "Thank you, Shigure." Rummaging in his coat pocket, Agnus retrieved a set of vials containing a red liquid which he handed over. He watched as Shigure shoved the vials into his own coat pocket. "One final request."

Peering up, Shigure noted the tired expression on his master's face.

"If Adam suspects Terra to be Arche, do not correct him."

Shigure bowed, a wide grin splitting his face. "Yes, Master."

The lands drift and we are cast aside.
In the sea, we are dashed against the waves, in hopes of appeasing One.
But the storms rage on and the winds whisper of Death.

- Lines from *The Time of Exiles, Scriptura.* Translated by H. Van de Berg

14

In the early sun up hours of their second week in Manna, insistent knocking on the front door woke Terra.

With a bleary eye, she watched from her spot on the woven mat as Lamina stumbled to answer the door, grumbling the entire way and earning a snort from Adam. Terra's eye darted over to Adam whose makeshift bed was on the other side of Lamina—the ox happily slept in between the two—and she grinned at him, suppressing a giggle as he imitated Lamina's irate expression and grumbles.

After fumbling a bit with the doorknob, Lamina pulled open the door, almost squawking in shock. "What are *you* doing here?"

"Master invited me."

Terra's ears perked up at the familiar voice and she shot up in bed, eye landing on the grey-haired gunslinger they had encountered while running from Magia. "You're that man who was with Death!" she exclaimed, jumping up to her feet.

"Shigure," proffered the man, amused. "I believe that you're the one I'm to train, girl."

Eyebrows disappearing up into her fringe, Terra's mouth fell open. "*You're* training me?"

Trailing behind Shigure on the path through the large cavern, Terra spotted Agnus from afar. He was deep in conversation with Nicholo who made several wild gestures as he spoke.

Agnus glanced at Terra from the corner of his eyes and inclined his head, mirroring her warm smile. Exchanging a few last words with Nicholo, he strolled over to the pair and fell in step with them. "I assume that Shigure has informed you of your training?"

Terra made a face. "Somewhat," she answered, brow furrowed. "Is this meant to replace my current training with you?"

Smiling, Agnus shook his head. "It will be complementary."

They passed by Talia who waved cheerfully from the farm field, a parchment and ink pen in hand while she hunched over the plants.

The trio began to ascend the stairs out of the cavern when Shigure spoke up, "I will go easy on you this week, but don't expect to be babied next week." There was a hint of mirth in his tone.

Terra wondered if his head would fit through the exit.

They reached the opening into a house and stepped out with Agnus motioning for Terra to seat herself. While they began reading through the runic symbols together, Shigure sat in the corner of the room and quietly reviewed a collection of parchments.

"*I gazed upon the ruins of man and beast. We had long drifted far away from One.*
The temple we still have. All of history had begun in this place.
But One no longer walks its halls. One's voice we can no longer hear.
Where shall we go then? And what shall we do in this Oneless age?
We shall turn swords upon each other. For is that not our greatest strength?
As we had split the lands long ago with our hatred and greed, so too, shall we split each other.
In my grief, I wander the lands.
Men and beasts whisper of magick, but I will turn my face to the lands of One. To Praeter Tempus and its doors. I will pray for the day when they shall open for me and I will walk within its walls and hear the voice of One."

Crinkling her nose, Terra tilted her head. "I don't really get why this story is included in Scriptura. The writer just sounds miserable."

Agnus' eyes lit up and he turned to Shigure with a smile. "What do you think that part of the story is saying and why is it included here?"

Sighing, Shigure scribbled on the parchment he held and set it aside. "Master, I hate listening to these stories."

"Why?" Terra surprised herself with how sharp her tone was.

"We did away with these stories. This is the New World that the Sominiums have established," tutted Shigure, folding his arms over his chest.

"Does that mean the stories Agnus is teaching me are wrong? Or does that mean the way things are done in the New World is wrong?" Terra found herself asking aloud, her leg shaking in agitation.

A broad smile spread on Agnus' face as Shigure rose sharply, pulling up two scabbards. Eyes twinkling, Agnus stood quickly, brushing dust from his pant legs.

With a wicked smile, Shigure tossed the sheathed sword at Terra, eliciting a shriek from her as she jumped up, desperately flapping her arms to catch it. "Our training begins immediately!" He unsheathed his sword with a flourish and pointed it at Terra while she stooped to retrieve her fallen sword.

Following suit, she removed the sword from its scabbard, tossing the latter to the side. "Why so suddenly?" She threw a pleading look at Agnus who had already begun to move the rug aside to descend into the underground cavern. "Agnus, you're not really going to leave me alone with this...person, are you? And you didn't even answer my question!"

"Shigure will be sure to answer it during your training," Agnus called over his shoulder. He sang to unlock the entryway, and trotted down the stairway, leaving Terra to stare incredulously after his shrinking form before the door slid shut.

Seriously?

Frowning, Terra spun the iron sword in her hand. "If I can wield the power of Spiritus, why do I have to learn how to properly use a plain sword?"

Shigure slowly paced around, blade still pointed at Terra. "Well, I can't fault that logic. Magians primarily use E132, which Spiritus can destroy. But your battles in this world won't always be as simple nor will they solely be against E132 users and each fight will always require personal effort."

Brows knotting, Terra picked at the frayed leather wrapped around the sword's guard. "I've always just relied on Spiritus to guide me."

"Sword up, please. And address me as your teacher."

Terra scowled but straightened, standing poised with the sword in both hands and her feet planted hip-width apart. "Sorry, *teacher*," she grumbled.

Shigure instructed her on how to position herself and to pay close attention to his body language when defending from blows. As he was speaking, he leaned forward and struck her in the side with the pommel of his sword while her guard was lowered.

"You need to be more attentive than this." He resumed his starting position, eyes sparkling and a mischievous smile playing on his lips. "Be discerning."

Grinding her teeth, Terra rubbed her sore ribs. "I told you. I've always just relied on Spiritus to guide me in fights."

"Yes, and I'm sure its power dwelt strongly within, despite the clumsiness of the vessel."

"I am going to ignore that slight. I still don't see why I need to learn to fight like this!"

"The wielder must make good use of the weapon." Shigure stepped forward, swinging slowly at Terra and allowing her to connect her blade with his. "Wielding and using the sword is part of your own responsibility as well. You must devote time to honing your understanding of it and put what you learn into practice."

"My understanding of it?"

With a flick of his wrist, Shigure spun his sword against Terra's, forcing hers out of her hands. He struck her again in the side with the pommel.

Terra winced, staggering backwards, hand closing over her sore side.

"Pay attention. You need to hold your sword properly and not block in a way that tangles you up. Put some strength in your sword arm too." Shigure stepped back into his starting position. "Every time I disarm you, you'll get another bruise."

"I'm just trying to understand!" Tears sprang into the corner of her eye. "I never ever fought until Spiritus appeared in me! I just believed in Agnus and all of this stuff has happened and now... and now..." Face red and chest heaving with emotion, Terra wiped the tears angrily away from her eye, words stuck in her throat.

Without warning, Shigure crossed the distance between them and thrust the pommel into her already bruised side, causing Terra to stumble. He swung his leg hard against her unsteady ones, sending her sprawling back onto the dusty earth. His cold expression came into view above her and Terra felt the tip of the sword against her throat while she struggled to catch her breath.

"We all must take responsibility for our own choices. If you truly believe in Agnus, then get up and show me that."

Terra shoved the blade aside and pushed herself up into a sitting position. Prepared to launch herself at this infuriating man, she found more tears spilling from her eye. "Why would Agnus pick someone like me to fulfill this prophecy?" she croaked, hanging her head and pressing a trembling hand to her face. "I'm so weak. I don't even know what I'm doing!"

"It's precisely that reason that you were chosen," chided Shigure, reaching his hand out to her.

Terra looked up at him, eye glossy.

"Because you're weak, you'll naturally rely on Agnus' power more." Shigure's eyes softened and he allowed the gentlest smile Terra had ever seen from him to light his face. "There's nothing wonderful or remarkable that you've done to be here. And that makes what you do even more important," he explained, hand still outstretched.

Blinking away further tears and sniffling, Terra begrudgingly clasped Shigure's hand, allowing him to pull her to her feet. "Teacher, you still haven't answered my question," she huffed, earning a loud laugh from Shigure.

"I have," he replied with a smirk and a wink.

For the first time ever, Terra found someone's smiling face punchable.

Shigure stepped back and allowed her a moment to dry her face on her sleeve before they resumed their training.

When Terra trudged back, covered head to toe in bruises, Lamina bristled with fury.

The young girl shrugged sheepishly. "At least, I learned lots today," she mumbled, hobbling towards the bathroom.

"Well, Shigure might learn lots from *me* today!" Lamina sprang from the worn couch he had been weaving a basket on.

Steering back in his direction, Terra urged him to calm down. She didn't need another reason for Shigure to gleefully thrash her during their next lesson.

Once a fuming Lamina settled back into his seat, Adam strolled into the house, juggling three loaded paper bags. He paused at the sight of Terra, eyes narrowing on each visible bruise. "Do I need to speak to Shigure?"

Terra shook her head insistently. "I can handle this."

Mouth pressed into a hard line, Adam strode to the bench, placing the paper bags down. "Are you sure?"

Lamina's rumbling voice joined in assent, "For once, Adam and I are in agreement!"

Again, Terra shook her head. "When I have mastered swordsmanship, I'll give him a beating."

Adam's eyebrows shot up and the corners of his mouth twitched up. "That's the most unforgiving thing I've heard from you yet. Make sure it's a thorough beating."

"It will be."

Lamina let out a deep, throaty laugh.

Grinning, Adam shook his head. "I'm going to prepare dinner, so tidy up if you need to," he said, turning to sort out the contents of the bags.

At Terra's request, Lamina left to fetch her some firewood while she nursed her bruises over a chamber pot.

When night came, Terra couldn't sleep, her body protesting with every move. Recalling her training, she wriggled agonisingly slowly into her makeshift bed, frowning as she remembered her question and the answer she felt she had missed.

While her mind wandered, Adam slipped into his own bed, muttering good night as he settled in. Rolling over to face him, Terra quoted her teacher: "Spiritus' power dwelt strongly in me."

Turning wearily to her, Adam returned her expectant stare blankly.

"Does everyone have a power?" Terra pressed, mind darting to Simeon's control of E132 and Adam's ability to prophesy.

Adam smiled sleepily. "They are not powers. They are gifts and talents."

Terra gave a slow nod, her face betraying her confusion. "So then, what is your gift?"

"My gift?" Adam's smile broadened. "I'm guessing you're thinking of the one where I hear people's thoughts?"

"You can read minds?"

The corner of Adam's mouth twitched as if he were tempted to laugh. "More along the lines of having the memories of those long gone flow through my mind." He yawned widely. "I have to actively listen though."

Terra inhaled sharply. "Are you saying that the dead are still around us?"

A small laugh escaped Adam's lips. "No, not at all. I meant to say the remnant thoughts of a life that has passed from this world."

"Like looking into the past?"

"Nothing that fantastical. But I suppose you could say that. Like listening to distant echoes."

Relief washed over Terra. "So then, you wouldn't be able to read my thoughts?" she asked curiously, praying he couldn't.

Adam's eyes held hers and he smiled softly. "I wish I could."

Terra looked away, stomach somersaulting. She stared at one of the windows in the wall she faced, the faint voices of Lamina, Agnus and Shigure drifting in. Heat rose in her cheeks when she thought of Adam's response and she couldn't bear to look at him.

Adam heaved a long, tired sigh and rolled over, mumbling another "good night".

Once Terra heard Adam's soft and even breathing, she peered shyly over at his sleeping face and shook her head, squeezing her eye shut and begging for sleep. She curled her fingers over the bridge that hung around her neck and eventually drifted into a light sleep.

The days in Manna passed into months and Terra slowly earned less bruises with each lesson. Shigure congratulated her on her Tortul paced progress and Terra learned to grit her teeth and ignore his pointed insults. The decrease in bruises was evidence enough to her that she was growing in strength and skill. But she was always thankful whenever Shigure was away on "business with The Conqueror"—it gave her time to rest her aching body. He was a merciless instructor.

There were moments in her training sessions where she couldn't help wondering about what Lamina had said regarding Colonel Simeon and the desperate need to heal her troubled mind and heart. In these moments of distraction, Shigure would clobber her and she was certain it amused him.

But Agnus didn't raise the issue regarding the Colonel. Instead, they'd sit together, Terra listening to Agnus read some of the ancient runic writing surrounding Spiritus. Sometimes the stories and words made sense to Terra. Other times, they seemed utterly nonsensical. But each time she came away from those readings, she'd eagerly share the new things she'd learned with Lamina.

Adam was always either making Terra new clothes for her growing body or ensuring his barrier around the area was sufficient to protect them the next day. But on the occasions he was around for her story recounts, he was able to retell the tales word for word.

"You've memorised the stories?" Terra stared at him, impressed.

"They're not stories. It's history." Adam traced the deep grooves in the dining table. "But even then it's far more complex than that. It's Scriptura."

Making a mental note of the name, Terra scoffed the rest of her food down as Shigure approached. Eager to leave before he could speak to her, Terra asked Lamina for some firewood to heat her bath.

"*I'll* bring you some, dear student of mine!" sang Shigure, striding away before Terra could protest.

When Terra received several water-logged pieces of timber, she chased her teacher with her training sword brandished, much to the surprise of both Lamina and Adam.

"So you *do* have a personality after all!" Shigure unsheathed his sword and deflected a fierce blow directed at his head.

When Shigure eventually disarmed Terra, she left in a huff, seeking out Talia to ask for some dry logs. As Talia handed some over to her—along with some supportive undergarments—, she found Shigure hovering around, attempting to make light conversation and commenting on Talia's "delightful eyes" while his own were very clearly not addressing hers.

This elicited another bout of infuriated sword swings from Terra who hissed, "what kind of teacher are you!"

"Your favourite teacher!"

"You're my *only* teacher, you moron!"

Adam added hot water to his teapot. "I don't think I've ever heard Miss Ridley insult someone before."

Brow furrowed, Lamina rubbed his chin. "I'm not sure it's a good thing."

"It doesn't bring a fatherly tear to your eye?"

The old ox shook his head, trying not to smile. "Okay, enough teasing for today." Lamina shooed a chuckling Shigure away. "You're probably the reason the young mistress' hair is almost all silver."

Still fuming, both over her teacher and for having stooped to his level, Terra stormed away and Lamina followed her to light the firewood.

Adam laid out two teacups on the table. "Would you like to join me for some tea, Shigure?"

"Why not?" Shigure replied with a grin.

While Terra made several trips to the well for her bathwater, she dwelt on the events of the past spell. Despite the nature of her training and circumstances, she had grown fond of the time that she was spending with everyone.

Maybe not my teacher, she thought grumpily, wincing as she ran her fingers over a dark bruise on her arm. Even so, she had to admit, she was thankful for all he had taught her. She certainly felt confident she could fight without needing Spiritus to take full control.

The time at Manna had truly slipped out of her grasp and raced ahead of her in a light so dazzling she had struggled to keep track of the days. Already she was nearing her second birthday outside of Magia.

At this thought, her mind wandered to a certain Magian officer while she crouched beside Lamina who lit the fire for her bath. She wondered where the Colonel was and what he was doing. Was he still as cruel as she remembered? Had he tried to change at all?

After the water had warmed up enough, Terra thanked Lamina and closed the door behind her. She slid into the bath and closed her eye, surrendering to the heat.

In the stillness of the room, she remembered Agnus' words almost a spell ago regarding Simeon and, with all this in mind, she prayed—like Agnus had taught her to—for him and for her; that he might change his ways and that she might heal and love like One loved.

She didn't know whether such thoughts would reach Simeon or whether what she was doing meant anything. But it felt right and her heart was considerably lighter.

That night, Terra dreamed of what she imagined a harlequin stage play would be like. Laughter that warmed the room, smiles that lifted spirits. There she sat in the audience with Lamina and Adam. But most importantly, she sat side by side with the Colonel. At one point, he turned to her and smiled, blood dripping down his face and onto her hands.

From the stage, Agnus stood, holding his hat as he bowed deeply. *'Don't lose your way,'* he mouthed from centre stage as the lights began to fade.

Sweat dribbling down her neck, Terra flopped back onto the ground, conceding defeat as Shigure stood over her, sword tip against her cheek.

Pulling out a silver pocket watch, Shigure glanced at it before snapping it shut and sheathing his sword. He reached down to help Terra up and she accepted with resignation. "It's almost night. We'll call it for now."

While Terra moodily examined her fresh bruises, Shigure paced over to the worn out door and peeled it open, sticking his head out.

"Teacher, what are you doing?"

Pulling his head back in, Shigure shot Terra a mischievous smile and wink. "Come on, live a little." He stepped over the door threshold, ignoring Terra as she called after him.

Gathering herself, Terra crawled over to the doorway. She paused, hesitating, and then poked her head out, not impressed by the amused look Shigure gave her. "Teacher, won't this disrupt Adam's barrier?"

Shigure shrugged, turning on his heel and walking away from the house, crunching through debris and pottery along the way.

Clenching her fist and glancing around furtively, Terra scrambled after her teacher, mentally berating him the whole way. When she finally came to a stop behind him, she gave an exaggerated huff.

Shigure had seated himself on what remained of the small stone wall at the edge of the ruined town of Manna. There he watched the sway of the trees beyond the town, their leaves stirring in the wind and framed against the black backdrop of the sky.

"I heard that you'll be of age soon."

Terra rolled her eye. People were obsessed with ages.

"Which means you'll get to see my work in Sominium soon."

Planting her hands on the stone wall beside him, Terra leaned over and Shigure turned slightly, laughing at her scowl of confusion.

"The coming of age ceremony," he explained. "It's held four times a spell in Sominium and you'll have to attend the next one."

"I have to?"

"Libertas. It's part of that law."

Swallowing her disagreements, Terra was reminded of the first time she had heard that word and her eyebrows creased together. "How many people will be there?"

Chuckling, Shigure clapped a hand on Terra's shoulder. "The world is a far bigger place than you can imagine."

Terra decided against her instinctual reaction of being irate and instead sat down on what felt like a stable part of the wall. The wind momentarily picked up and she scooted closer to her teacher for cover. "I've only ever heard of places others have mentioned while I was in Magia." The blood-red moon was reflected in her grey eye and after a beat she glanced at Shigure. "Can you tell me more about the world?"

"What do you want to know?"

"Anything."

Screwing up his face in thought, Shigure stroked his chin. "All I can think about is how the world was before the sun died." His expression softened. "A sky that was a brilliant blue. The striking colours of it when the sun set. The stars that lit up the dark night." The fond smile he wore faded. "Everything has changed now. Except men of course."

As Shigure fell into a contemplative silence, Terra's heart, to her surprise, sank. Despite his annoying antics, she was used to his playful mood and punchable smile. She racked her brain for a way to cheer him up and recalled when Simeon mentioned the Libertas law. "Have you ever heard of harlequins?"

"Hm? Is this something else you heard from Simeon?"

Abashed, Terra nodded mutely.

"Yes, they're a lot like jesters, jokers, clowns—whatever the word is nowadays."

Terra's face lit up in excitement. "Colonel Simeon said they entertain people. I thought that, if I saw one, I would really be free."

Hearing the elation in her voice, Shigure shook his head. "Don't put your hope in men," cautioned Shigure, his voice low. A light breeze blew between teacher and pupil and Terra found herself marvelling at the older man's nonchalant attitude. "It's best that you hold onto Agnus and all that you've learned from Spiritus."

Tucking several strands of silver hair behind her ear, Terra lifted a leg and hugged her knee to her chest. Countless thoughts raced through her mind. "You said that you hated hearing Scriptura."

The word made Shigure peer closely at her. "Where did you learn that term from?"

"Adam."

Shigure rolled his eyes, muttering "Mr Know-it-all" and Terra jabbed his arm with a finger. "You're right, I do hate hearing Scriptura. But not because I disagree with it," he mused, looking back out at the black horizon. "But because it's inconvenient for me. If I believe it all to be true, I can't really live however I want, can I?"

Terra hugged her leg tighter. The artificial sun began to sink, signalling the approach of night. "I had never really thought about it," she answered honestly. "But, I suppose, you can't." She paused again, and her eye widened as a thought struck her. "I finally understand what the answer to my question was."

Turning to her, Shigure processed her words for a moment before bursting out in laughter. "Well, we got there at least!" He wiped a tear from his eye.

Heart considerably lighter, Terra laughed, relief washing over her. She had a truth that she would not let go of now. Shigure was an odd but kind man.

"Oh, and I thought I would inform you." Shigure's eyes glittered with mirth. "I may have hinted to Adam that you're Arche Maremortum."

Jaw dropping, Terra was reminded of how punchable her teacher's smiling face was. "You—" She searched for a good insult she could bear to say, "—stupid brat! You can't lie to people like that!"

"It's not like you can tell him your real name."

"How would you even know?"

"Is your head in the clouds? Anyway, better to put him out of his misery. Maybe he might gain some sense and lose interest in you." Shigure winked at the fuming Terra. "Poor boy spent so much time sleeping, he ended up with poor taste."

Terra felt her face grow hot and her mouth pinching together in an angry pout. "You're so awful!"

Smile fixed in place, Shigure raised an eyebrow. "Well then, what are you going to tell him if he asks you?"

Opening her mouth, Terra felt searing pain tangle her name in her throat and a sharp stab like a knife slotting into her neck, pinning the words in place. She choked and spluttered, spittle covering the ground.

"You can't."

Terra glared up at Shigure but felt her heart thump at the sad but knowing smile he wore.

"Spare yourself the heartache. He told me he had prophesied that such an easy life wasn't for you. And besides, you may be separated and never meet again."

Remembering the prophecy Adam had shared in Initium, Terra's heart sank. "That doesn't mean..."

"And I have it on good authority that he will be meeting Arche in the future."

Biting her lip, Terra looked down at her feet, tears clinging to her eyelashes. Why was he pressuring her this much? Had Agnus told him something and he was trying to look out for her? Was Adam meant to meet Arche and fall for her?

At that thought, Terra felt as if a knife had been plunged through her heart. Maybe her teacher was right.

Shigure pressed a firm hand against her upper arm, drawing Terra's tear-filled gaze. His eyes roamed over her face and he murmured, "If he does like you, won't he be able to tell the difference when he meets Arche?"

Terra shook her head, heat rising into her cheeks again. "N-no. He doesn't like me that way."

Shigure chuckled lightly. "Think about what I said then. Save yourself from unnecessary heartache. This is why you're my pitiful student."

"That's not heartening at all."

"I'm not here to inspire you, I'm here to teach you, silly girl."

After their long bickering gave way to eventual laughter, Shigure patted Terra on the shoulder. "Keep up your training while I'm away."

"I will."

Terra waved farewell, watching Shigure kick up dust as he left, the azure sun sinking below the horizon. Skipping to the underground passage, Terra hummed as she descended the stairs, grateful to have seen a gentler side of her teacher. She made a beeline for the house, unable to deny the growling of her stomach any longer.

"The food's waiting for you on the table inside," Lamina said, ruffling her hair when she passed him and Agnus outside.

Thanking him, Terra headed in, giving a quick "hi" to Adam who sat hunched over a tunic, and collapsed onto the floor in front of the table.

Feeling as if she were being watched, Terra swallowed a mouthful of food and glanced over at Adam, catching his eye. "What is it?"

Adam looked hurriedly away. "Nothing." His hands ran over the fabric balanced on his lap and he continued mending the frayed hem of the tunic.

Terra frowned. It was difficult to read Adam. Maybe he was pondering Shigure's misdirection, believing her to be Arche. Terra viciously stabbed her lamb.

"You grew up in Magia under the care of Simeon Railesson."

Terra's brows rose. "Railesson? Isn't that the name of this country? The Colonel was only ever referred to as 'Simeon' or 'Van de Berg'."

Needle and thread wove expertly through the tunic without pause. "Yes, well…in any case you were under his care throughout your time in Magia."

"Yes." Terra's thoughts drifted back to the small outpost station when she had first met the Colonel. "He was not a kind person."

Adam's mouth pulled into a small, tight smile. "I assumed as much." He raised the tunic and bit through the thread. Setting his needle aside, he held the tunic out in front of him and examined his work. "All of that cruelty…" Adam paused, scratching his jaw, "…and you became kind. Silly. But kind."

Scrunching her nose up, Terra pursed her lips. "Thanks, I guess."

Satisfied with his work, Adam folded up the tunic. "It's strange," he murmured, laying the mended tunic out flat on the side-table beside him. "There are no memories or echoes that surround you, Miss Ridley. As though you have no past ties or relations…"

Adam's voice grew soft, but Terra was faintly aware that he was not lowering his voice. A light but sudden ache behind her empty left eye-socket drew her attention away. And as that ache began, the room shifted, becoming smaller and darker.

Shadows grew and shrank along the walls around her. The light above faded to a hazy orange, and the room bubbled and shifted each time the bulb flickered. A dark, hunched figure rose from the cracks in the concrete slab beneath Terra's feet and they stood beside her, its faceless head peering down at hers.

Frozen in horror, Terra watched as its hands reached out to caress her face. The dull throb behind her left eye-socket turned into searing pain and Terra let out an agonising scream, right eye squeezed shut and hands flying up to press against her empty left eye-socket.

Even though she had closed her eye, she could still see the figure beside her in her mind, its hands running over her face. The shadows from the walls peeled themselves off, shuffling towards Terra with their hands outstretched.

She shrank back, desperate to make herself smaller. But the shadows crept closer, and soon their fingers touched her skin and the pain behind her eye became unbearable; like someone had taken a hot metal rod and slid it through her head over and over.

Images burned in her mind. A woman being torn apart. A man bludgeoned with a bat. Another plummeting from a high height. A child, offered up to the yawning mouth of a fiery oven. Instances of death burned like the orange light on the back of her eyelid as more shadows crowded around her hunched body. She leapt to her feet unsteadily and screamed as image after image filled her mind. "Make it stop!"

Adam caught her as her knees gave way. "Miss Ridley!" He shook her, voice filled with panic. "Miss Ridley!"

A man was stabbed. Another hung. Children beaten to death.

Terra tore herself away from Adam and flung herself on the floor, clutching either side of her head as a long scream ripped through her throat. She clawed at the sides of her face, wet from her tears, drawing blood as her mind filled with countless depictions of death. She beat her fists repeatedly against her temple, sobbing from both the pain and the images.

Desperate, Adam threw himself at her, wrenching her hands away from her face and yanking her up so that he could place his arms around her, securely pinning hers to her sides. Murmuring gently, he held her close and faint runic words emanated from his body as he tried to soothe her. But she couldn't stop screaming and her body thrashed violently against Adam's, throwing him back against the legs of the table as he continued to wrestle her.

The door flew open, almost unhinged as Lamina raced across the room with Agnus in tow.

"Lamina, the eye-patch!" shouted Agnus as they reached Terra and Adam.

Stumbling forward, Lamina thrust a hand into one of his trouser pockets, pulling out a handkerchief along with the eye-patch from Hitori. Falling to his knees, he clumsily threw the eye-patch over Terra's head and with shaky hands, adjusted it so that it fell over her empty left eye-socket.

As soon as the eye-patch covered her left eye, the shadows and the dark figure dissipated and Terra took desperate gulps of air to fill her aching lungs. She trembled uncontrollably and didn't realise she was sobbing until Agnus was pulling her up into his arms. He calmly held her until her howls became small sniffles, at which he pulled away and handed her Lamina's handkerchief.

Snot dribbling down her front, Terra murmured a thank you and tidied herself up, blowing her nose loudly.

She hadn't noticed that Lamina had left until he stepped back into the room, breathless. "Agnus, the people of Manna are on edge."

Agnus reached over and briefly squeezed Terra's hand before he stood. "I'll ease their minds, thank you Lamina."

Reflexively, Adam stood and crossed the room, rummaging through their supplies until he pulled out a palm-sized tub of ointment which he carried back to Terra's side. His eyes reflected pain. "Are you alright?" he whispered, gingerly brushing her tears away with the back of his hand. Once her face was dry, he dabbed the ointment onto the deep, red scratches on Terra's face, ignoring her flinches.

Terra quietly noted that his hands were trembling. She had never seen him so shaken before and felt a pang of guilt. "I'm sorry for worrying you."

"Never mind me," grumbled Adam, eyebrows in a knot. "I just want to know if *you're* okay."

Opening her mouth to reply, Terra paused, recalling some of the images she'd seen. She shuddered, hugging herself as her chest tightened. "No, that was frightening," she whispered, body trembling.

Lamina sank to his knees beside her, wrapping his arms around Terra and pulling her into a tight hug.

"What was that?" she rasped, fresh tears filling her eye. She reached her arms around Lamina, hugging as much of him as she could. "Why did I see all of those things?"

Lamina squeezed her. "It's because of your connection to your missing eye. Perhaps you experienced what that person saw."

Terra remembered seeing things with her eye previously. Did something happen to Arche? Or was this the 'gift' that she had heard about?

"Do you want to talk about what you saw?" Lamina asked into the top of her head.

Terra's eye glazed over, her thoughts rushing back to the onslaught of imagery she witnessed and the shadowy hands that groped her. She shuddered again, making herself smaller in Lamina's arms. "No." She buried her face in his fur and closed her eye, trying to chase the images away into the far corners of her mind.

Ω

Across the grassy fields leading to The Mare, a young girl desperately ran, her bare feet covered in cuts and sores. Red lines like scratch marks trailed down both her cheeks and arms, a stark contrast to her pallid complexion.

Swooping past her, a large black bird descended upon Joseph's boat and he looked about in curiosity, eyes falling on the stumbling figure of the young girl. He was silent, noting her shoulder-length silver hair, unmistakable from afar. Blood wept from several scratches above and along the eyelid of her left eye which she kept closed, leaving only her right grey eye visible as she came to an eventual halt before Joseph.

181

He watched her double over, hands on her knees as she retched onto the grass, her breathing short and fast, intermingled with choking sobs. Joseph looked back over at the bird which deposited a collection of small round metals, stamped with the faces of familiar figures from across the ocean.

Pocketing the payment, Joseph cleared his throat, drawing the exhausted girl's attention. "Payment received. Hopping on, Miss—?" He paused, aware that she was not the brunette girl he had encountered almost a spell ago. They would be twins in appearance aside from the hair colour and that her left eye appeared to be intact behind the closed and slowly swelling eyelid.

'From the other, division and death.'

The girl wiped her mouth on her shirt sleeve, grey eye unfocused as she staggered into the boat and sat down, leaving room beside her for another. She glanced up at Joseph, face vacant of all emotion except pure fatigue. "Arche." The boat gently rocked with Joseph's rowing. "Just Arche."

Now in those days, there was a seer known throughout the land of
Paegaelai named Veirya, daughter of Zaehaylai, the Ashen Prophet. She
would guide humans and beasts over The Mare in her family's boat.
One looked favourably upon her and her family and no harm came to
Veirya even though those days were full of evil.

- Lines from *The Time of Exiles, Scriptura.* Translated by H. Van de Berg

15
4 ASD

"In your hearts, you know," Agnus said, carefully resting Simeon's head on
the floor, "that the girl I left in Magia means something to you." He rose to
his feet, dusting the bottom of his pants.

Around him, the scarlet shards he had touched had melted away into
pools of pure white liquid, shaking Mrs Maremortum out of her stunned
stupor. She had seen this before—the remains of E132, destroyed by Agnus'
blood—, a sample was retained for study in The Lost Languages.

Allowing his words to wash over her, Mrs Maremortum felt her stomach
drop. She shook her head, wrapping her arms around herself. "No." Her
voice was faint in her own ears.

Searching her face, Agnus gave a sad smile. "Dinah, she is the third."

His words that day haunted her, clinging to her when she travelled back
with her husband, both of them supporting an unconscious Simeon. Mr
Maremortum had wanted to continue fighting but Mrs Maremortum
dissuaded him, holding him back when Agnus departed.

It was a shaken and dishevelled trio that returned to Magia where Lachesis directed cadets to relieve them of Simeon and have him cared for.

"Mama, why couldn't you kill the doll?"

Lachesis peered closely at her mother, scarlet eyes piercing and scanning.

Mrs Maremortum fidgeted. Guilt rose like a coiled snake from the pit of her stomach, ready to strike her down. She had been told to kill Simeon's doll but found she couldn't. The what-ifs she had suppressed after leaving Agnus that day bubbled up to the surface and plagued her every train of thought.

What if—?

What if—?

Aware of her daughter's scrutinising gaze, Mrs Maremortum attempted to shake the stream of thoughts from her mind and feigned a smile. "I'm sorry sweetheart, I'm afraid I'm too tired to discuss this further."

Lachesis gave a slow nod, her eyes still fixed on Mrs Maremortum's face. "Get some rest."

Mrs Maremortum inclined her head in thanks and hurried away, her heart thumping in her chest.

5BSD

Mrs Maremortum stared listlessly from her window. Unblemished children filed along, carrying materials towards the damaged buildings around the tower of Lost Languages.

"Before I leave, there are letters for you."

Sighing, Mrs Maremortum turned, extending a hand to the Brigadier. Taking an envelope, the royal seal of the Avarosan sultana caught her eye and she tore it open, mouth pursed while her eyes scanned the letter within. It feigned concern for the wellbeing of Magia's people. But beneath this, the sultana wondered if Magia could be trusted to meet Tempus' continual demand for Resinn.

'Avarose would be honoured to gift you with aid for a price.'

The price being the knowledge on how to make their own functioning sun. Mrs Maremortum scowled and scrunched the letter up, tossing it aside.

"There are more from other leaders."

"I presume they're of the same variety." Mrs Maremortum massaged her temples. "I have too much on my plate to deal with this nonsense."

"Delaying a response can reflect weakness. Perhaps it is time to train up Lachesis to fulfil her role as Marshal."

Mrs Maremortum turned away. "No. She's not ready. I will reply to the leaders tonight and meet with The Conqueror later."

"Very well. Remember that protecting your child is not your priority in your role as leader of Magia."

Eyes dull, Mrs Maremortum glanced back at the Brigadier. "Yes. Just as serving me is not your priority."

The Brigadier's mouth twisted, her eyes gleaming angrily. "I serve you to the extent The Conqueror allows."

"And I appreciate that." There was a beat where Mrs Maremortum cleared her throat and The Brigadier's face settled back into its usual glare. "There is an urgent matter that I need you to handle. I know that dealing with the beastmasters is more Wayman's duty, but we lost so many blemished last spell...the world is not producing enough for us to meet E132 demands."

"I'll look into it." The Brigadier's eyes darkened. "We may have to make special requests."

"I've heard that Keira is moving in Liberia again. I would be careful of who you make special requests to."

"Her distractions benefit us. Liberia and Avarose may stop asking about the sun."

Inclining her head, Mrs Maremortum turned back to the window. "I really do appreciate you, Grüber," she murmured, mindlessly watching the unblemished slowly cement bricks into place.

"Will that be all, Oracle?"

Below the tower, Mrs Maremortum watched as an unblemished wordlessly directed the brick work. Their black collars were visible from this angle. She frowned. Being indebted to Tiamat and Avarose by extension was not a pleasant thought. Her mind returned to the sultana's letter.

"Oracle?"

Mrs Maremortum continued to stare at the work outside. "Grüber, do you think any of the leaders of Tempus are right?"

"About what?"

"In any of their stupid theories on how our world survived through The Stillness. How the world continued to turn despite the scientific impossibility."

Folding her arms over her chest, The Brigadier furrowed her brow. "You've denounced the theories as stupid. Why ask if they're right in the same breath?"

Sighing, Mrs Maremortum turned, wringing her hands. "I could never understand how Kaishi knew her artificial sun would work," she said, shaking her head. "Where did she get the idea from?"

The Brigadier raised an eyebrow. "Didn't she say that it was from a well-known lullaby in her country?"

"That's more preposterous than the theories I've heard the other leaders espouse," Mrs Maremortum grumbled, rubbing her head again.

"Those were her words," replied The Brigadier with a shrug. "Besides, all credit for the creation of the artificial sun should go to our lead scientists of the project. And as long as the artificial sun works and the world continues, what does it matter?"

Mrs Maremortum nodded, a thoughtful expression on her face. "You're right. I'm sorry to have bothered you," she murmured, turning back to the window. "That will be all for today, Grüber."

Saluting, the Brigadier left the remaining envelopes on a table near the doorway and slipped out of the room, letting the door click shut behind her.

Lost in her own thoughts, Mrs Maremortum failed to notice the door open again.

"Dinah?"

Mrs Maremortum heaved a long sigh.

"Dinah, you can't truly believe what he said?" Mr Maremortum's arms coiled around his wife's waist from behind. He rested his chin on her shoulder. "You're letting him get to you just because he knew about the other one?"

Mrs Maremortum shook him off, whirling about to face him. "And you just think it's a coincidence that the doll looks *exactly* like Arche?" she cried in amazement, her lips pressed into a thin line. She wrapped her arms around her body as if to brace herself from a sudden chill. "And I tried to kill her! What if she really is—?"

Her words broke off when Mr Maremortum took her hands in both of his, squeezing gently. "Please," he murmured. "Please, you know what she is."

"I know what she was meant to be!"

"You didn't feel like this before Agnus said that nonsense!"

Ripping her hands away from his, Mrs Maremortum levelled a tear-filled glare at her husband. "Because I didn't know the truth!"

Mr Maremortum heaved a sigh of exasperation and ran his hand roughly through his hair.

A small sob escaped Mrs Maremortum's lips, "And now Arche is gone!" Head sinking into her hands, her body shook with her cries.

"Sweetheart." Mr Maremortum's eyes began to glisten. "I promise you that we will find her. In the meantime, Lachesis will attend the coming of age ceremony for the both of them." He edged towards her, arms hovering around her trembling frame.

Peeking up from her hands with her face twisted in agony, Mrs Maremortum flung herself into his arms and wept. "I'm sorry."

Mr Maremortum held her tightly, his hand moving soothingly against her head. "We have to finish making preparations here," he murmured, "so, I need you to be ready to help. We have to make sure we're ready for when Agnus attacks us." He pulled back to cup his wife's face in his hands, his eyes unable to see the trepidation in hers. "This is part of finding Arche, I promise you. From the lips of Daniel Sominium himself. So please, trust in me, my love." He ran the pads of his thumbs in circular motions on her cheeks.

Lowering her gaze, Mrs Maremortum nodded against his hands and sank back into his arms.

"When Simeon is back in Magia with some semblance of sanity, we'll be able to do so much more. Just hold on a bit longer." Mr Maremortum pressed his lips against the top of her head.

Laying her cheek against his chest, Mrs Maremortum allowed her thoughts to wander to Arche and then eventually to a girl who had escaped the clutches of Colonel Simeon and Magia.

Gathered around the table, Agnus, Lamina and Adam sang a rousing rendition of a Gershomite "Happy Birthday" song to a very rosy-faced Terra.

"Thank you." She smiled, heart full. "I didn't think I would ever enjoy growing up."

There was an exchanging of hugs and gifts; a delightful pair of cream sandals from Adam, a book on the alphabet that Lamina promised to walk her through and a silver sword left by Shigure. The latter had a note attached to it reading: *To my pitiful student.* Adam had to catch the sheathed sword when Terra tried to toss it out the window.

Agnus smiled broadly as he watched Terra excitedly receive her gifts. "My child," he began, drawing everyone's attention. "My gift to you will be given after you return from the coming of age ceremony, next week."

A lull fell over the group and Terra slowly nodded, chewing her bottom lip. "Can I avoid going to the ceremony? I haven't served under a master since I left Magia." She glanced up at Agnus, hopeful. Her stomach dropped when he shook his head.

"The purpose of the ceremony is not just for securing Libertas."

"But Agnus, it can be circumvented by paying the large fine associated with it," said Lamina, grim-faced. "I know that's how the people of Manna have been able to keep their children here. You have been covering their fines."

Terra recalled Talia's words when she had shown them around the cavern.

Agnus' looked suddenly tired and worn. "I will not do this for Terra. She must attend the coming of age ceremony as the next step in bringing about Magia's downfall."

Lamina nodded in muted agreement and Terra, wary of Agnus' sudden fatigue, spoke up: "What do you want me to do?"

Grimacing, Agnus held her gaze. "At the ceremony, when they ask you where you intend to settle, you must answer in Magia."

"Agnus, what?" barked Lamina, his expression darkening.

Terra stared, stunned. Shadowy claws inched across her, grasping her heart and filling her with dread and doubt. Why would he even suggest this? How could she ever return to that hateful place?

"You will tell them that you will claim your right to the title of Marshal of Magia."

Growling, Lamina shook his mane in furious disbelief. "What are you suggesting, Agnus? To do that is for her to claim to be a Maremortum!"

"And it is what she must do!" exclaimed Agnus sharply, his expression pained. Taking a breath to steady himself, he turned to Adam. "Adam, you will attend as her master."

Knees banging against the table, Lamina stood, towering over Agnus. "Why won't you go, Agnus? Why must Adam act as her master? And will The Conqueror even approve of such a claim by her? You know what he will do if he doesn't approve!" Lamina's voice broke in frustration and desperation.

"I will remain," continued Agnus, without addressing Lamina, "and negotiate with Gershom to secure provisions for the upcoming battle with Magia."

Lamina slammed his hands onto the table. "Agnus!"

Agnus turned pointedly to the old ox, lips pressed firmly together. "My friend, do you not trust me? There are things that must happen even if they cause you discomfort."

"You're letting these two walk directly into the hands of The Conqueror!"

Biting her lip, Terra reached over and patted Lamina's trembling arm. Her body and her head felt disconnected, as though she were peering into a life that were not her own. "It's okay Mr Lamina, Adam will look after me." Her voice was thinner and shakier than she hoped. She peered over at Adam who quickly nodded. "We will be okay."

Fist clenched, Lamina breathed deeply and ran a shaky hand through his mane of hair. "I'm sorry, Agnus. I…shouldn't be doubting…" He sat back down on the ground and gripped the sides of his bowed head, sinking into silence.

In the depths of her being, Terra felt sick to her stomach and found herself questioning both Agnus and herself. Why was he entrusting this task to her? That question she could answer logically if she was a Maremortum but she could not reconcile the paralysing terror that gripped her at the very thought of returning to Magia. Had Agnus forgotten all the suffering she endured there? Why would he ask her to do this when he could spare her from it? Was she even strong enough to go through this?

These thoughts plagued her as she sank into a fitful sleep that night.

In the second sun up hour, on the day of the coming of age ceremony, Adam helped Terra adjust a plain cornflower blue dress that she had purchased long ago at Mathelda's clothing store. He pinned some yellow azaleas to the dress—flowers he had specifically picked for Terra during the last sun down hour in Taliph. Taking her shoulder-length hair into his hands, he carefully pinned up the silver locks into a chignon and slid white myrtle, like a patch of stars, into her hair.

"Thank you," Terra said tonelessly. She touched the azaleas hesitantly, uncertainty consuming her.

Studying her briefly, Adam opened his mouth to say something when the door clicked open.

"I'm sorry that you two must journey alone." Agnus stepped into the room, followed by an unhappy Lamina.

Adam gave a weak smile. "Agnus, I promise that I will protect her with my life."

Expression tender, Agnus approached the pair and held his hand out to Adam. "These are the annual tithings for Manna." In his hand sat multiple vials of red fluid.

Adam, who Terra always believed to be almost unflappable, began to tremble. "Agnus." Adam's face screwed up in pain. "Must you give your blood?"

Agnus closed Adam's fingers over the vials and gave a tight smile. "Yes."

Nodding morosely, Adam pocketed the vials.

Turning to Terra, Agnus placed a hand on her shoulder and she raised her eye to both of his. "My child, stay strong. Remember to claim your right to Marshal of Magia."

"Will this even make a difference?" she asked, unable to mask the bitterness in her voice.

Cupping her cheek with his other hand, Agnus smiled apologetically. "Yes, my child. We cannot allow Sominium to intervene with the fall of Magia. Should The Conqueror agree with your claim, Magia will not be allowed to seek aid." He spoke in hushed, reassuring tones and Terra felt her spirit rally a little. Until she looked into his eyes and watched them grow misty, a lump gathering in her throat.

Laying her hand on his, she mirrored his smile. "I'll do my best," she murmured, heart still heavy.

Sliding her feet into the cream sandals Adam had gifted her, Terra braved another smile. She exchanged farewells with both Agnus and Lamina, the both of them hugging her tightly. Then, they parted ways, heading towards the stairway that led to the surface.

At the foot of the stairs, a couple of familiar faces, including Talia, Nicholo and Cecilia wished them well.

Talia clasped Terra's hand tightly. "We will pray for your safe return, Ridley."

With a troubled heart, Terra thanked them all and left.

Nicholo watched the two young adults disappear up the winding stairs and when their footsteps faded away, he turned, nodding to Agnus who slowly approached.

"Nicholo," greeted Agnus, expression grave. "Gather the people of Manna. I wish to share some news with them."

Trudging through the seemingly endless fields of grass, Terra wiped the sweat from her brow, the muggy weather causing her dress to stick unpleasantly to her skin.

They silently plodded past a replica of the Lost Languages that stood far in the distance to the east. On the odd occasion, Adam would make a passing remark about the places they were travelling past which Terra would impassively listen to. Otherwise, the squawk of a bird and the trickle of a stream were some of the few things that broke the still air between the two.

When the small dot that was Sominium to the north gradually grew on the horizon, a suffocating realisation dawned on Terra and doubt gnawed away at her mind. Legs wobbling beneath her, her feet dragged to a halt, unable to budge.

"Adam."

The young man spun around, white eyebrow arched quizzically.

Terra blinked rapidly, lower lip quivering and eye resting on the floor. "I don't think...I don't think I can do this," she quavered in an unusually high voice, wringing her hands. "Why does Agnus keep choosing me for these things? I'm not good at this." Taking a deep shuddering breath, Terra buried her head in her hands, her heart unbearably heavy. "I don't even want to be here!"

Firm, yet gentle, hands gripped her shoulders and Terra looked up at Adam before quickly averting her eye, unnerved by the intense emotions in both of his. "Miss Ridley, you're right. You aren't one for confrontation."

Terra's heart sank.

Adam gently squeezed her shoulders, prompting her to glance at him, her stomach in knots. "But you're wrong if you believe that you're not the right person for this. Agnus chose you. Not because you can do this on your own. But because you'll trust him, even as you struggle."

'It's precisely that reason that you were chosen. There's nothing wonderful or remarkable that you've done to be here. And that makes what you do all the more important.'

The vice-grip on Terra's heart loosened and she nodded in appreciation, lightly touching Adam's hands. She had learnt so much from Spiritus and the people around her who also believed in Agnus. Her gratitude swelled at the idea of her making a difference in the world of Tempus. And she held onto this idea, a numbing calm falling over her. It made the nightmares of Magia more bearable if she were making a real impact.

They continued their journey towards Sominium, this time with light banter and a warm conversation.

Small white stone walls wound all the way through the pearl-coloured town, delineating the public pathway and residential districts. At the very centre of this pristine city rose a palatial building, standing high above everything, grand in both size and beauty. It appeared to be carved out of white stone similar to that used throughout the town, with finely chiselled columns that was reminiscent of those in Initium. This was all topped by its ornate gold-painted rooftop that shimmered in the light of the artificial sun.

Terra's eye was instantly drawn to this building, glittering like a jewel in the heart of the town of Sominium, its outer walls lit by the hanging oil lanterns that shone like gems in their own right.

The town was abuzz with the throngs of travellers wandering about the city all dressed in varying styles, some that Terra recognised as being local to Railesson and others in colourful and distinctive garbs. A young woman slunk past, tailing an older man, both in fine looking robes stamped with pink flowers against a blue fabric. Her wooden sandals clopped loudly along the paved pathway.

A horse-drawn carriage rolled past and Terra peeked through the mauve curtained-windows. There were beautiful olive-skinned people adorned with an array of colourful jewellery on their necks, ears and pierced into their faces.

Recalling Shigure's words on how vast the world was, Terra continued to turn her head this way and that, admiring the differences and similarities between her and those that appeared to be in Sominium for the ceremony.

She wondered what their stories were; what hardships had they faced to be here?

A tall young man with a hooked nose strolled ahead with his guardian hollering at him, attempting to keep up with a cane.

In a fine suit, further along the pavement, a young man stopped to order some snacks, eliciting loud grumps of disapproval from the muscular older man tailing him.

All along the path to the Sominium temple—what Adam called it, instead of a palace—, Terra reflected on her life. She wondered what the likes of 08387 and 08385 would have made of such a lavish place. The world was not as dark and dank as the metallic-smelling mines they spent hours working in. She tilted her head back, soaking in the light warmth of the artificial sun and gave thanks with every fibre of her being for her life. The good and the bad. Even as she shook at the very thought of the ceremony, there was a sense of purposeful peace.

While all these thoughts filled Terra's mind, moving her to tears, the pair soon found themselves at the foot of a long flight of stone steps. They paused briefly while Adam quickly massaged his temples, mumbling about how loud the thoughts were.

As they climbed the stairs, she realised that these too were similar to those in Initium.

The tall wooden double doors stood wide open and, following the crowd, the two passed through, taking note of the lines forming to pass by five different marble desks, each with an armed attendant seated.

Adam wordlessly slipped into a queue and Terra followed suit, casting her eye around. At the desk on the other side of the foyer, a blonde-haired lady listened to the hooked-nose young man standing before her, bored. She held up a device, a sliver of red embedded in its surface catching the lights from above as she hovered it over the man and the E132 assumed a soft green hue.

In the shadowy corners of the foyer, there stood armed guards dressed in bright white uniforms, surveying the crowd.

Sidling closer to Adam, Terra gingerly touched the back of his hand with her own. "What are these lines for?"

"Registrations. They run checks before we can meet The Conqueror and his advisors. They personally assess each new adult." He leaned closer and lowered his voice. "It's part of them keeping a record on everyone in Tempus."

A hush fell over the two as they neared the front of the line and Terra took note of the man serving at the desk in front. He had a well-kept moustache which complemented the rest of his tidy appearance despite the lack of hair on the top of his head.

They came to an eventual stop in front of him and, without even looking up from the parchment he was busily scrawling on, he grunted, "Name?"

Shifting forward, Adam dipped down and lowered his voice to a whisper, "Adam Railesson."

The man's head snapped up to peer closely at Adam. A leering grin crept across his face. "Railesson? Blood that's worth bottling!"

Adam merely nodded and motioned to Terra. "And this is my slave girl—"

"Ridley." Terra rustled forward in her dress. "Ridley Maremortum."

The man's head snapped towards Terra this time. His unsavoury look up and down her slender frame made Terra's skin crawl. "A Railesson *and* a Maremortum? Kings of Old have gathered." He bowed in an exaggerated and mocking manner. "Never knew the Maremortums had a third!" The man sneered, eyes narrowed at Terra. "Or should I inform Levi and Dinah that their oldest has escaped Nyx to masquerade as some relative?"

Terra gulped, lowering her eye.

Cackling, the man returned to the parchment on the desk, scrawling their names onto the list. "No one can deny the silver hair and grey eye. Given that, I won't comment on your blemished status, *Ridley*." He jabbed his stubby finger towards Terra's eye-patch.

Twitching nervously, Terra murmured a thank you, eliciting a derisive snort from the man.

He held up the same device Terra saw the blonde lady use and she watched as he quickly hovered it over the both of them. The speck of glowing green on its surface returned to scarlet. "No weapons. Good. Head in and find the curtained door with your number. Your *master* will be questioned separately. Welcome to the old Ben'min temple," he jeered, tossing a numbered card at Terra. He jerked his head to the right, motioning for them to head in.

The two stepped into a room that had been outfitted with makeshift square tents that lined the sides of the room, forming a small hallway which eventually led down to a gilded doorway. The front of each tent bore a heavy felt curtain, each numbered from one to twenty.

Terra nervously glanced down at the four in her hand and looked around, trying to swallow down the ball of anxiety caught in her throat.

"What a jerk," Adam growled under his breath, glaring back at the doorway they had stepped through. Shaking his head, Adam lightly touched Terra's arm. "In the tent, a beastmaster will examine you. Don't worry, they have more honour than most humans."

Head jerking in his direction in consternation, Terra had no time to speak as the number four curtain parted momentarily and another young woman with dark curly hair exited and passed her. Forcing back all her questions, Terra stumbled into the candlelit tent.

"You are in your 13th spell, is that correct?"

Holding back a scream, Terra stood rigidly against the tent wall, eye wide. "Yes!" she squeaked, unable to tear her eye from the humanoid in front of her.

It stood on two scaly hind legs with a thickset golden-brown body, each scale that was lit by the candlelight shimmered. Large, pointy teeth sat in a powerful set of jaws that tapered out into a snout. And set into its face were large golden orbs for eyes that blinked twice as they studied Terra. At its feet, a thick tail thumped impatiently.

A lizard man, Terra thought, attempting to rationalise the situation. *A beast like Mr Lamina.* The idea soothed her whirring mind a little.

The beast arched the hairless scaled muscle above its eye before returning to the parchment in his hand, ink pen running along it. "What is going to happen is a standard medical check up." He sighed, placing the parchment on a small desk in the corner near him before approaching Terra. He stopped in his tracks, eyes narrowing at the sight of the eye-patch but the shine of her silver hair in the candlelight drew his gaze and his mouth opened in a loud "ah". "Miss Arche Maremortum, please do excuse my behaviour," he murmured with a reserved bow.

Almost forgetting herself, Terra opened her mouth to protest but she quickly shook her head. "N-no, please excuse *me*. I forgot myself as I've never met a...um..."

"Liv'yatan," provided the beast as he began to take her measurements. "The beast descendants of dragons."

"Yes! And I am so honoured and pleased to have made your acquaintance." Terra obediently said "ahh" when prompted to. "May I know your name?"

Again, the bulging muscle above the beast's eye quirked. "Sarkany." He then instructed her to keep her eye open which he examined with an unusual contraption fitted with several lenses and gears. Once satisfied, he scrawled several notes on his parchment. Grabbing her arms to check them, Terra briefly thought about how relieved she was that her left arm had begun to gain a healthy hue when her hair had started turning silver.

The examination continued in relative silence, with an occasional question from Terra that was cut short with terse answers.

"Miss Maremortum, I'm not accustomed to being interrogated while conducting a health check," came Sarkany's response when Terra asked if all beastmasters were Liv'yatan.

"I'm sorry, Sarkany! I'm just…I don't know enough about the world," Terra confessed, bowing her head apologetically. She bit her lip and wordlessly obeyed any other request from Sarkany before he straightened and returned to his side of the tent.

"You are in a good and healthy shape. Aside from your blemish, which was recorded during the incident in Nyx, and a number of unusual bruises—I assume are from…private hobbies—"

Terra scowled, making a mental note to scold her teacher later.

"—you are doing well." He sighed and turned back to her, baring his teeth in what Terra hoped was a smile. "I apologise for my curtness, Miss Maremortum, but I must be businesslike today. Perhaps, we can become better acquainted another time."

Terra's eye brightened and she nodded, a small smile playing on her lips. "Thank you, Sarkany."

The Liv'yatan's eyes seemed to darken, his voice lowering. "You are now free to see The Conqueror."

With a stiff nod, Terra bowed out of the tent to find Adam awaiting her, and the nerves that had gripped her earlier took hold again. The way Sarkany had ushered her out to meet The Conqueror left her stomach in anxious knots.

Terra clutched her necklace, silently praying that her hands would stop shaking. Her legs felt weak beneath her as she awkwardly shuffled towards the gilded doorway, lagging behind Adam.

She stopped, closing her eye and praying under her breath as her heart hammered in her chest. The hum of the crowd around her did nothing to drown out the blood pounding in her ears. Despite this, she straightened her back and lifted her chin.

Realising he had left her behind, Adam returned with his hand outstretched to her. She stepped forward and felt his arm wrap around her trembling shoulders, her cheeks warming with his touch. He wordlessly squeezed her shoulder, keeping her close while guiding her over the threshold. Terra focused on the comforting warmth of Adam's arm as he steered them into the grand hall, following the swarm of bodies.

The gleam of golden chandeliers dazzled Terra, their numerous candles like jewels from where she stood on the marbled floor. Glad for Adam's arm around her, Terra gaped at the detailed painting that covered the entire ceiling. What it depicted, she could not tell, but it illustrated countless scenes that brought an idea to mind—a people, blessed by their Creator.

A people, she recounted mentally as if by reflex, *cursed by the wine of the Other.*

A young woman's dress snagged under Terra's foot and she staggered much to Terra's embarrassment. After apologising profusely, Terra settled on casting her eye around the room to watch her footing.

There was a sumptuous air of extravagance wherever she turned her head; magnificent and colourful artworks lined the walls, columns embellished with gilded patterns and intricately detailed marble statues of creatures and humans.

However, these sights that delighted Terra were checked with a darkness that drew her back to her senses. All along the long sides of the hall, armed guards in white uniforms were intermittently stationed and after a quick glance around the room, Terra noted how they carefully watched everyone, their hands casually positioned near the scabbards in their belts.

At the very end of the hall stood an imposing throne, positioned between two elegant columns rising into a lowered sculpted ceiling around the elevated throne vestibule. Up six steps of cedar wood, each adorned with polished wooden carvings of lions on either side, the white-haired and jade-eyed Conqueror sat upon the golden throne. The top of the throne was decorated with several wings and countless eyes. At his feet, two carved lions sat proudly on both sides. A white cloth was draped as a backdrop with intricate golden embroidery that Terra could not make out from where she stood. But in large sloping letters across it were the words 'ACCIPERE COR'.

Beside the throne stood two men: one with ebony hair and matching clothing, who leaned heavily against the right column, his eyes drooping as if in sleep, and the other was a familiar figure dressed in a deep rouge double-breasted coat. This man stood with squared shoulders and arms behind his back, his grey hair slicked back into a neat ponytail.

His dark, slanted eyes briefly met Terra's and the young woman noted the sparkle in them before he turned his gaze to the other side of the room, a smirk pulling at his lips.

Following her teacher's gaze, Terra met the piercing scarlet eyes of another young woman of similar stature and silver hair. A shiver zipped down Terra's spine and she involuntarily took a step back toward Adam. She was glad to turn to him instead, the tips of their noses inches apart as she whispered an apology, her heart skipping at their closeness.

Terra forced her attention back around the room—this time avoiding eye contact with the scarlet-eyed woman—and noted that the room was still larger than the number of people occupying it at that moment, even though she was certain there was at least 200 people.

The way that Shigure had spoken about the world to her, she imagined it to be vast and filled with a great number of people. Then why were there so few people of age here today?

Trumpets blared at the foot of the cedar steps and a hush fell over the crowd as they all turned towards the hooded figures who lowered the instruments. The man from the desk with the leering grin and well-kept moustache strode out in front of the trumpeters, holding sheafs of parchment and a pen.

"My Lord Conqueror. I present before you, 214 young adults from across Tempus," he bellowed, eyes gleaming as he addressed the figure upon the throne. "The break-up is as follows: 32 Railessonians, 67 Gershomites, 18 Liberians, 26 Tohi Ofans, 52 Kiryuuans, 19 Avarosans.

"Upon the announcement of your name, please step forward, allow for The Conqueror and his advisers to consider you and then announce your place of settlement and intentions for approval. Guardians and slave owners, please step back."

The sudden cold caused Terra to look up at Adam as he stepped away from her, a small smile of reassurance pulling at his lips.

From where she stood, Lachesis quivered with disgust. She bit her lip and continued to keep her distance from the silver and white-haired pair.

The man began to read the long list of names one by one and each time a young adult in their 13th spell would wordlessly step forward, awaiting the dismissive nod of The Conqueror in order to speak. At times, the young adults would be asked to turn slowly on the spot with the advisers whispering to each other. The whole ordeal made Terra uncomfortable.

"I will be settling in Liberia, to pursue further research in Old World technologies," declared a young woman named Camila Perez.

"Denied." The Conqueror gestured to Shigure beside him.

Shigure cleared his throat. "We already have enough people working in Old World technologies and we strongly encourage the growth of New World technologies instead."

Camila clutched handfuls of her gown and Terra could hear the tremor in her voice as she retorted, "No, I have no interest in New World technology."

Terra clasped her hands together, heart hammering in her chest and heat rising up her neck. She wanted to tell Camila to stop. She could almost feel the rest of the room pull away from this young woman with the air growing heavier.

But the young woman continued, insistent, "I will not take part in this technology that is decreasing bir—"

In the blink of an eye, Shigure bounded down the cedar steps and before Camila had time to react, he unsheathed his sword, beheading her in one fluid motion.

Flinching, Terra watched in horror as two of the hooded trumpeters shot forward and picked up her small headless body. They heaved it out of the room, blood gushing all over the patterned floor. Another hooded figure scooped up her head, her face forever twisted in slow realisation, while several others swarmed around the blood, mopping it up.

Yet there had been no screams from around the room—a willing and silent acceptance.

Terra squeezed her eye shut, gathering her resolve again, her blood thumping loudly in her ears.

"Sione Ngaue," the moustached man announced as if nothing had happened.

As Shigure cleaned his sword on a handkerchief, a tall, dark-skinned young man lumbered forward. Despite his broad frame, he stood in a mild manner, his hands together and head bowed.

"Chin up," barked Shigure, passing Sione and ascending the cedar steps.

Sione raised his chin, his eyes nervously meeting The Conqueror's and he swallowed thickly.

The Conqueror's eyes flitted up and down the man's body, narrowing on the size of his hands and shoulders. He asked the man to spin around before nodding lazily.

"My lord, I wish to settle in Tohi Ofa to help build up the land of my people."

"Denied," came The Conqueror's unhesitant response, causing a shiver to ripple through the room. "You will serve under me and train as a Sominium guard."

There was a pause where Sione lowered his head and Terra's heart ached at the sight of him blinking back tears. He clenched his fists, eyes fixed on the ground.

The Conqueror uncrossed his legs and leaned forward, his voice dangerously soft, "Did you hear me, Sione?"

Lifting his eyes back up to the throne, Sione nodded meekly. "Yes, my lord. I would be honoured to serve the Sominium throne." He bowed deeply and slowly moved back towards the grey-haired old man he had arrived with. They shared a wordless embrace. Silent tears slid down the old man's cheeks.

"Jonathan Woodbridge."

With a few dainty steps forward, a scrawny young man with hollowed out cheeks stood before everyone. He ran a nervous tongue over his cracked lips and his patchy suit jacket hung awkwardly on his too-small frame.

On the right hand side of the throne, the sleepy ebony-haired man pushed himself off the ornate column, his heavy-lidded eyes roaming over the young man's figure. "You're too thin." He crinkled his nose, mouth stretched thin like he had tasted something sour. "Master's name?"

The man with the parchments hurriedly ran his finger down the page in response. "Karl Moseley!"

A sallow-skinned man almost as thin as the boy bumbled forward, terror etched into the lines on his gaunt face. He dropped to his knees, his body shaking uncontrollably. "My lord, have mercy on me! I have not been able to feed myself let alone the boy!" wailed the man, prostrating himself before the crowd.

"This is a serious breach of the Charter of Protection," hissed the man with the heavy-lidded eyes, his reedy voice echoing about the still room. His feet thumped heavily against the steps as he descended them. "The Charter requires you to raise a healthy and robust unblemished."

Karl raised his head, tears streaming down his face. "Yes, I know, my lord, but—"

Reaching the bottom of the steps, the man with the heavy-lidded eyes snapped his fingers, his gaze fixed on Karl's wavering one. "Any children?" he demanded, prompting the rapid shuffling and flicking of parchment by the blonde-haired lady that Terra had seen manning one of the registration desks.

"No children of his own since 7BSD," chimed the blonde gleefully, peering over the parchments to beam in wicked delight.

"The beastmasters have blacklisted his entire family's name in the register during the health check," came the voice of a goggled man with parchments, however he referred to the face of a device connected to a chunk of E132 that sat on the top like a glowing green beacon.

A loud sigh escaped The Conqueror's lips.

"My lord, have mercy on me!" Saliva and snot dribbled down Karl's chin as he sobbed.

The Conqueror recrossed his legs and folded his arms over his chest, his face emotionless. "You purchased this adult as a child with an understanding of our law." His jade eyes narrowed. "Denied."

The man with the heavy-lidded eyes glanced over his shoulder. "Shigure."

Shigure drew his sword and as he made his way down the steps, Karl scrambled to his feet and began to run through the crowd, pushing through the motionless bodies of both slaves and masters who all turned their faces away from him as he passed by.

The wall of soldiers that had lined the great hall marched forward, encircling the crowd with their silver swords drawn.

The previously immovable crowd parted quickly for Shigure who paced through them with ease while they blocked off Karl who turned to face his pursuer and fell to the floor, cowering. "My lord!" he shrieked, raising his hands defensively.

Sword sailing through the air, Shigure sliced Karl's hands off and turned his wrist, bringing the blade back around to cut cleanly through Karl's neck, sending his head tumbling at the feet of the stricken crowd members who had barred his exit.

"Breaching the Libertas law is a grave offense," stated The Conqueror. "Let none of you forget this."

Feeling as though her mind had left her body, Terra internally screamed at herself to stop shaking, her breathing uneven and ragged. She could not bear to look up as more hooded people brushed past her to collect Karl Moseley's body parts. How could she reconcile in her mind that her teacher was ruthlessly murdering these people; was this really the same person who eagerly told her about the vastness of the world? How was this man so obedient to Agnus and yet capable of such cold-blooded actions?

'Don't put your hope in men.'

Shigure's words shook her out of her daze and Terra took a deep steadying breath.

Countless more names were announced, with the occasional beheading and Terra still found herself shaken to the core every time Shigure cut someone down. The room had grown deathly quiet by the time a familiar family name was called.

"Lachesis Maremortum."

Sweeping forward, Lachesis curtsied to the white-haired figure on the throne, her long silver hair falling about her face like a curtain. Glancing up, she smiled as The Conqueror nodded.

"I, Lachesis Maremortum will settle in Magia and I intend to fully claim mine and my sister Arche's position as Marshal of Magia."

The Conqueror waved in approval almost before her last word left her mouth. Pleased, Lachesis gave a deep curtsy before reclaiming her spot within the crowd.

Gulping nervously, Terra quickly looked away from her in case their eyes met again.

The man with the sheafs of parchment cleared his throat, simpering derisively. "Ridley Maremortum."

There was a flurry of movement with heads turning to look at Terra who took a few unsteady steps forward, stiffly bowing. She could feel all eyes in the room boring into her, devouring every inch of her flesh. Sweat dewed on her upper lip. For a moment, she forgot herself, her mind blank. Swallowing hard, she wished she could force down the anxiety surging up her throat.

Slight movement from the throne drew her eye and Terra glanced up to see The Conqueror shift in his seat. "Turn around."

Quickly spinning, Terra caught herself before she tripped from her sudden dizziness, her skin continuing to crawl from the gazes of the entire room.

The Conqueror cleared his throat. "Turn around, *slowly*."

Face flushed, a humiliated Terra wordlessly turned around, this time in a languid fashion. Her chest was tightening and Terra closed her eye, mentally praying for courage and strength.

Opening her eye, she nervously looked up at The Conqueror who was scrutinising her, his face unreadable. He gave a slight nod. Her eye then darted to Shigure who was watching her intently, his eyes filled with amusement. A wide challenging smirk split his face.

I want to punch his face.

Taking a deep breath, Terra looked up at The Conqueror, eye blazing. "I am a Maremortum." Terra's voice rang through the hall. "I will settle in Magia and claim my right to the Marshal title of Magia."

Stunned silence was followed by a ripple of murmurs amongst the new adults and their masters.

"Is she really a Maremortum?" a new adult near her whispered. "Is this Arche or Agnus' Curse?" asked an older adult in a low tone.

Clenching her fist, Terra lifted her chin higher, defiant eye fixed on The Conqueror. The chorus of voices around her seem to swell. Rather than quell them, the Sominiums watched on silently as if amused and Shigure grinned smugly.

The Conqueror evenly returned Terra's gaze, the corner of his mouth twitching up. "Very well, Agnus," he muttered under his breath. "Very well!" he repeated more loudly after a beat, his booming voice hushing the room. "You have my blessing to do so. The Sominium throne will not interfere in a war between the Maremortums and will not tolerate others doing so."

Heels clattering on the ground, Lachesis rushed forward, face red and contorted with fury. "My lord! This would be a declaration of war!"

"You have had your moment to speak, Lachesis," warned the man with the heavy-lidded eyes.

"But she is not a legitimate heir!"

Raising his hand in a silencing gesture, The Conqueror narrowed his eyes at Lachesis and she immediately fell silent, stepping back into the crowd when his cold stare remained fixed on her. Turning back to Terra, The Conqueror smiled and leaned forward in his seat. "I wonder how a bout between sisters shall end? Shall the older who refuses to use her true name be victor, or the younger and more doted upon finally crush all her obstacles?"

With a smirk, The Conqueror nodded, waving her away. He shot a pointed look at the man with the parchments who hurried to read the next name out amidst the urgent whispers of "Arche" and "war" in the crowd.

With a shaky bow, Terra stepped back into the crowd, heart thumping in her ears. She reached back and found Adam's hand and realised the sweatiness of her own. Despite that, she felt him gently squeeze her hand as if to say 'well done'.

"A time will come when my voice will no longer be heard. A time when the vineyards of the Other will flourish. A time where your children will be trampled, and your joy stolen from you."
- Lines from *Seers of Paegaelai, Scriptura.* Translated by C. Yelnorin

16

When the man with the well-kept moustache called out the final name on the list and his settlement and intention were approved, he passed the sheafs of parchment to the blonde lady behind him. "Those of you who remain have been counted and approved!" he exclaimed with disturbing satisfaction.

A succession of trumpeting and cheering from the people gathered at the foot of the throne ensued as the final pools of blood were mopped off the floor.

Terra felt a sickening hollowness at the pit of her stomach.

"Very soon, we will invite you to dine and dance to your heart's content! This is a celebration after all!" he shouted as, on cue, dozens of hooded figures swept into the room, carrying tables and cloth which they quickly set up in neat rows. These figures rotated out as new hooded figures marched in, trays of delicacies balanced on fingertips and delivered neatly until each cloth-covered table was filled.

"But before then," continued the man with the well-kept moustache, "The Conqueror will officially welcome you to adulthood and Libertas!" He slapped his hands together wildly, stepping aside as the Conqueror rose from the throne.

Looking out at the silent crowd below him, The Conqueror smiled mirthlessly, his eyes steely. "It is a privilege to live," he declared, folding his arms behind his back. "Because of this, those who have the ability to must seize it when they can. Such people are then responsible for the weak."

There was a round of insistent applause from the hooded figures and the desk people, prompting the crowd of surviving owners and new adults to weakly clap along.

"There is no meaning in any talk without action," continued The Conqueror, his words drawn out and the scattered applause stopping, "There is no value in power if you do not make good use of it. We live in a time of great need. A need in which you can play a role in resolving. Our world, as we know it, is dying."

The Conqueror paused, allowing the words to hang over the heads of everyone in attendance. "It is dying a slow and laborious death supposedly because of a prophecy long ago from an outdated text known to some as Scriptura."

Terra felt a tangled surge of discomfort and fury swirl up from her gut.

Placing a solemn hand on his heart, The Conqueror's eyes roamed over the crowd. "My family once believed in the shallow values of this morality book. For generations, my family denied the power of E132, Resinn, Runonami—whatever else the beloved scarlet jewel of our world is called. For generations, we denounced the one thing that could save our world—we insisted that E132 was evil and destructive. But that nonsense stopped with me."

Earnest cheers and enthusiastic applause followed these words but the Conqueror pressed on, building momentum:

"The New World thrives on the power of the sacred scarlet jewel. We will be the change that this world needs. We will be the ones to take history into our hands and correct it!"

The thunderous applause that filled the great hall stirred an emotion within Terra that she did not think she had. She hated what she was hearing. She hated the shouts of agreement. Glancing surreptitiously about herself, Terra had the sinking realisation that she was possibly the only adult to have survived the horrors of the Magian mines. Tears sprang into her eye, yet the Conqueror continued his rousing speech, undeterred.

"But we do not turn away our brothers or sisters who continue to cling to the values of the Old World. No, we will patiently teach them and point them towards the glorious New World. A world in which we can save Tempus. And the first step towards salvation is to be fruitful. Children are the future of production. They will be the footing to a healing world. And this healing all begins with you.

"So take heart—accipere cor. You are the reason that our world continues to live. You are the heartbeat that drives Tempus. The law of Libertas is the recognition of that. So take heart, for we will return this world to its former glory. And I am with you always." The Conqueror spread his arms wide in a welcoming embrace, his jade-coloured eyes glittering with delight and a softness that Terra instinctively reasoned he was not actually capable of.

She shuddered involuntarily but hurriedly joined in the deafening applause, her heart aching in discomfort. Peeking over at Adam, she saw him unmoving, his face stony as he studied the Conqueror. A sense of awe and disgust with herself surfaced and she folded her hands over her chest, embarrassed.

"At the conclusion of the banquet, Pyrrhus will provide directions to the ports and caravans appropriate to each intended country of settlement. So please, stay and eat your fill. For tomorrow, you will continue the great work of healing our world."

At this, the man with the well-kept moustache bowed deeply. As the Conqueror reclaimed his seat, Pyrrhus ushered people towards the tables at the other side of the room, away from the throne.

Both Adam and Terra silently followed the crowd of people with Terra unable to meet Adam's concerned gaze as she fought back the maelstrom of emotions within her and the whispers of "Arche Maremortum" that followed her.

Along the banquet tables, there was an array of decadent delights and Terra thought back to that time in the Lost Languages when she dined with Colonel Simeon and Major-General Tres. A memory that felt so long ago now.

She quietly took a savoury looking pastry and found a spot to herself a bit away from the table. Huddled against the wall and ignoring the guards who stood near to either side of her, Terra watched from afar as Adam glanced around the room. She wordlessly nibbled on her pastry as an older woman with red splotches for cheeks tapped him on the shoulder and greeted him with a wide smile.

You're too old for him, lady, Terra found herself thinking coldly before internally chastising her own thoughts.

The room swelled with the bodies in it as every morsel was lapped up and the last drops of liquid squeezed from the bottoms of cups. People in their merriment added a distasteful glow to the room that made Terra avert her gaze, her disillusionment heightening as the evening wore on. The banquet passed by in a blur of thrashing bodies and aromas that coiled around each awkward limb, uniting these otherwise strangers to this macabre ritual of growth and freedom. Terra made no attempt to engage in any conversation, instead choosing to observe others from a distance and dwelling on the darkness that loomed over the events of that day.

Looking out at the throngs of people eating and drinking their fill, their bodies twisting to the drawn out notes of the jaunty melody a band played, Terra felt an overwhelming sense of despondency. She recalled that hopeless time in the mines when the Colonel had told her that the world would continue revolving, regardless of who died. The world dulled, losing its colour and lustre with the truth of his words. The shadows along the checked floor stretched and yawned, their claws encircling her, their voices murmuring and sobbing.

"There you are!"

Terra jumped as a relieved Adam approached her. Her breath hitched in her throat and she swallowed thickly, blinking rapidly.

Adam frowned. "Is there something wrong?" He reached out to her, hand hovering uncertainly around her arm.

Shaking her head, Terra quickly brushed tears away from the corner of her eye.

Setting his jaw, Adam grabbed her elbow and began to steer the both of them towards the exit of the great hall. "Pyrrhus is beginning to give directions to those who are settling outside of Railesson. We're free to find our own way now."

As they stepped over the threshold, the voices fading to an eventual hum, they discussed the time and that they would need to stay somewhere in Sominium until it was morning again. Inattentive and almost uncaring, Terra agreed and Adam's frown deepened.

"Oh," Adam said, struck by a sudden thought. "By the way, you did well, Miss Ridley." He smiled, resting his hand on Terra's shoulder.

The shadow cast over her shifted, and Terra furiously batted it into a cobwebbed corner of her mind. She gave a small smile. "Thank you." Heat rose into her cheeks.

Nodding, Adam withdrew his hand, casting a glance around the town before they descended the stairs of the temple. Spotting a nearby inn, belted in a romantic red, Adam waved for Terra to follow him and began leading the way towards it, slipping through the few others who had gained approval to remain in Railesson.

Wordlessly, they strode through the pristine streets, weaving through people and beasts. Terra kept note of Adam's decisive movements and occasionally glanced away to take in the sights and sounds.

The rousing chorus of a drunken tavern unfurled through the dimly lit streets, beckoning wandering souls of a particular yearning to stumble through its wooden doors. Despite the nature of it, the tavern mirrored much of the rest of the town; white square houses and buildings, with splashes of colour, vibrant against the constant white.

In a salient part of the town, they plodded past a marble fountain on which stood the intricate statue of a proud wolf. The dangling lanterns of the night markets seemed to sway in welcome as people sold and purchased wares. In the midst of this was the rhythmic beating of percussions as a woman in a scant silk outfit danced. Around the gold and red embroidered carpet she danced on, came the claps and cheers of a ruddy-faced audience with several of their members sloshing their beverages down their fronts or on the shoes of a neighbour.

It still felt too foreign to Terra to have such freedom. Only a couple of spells ago, she had weighed up the options of life or death.

The sunny jingling of a bell attached to a door shook Terra from her thoughts and she hurried through the door Adam held open.

Stepping onto lavish, scarlet carpet, Terra spotted a sleepy-eyed lady at the reception counter who quickly straightened. She flicked a golden switch on the green-glowing device in front of her, deadening its chatter. The receptionist's hazel eyes darted from Adam to Terra and the corner of her red lipsticked mouth curled up. A band of dread slipped around Terra's belly, tightening as they approached the counter.

"How may I help you?" The lady patted down her braided hair, clasping her hands together. She stared intently at the pair.

Noticing her behaviour, Adam warily approached and cleared his throat awkwardly. "We're looking for a room for the night. How much would that cost?"

The lady glanced over Adam and Terra, her gaze deliberate and unsettling. "Little birds say that you're the pair who claim to be descendants of Pater's people," she said in a low purr. "With such distinct names like Railesson and Maremortum, I'd be more than happy to have a vial of blood." A leering grin pulled at her lips.

Adam's face darkened.

Tense seconds passed with both wordlessly holding the other's gaze.

The lady leaned forward, shadows lengthening across her face. Terra caught a whiff of heady perfume and felt it waft around her throat, slender fingers that threatened to close tightly over her windpipe. "The little birds do like to wander," she said lightly, her eyes gleaming. "Who knows where else they share their news and whose ears they may reach."

Reluctantly, Adam unbuttoned the cuff of his sleeve and rolled it up, his nose crinkled in disgust. "Only one vial." He held out his exposed arm to the lady. "And do not touch my woman."

Unhurried, the lady withdrew a needle from a drawer. "It's sterilised," she said with a toothy grin before plunging it into the crook of Adam's arm. She simpered in a foul manner as Adam winced, relishing the sight of the red bubbling into the vial attached to the needle.

Terra held her breath, mind reeling from the distinct difference in treatment "descendants" of Kings of Old received. Watching the lady's vial fill, Terra slowly let her breath out in a hiss between her teeth. There had been so much blood today.

As soon as the needle was removed from his arm, Adam quickly stepped back from the counter, pressing two fingers over the pinprick. "Little birds better keep their mouths shut."

"Of course. So wonderful to do business with your people." Storing the vial away in a small icebox within the cabinet behind her, the lady smilingly ushered the pair to follow her to their allocated room.

They scaled the carpeted staircase, Terra following closely behind Adam and weighed down by her thoughts. As if sensing her discomfort, Adam glanced back and wordlessly let go of his arm, holding his hand out to her. Immediately, Terra threaded the fingers of her left hand through the fingers of his right and she clung to him as they wandered through the floral papered hallways of the inn.

Entering their reserved room, Terra eyed the large bed tucked into one corner of the room, opposite the desk, chair and wardrobe. A door, beside a two-seater lounge, led into a tidy adjoining bathroom where towels lay neatly folded over the tub. A toilet with a seat akin to one Terra had seen in Lacuna occupied a small corner of the bathroom next to a vanity and inbuilt basin with an empty brass pot sitting beneath.

The lady left a key on the desk and practically skipped out of the room, leaving the pair to inspect the area.

Shuffling hesitantly back into the bedroom, Terra wrung her hands nervously together. "There's only one bed."

"Yes. You'll be sleeping in it. I'll take the lounge," Adam replied without batting an eye, busily surveying the town out of the room window.

"That won't be very comfortable."

Dropping the curtain back, Adam turned to Terra, eyebrow raised. "Possibly not. But how could I take advantage of someone in my care?"

"I'm sorry, I didn't mean to suggest—!" Terra stopped, face bright red.

Adam's lips twitched. "I didn't realise you thought so poorly of me."

"No! I didn't mean it like that! I'm so sorry—why are you laughing?"

"It's so easy to tease you."

Terra slapped Adam's arm, her face hot. "Stop laughing!"

Eyes sparkling, Adam chuckled and murmured an apology. He shook his head with a smile. "I'm sure that Agnus and Lamina expressed their love by protecting and caring for you. Let me do that too."

Late that night, Terra curled up on the queen-sized bed while a weary Adam carried one of the plush pillows to the lounge. (He had spent a fair amount of time removing the flowers from her hair, finding more with each lock he combed aside.) As the young, silver-haired woman cradled her necklace in her hands, her thoughts wandered to the inn lady's words, the mocking bow of the man with the well-kept moustache and the dismissive words of The Conqueror.

"Adam."

"Mhm?"

There was a beat as Terra rehearsed her words mentally, running her fingers over the bridge. "Who is Pater?"

Without missing a beat, Adam's muffled response came back: "That is one of the many names of the Creator of all things."

"And we're his...people?"

Turning over to face her, Adam mumbled tiredly, his eyes still closed, "In the past, yes. Nowadays, no."

Terra's eyebrows crashed together. "That's confusing." She let her necklace fall against her chest.

"He wants everyone to be his people."

"Okay...so, are Pater and One the same?"

"Remember what you learned...from Scriptura..." Adam's weak response was soon followed by his soft and even breathing.

After a long incredulous pause, Terra suppressed the urge to roll her eye. "I suppose I should sleep too," she said aloud and pulled her blankets up to her chin, envying Adam.

Storming up the elaborate marble staircase of a hotel, a disgruntled Lachesis withdrew a key from the sleeve of her gown as she strode down the candlelit hallway of the second floor, passing by precious artworks, tapestries and alabaster sculptures.

A nervous Lieutenant Wayman tailed her, unaccustomed to escort duties with the young Maremortum.

Upon reaching a gilded mahogany doorway with a particular number, she slid the key into the well-oiled, gold-plated lock and pushed the door open.

She nodded dismissively at the Lieutenant. "Go and bother the Major-General."

"Marshal, you know that he's currently engaged in discussions with Lord

Gorbeh. We need to secure a meeting with The Conqueror."

Impatiently, Lachesis waved him away. "My useless uncle can relieve you of your duties."

Lieutenant Wayman bit his lip uncertainly but stepped back and saluted Lachesis as she shut the door behind herself.

Relieved, she walked into the room, glimpsing a familiar figure hunched over in a winged chair near the corner of the room. She wordlessly strode behind a privacy screen and began to unbutton her dress. Allowing it to fall at her feet, she grabbed the nightgown she had left out earlier and slipped it on over her head.

"She's here," grumbled Lachesis from behind the screen. She waited, body tense. When she heard nothing, she shook back her long locks and continued, her irritation growing by the second. "The doll."

The words evoked a groggy groan from the figure in the winged chair. "0792?" rasped the dark-haired man, raising his chin weakly.

Stepping out from behind the screen in her sleepwear, Lachesis crinkled her nose at the man. "Has the medication not helped you, Colonel Van de Berg?"

Head lolling to the side, Simeon grimaced. "My primary faculties are functioning." He placed a hand to his forehead, groaning.

Lachesis looked down at him through narrowed eyes. "You were overexposed to E132 for far too long and the armour you created through your powers was the last straw. You're lucky that you have an ounce of sanity."

At her words, the Colonel forced out a harsh, bark-like laugh and gritted his teeth, slamming his fist down on the arm of the chair. "Lucky?" He bristled, and there was an unmistakable tremor in his voice. "I can hardly remember what happened. But the very thought of Agnus *helping* me is simply unbearable."

"Then don't fail next time," sneered Lachesis, already moving towards the bedroom. She paused at the open door, her hand resting on the frame. "You heard my father. We have instructions to kill them."

The Colonel gave a throaty chuckle. "And what about you? Going to keep letting your sister wander about? Or are you relieved to finally be rid of that burden?"

Lachesis stood deathly still, her back to Simeon. Then, without another word, she stepped over the threshold and slammed the door shut behind herself.

In the morning, Adam and Terra thanked the inn lady who merely snickered as the door snapped shut behind them.

Fuming, Terra stormed towards the door to give the lady a piece of her mind, but Adam wrapped an arm around her waist. He dragged her away, releasing her when she squealed loudly in protest.

"Why did you do that?"

"It stopped you from doing something silly, didn't it?"

Flustered and red-faced, Terra stomped across the pavement as she followed behind Adam. "I didn't like how she treated us. All because of our heritage," she grumbled, crossing her arms over her chest.

"Yes," said Adam with a mirthless laugh. He paused, their footsteps echoing in the quiet morning air. "I'm glad I got to spend this time with you, Miss Ridley. No matter the task, you're always faithful to Agnus and I've found myself—more than once—encouraged by your actions."

Raising her gaze to the back of his short white locks, Terra frowned and placed a hand on her necklace, the ring on her right hand glinting in the artificial sun's light. "I wasn't always…and there were plenty of times when I was filled with so much doubt…" She hung her head, ashamed. "And there's still so much that I don't understand."

Slowing down and falling into step beside her, Adam's hazel eyes were soft. "What is it that you want to understand?" he inquired gently, causing Terra's cheeks to flush.

Unconsciously, Terra drew closer to Adam, her stomach knotting as her heart hammered in her chest. "Talk to me about Pater," she replied, surprising herself with how high her voice sounded in her ears. "Pater and his people."

As they left the streets of Sominium, returning the same way they came, Adam spoke about the One with Many Names and how all of Tempus had come to be. The love that One wove into everything he created and the Other that had disrupted the sweet melody of creation.

"Why would people turn away from One's love?" Terra asked, her eyebrows scrunched together.

"Because people's hearts are darker than you know," answered Adam, his tone matter of fact. "We are all capable of being lured away."

Frown deepening, Terra trudged along wordlessly. She considered her next words carefully, rolling the unpleasant shapes around her tongue. She couldn't talk about her own dark thoughts just yet. "Shigure acted in a way I never imagined he would," she said quietly, her words drawn out. Patches of dry, faded yellow grass were crushed under her feet. "He calls Agnus his master—but does he really think that?"

"All who know Agnus obey his commands," came Adam's blunt reply. "Even someone like Shigure will work according to his purpose."

"And what purpose is that?"

Adam pressed his lips together in thought. "I can only surmise what it could be, but the more you understand Scriptura, the more you will trust that there is meaning and purpose in all things. Even the things that are most difficult or painful to explain."

Nodding slowly, Terra surveyed the green horizon before them, mind racing with thoughts. "It's hard to get over painful things," she whispered, her words almost inaudible.

Ears perking up, Adam peered closely at her, noting her darkened expression. He looked away to the artificial sun, voice morose as he spoke, "Don't turn away from the evil things in this world. Face them and overcome them." He glanced over at Terra, catching her eye. He forced a smile and instead appeared grief-stricken. "Easier said than done, of course."

"Is that why some people turn away?"

"It can be. But you can let it strengthen you. Help it reaffirm your resolve."

Terra lowered her eye to the grass at her feet, smiling somewhat bitterly. "Easier said than done." After a beat of her recalling the tale of the disruption of the melody of creation, she shook her head furiously, clapping her hands against the sides of her face. *This*, she mentally berated herself, *is how people turn away*. She clenched her fist, determined to dust away the cobwebs of resentment that clung to the corners of her memories.

They continued discussing stories that Terra had learned from her lessons with Agnus and time flew by so quickly that the pair found themselves entering a house where Adam sang in response to the chiming of the wind and they were soon descending the stairs to the underground.

Lamina was preparing a roast meal when Terra and Adam returned to the area their house was located.

"Welcome back," he murmured, throwing his arms solemnly around Terra. He nodded in acknowledgment to Adam who merely smiled in return. Releasing Terra, he sat back down at the fire and urged the pair to join him. "I thought you would enjoy something special."

Smiling brightly, Terra plopped down near the fire, accepting a plate of steaming meat cuts and potatoes. "Where is Agnus?" she asked as she pierced a slice of meat and blew on it.

"He needed some alone time to pray," answered Lamina, handing a plate of food to Adam who mumbled his appreciation. The old ox fell into a brief contemplative silence while slicing himself some lamb. "He said that it had to be done but was greatly grieved that he had sent you. I'm sure he would be apologising if he was here."

Terra felt an intense pang of emotions. She tried to smile but felt pained. "He doesn't need to apologise," she said, shaking her head. She shot Adam a meaningful look—which Lamina did not miss—before continuing, "I was safe. Even so, I will always owe Agnus my life. I understand that even more now after all that I've learned."

Lamina's dark eyes shone bright in the firelight and he cleared his throat, swallowing thickly. "Young mistress, there was once a time when I was reminding you to have faith and to believe and now I'm being encouraged in turn by you," he reminisced, dabbing at the corners of his eyes. "You have truly grown, haven't you?"

Beaming at the old ox, Terra reached over and patted his knee, her heart full. "I should be thanking you. Especially for helping me escape from Magia," she whispered, her voice wavering.

The old ox took her hand from his knee and squeezed it in his own. Letting go, they resumed dinner, chatting heartily about the trip to Sominium and all the different people and things Terra saw. Good or bad, Terra shared all of her experiences and Lamina quietly listened, occasionally asking a question or remarking on something said. Terra felt a lot lighter than she had in a long while.

After they finished their meals, Adam went to fill up a pail with water to wash up the pile of dishes and Terra decided to go and find Agnus.

"He will probably be in one of the houses on the surface," Lamina suggested.

Terra soon found herself wandering quietly from house to house in search of Agnus. She wondered what she would say to him, knowing what she did and decided that she would reassure him of his choices and how she was always grateful for him and his guidance. These words all died on her lips when she found him in one of the furthest houses. He was on his knees, his eyes closed and hands held tightly together as if earnestly imploring another. The carpet near his feet had been pulled aside to reveal another entrance that Terra had not been aware of.

At the soft shuffling of her feet at the door, Agnus slowly opened his eyes and turned his head towards her. Relief marked his face, the creases appearing to lessen and he bounded to his feet, pacing over to the young silver-haired girl and wordlessly wrapping his arms around her.

Terra eagerly hugged him in return, misty-eyed again. *I'm back. I was safe. Thank you for always loving me.* So many thoughts raced in her mind but when she parted her lips to share them, she found that her voice failed her each time. Instead, she squeezed his torso and pressed her cheek into his chest, hoping he could understand her.

Gradually, Agnus pulled away, gladly ruffling her hair. "Shall we read some Scriptura?" he asked benignly. At a nod from Terra, he pulled the carpet back over the hidden door and sat down, patting the spot beside him.

Scurrying over, Terra excitedly recounted all that Adam had told her in helping to understand how Scriptura related intimately with the world. They talked at length about the *One with Many Names* and his love for a world that he created but did not love him. They yearned instead for another path; one of their own choosing and making. The thought of this disheartened and frustrated Terra.

"If One really created the world, why have people turned away?"

Agnus sighed, aggrieved. "The presence of E132 should be enough to understand why—a stone that is veiled with different names across Tempus for a more sinister purpose." After a moment, Agnus pushed himself up onto his feet and dusted his pants off. "I think it's time that we did some sword practice. I will stand in place of Shigure."

Terra slowly stood, the burden of lingering dark thoughts weighing on her chest. She shook the dust from her pants, her eye fixed on the floor as her pulse quickened.

Before her stretched a dark abyss that she couldn't share with Adam earlier that day—but did she trust Agnus enough to tell him?

Biting her lip and clenching her fists, she took a deep breath. She plunged into the black below.

"Agnus, today I learnt about the darkness in everyone's heart...and I know there's a darkness in mine too.

"I've been fighting against this desire to see Simeon suffer. I wanted him to die a painful death." She fiddled with a frayed thread on her sleeve. What was Agnus thinking? She couldn't bear to look at him. "When I was first filled with Spiritus' power, I had a chance to kill him. But Spiritus wouldn't let me and I...I'm so ashamed. I'm no better than him. Will I ever be better than this? I want my heart to heal. I want to be...a kind person. And I'm scared that when I see him again, I won't be kind. I won't have grown as a person at all."

Agnus cupped her cheek and Terra looked up to find his gentle and understanding gaze. Tears welled in her eye.

"My child, all people are capable of change. Whether it is for better or worse is a decision that each person makes. Why do you doubt your heart?"

"Because." Terra tried to blink back tears. "I haven't seen him in so long. How will I know if I've forgiven him? Am I really healing?" The dreams of her hands being covered in Simeon's blood surfaced in her mind.

"The fact that you struggle, even now, against the flesh shows how strong your heart is becoming. Do not doubt it when you come face to face with

Simeon." Agnus rested his hands on Terra's shoulders. "Come, let us practice."

Wiping away tears, Terra unwillingly lifted Spiritus.

"Terra." Agnus took the young girl's free hand in his. "You must fight Levi Maremortum."

"Levi? Do you mean Mr Maremortum?" Agnus' nod prompted another question from Terra, "Why must I fight him?"

"In order for things to come to pass, you must fight him. If you do this, then you will be able to overcome the Magian's army."

Terra's eye lit up. Maybe she wouldn't have to face Simeon. "Really?"

Agnus nodded once more, slower this time.

"Thank you, Agnus!"

He squeezed her hand, his expression grave. "When you must swing Terra, do not hesitate. Do not lower your sword. Do not relent when you fight him. For in any moment of weakness, you shall perish."

Squaring her shoulders and meeting Agnus' eyes, Terra replied in a calm and firm voice, "I won't hesitate. I'll allow Spiritus to guide me."

Agnus resumed her training and Terra poured as much energy as she could afford into honing her swordsmanship, recalling all she had learned from Shigure. Memories of his execution of the people at the coming of age ceremony surged through her mind and she desperately suppressed them, pushing them to the back of her mind. She focused on her footwork and reading Agnus' movements instead, determined to confront her teacher the next time she saw him.

When the gates of Hrestia stood clear, the spirit that had been with
Mila'sey and her group departed.
The dragon of Xanadu, descended from the skies and sought the hand
of Mila'sey.

- Lines from *The Gates of Hrestia, Scriptura*. Translated by T. Lowenthal

17

At a gold-trimmed mahogany door bearing a detailed engraving of a wolf
baring its fangs, a young tortoiseshell Emau bowed to Mr Maremortum,
wordlessly gesturing with a paw for him to enter. Upon realising this was
fruitless, the Emau flicked his tail and reached forward, lightly tapping Mr
Maremortum's arm and stepping aside to allow him entry.

Heavy smoke wafted through the open doorway and Mr Maremortum
crinkled his nose. He edged into the smoky room, cane leading the way, and
threw on what he hoped was a warm smile. "Lord Gorbeh, I thank you for
your hospitality and willingness to help my brother."

A heavy silence followed.

Taking a breath, the silver-haired man continued, a bit more shakily.

"I'm sure that you're aware that we will soon be under attack from
this…thing that claims to be a Maremortum," spat Mr Maremortum, as if the
person in question were an illness. "You've done much to help us already,
but we also need assistance with securing a supply of particular weapons."

The pillow of smoke unfurled before Mr Maremortum's face and glided through the air, coiling around his motionless frame. Before him languidly sat the large silhouette of a long-haired, white Emau.

"I have repaid my debt to your father," came the white furred Emau's voice from amidst the cloudy haze, yellow feline eyes flashing warningly. He raised the pipe to his mouth again, taking a long draw before pulling the pipe away between his long-clawed digits. The smoke seeped out of both his flared nostrils in a steady stream that filled the air around him.

A bead of sweat trickled down the back of Mr Maremortum's neck and he opened his mouth hesitantly. "I received a dream from Sominium and you will want to ensure you're well placed in the future."

A deep rumbling filled the room and a low hiss issued from the Emau's mouth. "Do not speak to me of the vile magicks your people have brought into Ezer's world."

Mr Maremortum smiled stiffly and bowed, swallowing his retort. He opened and closed his mouth several times before finally finding his voice. "Thank you, Gorbeh. For housing both Simeon and my daughter."

Gorbeh made no acknowledgment of the Maremortum's words, silently observing him through the haze. He leaned over and placed a paw atop the bell on a small table beside his chair, ringing it once.

The tortoiseshell Emau slid back into the room. "Master Gorbeh?" He bowed lowly.

Waving a nonchalant paw, which momentarily parted the sea of pollution, Gorbeh's voice grumbled: "Please escort Mr Maremortum to Mr Van de Berg's room and see that they are assisted in their return to Magia."

Wordlessly, the young Emau waited for Mr Maremortum to fall in step behind him before picking up speed and leading the way to the guest room— down several winding corridors of the decorative and palatial hotel, up the stairs past the room that Lachesis had stayed in. Eventually they came to a stop outside one of the many similarly gilded doors—number 1011—and the Emau quickly unlocked it with a key from a collection that jingled on his belt. Standing clear of the open door, the Emau bowed, and tapped on Mr Maremortum's arm so that he would enter.

Within the room, Simeon rose from the lounge, greeting Mr Maremortum in a wan voice before they shared a brief boyish embrace.

"Simeon, we have overstayed our welcome." Mr Maremortum held the dark-haired man's face, acknowledging the heavy beard with his hands. "I'm grateful for the help we've received but we must go home now."

What little colour remained in Simeon's face drained away and his jaw tensed. "I'm ready to go home, brother."

Mr Maremortum attempted a smile. He pressed his hands on his brother's shoulders as if to reassure him. "Are you truly ready?"

Clasping his brother's hands, Simeon nodded, his eyes dull. "I'll kill her this time."

The week continued in a fashion: Terra studiously examined the alphabet with Lamina and at other times trained with Agnus both by learning to appreciate Scriptura more, complemented with basic sword stances.

"This rune is for One," Agnus explained one day when Terra began to recognise similar characters.

Excited at the prospect of learning how to read Scriptura on her own, Terra sat in eager anticipation for another story, her mind abuzz. But Agnus gave her a sad smile and said: "Terra, I need you to know that I will be leaving as soon as your training finishes."

Terra's heart sank. "Are you going far away?" she heard her voice ask, tiny and insecure.

"There is a battle elsewhere that I must be present for," he explained. "In my stead, you and Lamina must guide the Mannite army into Magia."

The young girl was already shaking her head long before Agnus finished. "Agnus, please don't say that. How can I lead anyone? I don't know anything!" She took a shaky breath, racing into her next sentence: "I don't even know who is part of the Mannite army! And how could they even listen to someone as young as me?"

Agnus shook his head knowingly. "My child, do not let your youth deceive you. Did Spiritus not come out from this mortal body?" He lightly prodded her chest with his index. "You are capable of far more than you know. And you will not be alone." He paused, studying the harrowed expression on Terra's face. "Do you trust me, Terra?"

Head snapping up, Terra's fearful grey eye met the older man's solemn dark ones and she felt a sheet of calm draping over the turmoil that roiled in her heart. Despite the terror that seized her senses, a peculiar understanding of assurance and peace encircled these emotions. Her mind recalled the hope Adam had spoke of and the certainty of the future. "In the past, I would never have said this. But after all that I've seen and all that I've been given…" Jutting her chin out with renewed confidence, Terra said in a tremulous yet vigorous voice, "Agnus, I put all of my hope and trust in you."

Eyes softening, Agnus whispered an almost inaudible "thank you" before he urged the young woman to follow him back down to the cavern. Once there, Agnus waved Nicholo over and the two rounded up a host of adults with some disgruntled by the interruption to their day.

A crowd of people surrounded Agnus, Nicholo and Terra in a half circle.

"My friends, I spoke of this previously while this child was away at the coming of age ceremony." He placed a reassuring arm around Terra's trembling shoulders. "While my spirit is with her and under Lamina's tutelage, she will help lead you in my stead."

Terra's heart hammered in her chest. Her throat closed up as she looked over a few of the faces in the crowd. There were several expressions of confusion and indignation. Her ears rang from their shouts of discontentment and Terra had to lower her eye to her boots, steeling herself as their voices rose together in a tumultuous roar.

"We will obey Lamina, but not her!"

"She's nothing but a child!"

"How will we even know that your spirit is with her anyway?"

Agnus removed his arm from around Terra's shoulders and raised his hands in a silencing gesture. Eventually the crowd fell quiet, attentive as Agnus' severe gaze swept over them. He turned to Terra, a small smile lighting his face. "Show them Spiritus."

After a moment of hesitation, Terra grabbed the hilt of Spiritus from within her chest and, in one fluid motion, unsheathed it, its light illuminating the awestruck faces of those gathered.

Many in the crowd fell to their knees, bowing so low their faces almost touched the ground.

Panic rose like bile in Terra's throat and she begged them to stand, feeling the spirit of the sword strengthen her resolve. "Don't bow to me!" she cried, her voice shrill. "I'm not Pater! Please don't bow!"

The crowd shrivelled at the mention of Pater, many turning to mutter darkly to one another. Some people's faces twisted mournfully. Fewer still raised their fists to her, seething, "Pater has abandoned us!"

Nicholo cleared his throat loudly and stepped in front of Terra, shielding her from view. "Silence! It was *our* people who abandoned Pater!" he spat, his chest heaving. "And again, you would have us do the same."

Several people shrank in shame, heads bowed low, but others scowled, shaking their heads.

Turning to Agnus and Terra, Nicholo dropped to one knee and bowed his head before them. "My Lord, we will obey your command. If you are leaving Lamina and Terra in charge, we will ensure to follow their guidance with discernment, wisdom and obedience to you."

There were a few grumblings of assent from the crowd, with some such as Talia plucking up the courage to heartily agree with Nicholo.

Agnus thanked Nicholo and continued to address the crowd, his eyes hard. "In the beginning, was the One with Many Names. He revealed himself to your Railesson ancestors as Pater. And many times, your ancestors readily chose to turn away from him. I stand before you to remind you of this truth. Because of this, the truth that was once shared with only your ancestors has now been shared with all who will accept it.

"When you look upon Spiritus, may it be a reminder to you of the hope that is available to all."

Following this, Agnus engaged in several discussions with people within the crowd and despite sensing that the formal part of this meeting had concluded, Terra remained to absorb some of Agnus' wisdom. Many of the conversations he had involved different interpretations and understanding of Scriptura and Terra found herself mystified with how Agnus calmly debated people, pointing to different parts of Scriptura to present the basis for his arguments.

"This battle must happen to cut off E132 from the rest of the world," explained Agnus.

"But we need E132 for our farming systems! Even the currency registers require it! We need it to live!"

So engrossed in the debate, Terra started at Adam's sudden appearance beside her. Her heart fluttered as he beamed at her.

"I see you're enjoying yourself."

Terra smiled brightly in return. "I'm learning and understanding more." Her ears perked up at Agnus' apologies as he pulled away from the crowd and approached them.

"Adam," said Agnus, an unusually tight smile on his face. "I need to discuss a matter with you." He glanced apologetically at Terra who obediently excused herself, humming to herself as she skipped away to help Lamina with cooking dinner.

While Terra and Lamina were excitedly babbling about the night's meal, Agnus returned with Adam trailing behind him, the latter with his face downcast.

"Sorry, Miss Ridley, I'll excuse myself from dinner tonight," he murmured, unable to meet Terra's eye. "The thoughts in the cavern are too much tonight." He retreated to the inside of the house, leaving Terra to stare after him.

Placing a delicate hand on her shoulder, Agnus smiled benignly at her raised eyebrows. "It was Adam's birthday yesterday."

Mouth full of hot soup, Terra reeled back, her eye wide in bewilderment. She gulped the mouthful down, ignoring the sudden tenderness of her throat.

"He doesn't like celebrating it, so I made no mention of it previously."

"You're telling me now?"

Expression tightening, Agnus held her gaze. "Yes." His hand weighed heavily on her shoulder. "There's something on his mind that's important for you to know."

Puzzled, Terra simply nodded and resumed eating, her mind filling with all sorts of conversation ideas for Adam later.

Lamina and Agnus exchanged a few light-hearted jokes over the fire and Terra, warmed by the meal and the company, gathered up the dirty dishes to wash up.

After the dishes were scrubbed clean, and with one final glance over them, a satisfied Terra turned away, lazily wiping her hands dry on her pants.

She tipped the contents of the wooden pail onto the dirt outside of the house, laughing as Lamina passed by with a dead chicken in hand, absently muttering about needing to grab something. Returning into the house with the pail wrapped in her arms, Terra hummed to herself as she placed it in the corner of the main room.

Wiping sweat off her brow and sighing in exhaustion, Terra stretched widely. She paced over to one of the windows to look out at the people quietly milling about outside. Contemplating the stillness of the night, her mind drifted to the blood-red moon hanging in the black sky above the cavern. Scratching the back of her head, she turned and noticed Adam sitting on a wooden chair by the other window, eyes glazed over.

Hesitating a moment, Terra shook her head and grabbed a spare chair on the other side of the room and carried it over to where he sat. The feet of the chair gave a muffled clunk as she placed it down opposite Adam, drawing his gaze.

"Miss Ridley?"

"Hey." She gave a bright smile. "Agnus mentioned it was your birthday yesterday. We didn't even celebrate it last spell! Happy birthday!"

Adam smiled politely.

Terra observed how his light-coloured lashes curled against his cheeks whenever he closed his eyes. "How old are you?"

"Now? 16."

Terra nodded slowly. *He's not that much older than me*, she thought, heartened.

In the silence, Adam turned away and resumed gazing out of the window.

Racking her brain, Terra cleared her throat. "So... what are you up to?"

"Nothing at the moment." There was a beat. "It's strange, waking up in a different time."

"What time are you from, Adam?"

Brow furrowed in thought, Adam replied, "I know it was before you were born."

Terra's mouth fell open. "Does that make you as old as Lamina or older?"

Pensive, Adam put his hand to his chin. "During my sleep, time completely ceased for me." He paused, screwing his face up in thought. "No, more like, I was outside of time...so, no, I'm not older than him."

"Outside of time?" Terra repeated, her mouth still hanging open in disbelief. "What does that even mean?"

"Outside of the constraints of the flesh."

"Like being a spirit? Wouldn't that be like death? How could you be alive then?"

"Have you read about hope beyond this world in Scriptura?" Adam continued to stare out of the window, fingertips pressed lightly against his temple.

"Yes, when the doors of Praeter Tempus opens."

Adam nodded. "You can't live another life unless you can be brought back to life." There was a slight glow in his eyes and a sliver of runic words escaped from his body. "These were the truths shared with Pater's people and now they are revealed to all." He sighed and closed his eyes.

Holding her breath, Terra leaned closer to Adam. "Are you okay?"

"I'm tired."

"Is there anything I can do to help?"

Adam slammed his hand down on the window ledge and sucked in air through clenched teeth. "What is your real name, Miss Ridley?"

Terra felt her stomach drop and she recoiled. "I can't tell you that," she whispered, heart aching.

A heavy blanket of silence fell over the pair and for a number of minutes they sat in the stifling awkwardness of it. Terra lowered her eye to the dirt beneath her feet, wishing it would open up and swallow her.

"I'm sorry to press you, I just..." Adam trailed off, his voice soft enough to melt Terra who still could not bear to meet his eyes. "Miss Ridley, I'll be leaving tomorrow at Agnus' behest," he sighed, pulling away from the window and turning to her.

Terra could feel the world grow silent as she stared, unseeing, at the ground. Her chest grew unbearably tight.

Why were they all leaving her? How could she do this on her own? Was Spiritus enough for her?

She did not realise she was standing until Adam grabbed her hand, his brow creased with concern.

"Miss Ridley?"

A crushing wave of emotion crashed over her and Terra tore her hand away, dashing out of the house with Adam's cries chasing her. She could not stop the panicked sobs that wracked her body as she ran. Where she was going, she didn't know, but eventually she was heaving her body up the stairs to the old ruins of Manna.

Crawling into a corner of the dark and abandoned house, she covered her face, unable to stop the tears from falling or the mad racing of her mind. The cold fingers of loneliness could not be pushed away this time.

She was going to be alone like she had been for spells in Magia. She was going to have to be brave and survive in whatever way she could. She was going to have the face the Colonel's cruelty alone again.

Terra grabbed her hair that was now fully silver, choking on tears, her body trembling uncontrollably. Heart painfully fast and breaths frighteningly short, the world began to spin and Terra rocked back and forth, vision narrowing as she wondered if it was okay to wish for nothingness rather than being alone again.

"Young mistress?"

Jumping back against the wall, Terra hurriedly wiped her face and looked around.

With a dead chicken slung over his shoulder, Lamina's hulking body stood, silhouetted against the blood-red moon. He crouched down before Terra, reaching out with his free hand to pull her towards him into the fragments of light piercing through the patchy roof. With one arm wrapped around her, he murmured softly in her ear, "Did they finally tell you that they were leaving?"

Eye widening in realisation that she had been the only one in the dark, Terra tried to pull back but Lamina held her tight, hushing her as she made a disgruntled noise.

"They don't want to leave you, young mistress. Please, understand that," he crooned, his voice thick with emotion.

At the sound of his wavering voice, tears welled up in Terra's eye and she sank back into Lamina's embrace, gripping his shoulder as she began to cry in earnest again.

"But I will be here." Lamina drew back to cup one side of Terra's face. "I'll be here to support you the whole way. And just because the other two won't be here, doesn't mean they don't support you either." He brushed away a tear with his thumb, continuing, "And it doesn't mean that they don't love you."

Terra screwed up her face in pain again, throwing herself back into Lamina's chest with a sob.

Lamina sniffed, stroking her hair. "They love you, young mistress. I love you."

He stayed with Terra, holding her until her tears dried and they both laughed at the chicken slung over his shoulder. They descended the stairs into the underground, hand in hand.

Lachesis was drifting through a dark space. In the far distance was a small speck of light. She spun, parting her arms and kicking her legs, trying to propel herself towards the light. Her heart hammered in her chest. She was suffocating in the inky black, her arms flailing uselessly like swimming through sludge.

The light grew as she approached and within it she could see three people sitting in a boat, slicing through the thick darkness. Her gut twisted into knots and her palms were slick with sweat. She recognised the silver hair of her twin, Arche, and the shabby, long hair of the seer, Joseph. But she didn't recognise the third being sitting beside Arche. A skeleton of a figure, covered in stretched sallow skin. Thin, dishevelled white hair crowned its head.

She shuddered, cold sweat accumulating on her brow. Was it even human?

What a rude child you are.' The creature turned its head towards her, its hollow eye sockets trained on her and its mouth pulled up into a wide toothy grin, razor sharp teeth glinting. *'Perhaps I should take my eyes back from you brats.'* It rose from its seat on the boat, but Arche and the beggar did not glance at it. In this space, only Lachesis could see the hideous creature.

"What are you?" Her voice was tiny in the large, empty space.

'Isn't this what you wanted? The power you envied. That Arche grieves over.' It raised a bony hand to her and she stared into the dark emptiness of its eye sockets.

Gooseflesh covered Lachesis' body. And yet, she found herself mirroring the creature, raising her hand towards it and reaching out, fingers outstretched.

'In Tohi Ofa, they buried a great beast. Listen to the lullaby. Know the truth of this pathetic world. And I will acknowledge you.'

"Who are you?"

The creature's fingertips met hers but instead of the feeling of bones, she felt the soft skin of small human fingers.

Her twin stood before her, a hand clamped over her left eye—the one that mirrored Lachesis' in its scarlet colour.

Everything else in the space had vanished, consumed by the abyss.

A single tear slipped from the corner of Arche's grey eye. "I'm Hades."

Azure burned over the black horizon and the artificial sun snaked out from the depths of the darkness. A great and terrible roar shook the earth.

Eyes slowly opening from sleep, Lachesis sat up in bed and touched her face. She was crying.

The next morning, Terra awoke to an empty house. Exhausted, she sleepily dragged herself out of bed and tried to force her unkempt hair down with her hands.

She squealed in shock when Lamina poked his head in through one of the windows. "Young mistress! Quick! Adam is leaving!"

Bolting up and out of the house, Terra raced to the surface with Lamina chasing after her. She threw the hidden door open, breathless as she heaved herself up the last few steps into the ruined house where both Agnus and Adam stood, saying farewells.

The men looked over at her, Adam's face crestfallen.

Terra clenched her fists and a mixture of anger and disbelief welled up inside of her, rising from the pit of her belly. Why was he trying to sneak away without saying goodbye?

But at the cold realisation that this was perhaps the final time that she would see Adam, Terra's heart sank and the sudden bubble of fury popped. She stepped back from the group, standing awkwardly behind Agnus and Lamina. Turning her face away, she stared off into the distance, Adam's conversation with Agnus but a murmur as her thoughts wandered.

"Thank you for all you have taught me, Master. I promise to carry out the rest of my duties."

Adam then turned and gave a formal bow to Terra, drawing her back into reality. "Miss Ridley, I pray that you'll continue to hold fast to Agnus' words. Let the sword guide you in difficult times."

Stomach in knots, Terra turned to Adam with a stiff smile. "Thank you. I hope that you stay safe wherever you go." After a beat of twisting her hands together and biting her lip, she stepped forward and reached her arms up uncertainly to the young man.

Without hesitation, Adam stepped forward and stooped down, wrapping his arms around Terra's small frame. They wordlessly stood like that for a moment before Terra pulled back, her face flushed and tears stinging her eye.

"I'm sorry for running off," she said, blinking furiously.

Lamina and Agnus exchanged looks, with the latter smiling and ushering the former out. The hidden door shut soundlessly over them as Terra continued to speak, flustered.

"Last night, I mean."

Adam smiled, his eyes gentle. "You're more than forgiven for that."

"Where will you be going?" Terra's voice was oddly high as she strained to hold back her tears. She stared fixedly at the floor.

"Shin'en Kiryuu. We know that they were involved with the ending of The Stillness, just not how."

Terra nodded blankly, her eye distant.

"Perhaps, you can come and visit me."

Face lighting up, Terra nodded with more enthusiasm. Chancing a glance up at Adam, Terra felt herself mirroring his smile, her heart bursting at the seams. "I was really happy when we were in Sominium together." She cringed, shaking her head. "I mean, thank you…for everything," she whispered, voice growing softer with each word.

Adam chuckled lightly, unable to stop smiling. "Well, look after yourself." He paused, noticing the sudden emptiness of the room.

Surprised by the silence, Terra glanced over her shoulder. Was this intentional? Terra scurried after Agnus and Lamina, the red in her cheeks deepening as a sense of awareness flared within her.

"Please, wait!" Adam, stumbled after the young woman, his hand closing over her arm.

Closing her eye briefly in agonised defeat, Terra bit her lip and turned to face the young man, cheeks rosy. "Y-yes?" She mentally pummelled herself for not maintaining her composure.

"Would you," he paused, hesitating, "do one thing for me before I go?"

There was a beat where Terra returned Adam's gaze with uncertainty and confusion. "What is it?"

Ears flaming red, Adam opened his mouth with much difficulty before closing it just as painfully slowly, the lump in his throat bobbing visibly as he gulped. "Have you ever heard of the prophecy of the slumbering guardian of Initium?"

In the back of her mind, Terra recalled the tale that Lamina had told her and of their correlating discovery of the man standing in front of her. She swallowed nervously, lowering her eye to the cracked floor beneath her feet, face beet red. "Yes, I have."

Encouraged, Adam hastily stepped forward, grabbing Terra's left hand before she could leap back. "They say that the person to claim the rib of the guardian is to be joined to them."

Despite the brave face Terra forced, her hand trembled uncontrollably in Adam's, her legs like jelly beneath her. Her lips remained glued together and she continued to study the small cracks under her feet while her face, if possible, steadily grew hotter.

Adam watched Terra's face intently, choosing his words carefully. "And so, if you're to continue on your own journey, then I will wait until our paths cross again. Whenever that may be."

Terra glanced up at him imploringly, opening her mouth to speak but was cut off by the young man.

"I don't mind," he murmured gently. "I will be content simply with your name until then. That's all I want to have before we part ways."

Terra gulped and lowered her gaze to the floor once more. She couldn't give him her name. She still bore the brand on her tongue that prevented her from even mentioning it. And yet, Terra could feel heat shooting up through her fingertips from where Adam lightly held her hand. How could she disappoint him again?

Her teacher's face flashed through her mind.

Slowly and resolutely, Terra raised her head and Adam noted the odd look in her eye.

"Arche," she whispered hollowly. "My name is Arche."

After a beat, Adam squeezed her hand gently—the hand that belonged to him. "I'll look for you in the future then, Arche."

Terra smiled, yet it did not reach her eye. "Yes," she whispered, blinking back tears. *I hope Arche is kind to you.*

Heart wavering, she stood on tiptoe, pressing a soft kiss on Adam's cheek. His hand tightened, almost painfully, on hers. "I hope you'll find me."

It was a puffy eyed Terra that returned to the cavern. She sniffled an apology to both Lamina and Agnus who patiently awaited her at the bottom of the stairway.

The trio walked in silence through the cavern towards their house with the occasional sniffle from Terra breaking the quiet.

After some time of contemplative silence, Agnus spoke up, "Do you recall that I told you my gift would be after you returned from the coming of age ceremony?"

"Yes?"

Agnus reached into his pocket, revealing a small silver hair clip that he placed into Terra's upturned hand. "This is not the gift itself," he said at Terra's blank stare. "It is a means for you to visualise and summon the gift."

Peering up at him, Terra noted the twinkle in Agnus' eyes and a thrilling idea surged through her. "An armour piece?" At the broad smile Agnus gave her, Terra fumbled excitedly over her next question. "What is the name of the piece?"

"Salvatus. Use it wisely to protect when you cannot."

Terra slid the hair clip into the side of her silver waves and screwed up her face in concentration, heart beating wildly. The name of the piece brought to mind all that she had learned and studied under Agnus. The memories of Adam's words regarding One and the strengthening of Terra's resolve bubbled to the surface. "Scriptura Salvatus!"

Glowing runic symbols burst forth from Terra's head, whirling about and weaving together to form a helm that was akin to an over-sized crown. The helm was covered in brambles and thorns and runes covered every inch of the fine armour which sat snugly over her forehead.

The helm seemed to resonate with Spiritus and she felt it stir powerfully within her.

Eyes lighting up, Agnus smiled heartily, clapping Terra on the shoulder. "Well done, my child!"

Flushing with pleasure, Terra parted her lips to respond but felt a pang of pain as an image of a desert plain flashed through her mind. Shaking her head, she reached up and pulled the helm off and it dissipated in her hands, the grains of which fell back into her body. Her legs wobbled.

There was a rush of footsteps as a reassuring hairy arm circled her shoulders. "Are you okay, young mistress?"

"Yes, I'm okay. Thank you, Lamina."

After a beat, Agnus reached over and patted her head, eyes soft. "With that, your training is complete. And I must go to Sominium." Agnus pulled away, throwing his great coat on.

Terra watched him wondrously, the exciting taste of adventure on her lips. "When will we be leaving?"

Pausing, Agnus cast a glance at Terra and then to Lamina. "I will be going alone."

It felt as if a hand tightly gripped Terra's heart. Automatically, words flew from the youth's mouth. "Please Agnus—please don't send me from your side. Please don't send me away from you," she begged, the hand holding her heart squeezing it painfully tight. She held Agnus' gaze, pleading with him.

"Terra, you cannot come," he answered after a beat, his mouth twisting into a grimace. "You already have all that you need." He reached out, tapping her chest lightly.

Brow creased under the crushing weight of her emotions, Terra watched as Agnus wordlessly slipped his hand around hers. Tears formed in her eye and her hand sat limply in his. Within her breast, Spiritus flamed and Terra allowed its warmth to spread through her, a small amount of energy returning to her.

She had real hope. Hope worth clinging to and trusting in.

"Agnus, before you…" She struggled to force her mouth to shape the words that sat on the tip of her tongue. She pursed her lips and her eye met Agnus' which shone brightly, so her voice wavered when she continued, "I know that I shouldn't worry about this sort of thing but still…did I…have I made a difference in the world?"

A kind smile spread across Agnus' face. He placed his hands on either side of her head and planted a gentle kiss on her forehead. "My young one, you made *all* the difference in the world. Don't ever think differently. You being here today is so incredibly important—please don't ever doubt your existence. The things you have done and will do in my name will never be made worthless." Taking Terra's hand, he squeezed it reassuringly, tears glistening in his eyes.

Terra sniffled, and she nodded her head, throat closing up with emotion.

Agnus patted her hand and let go. He turned to Lamina and they shared a warm embrace. "Please look after her as best as you can, Lamina."

"I promise you, I will."

With those words, they parted and Lamina wrapped his arm around Terra's shoulders. Terra waved a farewell to Agnus' retreating back, heart full and tears streaming down her face.

"A King's hands are to build up his people. His life is one of holiness;
an example for all."

- Lines from *The Wisdom of Aurelius, Scriptura.* Translated by T.
Lowenthal

18

Lachesis descended the stairs, her heeled boots echoing through the Lost
Languages. She internally grumbled about how high up the Maremortum
living quarters were.

As her boots continued to ring out in the stairwell, the door she had left
from burst open.

"Lachesis!"

The corners of Lachesis' mouth tightened. She didn't stop. The clatter of
high heels followed her down.

"Why are you so determined to go to Tohi Ofa?"

Sighing, Lachesis didn't look back. "I want to see what Hades said is
buried there."

"Hades? You've spoken with Arche?" The heels were behind Lachesis
now and she felt her mother's hand grab her shoulder, dragging her back to
a halt. "Where is she? Is she okay?"

Throwing a glare over her shoulder, Lachesis shook Mrs Maremortum
off. "Aren't you about to receive some guests?"

Mrs Maremortum's eyebrows knitted together. "Sweetheart, please. I can't lose you too."

"When you say that, are you counting that doll?"

Silence fell between the pair and Lachesis slowly nodded her head, her mouth twisting into a sneer. "Arche reached me in a dream. I only know two people who can do that trick. Daniel Sominium and Agnus Dayton. And I doubt she had much contact with the former."

Mrs Maremortum's hand flew to her mouth, her face fluctuating between fear and anger. "Lachesis," she said after a beat, "it doesn't matter if you don't have the same gift Arche does. You're just as important."

Lachesis laughed but it did not reach her eyes. "Mama, I'm *more* important than her."

"Don't say things like that." Mrs Maremortum wrung her hands, unable to meet Lachesis' glare. "How will you manage when you get to Tohi Ofa? Unless you're The Conqueror or a Kiryuuan, the Tohi Ofans won't welcome you."

Turning back, Lachesis resumed her descent, relieved to not hear the clack of heels behind her. "I learnt of a strong looking Tohi Ofan recently."

"What about the title of Marshal?"

"You keep your end of the bargain and I'll keep mine." Lachesis raised her hand in farewell, continuing her descent to the bottom of the tower. "I'll wait to hear of your victory. So, don't lose."

Terra rose early to help Lamina make breakfast. They sat together, poring over Terra's alphabet book while munching on eggs and flatbread dipped in sauce.

"L-A-M-I-N-A. Lamina."

Beaming with pride, Lamina leaned over and affectionately gave Terra's cheek a pat. "Well done, young mistress."

Terra's face broke into a grin. "I have an excellent teacher." Taking a chunk out of her flatbread, she chewed pensively. "Do you think I will ever be able to read Scriptura on my own?"

"Perhaps you shouldn't speak with your mouth full," advised Lamina, earning a sheepish smile from Terra. He tutted when she poked her tongue out at him with a giggle. "But, I can't see why not. There are even some translated fragments out in the world! Who knows what will happen after this week."

Swallowing, Terra nodded wordlessly, her stomach suddenly churning at a sudden thought.

The old ox tilted his head to the side, onyx eyes studying her. "What is it?"

Am I ready for war? Terra felt the words on the tip of her tongue but merely shook her head. "We'll be meeting with Nicholo soon, right? I'll go ahead and have a bath if that's alright by you, Mr Lamina."

It had been two weeks since Adam and Agnus left Manna. Since then, Terra would try to find quiet moments during her days to recite Scriptura.

It's history. Adam's words from month's ago echoed in her ears. It made her smile to herself.

Recalling the stories Agnus had read to her felt reassuring, like she was still connected to him. Sinking into the warm bathwater, she blew bubbles beneath the surface, mentally recounting a story of an old Pateran prophecy of a great lion's throne in the home of the wolves. As time whittled away, Terra renewed her vow to learn the old runic language. She didn't want to forget all she learnt.

When Terra was dressed, she and Lamina made their way across the cavern pathways, waving occasionally at the smiling faces they passed by. Upon reaching Nicholo's door, Lamina rapped his knuckles on it and it wasn't long before the door swung in to reveal the haggard face of Nicholo who quickly ushered them in. Inside, Cecilia rushed to the squealing kettle over the fire, throwing a "Hello!" over her shoulder.

Terra sat down at the table with Nicholo and Lamina while Cecilia poured out cups of tea, anxiety fluttering in her stomach. She resolved to pay close attention to the conversation, even if she contributed nothing.

Lamina rested his hand on Terra's shoulder. "I have spent the past two weeks informing Terra of the situation at hand and it is approaching the settled date Agnus and I had discussed for the attack on Magia. I want to make this clear: this is not a revenge battle for Manna—"

"I have no illusions regarding that," Nicholo cut-in flatly.

Lamina nodded. "Yes. And I would like that repeated to anyone else who intends to join before we depart tomorrow."

"I will do so."

"I appreciate that. Now, about the plans for tomorrow, have your scouts surveyed the areas we discussed? We'll need the element of surprise if we're to start this battle."

Pulling out a worn parchment, Nicholo unfurled it to reveal a map with names of cities that Terra recognised. "Well, considering our numbers, it shouldn't be too hard to move discretely to Magia."

Brow furrowed, Terra glanced from Lamina to Nicholo. "How many fighters do we have?"

Lamina grunted, scratching his head in an awkward gesture. "Not many, young mistress."

Terra felt her heart sink.

"Not all in Manna are able to take part. And even less from outside of Manna are willing to rally under Agnus." Lamina spat angrily on the floor. "If this were Gershom, we would have an army that would strike fear in The Conqueror's heart—if he has one."

Lips pressed firmly together, Nicholo reached over and patted Lamina roughly on the shoulder. "We will manage, Pater willing."

Nodding his large head, Lamina gave a small smile. "You're right. Agnus' spirit is with us. And we have the throne war and Sominium to thank for Magia's reduced numbers."

Still somewhat numb, Terra closed her eye and took a deep breath, allowing Spiritus' strength to spread through her body. "So, how will we get to Magia? I imagine ferrying across The Mare would take far too long."

Nicholo cleared his throat, running his fingers along the aged map. "We'll need to travel in a number of small groups to the Lune ruins on this side of The Mare. I've confirmed with several sources that the old underground passage that connected the two halves of Lune have been cleared of debris and are safe enough to travel through."

"We do have the assurance that anyone who interferes from outside of our forces or Magia are answerable to the Conqueror." Lamina ran a hand over his mane and sighed heavily. "I'm able to pose as a beastmaster if we go ahead with this plan. I can travel with anyone small enough to pose as a child."

"I didn't want to upset you by making the suggestion."

"I once served the beastmasters in Sominium—no upset feelings here."

"Most of the woman can travel with you then."

"Well, that certainly makes it easier for Terra to remain by my side," said the ox, briefly smiling at the young silver-haired woman.

Attempting to smile back, Terra merely grimaced, prompting a look of concern from Lamina. "I'm sorry, I just feel incompetent here. I wish I could offer something of use," she mumbled, lowering her eye to the table.

Nicholo shook his head, face stern. "Young Ridley, we don't expect you to have combat experience. Your value will be in speaking truths to the army."

"Speaking truths?" Terra repeated blankly, her eyebrows knotted together.

Nodding, the older gentleman took a swig from his cup. "Agnus' spirit is with you and you've committed much of Scriptura to memory. That is invaluable to a sleeping generation of Paterans."

Heartened, Terra sat up straighter, listening carefully as Nicholo and

Lamina detailed their movements and the transportation of weaponry and defences over the next couple of nights. When her thoughts drifted to who she would fight in the battle, she shook her head, determined to keep her mind clear. All that mattered was cutting the world's supply of E132 at the source.

Ω

Mrs Maremortum strode through the highest room in the Lost Languages, surveying its occupants: several large magitech machines attached through long, thick metal tubes to a central scarlet vessel that rose up through the centre of the roof. Stopping by one of the machines, she hesitantly placed her hand into the scarlet hand-shaped mould beside it and closed her eyes as it assumed a purple hue. After some time, she shuddered and drew her hand back.

"No matter what happens with Magia, these machines must continue to run."

Turning to the owner of the voice, Mrs Maremortum inclined her head in agreement. "I will maintain the peace with whoever claims leadership." She glanced sideways at Grüber by her side. "The Brigadier will keep in contact with Shin'en Kiryuu. And Lachesis has already agreed to sustain the supply of E132 to the artificial sun. We're grateful for your supply of weaponry. Please assure your leaders that we will do everything to fulfill Kaishi's wish."

"Assurance for Shin'en Kiryuu is only found in blood."

Mrs Maremortum flinched. Gathering herself, she smoothed out a wrinkle in her cotton blouse and nodded in calm assent. "You're right." Holding her arm up, Mrs Maremortum took a scarlet shard from her pocket and ran the jagged edge along her forearm, wincing as blood trickled down onto the ground. "I swear on the blood of my forefathers, the People of Old."

A runic circle momentarily lit up beneath her feet, words swirling about her feet like tendrils before fading along with the blood.

A young man with sleek, shoulder length black hair and almond shaped eyes bowed deeply to both Mrs Maremortum and The Brigadier. He wore what appeared to be an open blue gown over the top of a white blouse and a long, grey pleated skirt. Beside him, a taller individual wearing an ornate azure dragon mask mirrored him with a deep bow. He wore a robe-like tunic, that flowed out in three long strips from high side slits that exposed white, baggy pants underneath. A wide azure sash held the robe together and two slender sheathed swords sat snugly against it.

"Thank you. I will inform Sora Haruhi that you will be upholding Sora Kaishi's wish," said the young man, heavily emphasising the title 'Sora' which Mrs Maremortum had dropped. "Should you need replacements for the magitech machine, the Sora line have disposables. For a price." His face was unreadable as he proceeded to exchange foreign words with the masked individual beside him. They both nodded, swept their arms in a circular motion and pressed a closed right fist into the palm of their left before departing with a muttered, "Arutana".

As the sound of their retreating footsteps faded down the stairwell, Mrs Maremortum heaved a long sigh and sagged atop of a nearby stool, binding her wound up with a handkerchief.

"Oracle, a promise involving blood cannot be broken," said the Brigadier, breaking the silence that hung over the room.

"Yes, but what else could I do? We need to placate the simmering tensions between Railesson and Shin'en Kiryuu, never mind their existing partnership with Gershom." Mrs Maremortum sighed loudly again, running an irate hand through her silver hair.

The Brigadier closed her eyes, face impassive. "It's believed your father died from breaking a blood promise."

"Anyone with any sense knew that was the case with that oaf!"

"Harsh words regarding your father."

"I have no love for falsehoods."

"Even so." The Brigadier shook her head. "Are you setting you and your daughter up for failure? If she draws Keira's ire—even The Conqueror won't interfere with her."

Fists clenched, Mrs Maremortum pursed her lips. "My people are Pater's chosen. He will protect us because of this truth."

"Now you've deigned to call yourself a Pateran?"

Mrs Maremortum's eye twitched when a familiar Magian Colonel swaggered into the room, a look of pure disdain on his face. "I'm simply stating the truth."

"When it's convenient to you," Simeon snorted derisively. He approached Mrs Maremortum, eyes glinting maliciously. "And why should he spare a sinner like you?"

Mrs Maremortum stretched herself up to her full height, a snake prepared to strike. "How dare you," she hissed, voice low. "I saw your lingering looks at my daughter."

"Your daughter?"

Closing the distance between them, Mrs Maremortum jabbed an angry finger in his face. "You're sick," she seethed, her face, a mask of fury, inches away from Simeon's. "You wanted to make her your own. You incestuous freak."

The muscles in Simeon's jaw visibly clenched. "I'm the freak?" He sneered, nodding his head slowly. "How ironic your words must sound to you!"

"Don't involve Levi in this!"

"You're the temporary General by blood, not by ability. I have no reason to tolerate your abuse any longer." Turning on his heel, Simeon marched away.

"Simeon!"

At the doorway, the Brigadier barred his exit. "Regardless of your claims, we've been informed that your doll and her army are on the move. Will you fight for Magia?"

"I will stand by my brother and the instructions he has received."

"I told you that I would hold you to your word." The Brigadier's voice was dangerously soft, her eyes scrutinising the Colonel. "Do you recall what you said in return?"

Simeon ran his tongue along his upper lip, inwardly steeling himself. "Yes."

"I expect no less than your death should Magia fall." The Brigadier held Simeon's gaze. "Or I will end your life for you."

Smiling weakly, Simeon bowed his head to hide the anger that flashed in his eyes. "You are the very opposite of The Oracle." He closed his eyes, willing his nerves to calm down. Raising his gaze to the Brigadier, he smiled. "Thank you for your reminder."

The Brigadier inclined her head and stepped aside, allowing Simeon room to leave. She inhaled deeply and let out a sigh that was almost inaudible to Mrs Maremortum who had turned back to the machines in the room, moodily looking over them for any maintenance concerns. They beeped out of sync, a strange and lonely tune that filled the quiet.

Boots slapped against the stairwell, ringing up through the open door and after a prolonged couple of minutes, Lieutenant Wayman stumbled into the room, chest heaving while he tried to catch his breath. "Ma'am!" he gasped between breaths, weakly saluting.

The Brigadier unfolded her arms. "Breathe, Lieutenant."

Gulping in some air, Wayman continued. "Major General Tres was successful in obtaining permission."

"Good. And the E132 mines?"

"All in place."

The Brigadier nodded in appreciation. "With no allies to depend on, we'll do what we must." She glanced over at Mrs Maremortum, her lips pursed. "This war will not be one of honour, remember that, Dinah."

Mrs Maremortum stiffened. Without returning the Brigadier's gaze she nodded, her glossy-nailed fingers absently running over the head of a machine.

The Brigadier nodded dismissively to Lieutenant Wayman and with one last glance back at Mrs Maremortum's slouched figure, she followed Wayman out onto the long spiral staircase, descending one floor.

Rapping her knuckles on the floor's door, the Brigadier stood back, threading her fingers together.

The door swung in and behind it stood a bespectacled young man in a long, thin, white coat with the sleeves rolled up to his elbows. He blinked rapidly several times, stammered a hello and mixed a bow with an awkward salute.

"I'm sorry, Brigadier, I was not expecting you," spluttered the white coat, his brown eyes looking anywhere but her.

Peering over his shoulder into the room beyond, the Brigadier noted several other white coats working; studying charts pinned to the walls, writing note on clipboards, monitoring several tubes descending from the ceiling. The tubes were connected into several large deposits of glowing scarlet crystals in metal containers.

"Are the bodies holding up?"

The white coat pressed his lips together and folded his arms, trembling hands holding his elbows. "The blemished are displaying signs of Tophetication," he answered, downcast. "However, those from the Sora bloodline are holding up incredibly well."

"I'll inform our contacts at Shin'en Kiryuu. And when are you taking leave? I noticed you hadn't handed in your mandatory leave paperwork."

The white coat blanched.

Eyes narrowing, the Brigadier took a step forward and studied the white coat's face more closely. He had dark, sunken eyes and his fingernails were bitten right down. "You can accompany me to Shin'en Kiryuu."

"Shin'en Kiryuu? When would that be?"

"Right now." The Brigadier turned to leave. "We can't lose an invaluable member of the Council of Magia to overexposure."

"But I'm monitoring temperatures and light!"

Pausing, the Brigadier slowly looked over her shoulder. "If you want to Topheticise, by all means stay. I'll ensure someone cuts you down while I'm away." The stairs rang with her footsteps as she began to descend.

Running a hand down his unshaven face, the white coat waved farewell to the others in the room and shakily stepped out, shutting the door behind himself and following the Brigadier down the stairs.

Ω

Under the cover of night, Lamina's group trekked to the eastern side of The Mare where the ruins of the northern part of Lune remained. It was a smaller city than Manna once was, claiming less than a third of the land when Terra reflected and compared the remains there.

"They were the devoted keepers of The Mare and a long line of seers blessed with the gift of Pateran prophecy. The place given to them by Pater's blessing," Talia explained as Terra looked in wonder at the broken remains of what she imagined were once beautifully crafted statues and columns of towering marble. "Most of the survivors fled to Taliph, with many others running through to leave by Railesson's spiritrest port."

The crunch of rubble underfoot dampened Terra's spirits and she tried to imagine how the city had once been in all its splendour. "Where did the others go?"

"Mostly Gershom. Many were fortunate to have had family already settled there from the age of exiles."

Terra felt the corners of her lips lifting. "But Mr Joseph remained with his son."

"He did."

"Do you have family waiting for your return?"

Talia smiled. "My parents." After a pregnant pause, she continued, "There's no man waiting for me, if that's what you're asking."

"I'm sorry, I just thought that someone as beautiful as you would have…" Terra trailed off, mumbling incoherently to herself, face red.

Letting out a light, airy laugh, Talia slipped a reassuring arm around Terra's shoulders. "I'm flattered." She looked ahead thoughtfully. "I suppose with how dire numbers have become across the world, it's just expected that everyone would be 'contributing' to keeping this world alive." She paused. "Do you recall what Scriptura says?"

"It says that if you need to get married, then you should. But you don't need to if you can help it."

"Kind of contradictory, right?"

Terra shook her head. "It makes sense. If you have no desire to, or are unable to, then you just don't marry."

"You make it sound so simple!" Talia laughed. "Isn't that a bit sad though?"

"Do you find it sad?"

Shifting the bags on her shoulders, Talia mulled over the question. "Sometimes, yes. Sometimes, no."

"Not to be impolite but I think that's what everyone's experience of life is. And I know that understanding the reason for your existence is far more important than whether you marry or not."

"What is your reason for existence?"

Terra flashed a brilliant smile. "Trusting Agnus and following him." The black of the sky could not dampen her mood as she reached up to it, her eyes sparkling. "I know that a lot of people would believe such an existence to be meaningless, but I have never felt so free and so hopeful for the future." Hair blowing about her in a gust of wind, Terra closed her hand, as if grabbing hold of something.

"Well," Talia said with a soft smile, "I think it's a beautiful existence."

The two women linked arms, giggling softly as they chatted all the way to Lune and Terra's heart soared. These moments of peace, of enjoying another's company, she treasured and wondered if perhaps her heart could overflow with love like One.

In the ruins of old Lune, the separate groups of the Mannite army convened and they huddled quietly together in the cramped underground tunnel, prepared to sleep before the battle ahead.

Lune had taken care to construct their underground—it had been paved with slabs of grey stones, interspersed with colourful tiles, arranged in patterns of various shapes and designs. The tiles were carefully labelled with painted letters and directional arrows that were now flaking with neglect.

Sinking to the cold stones beside Talia, Terra laid her head back against the stone wall, her mind racing endlessly with thoughts of Magia and this strange return to it.

"I worked in Shin'en Kiryuu as a child," whispered Talia, cutting through Terra's train of thought.

Allowing her words to register, Terra screwed her face up in bewilderment. "I thought Agnus paid the fine for Manna's children not to work?"

Throwing her head back and laughing, the corners of Talia's eyes crinkled merrily. "It was long before that, Ridley. My appearance does not portray my age." Winking, Talia leaned back against the old stone wall behind her and closed her eyes. "Back in Shin'en Kiryuu, my master's wife often sang a song during the war with Gershom." Without warning, she quietly burst into song, causing several close by to shoot looks of concern and confusion at her.

In the twilight of the land,
The heart slumbers.
Softly murmuring as it dreams
Of a sinking sun.
Spreading wide its wings to soar,
Scarlet everywhere.
And the dream it dreamt within the time that past
A fading dream never meant to last.

Mesmerised by the mournful tune, Terra struggled to feign a smile once Talia's eyes fluttered back open. "That's a sad song. What's it about?"

Shaking her head, Talia shrugged. "It's an old Liv'yatan lullaby. They sing it to their young. Some say it's prophecy and others claim it to be heresy because it's Liv'yatan folklore—they don't believe in Pater." She laid her head back against the wall, her eyes closed once more, her voice growing softer with fatigue. "But I simply thought the song was beautiful."

When quiet settled over the company, the night trickled by in an amalgamation of neck pain, interrupted sleep, loud snores, grunts and sore backs.

For Terra, she sat quietly, recalling parts of Scriptura as she rolled her ring over her finger endlessly. Sleep would not easily come and she whispered Agnus' promises and reminders to herself, praying earnestly for everyone to rest well, to be refreshed and that they would achieve what Agnus had sent them to do. Mid prayer, her head lolled to the side and she drifted off, her dreams haunted by the shadow of a familiar Magian officer chasing her through the night into the late hours of sun down.

Long before the light of the artificial sun spilled over the horizon, the Mannite army marched through the Lune underground, descending further into the earth, the air slowly thinning and the smell of mildew filling their nostrils. Terra found herself stifling several yawns as her feet stumbled over stone after stone. She readjusted the strap that held the scabbard of Shigure's sword around her waist, idly wondering when she would need to make use of it over Spiritus.

After following the sloping tunnel down, it plateaued and a couple hours passed to the drone of shoes pattering against the stone floor. The ground steadily inclined up and several more flaky sloped names and arrows on the wall indicated they would soon reach the surface.

When Nicholo announced that they had reached the other side of The Mare, Terra curled her toes as far as she could in her shoes, her stomach churning in anticipation and anxiety. The company surfaced in an old, dilapidated building, crumbling from the devastations of an old war, with the exit still half obstructed by rubble, forcing the company to leave in single file. Ash covered much of the ground around Lune's southern houses streaking the tunnel end.

It was another couple of hours retreading the dusty, humid plains that Terra had once run along with Lamina. The young silver-haired woman's thoughts dwindled into past memories and she unconsciously placed a hand over her heart, recalling the suffering she had endured in the town she grew up in.

Could she finally put an end to this evil place?

Rising up from the ground, rot birthed from the wine of the Other, Magia appeared on the horizon, its appendages of overexposure stretching far all around the town. The closer the Mannite company got, the heavier the air became and the more violently Terra's stomach writhed. From a distance, a force of Magian soldiers far larger than their army stood before the broken gate and half-collapsed stone wall, dotting the landscape navy blue.

Terra's heart thumped so forcefully in her chest, she was convinced it would leap out. They were here at last.

"Form ranks!" Nicholo called out from somewhere to Terra's right.

Getting into formation, they slowly continued their march towards Magia, shields ready for attacks.

A deafening bang reverberated throughout the dusty plains, stopping everyone in their tracks and far to their left, Terra watched a chunk of flesh soar over, landing near Talia's feet. Muffled screams and a number of people scrambled away from where the explosion had occurred.

As Terra stared numbly at the flesh near her, she vaguely heard Nicholo repeatedly yelling for people to stop and the urgent cries for calm from Lamina. Humming beneath her skin, Terra felt the roar of Spiritus within her and plunging her hand into the bright light in her chest, she wrenched the sword out and held it high above her and took an unsteady step forward.

She turned to face the broken formation of Manna's army, the fear on their faces resonating with her feelings inside. Grounding her teeth, she mumbled a prayer and sucked in a deep breath between her clenched teeth. "Long ago, the Other sank his fangs into the flesh of Magia. It was here that the Other planted his roots and has since offered his fruit to the rest of the world. This fruit is rotting the world with overexposure, separating you from One—who long ago, revealed himself to our ancestors as Pater."

All eyes were on her now and Terra felt her heart swelling and she could not stop herself from speaking—she felt the need to shake people awake.

"Magia must fall to stop the supply of E132 in the world. Whether you remain here to fight Magia or not, I will see the prophecy fulfilled!" Terra turned on her heel with a huff, her gaze hard as she stared at the Magian officers stationed from afar who had begun to point what appeared to be bows and arrows. "Agnus, guide me." She inhaled deeply, hands shaking. "Scriptura Salvatus."

A burst of words erupted from her head before confining back into a thorny helm that moulded around her head. Closing her eye, Terra concentrated and prayed that she may be able to spread the protection of Salvatus as far as she could.

The heavy thumping and clanging of metal drew her attention and she looked around to find a body of long shields—scutums—, forming in front of and around her.

"We're with you, Ridley! We won't turn away again!" cried Talia as she stood poised with her own shield on the dirt before her crouched form.

Unbidden tears welled up in Terra's eye.

"Everyone, we march! Do not stop! Close the distance!" yelled Lamina as they all huddled behind the shields. "We move as one!"

The body of shields inched forward, picking up speed as a couple of eruptions sounded nearby and Terra glimpsed an insidious, familiar scarlet hue in connection with all of them. A few metres to her right, there was an explosion of blood, pieces of flesh and other materials that Terra refused to look at. She grit her teeth and continued onward, focusing on channelling Salvatus' shield to cover as many people as possible.

"Don't stop!" Lamina's voice bellowed above the sounds of explosions and screams. "Don't stop!"

The wall of shields continued to march ahead, closing in tighter together with each explosive disruption, until Terra no longer heard the thunk of arrows embedding into them and knew they would soon be reaching the Magians. Her grip on Spiritus tightened and she felt the deafening roar of her blood in her ears at the anticipation of battle.

There was a scream and a howl as the wall of shields were rammed into several bodies and they parted with Terra leaping out, whirling Spiritus readily about.

Focusing on her breathing, Terra filled her mind with memories of the words that swirled around the sword she wielded. She allowed the blade to direct her movements and danced behind it, pulling it through the body of an enemy and sliding it into the belly of another.

Lamina covered her back whenever it was exposed, deflecting blows and overwhelming attackers with his raw strength. He wrestled with two sword wielders, his hand gripping the wrists of their sword arms. Before the two could land a blow with their free fists, Nicholo swept their feet out from under them with a staff. Leaping back up, he swiftly caught a sword swing from the right with his staff and spun it, jerking the sword away from himself and crushing the man's nose with the other end of the staff. He dropped quickly to grab the sword, Terra jumping in to parry another swing directed at him.

Terra's eye darted across the battlefield at every opportunity, but battle stratagems were not her forte. At the sight of some of the Mannites struggling, Terra strained to push away an iron axe and ducked under the swing of another, shouting over her shoulder as she rose: "Lamina, rally the army and decide what's best!"

Lamina clenched his teeth, throwing off a bulky man who stumbled back into two other people who collapsed under his weight. "What about you, young mistress?"

"I'll cover her!" Nicholo roared as an arrow whirred past his head, cutting his cheek and embedding itself into the back of the man Terra was engaged with.

Terra flinched back as a man to her left lunged at her, nicking her arm with his sword.

A deafening bang resonated through the battlefield and the close proximity of it caused Terra to stagger back with a grimace, her ears ringing. "Lamina!"

Crouching on all fours, Lamina launched himself over the heads of the men surrounding them and charged through the sea of bodies towards the area where the sound had erupted, his horns striking any who stood in the way.

Staggering from the explosion, Nicholo snarled as a sword tip caught the side of his leather armour and soon found himself dancing between two soldiers, defensively using his staff and newly obtained sword.

"Mr Nicholo!"

"Focus on your own battle, young Ridley!"

From where she fought, Terra glimpsed several casualties from the explosion on both sides and could only pray that Lamina would know how to help.

Disarming a soldier in front of her, the hairs on the back of Terra's neck stood on end and she instinctively moved to dodge a shard of E132, biting her lip as it ripped through the skin of her forearm.

The bodies of soldiers parted and Simeon passed through the berth, his hand raised and navy blue coat billowing out behind him. The shard returned to his hand and in one fluid motion he unsheathed a silver sword and dashed forward, his strike almost catching Terra off-guard.

Positioning her right foot behind her body to steady herself, Terra's heart thumped uncomfortably as she met Simeon's cool gaze.

He looked her briefly up and down, his expression unreadable. "You really must be her daughter."

There was no anger or madness to simplify his movements; no wildness that made him predictable, his strikes telegraphed.

A niggling doubt entered Terra's head and Simeon pushed Spiritus down, his eyes flashing red momentarily. Shards of E132 rose around him, shooting out at Terra who jumped back and deflected some, slicing through a couple others. She cried out as two more scraped off a layer of flesh from each thigh. She leapt away again on the recall of the shards, breathless as she spun away from a sword swung at her from a nearby Magian soldier.

Simeon glared at the Magian, firing a small shard that pierced straight through the man's left shoulder. "She's mine."

A visible shudder rippled through the crowd of nearby Magians who proceeded to scatter away, Simeon's E132 piece rushing back to his hand when summoned.

Terra brushed back her bangs, sweat causing her hair to stick to her forehead. Raising Spiritus, she firmly planted her feet shoulder-width apart, steeling herself for another attack. "Colonel Simeon…we should talk." Terra blew hair out of her mouth, walking cautiously around the perimeter of the wide berth formed around the pair.

Simeon returned her gaze coolly, stowing the E132 into his pockets. "We've spoken enough, 0792."

He lunged forward, brandishing his sword and forcing Terra on the back-foot. While calm and collected, Simeon's ease and expertise with a sword was apparent; like an extension of his arm, it wove through the air, slicing and piercing.

Beads of sweat trickled down the back of Terra's neck, meeting together between her shoulders blades that ached as she barely managed to keep up with Simeon's relentless assault. There was no time to split her attention to Salvatus.

While he fought with a metal sword, he had the advantage. He swung against her defensive stance, forcing her arms up. He plunged his sword through the air towards her belly and Terra barely stepped aside in time, his sword catching her left side.

There was no time for her to think as three red shards shot forward, following Simeon's sword and embedding themselves into Terra's right side.

She shrieked as Simeon recalled the shards but she instinctively dove to the side at the sight of Simeon's blade reaching to strike her again.

There was a rumbling of cries from the Mannites nearby. They struggled against the barricade of Magians, forcing one of the soldiers near Terra's left to stumble backwards.

The ground erupted below the man in a deluge of scarlet, and Terra soon found herself soaring before colliding with another person far to her right. Disoriented, she struggled back to her feet with the help of a couple of Mannites who murmured words of concern. She swayed on the spot, a hand clamped over her ringing left ear.

She shook her head, trying to refocus her vision, unsure of which blurred uniform was the Colonel's. Groggily, she drove Spiritus' point into the ground, sending a shockwave from it as she bellowed with all the strength she could muster, "Libertas Spiritus!"

A force of words burst forth from around the sword, billowing out and throwing back many of the blue uniforms, to the relief of the Mannites. Several explosions went off in the process under the bodies of Magian soldiers as they fell from the blow of Spiritus, catching many others in the process. Showers of bloody matter and rocks splattered against the forcefield from Spiritus, unable to enter.

Terra took advantage of the moment to catch her breath and shakily reached into her trouser pocket, pulling out the silver hair clip Agnus had given her. Leaving Spiritus in the ground, she opened the hair clip with a snap and slid it into her fringe, pulling it a little to the side and pinning it down with a click.

The words that had burst from Spiritus, shrank back, surrounding the sword once more and Terra pulled it from its place in the ground.

At the sound of the blasts, Lamina glanced over his shoulder and recognised the runic symbols from Agnus' armour radiating out from a central point. "Nicholo!" He threw off some attackers with the scutum he and Talia carried. "Nicholo! Look after the young mistress!" he shouted into the scramble of shields and the flashes of silver and iron.

Grunting with effort, Nicholo bashed his head against the Magian soldier in front of him and swiftly gutted him. Gripping the sword tightly, he rammed the body against the people in front of him, shielding himself from a few blows before tearing his sword out and slicing two Magians near him. He moved towards where the explosions had sounded, parrying blows with both staff and sword in either hand and slitting a throat.

"Talia, can I count on you too?" Lamina yelled over the rabble, goring a Magian soldier and crying out as an arrow embedded itself into his shoulder. Roaring, he tore the arrow out, clenching his teeth and ignoring the rivulets of blood.

Talia thrust her scutum into the gored soldier, sending him toppling into his allies. "What about you?"

"I promised Agnus that I would take care of the young mistress! Don't let me become a liar!"

"Yes, Mr Lamina!" Talia inched back towards Nicholo as he knocked his way through soldiers to Terra, mindful of the skirmishes around her, with Lamina covering her where the scutum didn't.

Mr Maremortum plunged his sword into the belly of a Mannite, his teeth gritting as another charged at him.

Breathing deeply, he focused on the movement of air about him, clenching the fragment of E132 in his mouth between his teeth, drawing out its power. He could sense where the figures about him would move next. His feet slid to the left, dodging blow after blow and sinking his silver blade into one person and then another.

Tossing another fragment of E132 from his pocket in his mouth, Mr Maremortum leapt up high into the air to the astonishment of his next attacker. The balls of his feet connected with the jaw of the person in front of him, sending them sprawling into the dirt with a loud crack.

With the Magians still outnumbering their enemies despite heavy losses from the earlier explosions, Mr Maremortum pushed through the battlefield. He struck down any Mannite in his way as he edged to where he had heard Agnus' armour activated. A sudden yell from his right side drove him to leap hurriedly away, narrowly avoiding the swing from a sword.

"Silver hair," came the gruff voice of Nicholo as he followed up with several swings from both staff and sword. "Levi Maremortum."

Mr Maremortum growled, jumping and inching back to avoid several staff swings at his legs. He caught Nicholo's sword with his own and dodged when he did not have time to think.

Closing his eyes, he let his footing slip slightly. Red hot pain seared through Mr Maremortum's right thigh as Nicholo's sword pierced cleanly through it and in that split second, Mr Maremortum's eyes snapped open, glowing a malicious scarlet. He took his own sword in both his hands and spat one of the E132 fragments directly into Nicholo's eye. As Nicholo howled and flinched back with the shard protruding from his eyeball, Mr Maremortum brought his sword down with such force that he cut through Nicholo's wrist, detaching his hand from his body.

Screaming in horror, Talia blundered forward as quickly as she could with her scutum, running into Mr Maremortum and knocking him back. She stood protectively over Nicholo as he tore the shard out from his right eye with a howl. He desperately tore at his clothes for enough material to stop his arm bleeding, his right hand fumbling as tears mingled with blood streamed down his face.

Popping another scarlet fragment into his mouth, Mr Maremortum clenched his teeth, ripping the sword out from his thigh and tossing it aside. Knowing he was at a disadvantage while injured against two people, he turned and hobbled quickly away, providing time for Talia to dig her scutum into the ground at an angle over both her and Nicholo.

Finishing the poor binding on his arm, Talia helped Nicholo up gingerly but yelled in protest as he jerked away from her.

"Go to the young Ridley!" barked Nicholo as he raced after Mr Maremortum's retreating form with staff in his remaining hand, dodging several entanglements.

"Nicholo!"

From a distance, Terra watched the limping figure of Mr Maremortum and Nicholo giving chase, and Agnus' words rose to the forefront of her mind.

Her grip on Spiritus tightened and her legs were moving before it had registered in her mind that she was chasing him. She slashed the soldiers who rushed at her sides, her eye blazing blue as Spiritus hummed with urgency.

"0792!"

Terra cried out as a scarlet shard struck her on the left shoulder. Staggering, she cursed the continued ringing in her left ear and grabbed the shard, prepared to wrench it out when she spotted another sailing towards her with no time to react.

With a guttural roar a shield leapt out in front of her, absorbing the shard with a satisfying thud and Talia stood tall before Terra.

"I'll be your shield, Ridley!" Talia glared at Simeon who continued to stride towards them. Armed with the heavy scutum and a smaller rounded shield strapped to her back, Talia began to lug the shield backward.

Encouraged, Terra's eye returned to its grey hue. "Thanks." With a grunt, she ripped the shard from her shoulder and tossed it on the ground.

Soon the two women were pushing through the battlefield, Talia covering Terra's blind spot and keeping an eye on Simeon who continued to pursue them, his sword gliding through all passing bodies in indiscriminate fury. They rushed through the broken gates and into Magia proper and there, they spotted Mr Maremortum and Nicholo racing towards one of the closer caves; old mines that had long run dry of the coveted rocks even before Terra had arrived. Following Nicholo into the cave, Terra ignored the shout of Simeon who dogged their steps.

Within the first area of the cave, Nicholo's staff was cut clean in two by the long, thin scarlet blade that Mr Maremortum now bore. The Mannite fell backwards, his staff falling to the side and Terra shot forward, ramming Spiritus into the floor.

"Libertas!"

The brief shockwave rocked the cave and Mr Maremortum stumbled away from the forcefield as it reached Nicholo.

As the runic symbols began to retract back to Spiritus and Terra who continued to rush to Nicholo's side, Mr Maremortum instinctively turned, eyes flashing red and spitting one of the fragments in his mouth. It sliced deep into the flesh above her eyelid, narrowly missing her eye and she gasped as she tumbled to the ground near Nicholo.

Talia immediately ran at Mr Maremortum, shield out to beat him back but a scarlet shard shot from the cave entrance caught her left calf and another lodged itself in her lower back. She staggered and planted her scutum in the ground to stop herself from falling over, taking cover behind it as she glared at Simeon entering the cave.

In that moment, Mr Maremortum spun around and drew out a collection of fragments from his pocket and flung them at Nicholo's head as he tried to push himself back up.

Scrambling to her feet, Terra slashed through several, with a couple slipping past and two, like long needles, embedded themselves deep into Nicholo's chest. Nicholo crumpled to the ground with a feeble grunt.

Teeth grit, Terra cried, "Talia!" She cut loose the strap from around her waist, flinging her teacher's sword in Talia's direction.

Abandoning her scutum, Talia scuttled forward, scooping the scabbard up and detaching the round shield from her back. She screamed as the shards in her body were summoned back to Simeon's hands but still she darted forward to Nicholo's side as Terra charged at Mr Maremortum. "Don't you dare die on me, Nicholo!"

Nicholo gave a weak smile from where he lay. "Help young Ridley." His breaths were short and uneven.

Mr Maremortum flicked his wrists and the two needles of scarlet in Nicholo's chest tore themselves out with a loud cry, flying back towards the silver-haired man, with Terra within its trajectory.

Dropping down to the ground instinctively, Terra swiped at the blood over her eyelid before quickly rolling, narrowly avoiding Mr Maremortum's next attack.

She reflexively leapt up as Simeon entered the fray, his sword swung where her legs had previously been, her body aching in protest.

Mr Maremortum danced away from Talia's swings as she jumped forward with shield in hand. The silver-haired man was already moving towards the left of Terra. She could hardly take a breath before launching herself to the right to dodge the attack aimed at her left side.

He knew that there was no vision or hearing on her left.

Mentally, Terra scolded herself for having revealed the weakness.

The whistle of a sword swinging at her from her right side prompted a grunt from Terra as she tried to manoeuvre to dodge it and she grit her teeth as the E132 brushed hard across her already wounded forearm.

She closed her eye and took a breath to steady herself, clamping her hand over the throbbing wound in her side. *Agnus, I need your strength.*

"Ridley!" Talia lunged forward to block a hit from Mr Maremortum's blade with her round shield. But she was sluggish from her wounds and her screech pierced the air as metal met flesh, the sword catching her side.

Terra almost fell as she caught Talia who staggered back into her. Wrapping her arms protectively around Talia, desperation and terror filled Terra.

What had she been training for?

She could picture her teacher's wicked grin when he would taunt her, asking if the pain and fear was enough for her to give up. She ground her teeth. *No.*

Simeon launched himself at her, sword raised and Terra opened her eye glaring furiously at him.

"Scriptura," she said, voice crisp and firm, "Libertas."

Words encircled Terra's body and she closed her eye, allowing it to embrace her, her mind filling with images and memories of those which the words whispered of. The words brushed against her forehead, imprinting characters that blazed in the darkness of the mine.

Spiritus was a burning flame in her hands as it resonated with the thorny helm encircling her head, growing in strength.

The runes engulfed Talia and her whimpering quietened, temporarily soothed by the armour. Struggling back onto her knees, Talia rested her shield on the rocky floor, her breathing ragged.

Terra opened her eye, revealing it had turned a deep blue. Her eye met with Simeon's terrified ones. "Do not be afraid, Simeon," spoke a voice that was not Terra's. "I know that you have seen these markings before."

The spirit spun the sword in her hands and, squaring her shoulders, held it up near her jaw, point directed at Simeon. Spiritus plunged towards him and as he deflected it, there was a brilliant flash of light and jolt of electricity that sparked and leapt through the pair.

My songs go nowhere
The words are scattered away
Like sand blown by the wind
Voice caught in my throat
There is no meaning

- Lines from the *Laments of Lerielle, Scriptura.* Translated by J. Talis

0001
16 BSD (*Spells* Before Sun's Death)

The sharp stab of several pickaxes against rock resounded throughout the mine, a monotonous drone that hummed endlessly in the minds of the labouring children who lined the walls of the shaft, even long after they left to rest for the night.

At the far end of the mineshaft, a dark-haired boy squatted, eyes glazed as he mindlessly chiselled out the scarlet crystal embedded in the walls. His right hand was blistered from the arduous work, so he had switched the pickaxe to his left, his aim awkward as he continued to tiredly beat the rock before him.

"General Van de Berg is resolved on the decision to make deals with the beastmasters," murmured an officer within earshot of the dark-haired youth.

"Really? I hope that means good news for Bernadette...she's been considering injection..." A second officer shook his head. "No one knows if the magickal properties of E132 will return everyone's bodies to normal."

"We have to try whatever we can!" The first officer clenched his teeth.

"It's that scoundrel's fault! If he didn't interfere—"

He followed this with a string of words the young boy had heard his mother hurl at him when she was in a foul mood. And every night for the past couple of months, she had been so.

The second officer attempted a smile. He laced his fingers together behind his back. "What about your wife? How is she coping?"

The first officer sighed, his expression worn. "Aliza had always wanted a girl." He shrugged. "I guess now we'll never know whether what they say is true—that a girl lasts longer in the mines than a boy."

His companion gave an appreciative laugh. "We're all in the same boat. None of us can replenish the number of workers anymore."

He received a wrangled grunt in reply. "Why do you sound so happy about that?"

"Come on. I want the curse lifted as badly as any other Magian parent. If injection is the only solution, then what else can we do?"

"As long as we don't deal with those anti-E132 beasts. Our progress may be slower than before Dayton appeared, but it hasn't brought us to a standstill. I'd prefer we keep to ourselves until we resolve our own issues." A nod of agreement from his companion encouraged him to continue. "If we reach out to the beastmasters now for assistance in acquiring children outside of Magia for work, it'd reflect badly on the state of the place. Who knows if the talk in the west about Eli and Daniel Sominium is true?"

Over the noise of rocks breaking, the second officer inched towards the first, jerking his head subtly in the boy's direction. "Do you think Dr Railesson has made progress on a cure? I mean, he does have problems of his own..."

The first officer snorted derisively. "That boy? Aren't all children merely grief for their parents?"

The boy made no comment. His gaze was fixed on the mine wall while his left hand repeatedly moved back and forth, rocks crumbling under the abuse of the pickaxe.

On his makeshift bed of folded blankets, the dark-haired boy listened to the voices of his parents in the room next to his, whispering in urgent and hushed tones late into the night. The wall in between his and theirs muffled their voices and the boy could not make out all the words they spoke. He listened intently to their murmurs until without realising it, he drifted off to sleep.

There was a loud crack that shook the sleep from the young boy's eyes.

He sat up in bed, warily looking about himself, eyes still adjusting to the darkness. His heartbeat erratically in his chest.

"Mother...? Father...?"

The hairs on the back of his neck were raised as he strained his ears to hear any sound in the silence that had enveloped the house. Gulping, he pulled back his sheet and rose, tiptoeing across the room.

His ears picked up the sound of movement in the kitchen and he edged towards the sound, struggling to keep himself from shaking. "Mother...? Father?" The floorboards creaked under his feet as he inched towards the kitchen door that stood ajar. The sliver of light that slipped through the gap between the door and its frame illuminated the syringe tossed on the floor, with, what the boy recognised from spells of mining, the liquid remains of the scarlet crystal, Element 132.

Gingerly, he pushed the door open, a lump in his throat.

"Mother...?" The boy's voice quivered, his scrawny legs trembling beneath his tiny frame. His breath came harsh and sharp as he watched his mother, her body inhumanely bent over his fallen father's figure.

The woman's fingers were delicate as they tore into the throat of her husband, her head bent towards the blood that spouted out and her tongue, tainted red with blood, eagerly lapped up the viscous fluid.

The boy felt a scream rise into the back of his throat and, unconsciously, he took a shaky step back, drawing the blood red gaze of the creature that wore his mother's face.

Her lips pulled back, revealing her scarlet stained teeth in a horrific snarl and the boy took another step back, an overwhelming roaring filling his ears.

I don't want to die. I don't want to die. I don't want to die.

He leapt back, narrowly avoiding his mother's hands, clawing viciously at the air.

I don't want to die. I don't want to die, he cried desperately in his mind, slipping over the discarded syringe, his mother's wild shriek piercing the night. *I don't want to—*

Those thin, elegant hands slowly reached for the young boy's throat as the creature's red, macabre eyes glowed in the dark.

A scream ripped through the boy's throat: "DIE!"

The metallic smell of blood filled the air and it splashed across the boy's face and clothes like paint. The E132 in his mother's veins had torn through her flesh and gathered in his right hand where it solidified into a scarlet crystal shard.

He trembled uncontrollably, his eyes wide and wild and his breaths were quick and ragged.

In the sudden stillness that blanketed the night, the boy looked upon his mother's shredded form, tears streaming down his face.

"This is the boy, Gustav."

Two officers marched into the room with a dark-haired boy in tow. He trailed behind them tiredly, the cuffs around his wrist connected to chains an officer held.

Gustav sat up in his seat, taking note of the bloodstains covering the shivering boy from head to toe and the lifeless look in his eyes.

Two silver-haired children ran around a front lawn, laughing as they kicked a beanbag back and forth between themselves.

Approaching the lawn, the dark-haired boy's eyes were drawn to the pair as they darted about and a faint feeling of jealousy arose in him.

What a carefree existence they seemed to lead.

"Levi! Dinah! Come and say hello to your new brother!" called Gustav Van de Berg as he approached the door to his family's home.

The silver-haired girl near the front door drew her leg back, kicking the beanbag at the dark-haired boy and hitting his arm. "I don't need a brother! I already have one!"

The boy rubbed his arm but kept his eyes on his bare feet. An odd feeling of hollowness filled him. He would not like it here either.

"Don't be like that, Dinah," said Gustav, his expression stern. He put an arm around the boy and gestured to the silver-haired boy behind Dinah to come closer. "I want you all to get along. Say hello, Levi."

"Hi." The silver-haired boy gave a small, dimpled smile. He shuffled forward a little, hand outstretched and face filled with both uncertainty and warmth. "I'm Levi."

Intrigued by Levi's mixed emotions, the dark-haired boy hesitated briefly but reached out and took Levi's hand. "I'm Simeon," he murmured, lowering his gaze when he noticed Dinah's piercing one fixed on him.

Levi's hand slipped out of Simeon's and the latter glanced up to catch the look of shock on Levi's face. "Your name is like mine."

Confused, Simeon opened his mouth to reply but Dinah nudged her brother out of the way and thrust her hand out. "I'm Dinah. Nice to meet you." She grabbed Simeon's hand and shook it roughly, making the dark-haired boy uncomfortable. He shrunk away, hoping she would let go, but she held on, studying him closely. "I think I've seen you before."

Simeon jerked his hand out of hers and lowered his gaze to his feet again. "I've never met you."

Shuffling his feet, he could feel Dinah's grey eyes burning through the top of his head. Eyes that were too striking to forget. They were just like his mother's.

He swallowed thickly, his clenched fist shaking as his nails bit into the palm of his hand.

"I heard you killed your mother. Is that true?"

It was late in the day and the sun had sunk low into its bed of colours. Orange and purple wrapped comfortably around it, blending seamlessly as one blanket. The buzzing of insects cut through the otherwise quiet evening air.

Crouching low to the ground, Simeon kept his head down, ignoring the silver-haired girl.

The toe of her shoe dug into his ribcage. "Well, is it?"

Simeon turned his face away, hoping it would deter Dinah.

Rocks crunched under her feet as she crouched beside him, her breath lightly fanning his face. "You killed your mother and that's why Van de Berg adopted you. He's going to use you one day because of your power." Simeon swore he could hear the cruel smile on her face. "I bet you're a real monster."

Curling his toes, Simeon hunched over, his breaths short and sharp. He prayed that Dinah would stop and let him be, but every cold word from her lips that followed his prayer disheartened him more.

When Dinah finally left Simeon alone, he sat back, drew his knees up and hid his face behind them as the tears that had been building up fell from his eyes. A sob burst from his lips.

"I didn't ask to be born this way!" He trembled from head to toe. "I hate her! I hate her!" He ground his teeth together and placed his hands in his hair, pulling at the ends of them. "I *hate* her! I hate people." He paused, a fresh sob escaping him. "I hate myself."

He cried out to the darkness in despair but the darkness gave no comfort, it only laid claim to his heart.

"I wish I were dead."

After Simeon's tears had dried, his ears perked up at the sound of rocks crunching underfoot. He hugged his legs, shoulders visibly trembling.

A small, gentle hand touched him lightly on the shoulder and a familiar soft voice brought him to his senses.

"I'm sorry that my sister is mean to you sometimes..." mumbled Levi, crouching down beside Simeon's hunched form.

Simeon said nothing.

"She's really quite nice."

Still, Simeon did not reply.

"She's just angry at you...she found out that you really are our brother..." Levi eased himself onto the ground next to Simeon. "That lady you killed, she was our mother too."

Simeon twitched but did not say anything.

Levi continued. "They separated us from her when I was little but I remember her as a really nice lady."

"Liar."

It had been soft, but Levi was sure of what he heard. "I'm sorry." He rose to his feet. "I just wanted to help."

Simeon remained where he was even after Levi's footsteps had faded away completely.

The night air was humid and Simeon's shirt had already started to stick to his back. As unpleasant as this sensation was, Simeon made no move to adjust his clothing. His eyes remained fixed on the ground, dirt clinging to the sweat on the bottom of his feet.

The soft pad of returning footsteps steeled Simeon and he clenched his teeth as Levi spoke up again.

"We're having dinner now." Levi's gentle voice almost felt swallowed up by the darkness of the night. "Everyone in the family is there except you. Won't you come in?"

"I don't consider you family."

The words hung in the air like a heavy weight.

Simeon's heart hammered in his chest and the thought that Levi would hate him rushed back and forth through his mind.

Rocks crunched underfoot as Levi crouched beside Simeon. The latter closed his eyes in acceptance, bracing himself for the hurl of insults that were sure to fly out of the young Maremortum's mouth, or the slew of fists to really teach him a lesson.

But neither of these came.

Instead, Simeon felt the thin arms of Levi encircle him and he was drawn into an embrace.

"Don't say things like that," whispered Levi, hugging Simeon tightly, his cheek pressed against the back of the dark-haired boy's shoulder. "Because I consider you my brother."

Simeon's throat closed up. He heard the unmasked pain that strained Levi's soft voice. Tears stung his eyes and the darkness that had coiled itself around his heart fell away, dissolving in the night air. Returning the hug, he buried his face in the older boy's shoulder and cried, his body wracked by the wretched sobs that escaped his throat. He cried until his throat was raw and his face was red and puffy from the tears.

Levi pulled away and asked if Simeon would now join them for dinner, to which the dark-haired boy replied "yes" and the two walked back to the house, hand in hand.

Simeon clung to Levi. This boy would be his one semblance of hope in a world that seemed devoid of love. He would be an anchor in Simeon's times of uncertainty and fear; whenever he felt himself falling away, there Levi's hand would be holding his and keeping him from drifting.

In his mind, this broken world would finally meet its match with Simeon anchored in place. This world deserved nothing.

14 BSD

The clunk of heavy footsteps echoing throughout The Lost Languages announced the arrival of Brigadier Tres long before her lumbered into the Van de Berg quarters. He was a solid build with the beginnings of a doughy gut. "General Van de Berg, Eli Sominium has ordered the removal of women from Magia, with an exception for those within the military."

Perched on the edge of an armchair, Gustav inhaled deeply, nostrils flared. "The little Conqueror has only been on the throne for a handful of months and already he is barking orders." He clenched his jaw, a headache forming behind his eyes.

"What are your orders, General?"

Uncrossing his legs and resting his palms on his knees, Gustav shook his head. "We're too weak to oppose. With Agnus striking us and our loss to the Sominiums, what else can we hope to achieve?"

"With all due respect, this will be the final nail in the coffin for production numbers," retorted Tres, grimacing. "They have been plummeting since the curse."

Gustav tutted. "Tophetication."

"Yes. My apologies."

Rising from his seat, Gustav placed his hands behind his back and strolled over to the window, peering down on the rest of Magia. "Send out the order that all women outside of the military are to leave. We will have to meet with our little Conqueror to discuss the options for meeting the export demands across Tempus."

With a delicate 'ah', Gustav turned, peering at the corner of the room, a faint smile playing at his lips. "Could you possibly inform your siblings?"

Leaning back into the creaking armchair, Simeon scowled. "I will when you approve of my enrolment to the army."

Tres snorted. "You're not even of age. What use would you be?"

"I can manipulate E132!"

"Hardly," sneered Tres, crossing his arms and looking down his nose at the dark-haired boy. "You haven't achieved anything as grand since."

Chewing his bottom lip, Simeon fell into red-faced silence.

"Your beloved sister, Dinah, fares better than you." Tres shook his head. "We needed Dr Railesson to live that night, not you."

Simeon balled his fists, face twisted in fury.

Gustav steeped his fingertips under his chin, scrutinising Simeon. "I thought you despised Magia."

Head whipping towards Gustav, Simeon formed his lips into a hard line. "I do." He straightened, sitting proudly. "I hate this place with every fibre in my being."

Lips curling up into a smile, Gustav sat back in his chair. "Then, I'll approve your enrolment."

"General!"

Gustav raised his hand to silence Tres. He smiled broadened as he regarded Simeon's darkening face. "I want to see where your hatred takes you, boy." He shot a look at Tres who remained tight-lipped, his brows knotted together. Motioning for Simeon to approach, Gustav turned to the window and waited, hands clasped behind his back.

Swallowing a snide remark, Simeon rose from his seat and shuffled to his adoptive father's side.

"Do you see her?" Gustav's deep voice whispered in Simeon's ear. "Your sister is a splendid creature, isn't she?"

Simeon remained motionless, eyes trained on the silver-haired Dinah below. She smiled widely, eyes soft as she regarded the young silver-haired Levi next to her. They walked along the footpath below the tower.

Simeon could hear the leering grin in his father's words: "If you leave together with the both of them, she will be yours once you come of age."

Flinging her long hair back over her shoulder, the silver-haired

Maremortum looked up at her younger brother, eyes turning cold as she regarded the figure with him. She turned away and jogged off, hair shimmering in the light of the hot afternoon sun.

Simeon's lips were pressed together in a thin hard line, his eyebrows drawn down in anger. "I don't want her," he muttered stiffly, turning away from the window. "I'll tell them to leave but I'll remain here." He strode away, pausing at the door. "Besides, I'm sure the Old Laws forbid marrying relatives." He slammed the door behind him, intent on letting his words ring in his doddering father's ears.

A few days had passed since Simeon had officially changed his last name to Van de Berg and already the word "father" was like acid on his tongue. But he would learn to make use of it.

His hand came to rest on the scabbard that contained the E132 from his mother. Yes, he would use both of his parents to make this world right again.

"From the ashes of the dragon, my warrior will arise. She will point you to Ezer. And I will be with her and her people and my hand will deliver you from this age."

- Lines from *The Gates of Hrestia, Scriptura.* Translated by T. Lowenthal

19

On the far-side of a large, torch-lit ornamental room, Major General Tres ran his scabbard along the iron bars of the Tophet cages, listening with satisfaction at its clanking sound. Letting his scabbard drop back to his side, The Major General stopped and swung around to face the groaning grotesque figures, his mouth morphing into a hard sneer.

He had been tasked with releasing the Tophets for the battle. *A lieutenant's job,* he thought darkly. *I bet the Brigadier told The Oracle to have me do this while she's off with the beasts.*

Grinding his teeth, the Major General opened his arms wide in front of him. "Go out and maul Agnus' pitiful numbers." Stepping back, he reached beneath the table and pressed a switch. A mechanical clinking issued from the Tophet prisons and slowly the doors slid open.

The Tophets writhed but remained where they were.

Growling, the Major General marched up, banging the bars with the side of a clenched fist. "I said, get out of here!"

The hand of the Tophet before him shot out, grabbing him around the neck. It drew him closer, its foul breath fanning his face as a single word filled his mind: *PATER.*

Grunting, the Major General tried to reach his sword but the snakes around its waist launched themselves at his arm, sinking their fangs deep into his flesh.

He tried to shout, but the Tophet's grip on his throat tightened, squeezing out the last of his breath.

From the corner of his eye, he saw the other Tophets slink out of their cages with some rushing jauntily to the exit and those closest to him swarmed around his body. Their nails and teeth tore into his soft, supple flesh and he was unable to scream.

The second of crackling energy dissipated and both Terra and Simeon stumbled backwards, the former clutching her head.

Were those memories?

There was a flash of scarlet as Mr Maremortum brought his sword down on Terra from behind but a light ballooned out from Salvatus, bending the weapon away until Mr Maremortum's wrist twisted back. Grunting in pain, Mr Maremortum flung the two needle-like shards of E132 at Talia with his free hand, striking her in the chest.

With a shriek, Talia fell in a heap on the floor, thrashing about in agony. She placed her sweating hands on the thin, long shards, one planted deep in a breast and another lodged just beneath her collar bone.

"Talia?" Nicholo, breathed heavily, forcing himself up with his broken staff. He spat blood out of the corner of his mouth, almost vomiting from the effort. "Talia!"

A choked whimper was all he heard.

Shifting his arm away from Salvatus' radius of light, Mr Maremortum turned to Nicholo who let out a furious snarl as the silver-haired man recalled the scarlet shards from Talia's body, eliciting an ear-splitting cry. Closing his hands over the summoned shards, Mr Maremortum gasped as a deep gash was sliced into his back; Terra had spun and ran Spiritus diagonally across his back. Stumbling away, he fell backwards with Simeon darting forward to catch him.

"Thank you," murmured Mr Maremortum, pulling away from Simeon. He groaned, sagging momentarily as his back wound wept through the threads of his uniform.

Despite his concern for his brother, Simeon glanced at Terra from the corner of his eyes, his mind still muddled by the memories that had resurfaced when their blades met.

He watched as she wordlessly removed the helm from her head, carefully placing it between both Nicholo and Talia. The light that radiated from the helm seemed to bring some relief as Talia's trembling ceased.

Yet Simeon's own heart was unsettled, leaping into his throat when his eyes flickered up to Terra's face as she turned around. A bright light emanated from her brow and upon it was etched characters that struck terror in Simeon's heart.

Reflexively he looked away from it, body quivering. A suppressed memory of his mother in one of her few moments of sanity shot through his mind like a bullet. A time when he thought her capable of love.

"Colonel Simeon," the spirit spoke gently. "Don't fear these characters. I know that you've seen these before."

"I don't know what you're talking about!"

"Your mother." Terra's eye glistened with tears, fading back to their usual grey hue. She took a few steps forward, her eye locking with Simeon's. "I'm sorry."

Emotions bubbling to the surface, Simeon stepped forward, trying to slash her with his sword, but Terra swerved away, avoiding his blade. "Don't you dare—! Don't you *dare* pity me!"

His sword swings became more desperate and quick. Terra attempted to deflect a particular attack and flinched at the sudden pain that flared through her wrist. She leapt back resisting the urge to hold her wrist when Simeon threw himself at her again.

"I don't want to fight you!" she cried, placing her left hand against the flat of her blade to push back against the Colonel. The pressure against her right wrist increased as the Colonel's silver blade pushed hers back. The tears that she had been holding back from the glimpses of his past, slid down her cheeks.

Simeon paused.

Terra's eye locked with his. "I want to help."

"Help?" repeated Simeon incredulously, flexing his fingers on the grip of his sword.

Terra nodded and the weight against Spiritus lightened.

"Why?"

Eye still locked with the Colonel's, Terra slowly lowered Spiritus, her heart fluttering as Simeon mirrored her. "Because I understand." Terra's eye softened. "I understand what it is like to not know your worth in this world." There was a beat where they continued to gaze at one another. "Please let me help you, Colonel."

As if by reflex, Simeon's hands tightened on his sword and he raised it, the point directed at Terra. Cold fear gripped Terra but she remained with Spiritus lowered.

Simeon opened his mouth and appeared to struggle with his words. "After everything that has happened to you…after all that I've done…why?"

Terra's heart swelled.

'Let yourself heal. Only then, can you move forward, holding on to that gentle heart of yours.'

"Because the things you've done—all of the terrible things cannot be erased, but the things you decide to do from now on can be different." Terra lifted her right hand up and extended it to the man before her. "Stop looking inward, and start to look out towards the people around—"

"I have looked around and have judged this world and its people to be undeserving of true salvation." Simeon's eyes flashed angrily. "But even so, I will do what my parents could not. I will make things right in this broken world. This world will recognise Railesson again. The Ben'min throne will return to our people and the Maremortums will reclaim their rightful place as guardians to a Pateran king."

"You're right about this world being broken, but you can't hope to fix anything on your own."

Mouth twisting, a peculiar expression passed over Simeon's face and he licked his lips several times. "Then be with me."

"What?"

"Let's marry," Simeon blurted out. "My desire is for us to live together again. We can be fruitful like the world's needs demands. We share a blood lineage that is strongly attuned to E132. Imagine the powers our children would wield. We would subjugate all who opposed Pateran rule."

Terra's stomach churned and, despite the sword that pointed at her, she could not mask the look of pure disgust that crossed her face. "I was a child under your guardianship!" she cried, her trembling voice shrill. She lowered her hand, a horrid taste rising to the back of her throat.

"Many masters and guardians have been known to form families with the adults that were once in their care!"

"How could you happily form a family with someone who you lived vulnerably under—abused by for countless spells!"

"To save this world, we must do what we can! If you really care about this world, you would work towards its good and its good is to restore things to the way they once were!"

Shaking her head, Terra clenched her fists and a newfound strength urged her to defy this man whose hand she had long trembled under. "No! There is no way to restore things as they were. Our hope should only be placed in the plan that Agnus has! This world is ending—Scriptura forewarned us about this."

Simeon stared at her in disbelief. "Scriptura? You're brainwashed!" The sword drooped and he lifted his upturned hands to her, his face softening. "Let me look after you, 0792. I swear to love and cherish you. Why cling to Scriptura when we can rely on real strength—our own."

Mind reeling, Terra furiously shook her head and she unconsciously took a step backward. "No! I know the truth! I know there is real hope beyond this dying world and I don't want anything to do with your wicked dreams!"

"I have you!"

Terra's sword arm was seized from behind and twisted behind her back, eliciting a cry from her. Her other arm was pulled back and there was a small click of her bones as she was held firmly in place by Mr Maremortum. She tried to wriggle out of Mr Maremortum's grasp and gritted her teeth when his grip tightened. The pain in her wrist shot through her.

"Now, Simeon!" cried Mr Maremortum, his voice rising in excitement. "Kill her now!"

Simeon stopped, his eyes flickering between the struggling young woman and his brother. He dropped his silver sword to the ground, stricken with emotion.

"What are you doing?" bellowed Mr Maremortum, spraying blood and spit from his wounded mouth. "You said you would do it! Kill her!"

The Colonel's eyes rested on Terra who continued to struggle in Mr Maremortum's hold. "I can't," he breathed, voice weak. "Not this way."

For a moment, Mr Maremortum's grip slackened in disbelief and Terra tore her arms away, spinning around to face him.

Agnus' words flashed through her mind. *When you must swing Terra, do not hesitate.*

She raised Spiritus above her head, determination and adrenaline pulsating through her veins. She had to get him away. For a sliver of a moment, she took a breath, mind racing with doubts. Then her grip tightened on the sword's hilt and she made to swing at the blind man.

Blood dripped onto the floor before her. Yet it was not Mr Maremortum's.

It was hers.

A sharp pain issued from a spot just below her ribcage where Simeon had cleanly buried his sword through and vaguely the grey-eyed girl noted the malicious shine of the Element 132 where it protruded from her flesh.

Blood, instead of words, gurgled in her throat. It spewed forth from her mouth and rolled down her neck. A scarlet patch had begun to spread from the wound, staining her shirt.

Why did this happen?

There was a sharp intake of breath and Simeon wrenched the sword hurriedly out of her, catching her frail body before she fell. He trembled, his mouth opening and closing repeatedly and an odd noise escaped his lips. Drawing Terra close, he embraced her, his eyes closed in agony and regret.

"You shouldn't have. You shouldn't have raised your sword against him," whispered Simeon, more to himself than to the girl who steadily grew pale.

Terra merely twitched in his arms. Salvatus faded, disappearing completely from where it sat. Spiritus slipped from her grasp and vanished mid-fall. By this time however, her eye had begun to glaze over and her bloodstained lips quivered. "Ag-Agnus, did I really make a diff—"

Her movements stopped. Her eye stared, unseeing.

Simeon cried out, holding tighter.

Terra was dead.

When this shell of dust returns to whence it came, the breath within shall depart to those once lonely halls; made alive beyond that veil. Made brilliant in that presence.

- Lines from *Writings of the Kings of Old, Scriptura*. Translated by C. Yelnorin

0002
8 BSD

"You are blessed, Dinah," came the drawl of a woman's voice. Her fingernails tipped with scarlet brushed against the small bump that was a silver-haired woman's stomach. "You carry three children within you now."

"Triplets?" gasped the silver-haired woman, her cheeks rosy with joy.

But the joy was short-lived.

"Levi!" howled the silver-haired woman one night, stumbling out of bed. A trail of blood followed her. "Levi!" she screamed desperately, her hands pressing against her belly. Tears filled her eyes. "The babies! The babies! Help me!"

The silver-haired woman stoutly refused to be examined at Nyx, her reason being that the hospital examinations were done with Element 132. "I won't let them hurt my children," she declared fiercely, even with the fear for her children's safety gnawing away at her.

And so, her husband ordered a carriage and took her to Sominium, where its hospital was renown as the best throughout Tempus, no doubt due to their monopoly on particular technologies.

"I'm very sorry Mr and Mrs Maremortum…it appears one of the babies has been reabsorbed into your body. From the mech-nix scans we can see that there are only traces of the identical twin that has now vanished."

"Identical…?"

"Yes. See here? There are two separate sacs. One was for the two identical twins and the other, as you can see, contains the fraternal twin. Now if you look carefully here…"

The doctor's words seemed to fade away in the silver-haired woman's ears and she sat in stunned silence, staring off into the distance.

"It's okay, we still have the two that are left," her husband murmured to her in bed that night, wiping away her tears.

"We still lost one of our girls!" The woman lightly rubbed her belly. "Why did this have to happen?"

"You heard what the doctor said. It just happens sometimes…you couldn't have stopped something like that."

The woman stared into the distance, her eyes widening. "It's because of our sin, isn't it?"

"Our sin? Dinah. Don't be ridiculous." The man grabbed the woman's chin, forcing her to look at him. "We may have come from the same womb, but there is no other woman that I'm closer to than you." He drew his wife up to kiss her gently on the lips.

But even as the woman melted into her brother's arms her mind drifted to the words of her mother as she wept over her children's foreseen sin that she declared would bring a curse upon her descendants.

2 BSD

Market day in Lacuna was always busy and the silver-haired woman was not too acquainted with the rush on the streets. Nyx was a far quieter city but hardly a place to purchase goods for children.

There were several stalls set up along the paved streets and the woman found herself stopping by one of them to purchase a pouch of hair clips for her girls.

She continued along the road and found several people swarming towards the largest stall at the far end of the street. Children auctioned as slaves by beastmasters. She contemplated having a look but recalled her husband's adamant opposition to owning a slave.

Instead, she busied herself with looking at the displays in the shop windows, even stopping to order a coffee at a nearby café. As she exited the café, thanking a young man named Kouki for the coffee, she caught sight of a toy store's display window. Charmed by the collection of toys on display in the front window, the woman waltzed into the store to make a purchase.

At the front of the store stood a young auburn-haired girl, manning the counter.

The woman glanced surreptitiously around the store. "Where's the shopkeeper? Aren't they meant to be supervising you?"

"He's having lunch."

Perplexed, the woman simply nodded before turning to resume her search of the store. She settled on a pair of dolls that she felt strangely drawn to. A brown-haired doll wearing a colourful harlequin mask and a silver-haired doll. Satisfied with the dolls on examination, the woman took them with her to the counter and slipped a golden brooch from her pocket and handed it to the girl.

At the same time, the shopkeeper entered the store, with a brown paper bag in one arm.

The woman's attention remained on the child at the counter who wordlessly placed the brooch into the cabinet behind her after scanning it.

"What is your name?" asked the woman.

"Meiko."

"Well, Meiko." The woman reached into her bag. She pulled open the pouch of clips she had bought earlier and slipped out a jade-coloured one. "That's for you to wear." The woman smiled with a wink, placing the clip in the girl's hand. "I believe it matches your eyes."

"You can't have that," sneered the moustached man to the young girl.

Panicking, the girl held the clip out to the man. But as he reached to snatch the clip from her, the silver-haired woman slapped his hand, an expression of fury marring her face.

"Who said that was yours to take?" she demanded, nostrils flaring. "The very nerve! And right under my nose too!"

The man rubbed his hand, bowing humbly. "I'm very sorry, ma'am. It's just that she's a mere slave girl…you can't just give her something of value when she has nothing to offer…"

"That's not the issue here!" The woman waggled her finger at the man. "I take great offense that you attempted to take my gift to the girl for your own. Have you no shame? You have greatly insulted me! If you value your customers, you will think twice before trying to snatch a gift right before their eyes!"

"M-my apologies ma'am!" Beads of sweat accumulated on his forehead.

The man continued to apologise profusely to the silver-haired woman while the girl at the counter slid the jade-coloured clip into her hair, clipping back the auburn bangs that had framed one side of her face.

Terra drifted. She did not know where she was, but she floated across an endless white expanse her head filled with the thoughts and memories of a silver-haired woman that she knew she should recognise but could not name.

All the names she had heard were fading away and she struggled to grasp anything that remained.

"These images filling my head..." Terra rubbed her temple. She covered her eyes with her hands, exhausted. "What do they have to do with me?"

The haze of white surrounding her began to draw away like mist and before her eye a familiar scene appeared.

A dark cave, dimly lit by the twinkling scarlet gems embedded into its walls. Small, hunched figures lined the walls, hacking away with old pickaxes. The dull sound of rock breaking filled the cave and as her eye swept the area, Terra came to a stock still behind a small and familiar huddled form.

Why do I exist if this is all I'm meant for in life? wondered a younger Terra as she hacked tiredly away at the Element 132 on the mine walls. *What does this existence mean?*

She watched as a pale and frail-looking child was pulled forward. Blood poured over the mine floors. The officers had slit his throat.

Who are we, she thought, detached, *that this is our lot in life.*

An officer's head turned and his eyes met hers. She lowered her gaze and kept her head down.

Clouds swirled about Terra and the scene shifted and she felt herself plummeting towards a familiar desert plain. She soared over the pockmarked fields of Attero, her heart thundering in her chest as she scanned the landscape. Her heart leapt into her mouth as she recognised the top-hatted silhouette that strode through the ruined farmlands.

In his hand, he held the doll that the silver-haired woman had purchased for her daughter spells before. The brunette doll was marred with a large spot of blood against the side of its face.

Agnus came to a halt in the middle of Terra's vision and crouched down, pressing his right hand into the dirt at his feet, murmuring. He laid the doll on the ground nearby and lifted his hand, the dust from the part of the earth he had touched rose with the motion.

From this dust he drew up, a small figure formed; a shadow that rose from the blood-stained doll.

Agnus raised his left hand and a harsh wind whipped through the floating dirt. In a matter of minutes, the fine and delicate features of a small girl had been moulded.

The blood that marked the body of the doll rose as thin as string in a dark stream to the girl-shaped dirt mould. Then the doll itself began to disintegrate, each particle drawn into the dust. The body of dust was infused with colour—her hair became a light brown and strands of it separated from her head, encircling her bare body. It turned into silver thread and the pieces wove seamlessly together, eventually replicating the design of the doll's dress.

The doll.

Agnus' Curse.

This was her.

Agnus drew her into his arms, a sad smile on his face. "You, my child, are to be the Third."

With those words, he drew back, inhaled deeply and blew gently onto the girl's face.

The youth's sickly grey skin changed in colour, assuming a light-pink hue as blood rushed through her veins.

The older man studied her quietly for a moment and then, keeping a firm hold of her, he rose with her cradled in his arms.

"You are the Third of the Maremortum children. The one who was never born. The twin of Arche that could never be. Terra."

Tears filled Terra's eye as Agnus carried her through the destroyed land of Attero, holding her close while the bleak black canvas of the sky bore over them. Beneath his feet, there was spring even though devastation surrounded them.

Terra closed her eye and let her tears fall. She took a deep shuddering breath to gather herself and opened her eye once more, finding herself within the white space, drifting again.

Was I really alive? Terra's mind returned to the blood-stained doll that had formed her. She looked down at her left arm, the one that had been created from Adam's rib. Tears welled in her eye again when she remembered him. *Or am I just a doll? Am I not even real?* Her body shook and her breaths became short and fast. *What was the point of my existence? WHAT WAS THE POINT IN ME BEING HERE?*

She covered her face, her shoulders trembling with each anguished cry she gave. A pang of loneliness evoked sobs from her—in that lonely cavern she fought without Agnus, Lamina and Adam. And there she would die without them realising; the three faces of those she loved dearly arose in her mind's eye.

"Agnus, help me!" she wailed, gripping strands of hair that fell over her face.

No—thread, she corrected mentally, a bitter taste filling her mouth. It was blood.

Pain seared through her belly and the wound from Simeon's blade opened, blood falling through the white space.

Terra gasped through the pain and the tears, her hands reaching to cover the wound. "Ag-Agnus," she rasped, struggling to draw breath, the pain in her stomach increasing with each passing second. "Did I really make a diff-"

She could no longer form the words. Blood gurgled in her throat and the silence of the white space was filled with the young girl's desperate struggle for air.

Her vision blurred and the pain from the wound was crippling.

This was the end. The cold arms of loneliness embraced her..

But a voice rang out, as clear as day:

My young one, you made all the difference in the world. Don't ever think differently. You being here today is so incredibly important—please don't ever doubt your existence.'

Agnus' words before he left Manna.

And suddenly the pain began to fade and she could feel the warmth of a familiar light embracing her, drawing her away from the horrid situation she had been caught in.

"That is enough for now," spoke a voice that Terra knew in her heart yet could not put a face to. "My child, you made all the difference in the world."

A hand was outstretched to her from above and a gentle wind circled Terra as she reached out, her wounds fading away along with the dirt and sweat from the battle. Her clothing transformed into a pure white gown that billowed about her small frame, dancing with the wind.

She clasped the hand of the person in the light above her and a broad smile lit her face.

"Wake, Terra." said the person, drawing Terra upwards.

Terra closed her eyes, letting the light wash over her.

The pain stopped.

It was then that Veirya, filled with One's power, struck her eldest son. "I bind you with your blood in a vow unbreakable. You will serve your brother until the end of your days. And your children will labour under the command of his children. Their children will also be bound by your blood to serve. And so, your cursed line will live in service to your brother's because you drank the wine of the Other and in your drunkenness, you destroyed what was sacred."

- Lines from *The Time of Exiles, Scriptura.* Translated by H. Van de Berg

20

Lamina brought his sword down upon a Tophet that edged towards the cave entrance, hastily dodging the arrows of the archer that had relentlessly chased him from the battlefield. A loud cry issued from behind him and he glanced back to see a Mannite cut down the archer.

"Strike down the Tophets once the Magians are done for and secure them somewhere before they reform themselves!" Lamina called out. As he said this, a Tophet appeared from the open gates, its snakes and limbs squirming disjointedly. He gritted his teeth and rushed on towards the cave, knowing that he did not have time to waste on anyone else.

He had promised Agnus that he would take care of Terra. And he had now left her alone for far too long.

An odd idea gnawed at his insides as the sensation of a burden—like a restraint—lifted from him. It drove him to push through the pain in his limbs.

The ear-piercing screeches of the Tophets that the Magians had foolishly released left Lamina mentally thanking Pater. For some reason, the Tophets had turned the tide in the Mannites' favour, attacking countless Magian soldiers, many of which were armed with E132. He did not know what had possessed the creatures, but he was thankful regardless.

Leaping over small rocks, he ducked to avoid another arrow before running into the cave he had seen Terra, flanked by Talia, race into around twenty minutes ago. It took a moment for Lamina's eyes to adjust to the dark and his quick and ragged breaths awoke an impressive ache in a wound he had sustained in battle, leaving him muttering for strength to ignore it and carry on.

Hearing voices up ahead where there appeared to be some lights, Lamina raced forward, anxiety eating away at him.

"Leave her, Simeon. Don't cry over her, leave her!"

The old ox was breathless upon reaching the large cavern where a heavily wounded Mr Maremortum leaned against the rocky walls for support. Nearby, the broken bodies of Nicholo and Talia lay, struggling for breath. A couple of metres or so away from their bodies, Simeon sat hunched over, his back to Lamina. In his arms he cradled an unmistakable small body.

Her name escaped like a despairing howl from Lamina's lips and he blindly charged at the mourning Colonel, sword at the ready.

With the remainder of his strength, Mr Maremortum jumped forward, brandishing a shard of Element 132 which he transformed into a thin shield. It shattered from the sheer force Lamina exerted from his sword, throwing the silver-haired man back.

Simeon laid Terra gently down, his eyes blazing as he brandished his weapon at Lamina's approach. "YOU CAN'T HAVE HER!" There was a glimmer of madness in his icy-blue eyes.

"SIMEON!" roared Lamina, his blade clashing with Simeon's.

There was a brief struggle of power; the blades pushed heavily against each other until Lamina's rage and Simeon's fatigue surfaced with the ox's sword forcing back the Colonel's.

Anticipating his loss in the struggle, Simeon leapt back. "Get out, Levi. I'll follow soon."

Without hesitation, Mr Maremortum clambered to his feet and scrambled to the exit.

"Simeon, you…" growled Lamina menacingly, stepping toward the Colonel, his grip tight he felt his weapon would snap. "What have you done?"

"Only what I had to!" Simeon snarled swinging his sword forward.

Lamina's blade easily blocked the blow, knocking the Colonel's blade aside. He plunged his sword through the air, narrowly missing Simeon who had hastily dodged but Lamina followed this with a guttural growl as he swung his leg out and caught the Magian in the gut, sending him spiralling backwards. Vomit followed the Colonel to the cave floor.

Grimacing and howling in desperation, Simeon's eyes flashed scarlet and his sword scattered into innumerable pieces, flying towards Lamina who hastily closed his eyes and covered his face as the tiny shards ripped into his flesh.

I can't let him escape. Lamina gritted his teeth against the relentless onslaught of E132. But even as he tried to blindly stride through the pain of countless cuts, Simeon's grunts faded until there was nothing and even the shards departed, shredding through Lamina as it retreated to its owner.

"COME BACK HERE!" bellowed Lamina, prepared to give chase.

"Lamina."

The weak groan halted Lamina's movements. "Nicholo?"

With his eyes closed and breathing ragged, Nicholo coughed, fresh blood appearing at the corner of his mouth. "Leave them be. Talia needs help now."

The blindfold of fury slipped away and Lamina rushed to the cave exit, barking for medical assistance. As people in the distance hurried towards him, declaring that victory was at hand, he slipped back into the cave and paced back to Terra's motionless body. Lamina stooped down, scooping up the young woman's lifeless body. He held her close, burying his nose into her hair and howling as tears streamed down his face.

"Terra," he blubbered, cupping her still warm cheek with his hand. His large frame shook uncontrollably as he put a trembling hand to his mouth. Several more sobs wracked his body, his tears dripping onto Terra's unmoving face and snot dribbling into his mane. "What is the point in being able to finally say your name if you can't hear it?" The old ox cradled her tiny frame in his arms, rocking back and forth.

What followed was a blur. Many figures came and went, applying aid and gathering up Nicholo and Talia, stopping to console, solemnly sitting nearby, praying mournfully.

Mopping up the mess across his face, Lamina forced himself to his feet and slowly limped towards the cave exit, Terra's body still in his arms.

On the ground floor of the Lost Languages, members of the Mannite army found Mrs Maremortum sitting alone near the entryway. She rose when two Mannites entered, carefully reciting her rehearsed lines of surrender. She would remain to keep the peace to uphold her vow to the Kiryuuans.

When asked to raise her hands in surrender, Mrs Maremortum obeyed, apathetic. "If I could make one request—"

"You're in no position to bargain."

"I'm not bargaining. I fully surrender to the Mannites. I simply wish to speak with my daughter." She glanced hopefully from one Mannite to the other. "Could you please tell her that?"

The Mannite stared at her blankly. "Your daughter?"

Mrs Maremortum nodded. "Yes. Terra."

"Terra?"

"The girl who was with Agnus and Lamina—silver hair and grey eyes like me. Please tell her that I wish to speak with her," insisted Mrs Maremortum, growing impatient.

The men glanced at each other with the second Mannite who had not spoken yet finally blurting out: "She was your daughter?"

"Yes!" snapped Mrs Maremortum. "Can't you see that?"

The first Mannite cleared his throat. "Ma'am, with Magia having fallen to the Mannites, you're not in a favourable position."

The bubble of impatience in Mrs Maremortum shrank and she attempted a mild smile. "Can I please at least speak to her?"

"We had all assumed Ridley really was a Maremortum but we didn't know you had had a third."

Again, the two men exchanged looks and Mrs Maremortum felt her stomach sink. It dawned on her that she had been able to say her daughter's name.

The second Mannite swallowed thickly. "She's dead, ma'am."

The world spun and Mrs Maremortum found the ground rising up to her—or perhaps, she was sinking down to it. But none of that mattered. She cradled her head and a screech filled her ears and it did not register that the sound was issuing from her own lips until the men started to frantically shake her. She huddled into a small ball, wishing she could make herself smaller and smaller until she was nothing. "Not again, not again, not again, not again—," she chanted rapidly, her breaths short and sharp, her body cramping until finally the world darkened and she slumped to the floor, unconscious.

The light of the artificial sun streamed in through the open window and a light breeze stirred the curtains. Outside, a lady haggled with a shopkeeper's slave boy, her insistent voice carrying through the room to where Nicholo lay in a clean, white-sheeted bed. Beside him, an attentive nurse sat, replacing the bandages over the end of his arm. The lively hum of the streets outside Nicholo's room window led his mind astray, sending him back to the cave and his every regret.

He had been rushed to Sominium via beastmaster connections that Rebekah had maintained while helping with Lamina's café.

Yesterday, Nicholo was battling for his life in Magia. Today, he waged war against the dark recesses of his mind with Terra's—not Ridley—death looming over him.

Hanging his head, he sighed wearily.

The grey-haired nurse peered up at him, clipping the bandage in place. "Alright, love?"

Nicholo looked up, his smile tight. "Yes. Thank you."

She nodded and took her leave, reminding him to inform the staff if he needed anything.

When the tapping of her shoes faded away, Nicholo gazed out of the window, the weight of the bandages across his head heavy over his right eye.

"Look who I found!" a sing-song voice warbled from the doorway.

Nicholo turned to find his wife, Cecilia beaming at the open door and a despondent Lamina staring at the tiled floor behind her.

A grimace marred Nicholo's face and he groaned as he pushed his body up into a sitting position. "Cecilia, you haven't been causing any trouble for Lamina, have you?"

"Don't be silly, he asked to come see you. We were having a wonderful chat about all sorts of food we could cook up in Manna when you're able to return home."

Nicholo pinched the bridge of his nose and shook his head. He glanced up at the old ox, noting his quiet demeanour. "Well, you certainly don't look too happy to see me, if that's what you wanted to do, Lamina."

Clearing his throat, Lamina awkwardly stared down at his hooves, his brows in a knot. "I'm sorry. I did mean to check on how you were doing…" He shook his head, peering up and Nicholo noted the emptiness of his smile. "How are you doing, Nicholo?"

Despite the burning pain coursing through his body whenever he moved or even breathed, Nicholo waved the question away with a hand. "Of course. No need to fuss over me. I might be getting on in age, but I'm hardy."

Lamina merely nodded.

"And how is Talia?"

His gaze falling back to his hooves, Nicholo watched as Lamina's hands balled into tight fists and trembled. "Not good. The doctors said she might not be able to walk again…and she can hardly breathe without magitech."

"I see."

Silence fell over the room.

"And what about you, Lamina?"

Cecilia laid a gentle hand on Lamina's arm and Nicholo pressed his lips tightly together, a lump growing in his throat.

"I've been thinking that...Terra, she..." Lamina paused, his eyes overly bright. "She can't remain as she is." The old ox took a deep, shuddering breath, tears stinging the corners of his eyes. Looking up, his heart ached at the gentle expressions both Nicholo and Cecelia wore. "Nicholo. Cecilia. Please," cried Lamina, choking on his words. He could not bring himself to continue.

Cecilia gave a sad smile, hushing the ox as she ran her hand up and down his arm soothingly. Tears shimmered in her eyes. "Of course, we will help you bury her. We'll find her a lovely spot."

Nicholo wordlessly reached over to squeeze Lamina's arm, his face pained.

"Th-thank you."

On a grassy hill that overlooked the city of Babylonia, three figures gathered around a makeshift grave they had made for a beloved friend. They shared some quiet words, gave thanks to Pater for her life and wept for their loss. An azalea bush was planted above the grave as the marker.

Not long after, Nicholo excused himself apologetically, the strain of standing too much. Cecilia supported him as they limped away, leaving the lone ox to stare listlessly at the vibrant pink azaleas. Alone with his thoughts, silent tears fell from Lamina's face.

The soft thumps of feet on the earth broke the downward spiral of thoughts and Lamina raised his eyes, his gut wringing as a mixture of emotions surged through him at the sight of the approaching figure.

A weary Agnus wordlessly paced towards him.

Lamina's eyes widened incredulously at the flash of long silver hair behind him.

Mrs Maremortum was following him, her loose hair lashing about her pinched face. Her eyes were red rimmed and the tip of her pale nose was bright red.

Silence, a heavy blanket, draped over the three when both Agnus and Mrs Maremortum came to a stop in front of the grave. Agnus' tired eyes rested on the azalea bush, its leaves gently stirring in the wind.

"From the dust I created her and to the dust she shall return…"

Crossing the small breadth between them, Lamina cracked his knuckles against Agnus' jaw, sending the man stumbling backwards.

"Agnus! What was the point of you creating her if you knew that she would suffer so much?" Lamina seized the front of Agnus' tuxedo jacket and jerked the man towards him. "Why would you create her and allow her to endure such pain? Why would you make her grow up in Magia where they hurt her? Why didn't you protect her every step of the way? WHY?"

"Lamina, my friend." Tears filled Agnus' eyes. "I loved her too. Do not speak like I didn't. But know this." He paused, taking a deep and shuddering breath. "If she had not gone to Magia, she would not have saved a life during her stay there and subsequently enable the fulfillment of prophecy. She also would not have been able to save the current lives and many future lives of the so-called "blemished" children. Her service to me was pivotal."

Agnus looked away and the tears that he had been holding back fell from his eyes. "Many lives will be indebted to her and her work for me but it will not be recognised. However, she made all the difference in the world." There was a beat before he continued. "I want her to know that."

The old ox couldn't hold back his tears and turned away from Agnus. He watched Mrs Maremortum drop to her knees next to the azalea bush, murmuring "not again" in between gut-wrenching sobs. "Why are you mourning?" Lamina jabbed an accusing finger at the weeping woman. "You almost killed her yourself!"

"Forgive me!" Mrs Maremortum sobbed, flinging herself face down into the ground. "Forgive me, Terra!"

Lamina recoiled, uncertainty momentarily holding him. He hawked up phlegm and spat at his feet, his snarling mouth a veil for approaching obscenities.

There was a strange disturbance in the air beside the grave, like the very air itself shimmered, and in Lamina's eyes a white-haired figure stepped out into view, his fiery gaze slowly meeting the old ox's.

"WHO ARE YOU?" demanded Lamina, heart thumping from the abrupt appearance of the white-haired young man.

The pupil-less man turned to the old ox, sending an involuntary shiver down Lamina's spine. "I am *Death*."

Lamina opened his mouth and promptly closed it, stunned. Finding his voice, the old ox cleared his throat somewhat nervously. "What are *you* doing here? And why can I see you?"

"I was here for quite a time." His voice was deadpan and his eyes unblinking as he spoke.

Lamina spluttered incoherently, his legs weak beneath him.

"Fear not, Lamina," interrupted Agnus with a kind smile. "You experienced Death itself last spell. It is not uncommon for it to make you an acquaintance."

"But I still don't understand—why is he here?"

Hitori looked over at the makeshift grave, his expression unreadable. "Hades told me about this girl—that she was special. She said she foresaw her death long ago in the doll she once owned. She was under our care, and so died at the hands of one influenced by the allure that Death's powers have."

Agnus was silent for a moment before speaking, his voice wavering: "She *was* special."

Hitori turned to Agnus, apathetic. "I understand that now." He dropped to one knee and bowed his head low before Agnus. "Master, what would you have me do now?"

"That will be made clear when Terra speaks," Agnus turned to Lamina, his face set in determination. "Dig up her grave, Lamina."

"Agnus!" shrieked Mrs Maremortum, affronted. "What are you doing? She's dead! Leave her body alone!"

But Lamina, having seen the gleam in Agnus' eyes, dropped hurriedly to his knees, tearing desperately at the soft soil with his bare hands.

He recalled an image of an empty burial casing, that day when he stood side by side with Matthew and Meiko in Avarose; the tears and wonder in everyone's eyes as a figure stepped out.

The memory spurred him on and Lamina ignored the pain of the dirt pushing up under his fingernails the deeper he dug. The pain was meaningless while he drew on the memory in his mind's eye. His heart leapt when his nails scraped against the top of the wooden coffin he had purchased in Sominium.

Belatedly, Mrs Maremortum also crawled forward, hurriedly helping Lamina dig away the rest of the dirt that laid on the coffin until they were both able to reach in and grab the edge of the coffin lid.

Pulling away the coffin lid, inside lay the still body of Terra Maremortum. Her body had been cleaned before burial and her clothing replaced with a soft, billowy white dress.

Both Lamina and Mrs Maremortum sat back, breathing heavily, daring to hope, and watched as Agnus approached the coffin. He reached down, taking the young woman's marble cold hand in his.

"That is enough for now. My child, you made all the difference in the world." Agnus took Terra's stony hand and raised it to his lips. "Wake, Terra."

Eyelid fluttering, Terra's eye opened dreamily as if from sleep and she sat up, stretching widely. "Agnus?" She jolted upright, horrified, and grabbed

Agnus' shoulders. "Nicholo and Talia! Are they okay? I tried to give them Salvatus to protect them!"

"Oh, my Terra, you didn't lose your way." The tears shimmering in his eyes made Terra freeze. He cleared his throat. "Nicholo and Talia bear permanent wounds but are recovering well, thanks to you."

As Terra breathed a sigh of relief, a large pair of hairy arms were flung around both her and Agnus and they were pulled up into a rough hug by Lamina who sobbed in his gruff voice: "Terra! Praise Pater! You're alive!"

Puzzled but pleased to be wrapped in her dear friend's arms, Terra reached up, hugging both Agnus and Lamina. Her mind slowly whirred and as she pulled away from them, she looked around, noting a crying Mrs Maremortum and a motionless Hitori were also there. Lowering her gaze to the hole and box she currently sat up in, Terra reached up, touching her left ear where she could no longer hear anything.

It was almost impossible to understand, even with all Terra knew from Scriptura. She turned to Agnus, her eye wide. "It wasn't a dream. I really *did* die."

Agnus and Lamina pulled back, both struggling with tears.

As Agnus wordlessly squeezed her hand, Terra felt a lump rise in her throat, flashes of her memories returning to her. "You called me back," she whispered, the corners of her eye wet.

Unable to contain herself, Mrs Maremortum leaned over, throwing her arms around Terra, much to the younger woman's shock. Unsure of how to respond, Terra awkwardly patted her back, her eye darting from Lamina to Agnus for reassurance.

Remembering herself, Mrs Maremortum pulled away, wiping her face furiously on her sleeve. "I'm sorry! I just couldn't bear to lose you again." Sniffling loudly, Mrs Maremortum ran her hands repeatedly over her face, willing the tears to subside. "I know that…this may not mean anything." She took several gulps of air, her trembling hands pressed against her eyes. "But, I'm so sorry for everything…so, so sorry…"

Plagued by uncertainties, Terra bit her lip and wrung her hands. Her mind wandered to Scriptura and One's overflowing love. Deep in her heart, she felt she knew how she should respond. Yet she grappled with the looming recollections of resentment and confusion. "You are…my mother." There was a beat as she carefully rolled the next few words over her tongue, praying mentally. "I accept your apology." She paused, taking another breath to steady herself. "But please give me time and space. I just…this is too hard for me right now."

'Let yourself heal.'

Hanging her head and drawing back, Mrs Maremortum nodded. "I understand."

Agnus glanced from Mrs Maremortum to Terra, his heart aching at the sadness reflected in the latter's eye. "Dinah, as I told you when I released you from your cell, you would behold the power of Pater. And now that you have seen and heard the truth, will you still turn away from me?"

Silver locks of hair whirled about Mrs Maremortum's head as she vigorously shook her head. She bowed low to the ground and Terra noted the unmistakable quivering of her slender frame. "Please, have mercy, Agnus. I'll follow you wherever you go."

Studying her critically for a moment longer, Agnus' face softened. "You are forgiven, Dinah. Raise your head and do not stray again."

The words were like a small blow to Terra, who quietly watched Mrs Maremortum. She wondered if she should have said the same and her mind wandered back to her failure with Simeon. Biting her lip, she lowered her gaze to the ground, noting the teardrops that marked the place under Mrs Maremortum's bowed face.

With a genteel smile, Agnus turned to Hitori, allowing Mrs Maremortum time to collect herself. "The pieces are now in place, Hazael. I will be entrusting you with the next task—if Terra is willing."

Head snapping up, Terra's eye locked with Agnus' and a rush of strength seeped through every fibre of her being, her face lighting up into a wide grin. "Agnus, I told you I would trust you and I do."

"Remember the time when you were cross enough to slap Agnus' hand away?"

"Mr Lamina, don't tease me! I had my reasons!"

"Coming from the ox who just punched Agnus," Hitori chimed in flatly.

Lamina flushed and Terra whipped her head towards him, aghast. "I, too, had my reasons!"

Chuckling lightly, Agnus shook his head. "I'm thankful for all your trust. However, we will need those in Shin'en Kiryuu to move first before the true work begins." Agnus inclined his head to Mrs Maremortum. "They will call upon you to keep your blood vow."

"How do you—?" Mrs Maremortum shook her head as if dispelling her doubts. "I will have to uphold the vow."

Agnus nodded, smiling knowingly. "Yes, you will need to do so."

A look of utter confusion crossed Mrs Maremortum's face, but Agnus was already turning to Terra when her mouth dropped open with a "Hold on!"

"Terra, as Marshal, Magia belongs to you now. With Mrs Maremortum as witness, what would you have them do under your command?"

Stomach twisting into knots, Terra looked up at Agnus and she was grateful for the confidence and assurance reflected in his face. Taking a breath to steady herself, she raised her chin. "I would stop the mining of E132. And the abuse and murder of blemished." Despite her brave face, she felt tears clinging to her lashes.

Mrs Maremortum was already shaking her head, concern contorting her face. "The Conqueror will not approve of that!"

Biting her lip, Terra set her jaw, her eye overly bright. "We will have to contest him then."

"Contest him?" cried Mrs Maremortum, voice rising in fear.

Lamina stroked his mane pensively and caught Agnus' eyes with a sparkle. "We'll have to appeal to someone who *can* contest him and the Sominium family."

A smile played on Agnus' lips as he looked from Lamina to Hitori. "Hazael," he said, his gaze steady. "While Lamina and Mrs Maremortum wait for word from our friends in Shin'en Kiryuu, I would have you and Terra travel to Gershom. If Terra is prepared, she will go as the Marshal of Magia to appeal to the Lowenthals."

Lamina appeared taken aback, his eyes threatening to fall out. "The Lowenthals? Gershom's royal family?"

"Yes. If the Lowenthals agree to support Terra's request to stop the mining of E132, in her authority as Marshal of Magia, we have an opportunity to turn the tide on the corruption and overexposure across Tempus. Of course, this means the props holding up the world will fall away. What do you think of that, Marshal?"

Terra lowered her eye, heart aching. She clenched her fist. "The world shouldn't thrive on the sacrifice of children. I want this suffering to stop."

Agnus smiled softly. "I entrust this duty to you, Terra."

Meeting Agnus' eyes again, Terra felt a rush of gratitude and love. "I won't let you down."

"This is your wish, Terra. And I will give you the help you need." With a bright smile, Agnus glanced at Hitori and gave a small nod.

"Yes, Master," said Hitori, bowing deeply with a hand over his heart. He turned his pupil-less eyes to Terra and held his hand out to her.

Staring uncertainly at Hitori's hand, Terra decidedly slipped hers into his, allowing the young man to pull her up out of the coffin. Part of her mind marvelled at the fact that Death's touch was warm.

"May I call you, Hazael?" Terra found herself asking.

Hitori gave a slow, thin-lipped nod. "I suppose I should ask what name you would prefer." He paused, Terra staring at him expectantly. "I don't particularly care though."

"Hey, *Death*, be easy to get along with!"

Hitori gave Lamina a dry, sidelong glance. His pupil-less gaze slid back to Terra's. He made no comment on her flushed cheeks as she tried to hold her laughter in. "Master will expect me to behave. Alas, I will ask then: what should I call you?"

Smiling brightly, Terra answered: "I think, I'd like to be called, Terra Ridley."

"Terra Ridley," Hitori repeated without a smile. "I'll pretend it's a pleasure."

Feeling Spiritus' warmth fill her chest, Terra couldn't help but burst out laughing, her grip on Hitori's hand tightening. She could hear Lamina arguing with Agnus about Hitori's demeanour and her belly ached from the absurdity of her circumstances.

Here she stood, Marshal of the place she loathed, destined to travel across Tempus, with her new companion, Death.

For the first time in her life, she was certain of the future and content with the present.

"I look forward to working with you, Hazael."

EPILOGUE
5ASD

"May mother grace us."

Arche stood at a distance from Luke, who was deep in conversation with a Kiryuuan porter, praying she would not draw any attention to herself.

Luke had crammed a too small straw hat on her head which hid her silver locks, now in a tight bun. She felt that this, accompanied by the goggles he had lent her to wear, demanded unwanted stares. Still, Arche lightly touched the brim of the hat and practiced her smiles, followed by rehearsed small talk in her head.

Luke's cheerful voice burst the burgeoning bubble of Arche's thoughts which had devolved into imagining her sister, Lachesis, hunting her down to make a mockery of her. "Come on, Ar—aah, Lerielle."

With sweat collecting above her upper lip, Arche glanced at the porter, wondering if he thought her disguise to be as ridiculous as she did. But he had long turned away, ushering the rest of the passengers out onto the gangplank to the dock that connected into Shin'en Kiryuu's port city, Lon'ong.

She followed Luke off the ship, lungs full of salty air and ears ringing with the squawk of seabirds and shouts of the fish market nearby.

Peering up at the cloudless, black sky, Arche wondered whether her twin, Terra, would live happily now. She would die one final time, that much Arche knew, but she could not pinpoint when. She never could until their final week was upon them.

Raising a hand to her left eye, she touched the eye-patch squished beneath the goggles she wore, reminding herself it was still secure.

Slipping her other hand into her coat pocket, Arche ran her fingers over the small scrap of folded parchment within. She would need to get the new list of the dying to Hazael soon.

ACKNOWLEDGMENTS

First and foremost, I would like to thank everyone who made this story possible.

Kevin and Cara read the very first draft of the book I started many years ago. I'm so thankful that you tolerated my awful teenage writing.

Jessie was the only one who really liked the main character despite how lacking my writing was in the second draft. Thanks for assuring me that she could be likeable.

Jaz found the time to read my book in her busy schedule. I'm glad that you are looking forward to more books – I'm looking forward to writing more!

Pa blazed through the book in two sittings. Thanks for always taking an interest in my unusual ventures.

Sam always had the most interesting takes on characters and events. Your insight was always appreciated and your excitement was infectious.

Without all your feedback and encouragement, I never would've worked so hard on polishing and adding to this first book. I'm quite proud of the result and I have you all to thank for that.

To my youth group girls, thank you for being the greatest hype crew. What a joy it is to know that you have assurance and true hope in Jesus.

And Alanna, thanks for taking the time to proofread and give this book a much needed polish!

And thank you, reader, for taking an interest in this small, indie book! It means so much to me. Please look forward to more books from this series and from me!

Leave a book review on Amazon or Goodreads (or wherever you want to make a review!) to let me know your thoughts and help this book gain visibility! Reviews make a huge difference for indie writers and it would mean the world to me to read your thoughts and reactions to Tempus!

Visit my website and subscribe to my monthly newsletter for behind the scenes and updates: esolofoni.wordpress.com.au

ABOUT THE AUTHOR

Elisiva lives in Sydney, Australia and enjoys watching far too much anime and playing video games. There's less time for that now, but she loves curling up with a good book nowadays, finding inspiration everywhere.

She delights in being a child of God but isn't the greatest speaker. Instead, she hopes to write stories that can better illustrate her joy.

She is often in her own world, dreaming up more stories and furiously writing notes for ideas.

TALES OF TEMPUS WILL CONTINUE IN THE NEXT STANDALONE BOOK, *SORA*.

THE PATHS OF THE CHARACTERS IN THE THREE STANDALONES WILL CONVERGE…

WANT TO READ A SNEAK PREVIEW OF *SORA*?

CONTINUE READING…

Long ago, when the lands were still connected to Paradise, the Dawn goddess alighted from her long journey across the world on the snowy peaks of a mountain range.

At the foot of this mountain, a great dragon that protected the land asked for her to present herself before him, so that he may know that she was no threat.

So, the Dawn goddess descended the mountain and greeted the dragon.

"Why did you come to rest on this mountain?" asked the dragon, curious at the sight of this woman.

"I have journeyed very far to come here," said the woman. "Is there a place to rest my weary head?"

"You may rest here at the foot of the mountain, so that I might keep an eye on you," answered the dragon.

As the Dawn goddess rested her head upon a boulder to sleep, she found that it would not come to her. "If you are to watch over me," she said to the dragon, "can you fill this frigid silence in the air? I would find it easier to sleep if you did."

"Very well," replied the dragon.

The dragon began to sing a lullaby.

- A *Collective History III: Xanadu, A reflective approach to Shin'en Kiryuu's history* by E. Yelnorin

0001
28 BSD (*Spells* Before Sun's Death)
Or 183 EB (*Spells After the* Empty Ben'min throne)

There is a saying in Shin'en Kiryuu that the blood of the goddess atones for all sins.

It came to mind as a young and battered Kaishi stared at the blood dripping off the gleaming sword pointed at her.

The man before her flicked his wrist and blood splattered off the golden sword he held, overlapping the other red patches on the woven mats beneath their feet. He turned his gaze to the small, young woman kneeling before him.

One of his soldiers held her hands behind her back and kept her head in place by gripping a handful of her startling blue hair. Her face was lifted towards him, yet her eyes were lowered to the Kingsfang.

"You will be the next inheritor of the title of Sora," the man declared, taking a cloth from his pocket and wiping the Kingsfang clean.

Kaishi's eyes darted to the figures behind him. His soldiers had bound the hands of another, slightly older woman. One of her horns had been broken in the scuffle.

"We will be taking the current holder of the title of Sora and you shall replace her," the man stated, his tone matter of fact. Kaishi's eyes returned to him and he continued, "If you value your life, hers and those within your country of Shin'en Kiryuu, then you will agree to a peace treaty and never turn your blade against my country ever again."

Behind the man, the bound older girl began to softly weep.

Kaishi's eyes slid down to the Kingsfang again. She unconsciously ran her tongue along the gash on her trembling bottom lip. If she threw her head back, her horns could pierce into the soldier's gut.

But death by the Kingsfang was an unpleasant thought.

The man in front of her continued through what Kaishi assumed were clenched teeth, "The terms of the peace treaty will be decided by Gershom. If you do not agree to this, the line of Sora can continue to atone for its crimes with blood."

At this, Kaishi's eyes darted back to her bound cousin. Numb with terror, Kaishi hoped that Emeren would provide her with some guidance. But Emeren's face remained downcast and she continued to quietly weep.

The shine of the Kingsfang drew her gaze back to the man's. "Y-yes," she rasped, unbidden tears filling her eyes, "the line of Sora yields to you, king of Gershom."

After a brief pause, Kaishi watched the king pull his sword back, eyes fixed to hers. "Swear it by blood."

"I swear by the blood of the goddess and Shenryuu."

The tip of the sword was pointed back towards her and Kaishi felt a surge of panic rise from her belly.

"You will announce this treaty to your people once they declare you Sora. I will station some men in this temple to ensure you do not betray your word."

"I will!" Kaishi cried, a flash of earnest giving way in her voice. "The line of Sora shall atone, but not through death."

The king narrowed his eyes but sheathed the Kingsfang and turned away. "Let her go."

Kaishi felt her hair and hands released and she fell to the bloodied floor, her cheek aching against the woven mat.

"Jethro and Eliezer. You are to remain here and see that she is cared for while she stays true to her word. However, if she, like her aunt, chooses to raise her sword against Gershom, kill her," she heard the king instruct as he walked away.

Kaishi remained where she was, cheek pressed against the floor, her face wet with tears. She listened as Emeren's soft cries dwindled to a small hum and eventually that and the marching of boots could no longer be heard.

She clenched her fist as the two men the king had left behind asked for her to rise to her feet. Slowly, yet obediently, she pushed herself up onto her knees, mentally praying for her aunt's soul to be put to rest by the goddess.

Wiping her face clean on her sleeves, she allowed one of the men to pull her to her feet.

In the distance, she could hear the muffled roars proclaiming the death of Sora Rinkah from the steps of Shenryuu's temple. And from where she stood she could see the orange haze of a fire blazing outside.

The war between Shin'en Kiryuu and Gershom had come to an end.

Visit my website and subscribe to my monthly newsletter for behind the scenes and updates: esolofoni.wordpress.com

APPENDICES

Sun up (s.u.)/Sun down (s.d.)

These general time terms are based simply on when the sun is meant to be above or below the horizon, adjusted twice a year when the sun up/down periods are extended.

Clock times are 12 hour based.

GENERAL TIME TERM	TIME ON CLOCKS
Early sun down	1-4s.d.
Night	5-7s.d.
Late sun down	8-12s.d.
Early sun up	1-4s.u.
Morning	5-7s.u.
Late sun up	8-12s.u.

Element 132 (E132)

Known by this name specifically in Railesson and Liberia, the scarlet stone has several other names across Tempus depending on which country one should find themselves in.

In runology (the study of ancient runes), it is understood that old texts, such as Scriptura, referred to this stone as 'magick' or 'the wine of the Other'.

Listed below are the names and the relevant country this is used in:

- Resinn – Avarose & Gershom
- Runonami – Shin'en Kiryuu
- Kulokula – Tohi Ofa

The stone is known to exhibit magickal properties that allow it to interact with innumerable things, often assuming different colours depending on the type of interaction; green for operating within magitech and purple/velvet for communicating with other stones.

Liberian scientists have stated that E132 doesn't function well around excessive amounts of electricity.

In most cases, the stone retains its scarlet appearance, such as in combat or when manipulated by the blood of Vei. In the latter example, descendants of the great Queen and Seer Veirya have their eye colour affected by the stone when manipulating it.

Scriptura

Translated from the ancient Paegaelain language, Aelthaeom, the religious text was once revered as sacred to many during The Days of Old when it is said civilisation began in the lands around Initium.

The text is composed of six books:
- Writings of the Kings of Old
- Laments of Lerielle
- Seers of Paegaelai
- Time of the Exiles
- Wisdom of Aurelius
- The Gates of Hrestia

Due to the fragmented nature of the recorded forms of the text, these have all been translated into common language by different scholars.

The only known source where a full record of the text is believed to be found is within the Armour of Agnus, specifically the sword, Spiritus.

Currencies
By country (note that some locations take more than one type): Gold/Silver/Copper
- Gershom
- Shin'en Kiryuu

Blood
- Magia (Railesson)
- Nyx (Railesson)
- Babylonia (Railesson)
- Hinnom (Railesson)
- Liberia
- Avarose

Items of personal value
- Lacuna (Railesson)
- Hinnom (Railesson)
- Liberia
- Avarose
- Tohi Ofa
- Beastmasters anywhere in the world

Blood Values by Status/Race:
1. Deity/Dragon
2. Pure Pateran blood
3. % of Pateran blood
4. Liv'yatan/Hyu'yan
5. Satz'yan

6. Human/Beast
7. Slaves
8. Modified humans/beasts (Tophets)

Personal values ranking:
1. Item from deity/dragon
2. Name
3. Item (incl. coin)
4. Body hair/Nail clipping etc
5. Blood

Note that some payments can leave the payee in debt to the payor if the value far exceeds the service or item provided in exchange.

Name pronunciations

Key: *Asterisked names contain 'r's that are rolled when pronouncing the name.

Paegaelai – Payhe-gah-lay
Attero = Ah-terh-row
Lamina = La-me-nah
Railesson = Ray-yule-sen
Magia = Mah-jee-yah
Lacuna = Lah-coo-nah
Manna = Man-nah
Maremortum = Ma-rey-more-tem
Arche = Are-chay
Lachesis = La-kay-sus
*Shigure = She-goo-rey
*Hitori = He-tore-ree
Hazael = Hah-zay-yule
Initium = Ee-knee-shie-em
Dinah = Dee-nah
Levi = Lee-vai
Tiamat = Tee-yah-mat
*Shin'en Kiryuu = Shie-nen Key-ree-oo
Gershom = Gur-shem
Avarose = Ay-vah-rose
Sominium = So-min-knee-em
Tohi Ofa = Doh-hee Orh-fa
Liv'yatan = Live-yah-ten
Sarkany = Sarh-karh-knee
Resinn = Reh-sin
Runonami = Roo-no-nah-mee
*Sora = Saw-rah
Emau = Eh-ma-oo
*Gorbeh = Gore-beh
Pater = Pay-ter
Praeter = Pray-ter
Meiko = May-ko
Kaishi = Kie(like pie)-shee
Kouki = Koh-key

www.ingramcontent.com/pod-product-compliance
Lightning Source LLC
Chambersburg PA
CBHW030605120726
47904CB00006B/1779